Seducing the Spy

Spy Society, Book 2

Kelsey Swanson

Dragonblade Publishing, Inc. is an imprint of Kathryn Le Veque Novels, Inc.
P.O. Box 23
Moreno Valley, CA 92556
ceo@dragonbladepublishing.com

Produced in the United States of America

First Edition August 2025
Trade Paperback Edition

ARE YOU SIGNED UP FOR DRAGONBLADE'S BLOG?

You'll get the latest news and information on exclusive giveaways, exclusive excerpts, coming releases, sales, free books, cover reveals and more.

Check out our complete list of authors, too!

No spam, no junk. That's a promise!

Sign Up Here

www.dragonbladepublishing.com

Dearest Reader;

Thank you for your support of a small press. At Dragonblade Publishing, we strive to bring you the highest quality Historical Romance from some of the best authors in the business. Without your support, there is no 'us', so we sincerely hope you adore these stories and find some new favorite authors along the way.

Happy Reading!

CEO, Dragonblade Publishing

Additional Dragonblade books by
Author Kelsey Swanson

Spy Society Series
Courting the Duchess (Book 1)
Seducing the Spy (Book 2)
Marrying the Marquess (Book 3)

For J.
You are my sunshine,
My only sunshine.

Prologue

OLIVER BLACK, FORMER street urchin, thief, and gang-runner, had taken many beatings in his life.

The first he could remember with the most clarity was when he'd not yet been six years of age and tripped, spilling his father's stew on the way to the table while his mother finished the washing up. The wasting of precious food dashed across the dirt floor of their damp, cramped basement flat had earned him more than his usual cuffing about the ear.

He'd never been able to do right by his father's estimation and, as he grew older, the punishments grew more severe; the disgusted glares in his direction became outright hatred. Closed fists replaced slaps; bruises evolved into open welts from strappings. And matters only became worse for Oliver after his mother died. Fearing for his life without even the relatively ineffective shield his mother had offered, he fled to the streets at the age of ten.

Unfortunately for him, he proved to be a poor beggar; more than once, he'd been shoved by an annoyed passer-by into the busy street, saved only by his quick reflexes from being trampled beneath the plate-sized hooves of a cart horse driven by its screeching owner. Little did he know, Oliver had been under close observation by an older boy—another lad driven to the streets by the cruel circumstances of his birth.

So many children died on the streets from illness or starvation or simply disappeared, so the lad was careful not to invest too much energy or time into Oliver until he could ascertain whether he had any useful skills. He spent several days following him through the alleys and streets, watching Oliver's movements and determining how desperate the new boy might be. When Oliver proved to be a natural pickpocket with his nimble fingers and instinctual ability to make himself smaller and less obtrusive, he was quickly absorbed into the fold of the underworld. He was shown the skills and knowledge he needed to survive.

He was taught which alleys to avoid if he wanted to stay alive, which corners were the most lucrative, and that he should never, under any circumstances, alight into a carriage with anyone—man or woman—or risk never being seen again, suffering a fate worse than death. He was trained to hold his own in scuffles, and how to use and conceal a blade. He was protected within this little corner of hell, but that didn't mean his life was comfortable or safe. Food and shelter came and went; however, he wouldn't have given it up and gone back to his father for anything.

There was a carefully maintained hierarchy and honor among their group. His training involved a great deal of violence and exhausting nights, but Oliver had long ago learned to take (and survive) a beating at the hands of his father. And this was different. His training sessions were designed to build him up and make him stronger; his father's hands had intended only to break him.

Oliver was praised for his successes, corrected when he was wrong, learned a fairness he'd never before been shown, and was given an equal share of whatever spoils were to be had. He experienced a new type of camaraderie he hadn't known existed in his cold, cruel world. He and the other boys guarded one another's backs. They kept watch in the shadows and from the tops of buildings for the older lads and men of their group when they performed their business, sounding alarms through an intricate language of whistles.

As he grew older, he'd been trained in stealth, picking locks, and the proper use of other weapons. With regular food and encouragement, he'd grown tall and broad, strong in a lithe and graceful way. He became a valuable asset to the gang and used his skills in whatever form he was required.

Sometimes, he was called upon to rid the streets of a particularly violent enemy; other times, he was tasked with ferreting information through intimidation or stealth. Each new skill earned him his fair share of scars. Like many, he had to learn some lessons the hard way with the graze of a blade or the hard end of a cudgel, and he was left with scrapes, bruises, stitches, and the occasional broken finger or nose. Rather than discourage him, Oliver chose to take these incidents as reminders of his hubris and learn from them. A man truly found trouble only when he forgot his mortality.

Life continued thusly for Oliver and he worked his way up through the ranks until he and several of his partners were sold out by a coward hoping to avoid the hangman's noose. Ambushed, he'd been bound and beaten, left bleeding on the filthy stones of a Newgate cell reeking of piss and sweat, when a man dressed all in black had approached him. He had been lean and of indeterminate age, his mask-like features making him appear two to five years on either side of Oliver's eighteen years. It was unnerving how one minute he appeared no more than a harmless boy and the next, a tilt of his head and the worldly gleam in his eyes made him appear to be a cold-blooded predator.

He offered Oliver a choice: swing from the gallows or put his set of skills to a more honorable use.

Oliver spat a blood clot at his polished boot, missing it by an embarrassingly large berth. "Why should I trust you?"

The other man's lips twitched. "Because your other option is a short drop…after which you will likely kick and soil yourself until you black out. The current hangman is known to be a bit of a sadist—rather than snap necks, he likes to watch his men squirm." Oliver swallowed down the tang of blood and bile. "And…" the man paused, casting away any veil of refinement his voice once held to reveal an accent as rough and coarse and thick with jadedness as any heard in the London slums, "—'cause I was once right where you's now." He crouched down beside Oliver's prone form. "Life's funny, innit?"

Oliver accepted the only choice he could, if he wanted to live.

He was bundled into a canvas shroud and whisked away to recover in the country before embarking upon a new sort of training.

At first, Oliver had resented this strange group of men who had taken him away from the only life he'd cared to know, but it became apparent that his anger was futile. He was essentially a prisoner, free to roam the halls of the ancient stronghold, but forbidden from leaving the grounds. The man who'd pulled him from Newgate made only one appearance during that time. He reiterated, with his unnerving stoicism, how the terms of Oliver's survival were dependent upon his cooperation. Only after he left did one of the men brought in to assess Oliver's skillset comment on the importance that Adrian Ramsay, the Spymaster, himself, had taken an interest in him.

Initially a skeptical pupil, Oliver was eventually taught to read and write; his rough skills honed on the streets were further developed. He relished the hand-to-hand combat and his talents with a blade were sharpened to unsurpassed lethality. Next came training with a pistol until his aim with that weapon was nearly as good as when he wielded a knife.

Weeks bled into months and he was introduced to foreign languages he'd never before encountered. He was taught to recognize different dialects and pinpoint their regions. His brain— long starved of this stimulation—craved the knowledge and proved to Oliver that he was not half as stupid as his father had once made him believe he was.

He impressed his tutors with his ability to move as stealthily as a cat, to use shadows to his advantage, and to throw his voice to distract a target. In turn, they taught him how to change his speech, dress, and carry himself in a manner that drew no attention. They effectively taught him to become invisible.

Throughout his training and first few assignments, Oliver earned innumerable scrapes and injuries, adding them to the running tally he'd long ago lost track of.

Nothing he'd ever endured, however, quite measured up to the searing pain of a stiletto being rammed between his ribs.

Chapter One

London, 1823

THE RAIN FELL in nearly solid sheets of chilling grayness, turning what would have been an otherwise pleasant late-summer evening into the sort of bleak and dreary one that only London could create. Oliver flipped up the collar of his thick black coat, though it did little to protect the back of his neck from the chilly drops. His dark cravat was soaked and the melted starch made the skin of his throat itch, but he pushed the annoyance to the side to be dealt with later as he kept his eye on his quarry one-and-a-half blocks ahead of him.

The deserted narrow streets left few places for anyone to hide, meaning both he and his prey were vulnerable. Oliver, however, had the benefit of being a child of the shadows. He'd been trailing his mark from the docks and up through the winding streets of Covent Garden for what felt like an eternity. He'd been back in England two months now, after eight years abroad on the Continent and, aside from a few minor side projects here and there, nearly all of that time had been dedicated to investigating the man he now followed.

It didn't matter how hard the rain fell or how chilled he became, he'd be damned if he lost the trail now. He'd worked far too hard for far too long to allow him to slip through his fingers and, if his suspicions proved correct, a meeting was about to take place...and Oliver had every intention of intercepting the information before it could be passed along. With any luck, he'd be able to avoid continuing his exhausting masquerade as a ne'er-do-well heir to a small shipping company, and there would be no need to attend the house party being hosted by the man he trailed. These missions were always draining—more so when he was at the heart of them rather than an observer on the outskirts. He was vastly more comfortable in the shadows.

The man paused and, between one heartbeat and the next, Oliver smoothly sidestepped and melted into a shadow cast by the corner of a building. Not daring to move or breathe, he remained as still as the hunter he was while the other man listened, turning his head just enough to peer over his shoulder.

A plump rat chose that moment to scurry through the gutter and a crash sounded from a nearby alley. The sounds of life all served to further mask Oliver's presence and lessen the other man's unease. He continued on his path and, after counting to three, Oliver followed, careful to keep close to the shadows and move with silent feet.

The streets were lined with dank, narrow houses, dodgy pubs with ancient names, and filthy cobbles slick with material he'd rather not contemplate. Though he'd been removed from this world for years, it felt a bit like home.

Gradually, the streets became cleaner and the buildings less weary and worn. This was a more frequented part of Covent Garden where a toff might be lured into a sense of safety and believe that he wasn't putting his life at risk if he frequented a West End "Golden Hell" like the notorious duke's for a bit of gambling, spent the evening taking in a performance at the Mask & Lyre, or wiled away hours at any of the several exclusive brothels catering to the elite. That man would be wrong. Danger lurked even in these more well-lit streets. Oliver knew them as well as he did every mark and scar upon his body. His flesh was a roadmap of London—the city as much a part of him as the blood in his veins. His old territory wasn't all that far from where they walked; there was something oddly comforting about the familiar worn cobblestones, the same odors, seeing buildings he'd once walked past as a lice-ridden child.

A chill danced up and down his spine from the memories and he was grateful for the warmth of his expensive wool overcoat. His old, worn clothing would have offered a better disguise as he traversed Covent Garden, but (he hated to admit) he'd grown a bit soft in his old age, more accustomed to some fineries than he cared to admit. His body had taken enough of a beating over the years that every scrap of comfort was appreciated.

"What are you up to?" Oliver muttered to himself as the man made an abrupt turn and scaled the three steps to a narrow wooden door leading to a darkened building. It wasn't dilapidated, simply oppressively silent—especially when compared to the golden glow of the building next door. Just on the other side of the absurdly narrow alleyway sat the premiere brothel Covent Garden had to offer. Lady Night's establishment was one of the best worst-kept secrets in London. Men—and women—of social standing wished to patronize the establishment known for its willing employees, clean environment, and literal cutthroat dedication to utter discretion. As it was, several carriages were lined up before the building, their drivers and tigers adjusting tack or chatting and smoking to pass the time. Every clear glass window of the three-story building glowed, attesting to its owner's success and insistence upon providing only the best for her employees and their clients. In contrast, the black windows of the building beside it—into which the man had ducked—resembled a skull's hollow eye sockets, flat and foreboding.

Oliver paused and assessed his situation. Every bit of his training warned him that walking into that building without any sense of its layout or idea of its occupants was foolish. The other part of him wanted this to be done.

He wanted this man off the streets.

He wanted to uncover whatever potentially deadly threat this man and his information presented and neutralize it before any harm could be done.

And, when that was done, he wanted to finally—

What?

Where did he want to go? It wasn't as if he had a home or a family. He'd kept life at arm's length for so much of his existence that skulking in shadows and carrying out missions were all he knew. And he knew bloody well that he'd probably just do it all over again once he'd accomplished this task. He owed his life to this profession and he'd likely die for it in the end; that had been made impeccably clear from the very start.

Well, Oliver thought, *death comes for everyone.*

Palming one of the knives he wore strapped beneath his coat in a leather sheath, he began his examination of the building to locate an unobserved point of entry.

After discovering a poorly locked door off of the narrow alley, Oliver quickly confirmed the building was vacant. He waited in utter stillness until his eyes adjusted to the thick blackness. Ears pricked for any sound and eyes sharp, he maneuvered around the lower level of what appeared to have once been a boarding house of some sort. There were the typical rooms one would expect— the sitting room and narrow dining room with stairs leading below to the kitchens—each containing the odd bit of shattered furniture, healthy coatings of dust, and the faint stench of woodsmoke, mold, and animal waste. He moved from room to room, an occasional shaft of light filtering over from the busy brothel next door.

It didn't take Oliver long to confirm there was no one on the main floor or below in the cramped kitchens and he began to ascend the stairs as quietly as he could. Though his heartbeat slowed to a concentrated pace, each pulse was nearly deafening in his ears. It was always like this for him when the danger crept nearer. His senses heightened to a razor's edge, but everything else about him slowed along with the world around him. His grip tightened around the blade's handle in his palm and he took great comfort in its familiar balanced weight.

Room by room, Oliver made slow and steady progress throughout the narrow building. Silent and stealthy as a black cat, he slipped through the shadows, listened, and examined his surroundings for any signs of life or recent activity. It wasn't until he'd reached the top floor that he heard hushed tones and urgent whispers too muffled to make out the words. Creeping closer, he was able to discern three—no, four—distinct voices. One spoke in rapid-fire French; his thick country dialect would have made it difficult for many nonnative speakers to comprehend, but Oliver had been trained well.

And the man was irritated.

"We must go into hiding for at least a short while. You have become too visible—" A resounding smack cut off the first man's words.

"In English," snarled a familiar voice in a tone so low, it was almost inaudible from where Oliver stood. "Speak only in English," he repeated so dangerously that it brooked no argument. Oliver's every muscle tensed with the confirmation that he'd successfully trailed his mark. He'd found his man.

"Cancel the party," the first man begrudgingly repeated in remarkably smooth English.

"It is an unnecessary risk," chimed in the third.

His target scoffed, then said, "These contacts are far too important to alienate with such an offense. Ties to munitions production? A shipping heir? We would be stupid to turn away such opportunities."

"You, yourself, said you'd been followed," the fourth man added.

"He's at the bottom of the Thames now, isn't he?" sniffed their leader, the man whom Oliver had trailed since another spy's suspicious disappearance. At least now he could report back as to the agent's fate.

Oliver's hand tightened around his weapon and he continued to listen.

"But the fuse of suspicion has been ignited," cautioned the third. "We would do well to step away until curiosity dies down." There was a scuffle and a bang, the wall beside Oliver's head rattling as a body was shoved against it. It dislodged a shower of plaster and dust, coating his hair and shoulders in a gray powder.

Almost instantly, Oliver felt the debris enter his nose and set off the chain reaction indicating an imminent sneeze.

Damn and blast, he silently cursed, pressing his lips together, covering his face with his gloved hand, and pinching his nose shut to staunch the outburst.

"I will not give up and walk away from everything I've worked for," snarled the mark. "And you all had best remember who is in charge of this operation lest I be forced to gut each of you for insubordination."

The pressure in Oliver's sinuses built and his eyes began to water. No. Not now. He'd never live it down if word got out that he'd blown the reconnaissance due to a *sneeze*.

Or that he'd been killed because of it.

He managed to stifle the sneeze, though his head felt as if it might explode and he momentarily saw stars. Dust had always done this to him and it had been damned unfortunate and inconvenient…but never more so than at that moment.

He resumed listening in time to hear the men discussing the guest list for the upcoming party.

"Where are Henri and Paul?" asked man number four.

"Late, as usual," scoffed the first man.

Not thirty seconds into their discussion, a sudden, unstoppable, violent sneeze exploded from Oliver, thrusting the occupants of the house into shocked silence.

Oliver spat a curse before spinning on his heel and dashing back up the hallway. If he had any chance of salvaging this mission, he needed to escape without his mark recognizing him. It would undo months of ingratiating himself and gaining the man's trust. Who knew when or if another opportunity would present itself if this fell apart? Good men would die, and Oliver couldn't have that blood on his hands.

Heavy footfalls followed his progress, but he dared not look over his shoulder. He reached the top of the stairs only to hear the rapid creaking of boots ascending the flight before him. It appeared the tardy Henri and Paul had arrived.

He veered toward a narrow door he'd discovered during his earlier investigation and wrenched it open to reveal a dangerously steep set of stairs. He wasn't entirely certain what he would do once he reached the roof, he only knew that he needed room if he were going to have any chance of handling six men on his own.

There was a scuffle behind him as the men collided and attempted to squeeze through the doorway at the same time, buying Oliver another few precious seconds to heave his shoulder against the panel in the ceiling and climb up onto the roof.

He was instantly assailed by the bone-chilling rain once again and the air reeked of wet stone and filth, somehow even dirtier now that he was four stories above the ground. His eyes and brain worked frantically to analyze his options. Thanks to the clouds, the only light that night came from the glowing windows of the brothel next door.

"Nowhere to go," huffed the first man to reach the roof—not a voice Oliver recognized, so it was likely one of the new arrivals.

He held himself stiff, eyes still scanning the edge of the flat roof for any alternate methods of reaching the ground that didn't involve leaping to his death.

"Someone felt a bit nosy tonight," said another.

"What should we do with him?"

"Cut out his tongue so he can't repeat anything? Cut off his ears so he can't eavesdrop anymore?"

"Take his fingers?" suggested another.

Oliver counted five voices; the only one he had yet to hear was the one he most wanted to avoid. At least he had that going for him.

"I actually like all me parts, gentlemen," Oliver replied in a low tone, intentionally dropping all shine of refinement from his voice and allowing the rough accent of his childhood in the gutter to take over. "So you might want tuh turn 'round before ye get hurt."

"Hear that, Charles?" snorted one of the men. "This one thinks he can handle five of us on his lonesome." There was a glint of steel as a knife was drawn.

Five. That answered Oliver's question. His mark had fled and left his cronies to handle him. At least now he could defend himself without the fear of potential recognition. He hadn't blown the mission yet…at least, as long as he didn't die.

"He's either very brave or very stupid," chuckled the man called Charles. Oliver turned to face his opponents, disguising his knives beneath his wrists inside his coat sleeves. He sized them up. Two of them were taller than him but possessed less bulk. Another man had at least a stone on Oliver, while the final two were of average height and build. Oliver knew better than to underestimate any of them, though they seemed to fall prey to that fallacy when it came to him. Never discount an opponent simply because he *appears* to be at a disadvantage.

At once, the men charged, led by the one called Charles. In the blink of an eye, Oliver flung one of his knives into Charles's chest, dropping him in an instant with a sickening thud. Tall Man One and Two dodged his body with blades of their own. A well-placed kick with his boot sent one knife flying while he deftly fended off the other. His fist found the billowing fabric of a cloak and a sharp tug sent its owner stumbling to the edge of the rooftop. Before he could send the man over, another knife was coming at him. He caught his attacker's wrist in a crushing grip and rammed his second knife into his forearm. The guttural scream echoed between the buildings.

Ducking to retrieve another blade from his boot, Oliver smoothly swept the feet out from beneath the bleeding man clutching his forearm. He hit the roof with enough force to cause him to lose his breath, but there was no time to catch it before Oliver plunged his new blade into the man's chest.

The next attacker proved to be fairly skilled with his fists. They met one another blow for blow. Oliver deftly dodged a vicious right hook and blocked a jab with a swipe of his forearm before he was finally caught in the side of the head. The man's downfall, however, was the confidence the strike gave him; it made him sloppy. After a few more blocks, Oliver was able to catch him with a violent uppercut that sent the man's head snapping back and his eyes rolling back as he collapsed in an unconscious heap.

Oliver whirled, prepared to continue fighting, but froze when his gaze met a new kind of metal. The final man leveled a pistol at Oliver's torso. Judging from the man's steady hand and unflinching eyes, he knew what he was doing and he would most certainly use the weapon on him if it came to that. He wouldn't be able to reach another of his blades before the shot found his flesh.

"Enough," growled the man.

Oliver was in the midst of frantically weighing his options when his breath was stolen by a stab of white-hot pain in his left side. His hand flew to where the man who'd nearly toppled over the side of the roof had rammed a slim stiletto blade honed to deadly sharpness between his ribs.

"You tried to send me over the edge, you bastard," the man snarled into Oliver's ear from behind and twisted the weapon, earning an agonized growl from deep in Oliver's chest. Pain exploded within him, radiating from the blade's invasion like a flare of ignited gunpowder shooting throughout his limbs. His nerves were overwhelmed, his vision swam and blackened around the edges.

"We should keep him alive," cautioned the gunman as the blade was wrenched from Oliver's side, causing him to stumble and nearly drop to his knees.

His hand flew to the wound, a gush of hot blood instantly soaking through his glove. He took quick stock. It hurt, but he could still breathe. The wound was too low to have nicked his heart. Still, the amount of blood was more than a little worrisome.

"Like hell," spat the man whose knife dripped crimson with Oliver's blood.

"Louis won't like it."

"Shut it! Louis just wants to play with him." He leaned so close to Oliver that he could smell fish on the man's breath. "I'd much rather introduce him to the ground…after I cut his pretty face a bit."

Oliver's lip tilted in an approximation of a smile. "Thanks, but no." He surged forward and, with a practiced maneuver, he broke the man's wrist and forced the stiletto he held back into his gut. There was the crack of gunfire as Oliver ducked and rolled, hissing through the searing pain in his side. He just managed to catch the edge of the roof as his body rolled over, but his grip was slippery from the rain and his blood. Plummeting a few feet before he found purchase on the carved edge of a window, he cried out as a fresh wave of pain tore through him, made worse by the jolt to his shoulder. His heartbeat roared in his ears and his vision flickered. Rain pelted his body, plastering his hair to his face and scalp so he could barely make out the dirty stones of the building facade, the yawning pit of the alleyway below his dangling boots, the golden glow of the brothel at his back. And…was that a balcony? His perception was skewed by pain, darkness, and rain, but he thought the topmost rooms at the back of the brothel possessed a balcony. It was hardly deep enough to be considered thusly, but it was there. Too bad it was a full story below him and across the alley.

He looked up just in time to see the pistol-wielding man leaning over the side of the roof as he prepared to take aim and finish off Oliver. Was this how it finally ended? A bullet in his head and his broken body shattered on the floor of a filthy alley beside a brothel?

Likely, his father still would have believed this death to be too good for him. How odd that that was one of his last thoughts…

Suddenly, the gunman flinched as several shouts rang out behind him.

"Oy! Stop there!"

"Don't move!"

"What's all this?"

Rage and indignation flashed across his features as the man was pulled back from the roof's edge by officers who'd likely been on patrol and heard the fight. Lord knew no one else in this neighborhood would have summoned the law.

Fingers slipping one by one, strength waning, consciousness flickering, Oliver was left with no choice but to plant his boots and push himself off the side of the building and into the air.

The singular sensation of flight was nothing short of euphoric, right up until he landed.

Chapter Two

"U SELESS," GRUMBLED EMILY to herself.

The top-floor flat she and her mother shared was more than nicely appointed. She had stacks of books and cases of watercolors, more pens and sheaves of parchment than she could ever consume in a lifetime, and yet she couldn't help but feel…utterly and completely useless.

Her world was so irritatingly small—had been made to be so by her mother. Emily knew it was born of a desire to protect her and shelter her from the cruel world in which her mother had been raised, but it meant Emily saw and knew so little of it. She felt like little more than a child, though she'd already reached her twenty-second year. In her most morose and isolated moments, she often imagined herself a medieval princess locked in a tower with no prince or knight to come to her aid because no one knew she even existed.

Despite what her few friends among her mother's employees said, she didn't find herself a remarkable beauty. She'd been a quiet girl who'd grown into a relatively reserved young woman. More than once, she'd been told that she'd make a fortune if she became an official employee of Lady Night's, but she'd merely blushed, brushed off the flattery, and changed the subject. Emily wasn't delusional enough to believe the exaggerated compliments, and, even if it had been the life she'd wanted, her mother would never have allowed it.

And nobody went against Lady Night.

Emily's hair was halfway between blond and white, her eyes halfway between blue and green, her figure halfway between curvaceous and slim, and her height halfway between short and average. She was the very definition of middling. Well, except for her social status. As far as normal Society went, she was lower than even the muck on the bottom of a stableboy's boot. In Covent Garden, however, she was as close to a princess as it would ever see.

And her mother was its queen.

Lady Night, formerly Fran Tailor of St. Andrew's Road and child of the streets, had clawed her way up from poverty and victimization to form the right connections and obtain the building now inhabited by London's preeminent brothel. What had once been a fairly standard center of vice and carnal sin had been transformed into a den of luxury known for its lavish rooms, expensive spirits, and men and women who *chose* employment there rather than being forced to do so. The staff kept most of the money they earned, were fed well, clothed, housed, received medical care when needed, and were protected; above all, they were free to leave at will. Lady Night had created a new culture in her corner of Covent Garden and it drew clientele from the highest levels of Society, male and female alike. She'd also earned the loyalty and support of the neighborhood with her employment of many of its residents. Maids, cooks, barmen, burly men who ran security, grooms—not to mention the vendors who sold all the goods to them—all benefited from the steady employment. As such, Lady Night was one of the unofficial heads of Covent Garden…an institution all her own.

In direct reaction to her mother's horrific upbringing in the slums, Emily's life had been filled with every comfort and protection little Franny Tailor had never experienced. Her mother did everything she could to shelter her and keep her away from lecherous eyes, safeguarding her against the world of those who traded their bodies and their talents for money.

Unfortunately for Emily, that meant her life was unbelievably boring for someone who lived above a brothel. Despite the frequent squeals, moans, laughter, and music floating up from the floors beneath her living quarters, her existence was, for all intents and purposes, rather quiet.

She'd read every one of the books in her collection five times over—could recite centuries of English history as well as any man who'd attended university and studied it extensively. Though she never understood it, her mother indulged her interest in the lives and impact of female rulers, queens, and consorts, plying her nubile mind with as many books as she could find on the subject.

There were only so many watercolors she could create when her entire world was limited to the top floor of the building, her little balcony, and the small garden below. For that matter, there were only so many times she could take a turn around that small space before she lost her mind counting the number of blooms on the flowers.

Though her mother insisted on bringing in the best modistes, pretty gowns were pointless when there was nowhere to wear them and no one to see her in them other than her mother and the few employees with whom Lady Night allowed her to interact. Nothing exciting ever happened to Emily, especially because she was never in a position for exciting things to occur. Most of her time was spent in their flat keeping the books and managing inventory lists for the brothel while her mother spent evenings overseeing the business below; nothing was thrilling about Emily's life.

Just as the thought crossed her mind, several male shouts drew her attention. She'd opened the French doors to the little balcony off of her bedchamber to emit the cool, misty air of the evening. The topmost floor of the building often grew warm with all the fires, candles, and steamy bodies filling nearly every free space. There was a loud smack and thud as a large black mass fell onto her narrow balcony and then remained motionless. Emily was momentarily frozen in disbelief. Had her mind been so starved of entertainment that it had concocted this scenario? She blinked a few times to be sure she wasn't imagining it, but the body remained.

Gasping in shock, she tossed aside her book and rushed over to the door. Stepping out into the rainy, inky night, she thought nothing of her safety and only of checking on the unconscious person lying prone and…good heavens, *bleeding*!

His face was obscured by a veil of blood seeping from a cut at his temple and his dark hair was plastered to his head with both rain and more blood welling from at least one wound. Not knowing what else to do, she pressed a trembling hand to his chest to feel for his heartbeat and noticed the puddle around his body was turning pink with blood from yet another injury. Her fingers found a slit in this coat and her hand came away crimson. Had he been stabbed?

Emily squinted up through the raindrops at the pitch of her roof and instantly knew there was no way he'd come from that direction. The building to her left was too short, the balcony overlooked the small garden and there was no way up or down, to her right was the abandoned boarding house her mother had been considering purchasing for an expansion. That appeared dark and deserted as usual, but it also afforded the only angle she thought possible for this man to have come from. Had he leaped from the rooftop of the building next door to her balcony? And why? For that matter, why had a *stabbed* man done such a thing?

"Mary!" Emily shouted for her maid, repeating herself when she didn't immediately appear. The woman rushed into the room and screamed at the scene. Emily flinched, realizing what a sight they must have made. "Mary, I need you to send for a physician."

"Who's that?" the maid questioned frantically. Her face had lost its usual pinkness and her buxom figure trembled from the shock. "Where did he come from?"

"Never mind that. Send for the physician."

"R-Right," Mary stammered, her face paler than linen. She turned to go but hesitated. "Shouldn't we send for Dawson or one of the other men?"

Emily shook her head; the last thing she wanted was more witnesses to this perplexing scene—at least not until she could figure out what had brought this injured man to her balcony. Lady Night's guards were trained to keep the peace first and ask questions second. "Tell no one other than the physician."

A guttural groan rose from the prone man's chest a second before he clasped her wrist in his gloved hand. She gasped more out of shock than pain. His large hand was surprisingly gentle yet firm at the same time. And, when she looked up from where his long fingers held her immobile, she discovered the strangest, most piercing silver eyes she'd ever beheld.

"No doctor," he ground out, his voice thick with pain.

"You are hurt; you must see a physician—"

"No doctor..." He hissed a breath through his teeth and clutched his side. "No doctor other than Dr. McCullom near St. James's. Tell him Black is down." And, with that, his eyes glazed over and rolled back. He lapsed into unconsciousness once more. His hand fell limply from her wrist, taking with it its surprising warmth.

Black is down? What could that possibly mean? Black was a color, not a direction.

"Go!" Emily commanded the maid, deciding they hadn't the time to try to decipher the words of a man possibly delirious with pain from his injuries. With any luck, the words would make sense to the physician. "Find Dr. McCullom." She had faith that someone would be able to track down the prominent physician; nearly everyone knew his office's location.

Time was their only enemy.

She needed to take action or the man would surely perish before the physician could arrive. With no little difficulty, she hooked her hands beneath his arms and dragged him into her bedchamber and out of the rain. He was impressively long and heavy, but she managed. It took several tries and muttered curses, but she was eventually able to strip his fine wool coat from his body, proud when she only elicited a few groans of discomfort from him. Beneath the coat he wore a plain, well-tailored black suit and dark-gray waistcoat, the lines of which displayed a firm, trim body beneath. The man was lean, but it was clear that every inch of him was hardened with impressive musculature.

Biting her lower lip, Emily set about locating the wound in his side and quickly rediscovered the slice in his clothing, the slash where some sort of blade had penetrated deeply. Stumbling to her feet, Emily rummaged through her wardrobe's drawers to locate a pile of clean white handkerchiefs before scurrying back to the man's side. She pressed several to his ribs to staunch the blood flow and watched his face for any sign of pain. He didn't so much as flinch. Was that a good or bad sign?

With one hand firmly pressed to that wound, she turned her attention to the gash in his hairline. She used a new handkerchief to wipe his face clean and then pressed it to that injury. There, one hand on each of his most obvious injuries, Emily had her first proper look at the man.

While pale from pain and blood loss, his skin still maintained an olive hue complimenting the pitch blackness of his hair. A light stubble on his angular jaw was beginning to show and it accentuated the sharpness of his cheekbones. Even though it was clear his nose had been broken at least once or twice, it remained pleasing when taken in with the rest of his features. Dark brows framed deep-set eyes she wished she could see again—if only to confirm they were truly silver and not something more mundane. It could have been a trick of the light, but she thought they'd practically glowed.

"Who are you?" she whispered to the unconscious man. She expected no response and received none. "And where did you come from?"

Emily's head shot up at the sound of a commotion from the front of the flat. Mary rushed into her room and, rather than being followed by a man of obvious Scottish descent, a young man with black hair and eyes, golden skin, and long features entered, carrying with him a heavy black leather satchel. This was quite obviously not Dr. McCullom.

"You were to send for Dr. McCullom," Emily told her maid, trying to keep the panic from her voice.

The physician stepped around poor, flustered Mary and spoke in a gentle voice so heavily accented, it nearly obscured his English. "I am Dr. McCullom's apprentice, Dr. Bianchi. He was away attending another patient, but I was available."

Emily chewed her lip in indecision. The injured man had been impeccably clear that they sent only for Dr. McCullom...but he looked so pale and he hadn't opened his eyes in what felt like hours. It could very well be a choice between this physician or the undertaker. If his pallor was any indication, then there was no time to argue. She was generally a kindhearted, optimistic person, so she tried to give Dr. McCullom the benefit of the doubt, but it wouldn't be the first time a physician or other man of business refused to attend Lady Night's due to its reputation. To treat a prostitute with the same hands he used to treat the *ton*'s elite would not do. Still, Emily supposed a close associate of McCullom's was better than no physician at all.

Emily nodded and sat back on her heels to offer the physician space to begin his examination. She watched intently as Dr. Bianchi knelt beside her and checked beneath the handkerchiefs she'd applied.

"We must..." he made a carrying motion with his hands as his brain searched for the proper word, "...lift him and bring him to the bed."

"I'll call Dawson," Mary chimed in.

"No," Emily said, not wanting to alert the guard. Her mother would hear about it and then who knew what would happen to this man? "I can help."

Despite the maid's protests, Emily followed Bianchi's instructions and hefted the man's legs with a grunt as the physician lifted him beneath the arms and propped his lolling head against his chest. Good Lord, but the man was heavy. She was panting by the time they laid him atop her pale-blue coverlet.

She and Mary exited the room to give the physician privacy to examine his patient. Soaked through from her time spent out on the balcony, Emily gave a little shiver.

"Perhaps…I should help you change your dress?" offered Mary.

It was only then that Emily looked down and noticed that, not only was she soaked through, but her arms and sage-green gown were covered in streaks and splotches of dark-red and brown blood in various stages of drying.

Thank goodness she wasn't squeamish.

Chapter Three

ONE A LONG bath, a dry change of clothing, and an interminable wait later, Emily saw Dr. Bianchi exit the bedchamber. He found her and Mary seated beside the fire in the main living area. Her heart instantly skipped a beat at his arrival and she couldn't help but stand in an attempt to alleviate her anxiety. Her stomach performed one flip-flop after another.

Why did she care so much about the fate of this stranger who'd landed on her balcony?

"The gentleman has suffered a stab wound to his ribs, but he is extremely lucky," said the doctor in his heavily accented English. "The blade missed everything vital." Emily released a breath she hadn't realized she'd been holding. "I made sutures to the wound, and to the laceration to his scalp. He had a nasty bump on his head from his fall and he is likely concussed, but he should live." Earlier, Mary had retrieved clean linens and boiled water at Dr. Bianchi's request, so Emily had suspected that sutures had been necessary. Hearing it made her limbs a little weak, but she didn't falter. Bianchi continued, "I suggest we do not move him and let him rest as much as possible." He fiddled with his cuff, his hands pink from being scoured with hot water and strong soap. "I realize this may not be possible, but it could prove vital to his recovery." He watched her with his deep, dark eyes, a question there. How much was she willing to care for a stranger? It was her right to throw him out into the alley—she knew nothing about him and he could very well be dangerous—

but something about the careful way he'd grasped her wrist told her otherwise. She didn't know how he'd come to be there, but she refused to be the reason he didn't survive.

"How long will he be like this?" Emily asked, calmly clasping her hands in front of her.

"His side will take a few weeks to heal and he'll be sore from his fall. There are numerous bruises, but no breaks. Do...you know how this happened?" he asked curiously.

Emily shook her head helplessly. "I saw him only after he landed. I can only imagine he came from the neighboring roof, but I've no idea why or how he made it. The building is vacant and shuttered."

Bianchi nodded, looking thoughtful.

"Who is he?" she asked, watching the doctor's face carefully.

His shuttered, evasive reply was all the answer she required, especially when he could not meet her eye. "The man is a stranger." Bianchi may be a talented enough physician to train beneath Dr. McCullom, but a skilled liar, he was not.

"What if he's dangerous," Mary said, chiming in. Her sewing fell forgotten to the floor when she stood. "The man had no business being near Miss Tailor's balcony. It doesn't matter how fragile he is; he should be moved."

The twitch of the doctor's mouth told Emily just how bad an idea moving the unconscious man would be. "If at all possible, I would advise against it. I can offer you laudanum to help with his pain; it will also make him more docile—*not* that I believe him to be a threat. Sedation and sleep will help speed the healing process anyway." He met Emily's eyes and the pleading sincerity she saw there made her pause, especially when his next phrase felt as if he spoke directly to her. "If I were a man who made wagers, I would lay money down that this man would not trouble you—especially not with his injuries."

She trusted Bianchi with his kind eyes and gentle way of speaking; the fact that he also had the renowned Dr. McCullom's approval was another merit. If Bianchi was trying to impress upon her that this man's life depended on the sanctuary and care provided beneath her roof, then she believed him; if he insisted that this stranger posed no threat, then, as uncomfortable as it made her, she would trust him.

"Then he will stay," Emily said with firm finality, holding up a hand to silence Mary's ongoing protests. She knew she couldn't have imagined the relieved look in the physician's eyes.

Bianchi set about showing her how to carefully dose and administer the laudanum, explaining how and when to have the man's bandages changed, impressing upon her how vital it was that everything—including her hands—be as clean as possible. He left her with a bar of strong soap, doses of the drug, and instructions that he be called for if the man's condition worsened. "I shall return in a few days to see how he fares." Emily attempted to pay him for his services, but he held up a hand and shook his head. "*Grazie*—thank you, but no. It is handled." She frowned but didn't argue and Mary helped escort Bianchi and his bag out of the flat and to the back exit of the brothel.

Emily was left alone in the quiet apartment with only the flutter of music and the lilting voices below her feet.

No.

She wasn't entirely alone.

She nibbled her lower lip in a moment of indecision before heading toward her bedchamber. The door had been left ajar and a single candelabra remained lit on the desk beside her narrow bed. The man lay asleep beneath a fresh coverlet, though it was almost absurd how large he looked lying there. Mary had also fetched boiling water and fresh bedding at Bianchi's request and it seemed as if the physician had done an admirable job of swapping out the soiled linens, cleaning his patient, and settling him in to rest. The pungent medicinal scent of Bianchi's soap filled the air, mingling with the whisper of her rosewater oil and something deeper she slowly realized was the unexpectedly pleasant musk of masculine flesh.

Emily padded on silent feet to the bedside and, now that his face had been cleaned, she was afforded her first good look at the man's face. What she saw stole her breath.

He was impossibly handsome—not in the classical, statuesque way, but he was rugged, untamed, tense even in sleep. A bandage was wound 'round most of his head, but dark hair with just a hint of a curl peeked out from behind it. His jaw was strong and edged with stubble. The sturdy column of his neck and the sinewed firmness of his collarbone were the only things visible above the blanket.

She swallowed hard as she watched the rise and fall of the man's broad chest. She hoped Bianchi was right; even in sleep, she could sense this man's latent power. A shiver tickled her spine.

Just then, a bang of a door in their flat told Emily that her mother had arrived. She'd been able to convince Mary to delay the news of this man's arrival from reaching her, but it seemed Bianchi's request that they harbor this stranger while he healed had set the maid's conscience over the edge. Emily's stomach plummeted. Furious footfalls told her Lady Night was well aware of their uninvited guest…and she wasn't the least bit pleased.

Emily fled the bedside and quietly closed the door to her room behind her, immediately coming face-to-face with her mother.

Not yet in her fourth decade, the madam was still stunningly beautiful and impressively youthful. She tended to apply a touch too much rouge, but it could be overlooked when taking into account her painfully stylish hair and clothing. There were rumors that she bribed the best modistes in London to make her gowns of the latest fashions even before they became all the rage in the *ton*'s ballrooms. She denied it, but Emily knew her mother took pleasure in knowing the styles the snobbish gentry wore were exhibited first in her establishment.

That evening, Lady Night wore a gauzy crimson gown that displayed her pale decolletage and figure to perfection. Coupled with her dark-blond hair, curled and plaited and piled atop her head to better display her swan-like neck, the effect was nothing short of enticing. She no longer entertained guests—hadn't for many years at that point—but she always said it was excellent for business if the proprietor set a good example.

"Wha' the bleedin' 'ell is goin' on 'ere?" her mother demanded, every ounce of pretense dropping from her voice as her Cockney accent took center stage like it always did when she was furious. "A man? In yo' room?"

Emily barely resisted the temptation to twist her fingers like a child as she explained how this night had come to be so uniquely strange. She did her best to convey the gravity Bianchi exhibited when he requested they allow the unconscious stranger to take sanctuary with them, but she'd miscalculated the breadth of her mother's charity.

"Why is it ah business if this man dies?" Lady Night snapped. "'E shouldn't 'a' been on a rooftop anyhow." She turned to Mary. "Send fa a few men. I want 'im out in the streets tonight."

"No!" Emily lunged forward and grabbed her arm. Her mother had always been a warm and loving parent to her, but Emily held no illusions; Lady Night was a ruthless businesswoman with teeth and claws to match. She would do whatever it took to protect her business and her daughter. She'd destroy any threat and she had the means and loyalty of an entire quarter of London to do so. And she was as cold and ruthless as she was just. Ripping the man from his sickbed and tossing him into a faraway gutter to remove any hint of their business's involvement would be nothing to her; neither would having him dropped into the Thames, never to be seen again. "Maybe he was being attacked or chased. Maybe his only chance at survival was this balcony."

Her mother scoffed. "A balcony ain't a invitation to anyone. It don't give 'im the right to use it, and it don't mean we 'ave to nurse 'im. 'Specially not you."

"I don't mind—truly, I don't!"

"It ain't 'bout mindin', but what's proper."

It was Emily's turn to scoff. "Proper? Mother. I live above a brothel. I am the daughter of one of London's most famous madams. Any implication of propriety is merely a veil…a vain and futile attempt at maintaining an appearance." Her mother reared back as if she'd been physically struck by her daughter's words, but Emily stood her ground. "I won't have his death on my conscience." She stopped just shy of saying that she felt as if he'd landed on her balcony for a reason—like she was meant to be the one to find him and ensure he received the care he required for survival. For so long, she'd read about and admired the brave, resourceful women gracing the pages of history; saving one man might not equate to leading a revolution or martyrdom, but it was still an opportunity for her to make a difference. How many such chances would she have within the confines of her tiny world?

Her mother's color rose, even beneath the layers of artfully applied powder and rouge. "You live under my roof, 'n' everyone in this building knows I rule. My word's the law." Her posture was as tense as a feral cat's, but something in her eyes softened when met with her daughter's unwavering gaze. "I'll 'ave Liza or Jenny take over from 'ere. 'E can be moved to another of the rooms."

"No!" Emily rushed to respond, then repeated herself more gently. "No." She was the first to admit to herself that it was terribly silly, but she'd instantly balked at the thought of those ladies' practiced hands taking care of the man. Besides, this was quite the most exciting thing that had ever happened in her life. Thinking quickly, she added, "They're so busy. All of them are. And, as the daughter of this business's proprietor, I feel…responsible for him." Lady Night flicked away the words with a careless hand, but Emily forged on. "I understand and I appreciate your desire to protect my innocence, but really…I grew up in a *brothel*. My caretakers were prostitutes; my earliest friends, the fatherless offspring of those women. I have no illusions about what takes place beneath this roof. Who are we trying to fool?"

At their cores, both women knew the only thing innocent about Emily was the fact that her mother had been very careful to ensure Emily guarded her maidenhead. Why, in this den of iniquity? Emily had always thought it was her mother's attempt to give her a better future, though Emily had truthfully never felt even the slightest inclination to toss it away. She'd witnessed firsthand how her mother had struggled to raise her alone after one of her unnamed clients had planted his babe in her belly and gone on his way. Emily knew her mother harbored a hope that Emily would find a husband and a stable home, but it was futile with her dodgy lineage and unconventional upbringing. She knew who she was and where she came from.

In the end, the argument was cut short by a knock at the door to their flat; one of their longtime patrons had arrived. Lady Night left the flat to return belowstairs to oversee her business. Despite appearances, it took a great deal of coordination to run a business such as hers, especially when she so carefully ensured the comfort of her employees. Guests who didn't respect the boundaries set by the employees or failed to follow the rules clearly outlined before admittance were dealt with swiftly. In addition, it took a great deal of artful scheduling to ensure each guest was paired with the proper employee. Men who preferred to be dominated in ways they never could be out in the real world would do better with those who were trained in the use of a crop or a rope, and wouldn't appreciate the tender art perfected by others. Those patrons who lacked comfort and joy in their lives required just the right touch to give them what they needed. It was a delicate dance, and one Lady Night had perfected over the years.

Emily was determined to turn her head back to the man in need and leave her disagreement with her mother for another time. As far as she was concerned, the man was safe for now and she'd throw herself across his body if it meant saving him from certain death on the streets.

She returned to her bedchamber and set up a chair near

where he lay prone on her mattress. Before sitting, she plucked a book from the nearby desk, deciding reading might do her some good. She didn't make it very long, however, and was soon lulled to sleep by the even rhythm of his deep breaths, so like the ebb and flow of the tidal ocean.

Chapter Four

EMILY WOKE EARLY the next morning, as was her custom; unfortunately, she experienced several unfamiliar aches and pains from sleeping in the chair. She tried in vain to stretch the weary muscles of her neck and back, but an unfortunate tug between her shoulder blades made her grimace and deflate.

All at once, the previous night's events came rushing back. She looked back at the man still resting in her bed and realized he hadn't moved so much as an inch. His chest still rose and fell in an even rhythm, though. She hoped all of this pointed to a restful, healing sleep. She gently laid the back of her hand across his forehead and stubble-roughened cheek, noting that his skin was cool and dry, if still a little pale.

Gingerly, she rolled down the coverlet to find his torso was still neatly wrapped in a clean white bandage; there was no sign that the bleeding had continued. It didn't take a great deal of medical training to know that was encouraging.

The next thing Emily noticed was the strength evident in the muscles of the man's chest and abdomen. Dark whorls of hair dusted the skin both above and below the bandage encasing his sculpted chest and highlighting the defined ridges of his abdomen. Her eyes began to stray and count the hard muscles trailing lower, but she wrenched them back up with a gasp. She wouldn't ogle the man while he was unconscious!

Still…who knew men could look like this!

Not her.

Focusing elsewhere, her eyes snagged on silvery scars here and there, marking the olive-toned flesh and presenting evidence of a very interesting past. It took everything in her not to trace the marks with her fingertips and wonder at their origins. Despite a few new, cleaned scrapes not deemed serious enough for bandaging, the scars were all old and long healed; some bisected others. What had happened to him? And on more than one occasion?

Deciding to make herself useful, Emily began gathering what she needed to change the man's bandages per Bianchi's instructions. After scrubbing her hands pink with the cake of soap the physician had left behind for this purpose, she prepared a new bandage and carefully cut away the old one. She examined the wound with its even stitches and dark dried blood, thanking God for her strong stomach. After dabbing at it with a clean wet bit of linen, she was pleased to note that there was none of the redness she'd been told to watch for. As she worked, she ignored—or did her best to ignore—those remarkable muscles of his torso, the dark hair as it stretched down to his navel and disappeared below the edge of the sheet.

The old bandages were caught beneath his body and she had to pause to assess how she would solve the situation. It wouldn't have been an issue had he been conscious and in an upright position. This, however, presented an issue. She gave a cautious, experimental tug of his arm, but he was astonishingly solid and heavy. And he didn't stir. Hands on her hips, she decided the only way she would get anywhere was through a slow and steady process of pulling and sliding and lifting his shoulder as best she could. It wouldn't be a graceful process, but she took comfort that no one would bear witness to her fumbling attempts at nursing.

She reached beneath his trim side and balanced with a careful palm rested lightly against his steadily thudding heart. If she could just get the last bit from beneath his arm then—

Emily was caught between powerful hands as silver eyes flew

open, wild and confused. Long fingers encased her upper arms with such strength that she knew she had no hope of escape…but she would have been a great deal more frightened had he not elicited a groan of pain and a powerful curse. One of his hands released her to reach for his wounded side, but she grabbed his wrist.

"Don't!" He'd been bathed following his medical care, but Bianchi had told her never to touch the wound without freshly washed hands. He'd made it through the night without fever and she didn't want to risk it. "You've had a fall and you've been injured, but you're safe now." She hoped her voice was more reassuring to him than it sounded to her ears. Those piercing eyes made her heart race. "You need to rest." Despite her protests, the man struggled to a seated position only to screw his eyes shut with a hiss of pain and place a hand on his pounding bandaged head. "Your head was wounded as well," she added lamely.

Emily recognized the moment nausea overtook him and leaped to retrieve the basin Bianchi had so thoughtfully left nearby for this purpose. The man snatched it from her hands and relieved the meager contents of his stomach, groaning when the movement seemed to cause a fresh wave of pain in both his head and his side. Bianchi had warned her that this sometimes happened with head injuries, and she was grateful she'd been prepared.

Wanting to afford him some dignity, Emily averted her eyes and placed a hesitant, comforting hand on his shoulder. The wave passed with relative speed and he relaxed back against the headboard. He kept his eyes closed as he released a nearly unintelligible string of foul words in a coarse accent so thick, she could barely comprehend any of it.

And what she did understand was particularly vulgar.

She supposed she couldn't blame him; he did appear to be in a fair amount of pain.

Emily took the basin from his unsteady hands and set it aside before helping him readjust the pillows to a more comfortable position. She judged that the rebandaging of his wound could wait until he'd regained his bearings. The last thing she wanted to do was cause him additional discomfort.

When he finally reopened his eyes, confusion knitted his bold, dark brows together and, when he spoke, it was in a much more refined accent with enunciated consonants and elegant vowels. How interesting. The shift was distinct, but she made no outward comment; her mother had her reasons for masking her native accent, and Emily was sure this man did as well. It wasn't all that uncommon a thing to do. People tended to treat you better if they believed you were of finer stock.

"You said I was injured?" he croaked. His voice was hoarse from sleep and pain, but still deep and rich like quality tobacco smoke. It rumbled like thunder in the distance and rambled through her chest in a way that was not at all unpleasant. It was only when she realized that he was gazing up at her questioningly that she was startled back to herself.

"Oh, yes! You fell. And landed on my balcony." She gestured to the doors leading out onto the narrow space. The flatness of his expression might have been amusing had his eyes not been so intense, urging her to continue with more details. It was clear he was trying to remember, but his memory was lagging. He relied upon her account of things. She cleared her throat and continued to detail how he was now beneath Lady Night's roof, being tended to. She reassured him that he'd already been seen by a physician. His body tensed momentarily, but relaxed when she provided Dr. Bianchi's name, as if relieved that she'd followed his instructions and sent for the Italian rather than a nearer physician.

His eyes looked over her shoulder, growing unfocused as he scoured the corners of his memory—likely for any hint of what had occurred the prior night. Long minutes passed this way until she asked, "Might I finish replacing your bandages now? Dr. Bianchi did such a lovely job of your care and I'd hate to undo it all."

The man nodded somewhat reluctantly and allowed her to

resume the task that had been interrupted by his waking. He remained steadfastly silent and as watchful as his condition would allow while she went about her task. He allowed her to aid him by slowly leaning forward, and Emily barely stifled a gasp.

The scars on his chest and arms were nothing compared to the silvery web marring the otherwise smooth, muscular planes of his back. She had to force herself not to touch them or ask him what had happened. It was tempting now that her patient was awake, but she shouldn't pry. Those old scars had nothing to do with the reason he'd wound up on her balcony, so they were none of her business.

Instead, she asked him his name.

His only reply was a consternated silence.

"You *do* know your name, do you not?" Perhaps his head injury was worse than Bianchi had believed? And where did that leave them?

"Marcus Holden," he replied grouchily. "Yes, I do know my name."

Emily nodded and continued winding the bandage around his torso, trying not to touch his warm, naked flesh more than necessary—not out of repulsion, but because it felt too tempting, too dangerous to do so. And she was afraid that once she started, she wouldn't be able to stop.

"I am Emily Tailor," she offered without prompting. He made no further overtures at conversation. "Were you in the Wars?" she asked as innocently as possible. She couldn't help it; he intrigued her.

"Yes," was the curt answer. This might explain a few of the younger, pinker scars, but not the multitude of older ones. And he was so young—younger than she'd first thought him to be when he was covered in blood and drenched by the rain. She'd wager he was barely more than thirty years of age—if that. Despite this, there was a definite air of experience about him and she had yet to lose the sense of danger whenever she looked at him. If anything, it was intensified now that she could look into his intelligent, hawk-like eyes.

"Are you one of the…employees of this establishment?" he asked suddenly as she secured the end of the wrapping beneath the arm opposite of his injury.

"No." Her reply was light as she began tidying up.

"My apologies," he said quickly. "I meant no offense."

"None taken." Emily smiled reassuringly as she collected the materials and soiled wrappings to be disposed of. "My mother owns this building and runs the business within its walls."

"Lady Night has a daughter?" He was still sitting up, though the tautness of his face told her it was costing him a great deal of what remained of his depleted strength.

"Are you a patron of Lady Night's?" she asked, rather than answer him directly—not that she really wished to know if he'd frequented the brothel below. It wasn't common knowledge that the infamous madam had borne a child. Emily could have kicked herself for saying that much, and the last thing she wanted to do was draw attention to the slip.

"No." He shook his head and winced in instant regret of the motion. "Everyone in Covent Garden knows of Lady Night's."

"Are you a resident of the Garden?"

He narrowed his piercing eyes at her, making her heart flutter in her breast. "You ask a great deal of questions of a man who has only just woken."

Her cheeks flushed. "Apologies."

He sighed and tested the motion of his arm. "If you will hand me my clothing, I shall dress and be off. You have my gratitude for everything you've done, and I will, of course, provide compensation for the inconvenience."

"You intend to leave?" Emily's alarm grew as she watched Mr. Holden struggle to a more upright position and prepare to swing his legs off the edge of the bed. "But Dr. Bianchi said you should rest as much as possible." She rushed back to his side and placed a hand on his shoulder to try to keep him from rising. Though weakened by his ordeal, he was still impressively strong and much larger than she. She wouldn't be able to keep him there against his will, even in his current state. His brow was pale and damp with sweat, and she could see the determination in his eyes would soon push him past his physical limitations.

"Yes," he grunted. "I am sure I have imposed too much already and I would like to return to my own home to recuperate." Gathering the coverlet in his large hand, he met her eyes. "And I suggest you turn around or leave because you will otherwise soon receive an eyeful."

Emily's cheeks burned hotter than they ever had before in her life. Mortification and intense curiosity warred within her breast.

What could she do? Her eyes frantically searched the room for an answer before landing on the dark glass bottle the physician had left for her.

"A drink!" she said a little too loudly. "Surely you are parched. At least allow me to prepare a drink for you before you leave. You must take plenty of fluids—doctor's orders." Her smile felt forced, but it seemed to appease Mr. Holden. He narrowed his eyes at her for only a moment before huffing an exasperated sigh.

"Very well."

While he busied himself finding a position that did not cause him too much pain, Emily very quickly prepared a drink of tepid tea, plenty of sugar, and a very carefully measured dose of laudanum. Turning back, she saw that Mr. Holden had propped his head in his hands, his eyes shut tightly. This reassured her that she was doing the right thing. If she allowed him to leave, then he'd collapse as soon as he reached the street—if he even made it that far. Yes. This was for the best.

"Here you go," she said softly, guilt somewhat assuaged, as she held the cup out to him. "The tea has cooled, so it should not—"

He tossed it back before she could finish her sentence. This was to her benefit, though, because it also meant that he hadn't tasted so much as a hint of the drug's bitterness. He handed the cup back to her.

"My clothes." It was not a question.

"Of course; let me step outside and ask my maid where she's stored them. They had to be cleaned." She collected the rubbish and slipped from the room before she could ramble on any further.

Mary was so startled by Emily's abrupt entry into the parlor that she dropped the stack of linens she'd been carrying.

"Christ, child!" she hissed, pressing a hand to her throat. "You nearly scared the life right out of me."

"Apologies, Mary," she said, hurriedly walking to the dumb-waiter on the far wall and sending the items belowstairs. "Our guest is awake."

Mary's eyes widened and darted to Emily's bedchamber door. "He hasn't harmed you, has he?"

"No! Not at all. He's merely…trying to leave."

"Well, let him," Mary sniffed, stooping to gather up the linens she'd dropped. "His clothes should be clean and dry by now. I can fetch them once I put these away."

"I cannot allow that. If you only saw him, you'd understand that to send him away now would likely mean further injury or even death. I'm merely killing time until the laudanum sets in."

Mary eyed Emily for several heartbeats before huffing an exasperated sigh and turning away, all the while muttering something about Emily's bleeding heart. Emily remained in the parlor until a glance at the clock above the mantle told her she'd likely waited a sufficient amount of time for the laudanum to have its intended effect.

Inhaling a bracing breath, she reentered her bedchamber and was greeted by a pair of glowering, storm-gray eyes. She hadn't expected that. Could she have gotten the dosage incorrect? No. She'd followed Bianchi's instructions to the letter. Then why did he appear so awake? And grumpy…

"I don't see my clothes," he growled, but the effect was lost on the slight slur of his esses. Looking closer, she could see his pupils were so wide they nearly swallowed the mesmerizing irises.

"They're trying to track them down," she said, stalling just a little longer.

"I'll walk out of here stark naked if I must." He followed the threat with a lunge toward the floor, revealing one long, muscular leg to her. She caught him before he could either fall or bare himself to her entirely.

"Mr. Holden!" She grunted from the effort of propping up his large frame, barely managing to settle him back down before she had an entirely new set of problems on her hands. "Please. That is entirely unnecessary." All at once, his muscles gave in and they flopped together back onto the mattress. The laudanum must have been doing its job because he barely elicited a moan of pain. She blew a loose curl from her face and scrambled to sit up once she realized her hands were splayed upon his naked chest. His very hot, very hard, very masculine chest.

"J—just allow me another few minutes to obtain your garments and then you may be on your way." His thoughtful sound of assent was reminiscent of a groan of pleasure and it did the funniest things to Emily's stomach. Something flickered to life inside of her. "I think it's best if you lie down until then."

"Jussst a few minutesssss..." he said, closing his heavy eyelids and drifting off into a very deep sleep.

Chapter Five

THE NEXT FEW days for Oliver were nothing more than snippets of sounds, smells, feather-light touches, and oversaturated images. He felt at once lost and safe; even though his limbs felt impossibly heavy, he was also lighter than he'd ever been in his life.

The muffled grunts and moans of sex occasionally echoed in the distance, creating a hazy, confusing atmosphere in his head and teasing his most basic instincts. It made his body ache and throb uncontrollably during those brief moments when he wasn't floating in a dreamy mist.

Whiffs of delicate rosewater were usually accompanied by gentle caresses on his flesh, cool fingertips that ran through his hair, and traced the ridges of his ribs to leave gooseflesh in their wake. They never trailed lower, no matter how desperate his silent pleas for relief were.

A gentle voice spoke again and again, but the words were muffled as if they were being spoken underwater; still, the tone was soothing even if he struggled to understand them. He knew only comfort.

The few times he gathered the strength to peel open his leaden eyelids, a golden-haired angel floated above him. He experienced a profound sense of peace as he waited for her to take him into her milky-white arms and bring him to a heaven he'd never believed in…or to the hell he deserved. He didn't care where she took him, as long as she continued touching him and carrying on one-sided conversations over his inert form.

Nightmares came for him, as they sometimes did when he slept deeply. Faces from his past sneered and spat, closed fists pummeled his battered body. His father's slurring voice taunted him. Wide, unseeing eyes of the dead accused him of not being good enough to save them—fellow children of the streets and fallen agents, alike. The only friendly face he saw was that of Sterling St. John, the man with whom he'd spent the better part of a decade on the Continent as they worked in secret to obtain intelligence integral to England's stability. Even those dreams haunted him, fraught with a constant undercurrent of danger and the unknown as the two of them worked tirelessly to put their mission above everything, even their own safety. He nearly drowned in the thickness of the memories and their torturous reminders of his shortcomings and fears, of all the ways he'd struggled.

When lucidity finally came to Oliver, it was a painfully gradual process. His limbs felt heavy and his mouth stuck and tasted as if it had been packed with rancid wool. His vision took several minutes to adjust, but, when it did, he found his angel across the room. It took him longer than it should have to realize she'd shed her wings in favor of a plain pale-pink muslin morning gown, her rosewater-scented hair pulled back in a simple chignon with a matching satin ribbon. One tug and the waterfall of spun pale gold would cascade around her slim shoulders like liquid sunlight. Rather than greeting him with open arms to take him away, she was seated at a small writing desk, scribbling in what appeared to be a leather-bound ledger and utterly consumed with the task.

Recognition dawned on Oliver almost as slowly as consciousness.

Her name is Emily.

As plain a name as she was lovely.

And, when she looked up to find him watching her, the smile she gave him made it clear the title of "angel" did not do her justice.

Miss Tailor was remarkably pretty—beautiful, even. He held perfectly still except for his eyes, which danced over the delicate slope of her nose, the dainty point of her chin, her blue-green eyes slightly too large for her heart-shaped face…then down to the delicate curves of her body. She was soft and welcoming and she moved with all the grace of a trained dancer, except hers was more remarkable because it was innate. She'd been born for elegance.

Oliver fought to swallow. There he lay injured, drowsy, and half-naked—no, *entirely* naked—beneath the coverlet. It had been decades since he'd felt so vulnerable, and never had he felt thusly in the presence of a woman. He didn't care for the sensation of not having the upper hand, so he began to struggle into a seated position. The task felt as if he were pulling his limbs through molasses. Though Emily had risen and come to his side, he waved off her offer of the basin. The room didn't spin and he was not overwhelmed by nausea.

Thank God.

"I'm so pleased you are awake, Mr. Holden." There was that melodic voice that had come to Oliver in his dreams. So focused was he on the sound of it that it took him several seconds longer than it should have to register the words. He'd given her his current alias instead of his real name. "Dr. Bianchi should be by shortly to check on you."

"How long was I asleep?" he asked, his voice hoarse and his throat dry.

"Three days."

What?" he demanded, pushing away the tin cup of water she offered even though his parched mouth begged for it.

"T-the laudanum Dr. Bianchi provided seemed to help your pain…and I didn't want to risk you suffering further injury by allowing you to leave in your condition." She had the good grace to appear more than a little ashamed. "I continued dosing you per the doctor's instructions."

"Are you saying that you drugged me…for three days…to

keep me in your bed?"

"Yes," she said with a nod and then froze. "No. I mean, that is, yes to keep you in *a* bed, not necessarily *my* bed. Though that is where you are. My bed." She twisted her delicate fingers together as he inhaled as best as his injuries would allow. Her scent tickled his nose and caressed his memory.

That explained why the delicate aroma or rosewater flirted with his senses and danced through his dreams.

Still.

"You held me against my will."

"I acted in your best interests."

"I am not your responsibility."

"You landed upon my balcony; therefore, I would beg to differ."

Oliver's hand fisted around a fold of the coverlet. He opened his mouth for another retort but was forestalled when Dr. Bianchi strode into the room following a perfunctory knock.

Despite his annoyance, it was good to see a familiar face as the young Italian greeted Oliver with a warm smile.

"Ah. You are awake. *Molto bene.*" He turned his dark eyes toward Emily as he set aside his bag and shrugged out of his dark-gray wool coat. "It seems Miss Tailor has proven to be most capable in her nursing abilities."

"Thank you, Doctor. If you don't mind, I will leave you to perform your examination in privacy and take this opportunity to freshen up." She ducked from the room before either man could reply—possibly to save herself from any more of Oliver's ire. It was probably for the best, but the room suddenly felt dimmer, staler without her.

Silently, the Italian physician removed a canvas sack from his bag and set it on the foot of the bed. He didn't have to explain that it contained all the weapons he'd discovered on Oliver's person the night of his injury. It was protocol for all weaponry to be removed and hidden lest anyone discover it and question its need. As one of only a few physicians deemed worthy of caring for those within the ranks of England's elite spy society, Bianchi was returning them now that Oliver was conscious. It would feel good to have his knives and pistol strapped to him once more.

"Now," Bianchi began after cleansing his hands, "let us have a look at those injuries of yours."

After having his head prodded and declared much improved, Oliver allowed the doctor to unbind his chest and examine that wound.

"Do you carry any messages for me?" Oliver asked in a low tone, switching to Italian as easily as he breathed. His world was one of shadows and suspicion, but there remained a few individuals whom he knew he could trust. Bianchi's employer and mentor, Dr. Ian McCullom, had been appointed special physician by the Crown to treat the agents on home soil. This was not his first meeting with the trusted Italian apprentice and, if anyone were to try to get a message to him in these odd, frustrating circumstances, then it was highly likely that Bianchi would be carrying it.

"There are indications that you should abandon your task and rest," the doctor replied beneath his breath. *"Take time to heal."*

Fury bubbled up within Oliver's chest with shocking ferocity. How could his superiors think the best option was to remove him from his mission? He hadn't been recognized, he knew that much. His identity as Marcus Holden remained intact; to abandon the mission for this injury was a tragic waste of his efforts and time spent over the last few months. He knew he could not allow it to happen—not when he'd worked so hard and he was only days away from the house party he knew was one of his best chances at obtaining everything he needed to be successful.

He'd spent interminable weeks and done a multitude of un-savory things to gain the trust of one John Hayes—or "Louis" as he'd been addressed by his cohorts—to obtain an invitation to this bloody event. Now, if he followed orders, he'd be removed from the mission forever and another idiot would be sent in to bungle it. He'd picked up the pieces left behind by other men who'd failed in the task and he had little confidence there was another man who could take his place.

If he continued with his mission as if nothing had happened, however, then he would be going against direct orders.

It was tantamount to treason…and he'd have no assistance if he required it.

There would be no physician to sew him up.

There would be no other agents sent in if he wound up in a pinch.

His prospects were bleak, indeed, but Oliver's mind was like a hound with a scent; he simply could not let go. He was so close to the end and success in this assignment that he could taste it like a sweet on his tongue. More than a sense of accomplishment or duty, he couldn't stop thinking about the lives that could be saved if he were to achieve his goal and stop the forces at work seeking to shred England apart from the inside out. Powerful, dangerous men worked in the shadows to topple the delicate balance of peace; it was Oliver's job to ferret them out. He'd begun with very little to go off of and had gradually been able to narrow the scope of the investigation. Unfortunately, there was still a great deal left to discover.

What intelligence they did have indicated there may have been a leak from inside the spy society; several retired agents had disappeared in recent months. Additionally, there were rumblings that political unrest was being stirred up throughout England. Not everyone cared for the monarchy's direction and there were those who sought to capitalize upon it.

Like the French.

Oliver stewed over it throughout the rest of Bianchi's visit and his foul mood remained even after Emily poked her pretty blond head back into the room. His mind was still turning the matter over again, so occupied with it, that he didn't realize at first that she held in her arms a stack of neatly folded clothing.

"Dr. Bianchi said you've healed enough to leave," she said gently, as if unsure of her welcome in her own room. "I've brought you a fresh shirt since, well, the other was destroyed. Everything else has been washed and mended."

Oliver took a deep breath before replying. Did he appreciate being drugged these last three days? Certainly not. Would dying have been less preferable? Perhaps. Had she just been doing what she was told? Yes, he begrudgingly admitted to himself. Bianchi had confirmed as much and reiterated that, before that day, he'd been in no shape to care for himself, let alone leave and find his way back to somewhere safe. By all accounts, Emily had saved his life.

"Thank you," he murmured. She proceeded to help him shrug into his shirt and he began doing up the fastenings. For a shirt of unknown origins, it fit him rather well. She had a good eye. She turned to allow him privacy to don his smallclothes, breeches, and stockings. His body protested at the movement, but Oliver gritted his teeth and pushed through. He needed to be back to his normal activities as quickly as possible. A wounded and incapacitated spy was a dead one. Despite his determination, the motion of standing made his head ache and the fiery pull in his side caused a slight groan to squeak free from his throat.

"Who are you?" she asked in a small voice without turning around.

Oliver frowned while busying himself with tucking the fabric of his shirt into the waistband of his breeches. "Haven't I already told you?"

"Who are you *really*?"

"What is that supposed to mean?"

She peeked over her shoulder to confirm he was decent before fully turning around. She still held his coat draped over her folded arms and made no move to hand it over. There was a moment's hesitation before she continued. "Several times, you spoke while in the laudanum stupor. You spoke French." The room was silent as her wide eyes searched his. "It was so clear I almost believed you to be a Frenchman hiding here in England." She emitted a small awkward laugh. "Then you used another language I did not recognize. A nightmare came on the second night and…you spoke in one of the thickest Cockney accents I've ever heard—and that says something, given my current living arrangement."

Though his face remained emotionless out of nothing more than training and sheer will, his gut roiled. This was precisely the reason he'd always refused powerful drugs—no matter the severity of his injury—and why he never drank more than a sip of alcohol here and there for appearance's sake—no matter how his demons plagued him. He needed his wits about him at all times, and these substances could so easily cause slip-ups. A foggy mind could make for loose lips.

"You must have been mistaken," Oliver replied as he focused on fastening his breeches with his clumsy fingers, attempting to deflect and wishing his wits were sharper for this type of situation. All the sleep and inactivity had rattled all his faculties.

"I assure you, I am not. I know what I heard."

Oliver made a point to ignore her insistence and focused on pulling on his boots. The sooner he could get out of there, the better. He needed to get his mind straight and, most importantly, he needed to figure out what he was going to do about his mission.

He held out his hand for his coat. Emily complied but didn't release it. Instead, she met his eyes with the bravest fire he'd ever witnessed.

"Who is Sterling?"

Oliver froze along with the blood in his veins.

Damn.

How much had he revealed?

He'd been trained to withstand immense levels of pain and torture, but the one thing no one could account for was how one's mind and body reacted beneath the influence of certain substances. Laudanum, it would appear, was something from which he needed to stay far, far away.

"For that matter…" Emily released his coat and turned to

gather up something from an armchair in the corner. "You wouldn't want to forget this."

Dammit, Bianchi.

The Italian had forgotten to check his boots.

Emily now held out to him an ebony-handled stiletto in a plain leather sheath specially designed to fit beside his calf inside his boot. He didn't know how it had been missed, but that was beside the point. The weapon looked particularly vicious in Emily's small, pale hand.

"I know it is yours. I discovered it on the balcony and you are the only one who has landed there as of late." She met his eyes unflinchingly—she was remarkably brave, he had to give that much to her. "What is your real name? You owe me that little bit of honesty after leaving a large bloodstain on my balcony and ruining my favorite bedding."

Oliver knew she was probably correct; he owed her a debt he could never fully repay. The woman had saved his life, sacrificed her comfort, cared for him without so much as a question. She had every right to know exactly whom she had saved and brought into her space.

But he couldn't.

This angel of mercy deserved honesty, but she didn't need to be drawn into his world of danger and shadows—no matter how enchanting her wide eyes, how kissable her plump lips, how enthralling the sound of her voice.

"My lady—"

"I am not a lady."

"Miss." Oliver's jaw flexed. "I thank you again for your assistance and tireless efforts. I think it is simply for the best that we end our association at this point." His breath hissed through his teeth as he moved too quickly to retrieve the weapon from her hand and stash it in the canvas sack Bianchi had left for him. He gritted his teeth against a wave of pain and dizziness as he rummaged around until he located his purse. Without bothering to count them out, he held a number of coins out to her, then dropped them on the desk with a metallic clatter when she didn't accept them. The glint of gold and silver caught the light. "I must be off."

"You are truly going to walk out of here without answering any of my questions." It was a statement of disbelief rather than a question.

Oliver didn't know what made him halt his exit and respond. "I am."

She had the temerity to scoff. "Very well. Best of luck to you, *Mr. Holden*." He didn't need to see her eyes to know she rolled them in sarcasm.

He narrowed his gaze at her, barely staving off the urge to continue their verbal sparring. "Good day, Miss Tailor." He turned to leave.

"Take the stairs to the right when you exit the flat if you wish to leave unobserved. The stairs to the left will take you down into the main building. Pass through the kitchens and one of the maids will show you to the back alley."

He nodded and continued on his way. He could feel her enchanting eyes following his every move as tangibly as if she'd run a finger down his spine.

Chapter Six

OLIVER PUSHED THROUGH his aching head, throbbing ribs, and near-overwhelming fatigue to arrive at Scotland Yard from Lady Night's Covent Garden building in record time. He accessed the building via the back entrance off Scotland Yard rather than the main one on Whitehall. Though he avoided the bustle of the public this way, it was no less busy.

Messengers and secretaries darted to and fro to deliver their missives and attend meetings. Despite the chaos, everyone gave him a wide berth. Few knew his true identity, but his scowl and imposing size managed quite well in convincing people to leave him alone—as did his air of belonging. He knew precisely where he was going.

Bypassing the first and second desks, he paused in front of the wiry man bent nearly in half as he scratched away at his parchment. He paused as Oliver cast a shadow across the desk. He looked up and up into Oliver's face.

"I am in need of a file." Oliver's voice was a deep rumble beneath the din surrounding them.

"What file might that be, sir?" asked the man as he set aside his quill in anticipation.

"Windsor, 1791."

The man nodded once and pushed up from his desk to disappear around a corner. Not five minutes later, a tall, lean man dressed all in black appeared at Oliver's side.

"Pleased to see you up and about." The man's voice was cool

and even, so much so that it felt almost ethereal. Oliver turned into the very same face that had visited him in the London gaol all those years ago to pluck him free and drop him into his new life no less fraught with danger. "Come. Let us speak in private."

Oliver followed as they walked through a nondescript door before taking a winding path to an upper office overlooking the street below. "Jonathan Smith" read the engraved sign on the door. Rather than the man's real position, it listed him as an accountant. He knew Adrian Ramsay, the leader of England's elite spy society, spent a great deal more time away than he did in this office, but it served him to have a touchstone in the head-quarters of the Metropolitan Police.

Ramsay gestured for Oliver to sit in the wooden chair facing the sparse desk, which he did. Oliver chose to immediately launch into the purpose of his visit.

"Three dead and at least two neutralized in Covent Garden this past weekend."

"I know. They came through here."

"They were French."

Ramsay's elegant, angular face remained utterly still. He was silent.

"Bianchi said the mission was going to be called off."

"Yes. You are obviously injured, even if you are trying to disguise it." Oliver's jaw clenched at the comment. "We will not be moving forward with you. Recover and you will be reassigned next month."

"That is unnecessary," Oliver ground out. "I have a few days left before I need to leave."

"You have been compromised."

"Like hell, I was!" Oliver snarled and slammed his fist upon the desk that separated him from Ramsay. "Hayes did not see me. This can still happen."

"But you are injured." Ramsay's voice remained as even as ever, entirely unaffected by Oliver's outburst. They'd known one another for more than a decade, knew each other's mannerisms and personalities, but they'd managed only a stiff formality as far away from friendship as one might be. They were two formerly feral alley cats eyeing one another with suspicion and tolerance while offering no opportunity for any hint of companionability.

"I will heal. There is no reason to drop everything I've worked toward because of this."

"But I will not place another agent in jeopardy."

Oliver's heart skipped.

"Siren will not be attending the house party." Oliver's stomach careened off a cliff at that statement. The female agent was one of the most skilled females in Ramsay's ranks. She was intended to accompany Oliver as his paramour; together, their combined skills would have been unstoppable. Oliver knew Siren wouldn't be pleased with this turn of events, but she was nothing if not a devoted member of the spy society. He expected she would grouse but she'd eventually do as she was ordered. Unfortunately, Oliver had never quite learned to be so accommodating. "Neither will you," Ramsay continued gruffly. "When things quiet down, we will approach the mission with different agents. This is not up for discussion." There was an icy edge to Ramsay's voice that hadn't been there earlier.

"I've worked with Siren before. She won't want to step away either; not when—"

"She has already been reassigned." Though his voice was raised only slightly, this was the loudest Oliver had ever heard Ramsay speak. "And I strongly suggest you drop the matter. You are in no position to protect yourself, let alone look after another agent."

Oliver wanted to hit something. He wanted to throw the desk into Ramsay's unflappable face and demand that he allow him to continue his mission.

But, not only did he know from experience that there would be no changing Ramsay's mind, he was, indeed, injured.

Hadn't he been out of breath merely from the brisk walk to Scotland Yard?

Wasn't he already drained?

No.

His fists flexed.

Oliver would not allow himself to succumb to the weakness—not when there was so much on the line.

"Go home and rest. You will still receive compensation for the work you performed."

"It isn't about the money," Oliver growled.

"I know." Ramsay's eyes bore into his. "Believe me, I do." He leaned back in his chair and steepled his long fingers. "I was not alone in coming to this decision and it was not made lightly."

Oliver ached to bellow in frustration, but he knew the physical pain that would cause would serve only to underscore Ramsay's point. That was the last thing he needed. His gaze slid to the vista outside the window. Rows of buildings stretched as far as he could see; chimneys billowed gray and black smoke that drifted lazily toward the overcast sky. Each of its inhabitants went about his or her business entirely unaware of the complex network humming with secret efforts to keep their country afloat in the ever-changing world.

"You've done well." Oliver's eyes snapped back to Ramsay's face. Maybe Bianchi had underestimated his head injury, because not once in all the years he'd known him had he ever heard Ramsy utter such words. "You are one of my best and most capable agents." Well, now he knew he was hallucinating. "And I will not allow you to run reckless and roughshod into this scenario." Ah, there was the Ramsay he knew. His superior leaned forward, adding, "Go. Home."

"You look like an ill-trained hound took hold of you and spat you out after a good romp."

Oliver barely missed a step when the droll voice caught him as he rounded the corner from Ramsay's office. He did, however, roll his eyes when he replied, "You take a blade and a fall from a roof, and we'll see how handsome you are." The well-dressed man met his long stride with ease as they traversed the halls of Scotland Yard.

"Fair enough."

Oliver looked over and met the hazel eyes of none other than Sterling St. John, Duke of Morton, and former spy in Ramsay's ranks. He was also one of the few men Oliver considered both trustworthy and a friend. It was difficult to work closely with someone for eight years and not develop a relationship—out of necessity or otherwise. To be sure, Oliver never would have guessed that he, a street urchin, would one day count himself as a friend of one of the most powerful dukes in the kingdom. Ramsay's society did that, though; it threw together people of varying backgrounds and social standing, all in the name of safeguarding England's integrity. Oliver had been skeptical at first when he'd learned he'd been partnered with a young duke, but they'd learned quickly that they shared a similar quick wit, sense of humor, and unwavering sense of duty. Their time had been spent in foreign courts with Sterling playing the role of a debauched duke and Oliver, his loyal valet. They'd traveled extensively, lived in close quarters, and risked life and limb daily for years, but that had all changed a few months prior upon their return to London.

He'd seen little of the duke since the conclusion of their intelligence-gathering mission on the Continent, both returning to their lives. Sterling had retired from the spy society and reconciled with his wife before taking up his place in the government; Oliver, having no family or better options threw himself into new missions for Ramsay.

"Couldn't stay away?" Oliver muttered and stretched his neck in an attempt to relieve some of the tension there.

"I heard through certain channels that you'd been injured. I wanted to see for myself."

"You've seen me, now return to your wife."

If any other man had grabbed Oliver's shoulder to stop him from walking, he'd have been laid out and bleeding on the ground. With Sterling, however, Oliver halted his steps and, jaw set, met his friend's gaze and saw there the concern he'd been avoiding.

"I am glad you survived," Sterling said earnestly. "If anyone can take care of himself, it's you, but do let me know if you have need of anything."

"You wouldn't be up to convincing Ramsay to allow me to press on with my assignment, would you?" There was a sardonic tilt to Oliver's lips which the duke matched with a hint of empathy.

"You and I both know how damned unlikely that is. It isn't what you want to hear, but perhaps you should take the opportunity to recuperate and take on a different assignment once you're well again."

Oliver was already shaking his head before Sterling had finished speaking. "There is too much at stake."

A thoughtful silence fell between them, both knowing how vital their work was without needing to discuss the specifics of the assignment. If anyone knew and understood him, it was Sterling.

"Then," the duke began resignedly; "you do what you must."

OLIVER'S LONG STRIDES ate up Whitehall as he seethed on his path toward the river. Ramsay had told him in no uncertain terms that Oliver's continued involvement in the operation would not be tolerated; he had been given a direct order to step away.

He'd followed countless orders without hesitation for years. He'd thrown himself into life-threatening situations one after the other; he'd traveled to far-flung cities and countries all in the name of duty.

But this...

It was everything he could do not to rage right there and curse fate for its cruel hand. He knew in the very depths of his soul that to follow Ramsay's orders would be a mistake.

The gray-brown water of the Thames drifted lazily beyond

the line of trees and pedestrians, carriages, and hackneys in the street. He screwed his eyes shut and turned his face toward the beginning of the drizzle drifting from the overcast sky.

The conversation with Ramsay had been just about what he'd anticipated, but that didn't make it any less maddening or disappointing. It was one thing to imagine and another thing to have his wings well and truly clipped by his superior. Ramsay represented more than just someone who coordinated an elite group of men and women—he was a power unto himself. He wielded more sway than most dukes in the kingdom, and some might argue his arms, unbound as they were by the same rules and restrictions as the Crown, extended further than comprehension.

To go against him would be suicide.

But Oliver had never before abandoned a mission—willingly or otherwise—and being made to do it now was beyond galling. Not to mention he would now have to live with potential casualties on his head if, once the mission resumed, the person assigned to take over for him failed in his task.

Then, there had been his brief conversation with Sterling. They had often repeated the statement that they did what they must. They did it when they were homesick. They did it when they were in pain. They did it despite the peril.

How was this any different?

No.

Oliver's eyes snapped open.

He refused to accept this.

He'd spent the first years of his life without so much as a hand to hold; he knew how to work alone—how to survive.

He had every confidence that he could see this through to fruition. All he needed was a woman to fill the companion role intended for Siren.

And he had a certain beauty with white-blond hair in mind.

THE MYSTERIOUS MAN had slipped from Lady Night's hours before, but Emily had found it nearly impossible to stop herself from thinking of him. Each time she closed her eyes, she heard his shiver-inducing voice, saw his glowing silver gaze, felt the heat of his skin beneath her fingertips.

All signs of his stay in her room had been cleared away. Mary had swapped out the sheets and coverlet, the dishes and medical items had been cleared away, but there was no eradicating him from Emily's mind. The man had been hiding something, that was certain; it didn't take a brilliant mind to reach that conclusion. She, however, suffered from a condition that made her incurably inquisitive. Whenever she was presented with a mystery, she couldn't help but question it, turn it over, and examine it until she reached a satisfactory end. The man, however, had committed the worst sin imaginable: He'd left her without a single answer.

It was intolerable.

What was worse, even as she lay in her bed staring at the dark void of the ceiling, she couldn't escape him.

While the bedding had been changed, her pillows still smelled of him. The clean male musk of his skin, the brisk hint of rain on conifers and night air, clung to her bed like the whispers of a lover. So handsome. So mysterious. So intense.

There had been something about him that, even then, remained deep inside of her, tangled and knotted, impossible to dislodge no matter how she tried. It lingered, taunting her. And each time she heard the echo of his voice in her mind, it strummed her body a little bit tighter, made her skin dance with gooseflesh, and caused her nipples to pebble with awareness against the soft fabric of her nightshift. Something about him had spoken to a very primal part of her. It still did, even now that he was gone…and she'd likely never see him again.

The way he'd watched her every move made her feel at once intensely protected and an object of fascination. His gaze had curled around her as palpable as if he'd reached out and ran his large, calloused hands along every inch of her body.

Emily swallowed hard and—suddenly uncomfortably warm—she kicked off her coverlet in a flurry of fabric. The cool evening air did nothing to temper her growing fever or the ache blossoming between her thighs. She bit her lip in a moment of indecision before allowing herself to become lost in the fantasy of it.

Her eyes slid shut and she imagined the dark, mysterious stranger had returned for her, desiring to show her his gratitude with his poetically hewn body and sinfully curved lips. She cupped the weight of her sensitive breasts, catching her nipples in the vee of her fingers. Light pinches made her squirm as bolts of desire sang straight to her throbbing core.

The women of the brothel had whispered secrets to her about this part of her anatomy, and she'd learned over the years, through practice in the privacy of her bed or her bath, the ways in which it could deliver her blinding pleasure. Already the mere thought of the swollen pearl of her sex made her thighs slick with her anticipation.

Emily's fantasy took over. She imagined the mysterious man returning to her balcony—the logic of how had no place in this scenario—and he let himself into her bedchamber. She imagined she could feel his warm breath on her lips just before he claimed them. She turned her head to the side and buried her face in her pillow, imagining the scent there came directly from his heated flesh rather than just the lingering ghost of his presence.

As if of its own accord, her arm snaked down her body, beneath the hem of her nightshift that had ridden high on her thighs. She parted the tender, throbbing folds, spreading the sweet nectar with the pads of her fingers, up one side and down the other. She swirled around her entrance, imagining the man's long, capable fingers were the ones exploring her, learning what she liked, what made her squirm. One hand working between her legs and the other plucking and rolling her nipple, she felt the desire and arousal as it began to sing through her. Soon, she felt so hot, she was certain her very skin glowed with her need.

In her mind, he pressed his lips against her neck, his panting breaths matched her own, and he groaned in satisfaction when he found her wet and wanting. His were the fingers circling closer and closer to the sensitive bundle of nerves demanding attention, making her legs twitch in a rising tide of pleasure. Emily released a cry of relief into her pillow when the pressure finally reached that singularly magical place, unleashing a barrage of shooting stars behind her eyelids. The fingers worked her in quick, tight circles as her body rocked against the bed, seeking more of something it could not name but instinctively demanded.

Those fingers slid lower, teasingly dipping to her entrance, sliding inside with ease. In and out. In and out. Back to the throbbing bud of desire.

A sensuous rhythm was established until Emily's body quivered. She could practically feel the heat of the man's body against her back, the delicious weight of him pressing her into the mattress and holding her at his mercy.

A third finger slid into her tight channel and she whimpered at the stinging pleasure of it.

More, her body demanded. *More.*

She rocked against her hand, the mattress growing damp beneath her as she sought the sensations she craved. It made her frantic as she climbed higher, reaching, stretching, climbing, clawing her way to that pinnacle of perfect bliss.

The sounds of broken breaths and fingers gliding through slick flesh filled the room and the air grew thick with potent need. She wanted more—more than she could give herself. She burned for it; moaned in desperation for it.

"Yes," Emily gasped, her breath hitching. She heard the man's deep, rough voice as clearly as if he were in the room with her, urging her on, praising her for her wanton pleasure, reveling in how wet she was for him. How good she was.

Her entire body clenched, every muscle coordinating its collective shattering in the most exquisite of pleasure, the highest pinnacle of bliss. Her body shuddered and quivered, breaking apart and coming together once more in tingling, throbbing glory.

Emily floated down slowly, her fingers stilling gradually as the last tremors of her release rolled through her. She deflated with a sigh, her limbs heavy with delicious rapture.

She'd hoped acting upon her irrational desires would get Mr. Holden out of her system, but, when she closed her eyes, she still saw intense silver eyes that saw straight through her, heard the deep voice that resonated down to her very core. Even with her ill-advised desire temporarily slaked, his image lingered with her long into the night.

EMILY HAD JUST finished lacing the side of her pale-pink morning dress when the door to her bedchamber creaked open behind her.

"I wasn't expecting you yet, Mary," she said brightly as she began the process of plaiting her hair. "An early morning?"

"I take it this Mary is not normally one to rise at an early hour?"

Emily's heart leaped into her throat at the deep masculine timbre. She whirled around, hair forgotten, to find *the* man standing in her doorway, dressed all in black like an angel of death. The skin of his angular face was still wan and taut, but he'd scraped the dark stubble from his jaw and appeared more refreshed than he had been when he'd left just the day before. Emily's lips parted in astonishment, but she was unable to speak for the pounding of her heart.

"Do not scream," he cautioned her, low and evenly.

"I-I wasn't going to." At least, she didn't think she'd been about to do so. He stepped closer and she caught a hint of chilled pine boughs and masculine musk—the same one that had sent her over the edge as she touched herself in bed only hours before. The mere memory of it heated her cheeks with fire born of equal parts embarrassment and arousal. She tilted her head, grateful that she had the veil of her hair—and that she'd at least brushed it before he'd come upon her. "How did you find your way in?" she asked. "There are locks."

"Locks which may keep most men out, but not someone like me." His tone made it difficult to swallow. The thought that he'd been able to enter their building and make his way to their flat and into her rooms without being seen was…exciting? Shouldn't it have been terrifying? If he could manage to do so—all while passing through no less than three locks without issue or detection—what else could he accomplish? She'd been pining for excitement in her life, and it seemed she'd certainly found a bit of it.

Emily barely managed to stifle a little thrilled shiver at the thought. Since when had the thought of danger been such an aphrodisiac?

She met the man's eyes.

Apparently when she'd met *him*…

He was so tall and broad, yet he moved with a lithe grace that made it seem as if he floated across the floor. His boots were silent as he approached her.

"Why are you here?" Emily asked, proud that she managed to keep the quaver from her tone.

A heavy silence held the air between them as his eyes scanned her bedchamber. He'd been there before, but she had the distinct sense that he was taking it all in once again, memorizing its layout, reviewing potential entries and exits—of which there were few. Her blush intensified when she saw his gaze pause on the rumpled bed and her discarded nightdress. She imagined he could scent the lingering aroma of her arousal from when she'd given herself a blinding orgasm…with him on her mind.

"What I am about to say will seem wildly improbable, but I ask that you remain open-minded and allow me to finish speaking before you ask questions. After that, I will answer what I can." He fell silent, looking her up and down as unease edged its way inside her. "Agreed?" he asked when she remained silent and motion-less.

Emily nodded, for what else was there for her to do? He'd

proven uncommon stealth and skills in breaking into the building, bypassing all its residents and security measures. He stood alone with her in her bedroom, barely an arm's length away from her. If she cried out for help, there wasn't a doubt in her mind that he could dispatch her even before the sound was fully free from her throat, let alone before Mary, her mother, or anyone else might fly to her assistance. Oddly enough, despite his menacing presence and serious expression, she didn't fear that he intended to do her harm. She desired nothing more than to hear him out— to find out what had driven him back to her.

"I thank you again for what you did to save my life, Miss Tailor. I am in your debt. However, I fear I must ask more of you yet." Emily's eyes widened, but she listened. "I am due at a very particular house party in a matter of days, and I find myself in dire need of a companion. I can see what you are thinking, but it is nothing of the sort. This is not some poorly veiled attempt at getting you alone or taking advantage of you. I think we both know that would have happened already if it were my aim."

And did she ever. The ease with which he'd infiltrated her bedchamber was proof of that. It was terrifying and…unexpectedly thrilling. She clenched her thighs together and silently berated her wayward thoughts. Now was not the time.

FOR OLIVER, THIS entire situation chafed at him—more than that, it felt like a fire had been ignited beneath his skin and it caught and spread like powder had been peppered throughout his veins. Even contemplating saying what he planned to do went against everything he'd been trained. But there simply was no other way.

He didn't know what had finally tipped him over the edge— Ramsay's pulling him off the mission, the persistent pain, the grogginess, or a lingering sense of indebtedness to the woman who had saved his life (and he was a man who was meticulous about balancing his ledger)—but he took a breath and decided to answer her questions.

"You made inquiries before I left yesterday, and I feel I owe it to you to respond."

There was a long pause before Emily tilted her head in disbelief. "You…came back to answer my questions?"

As awkward as he felt, Oliver forged on. "You asked how I wound up on your balcony. I was following someone and he ducked into the vacant building adjacent to yours."

"Are you a pickpocket then?" she asked with…was that disappointment? "I thought you dressed far too well for that and the knife I found was of excellent quality."

"Now you are an expert on blades?"

"I've been tutored on recognizing quality." She didn't back down from his glare.

She was remarkable.

"I followed him because it is my job."

Silence, you imbecile! His mind screamed at him. *What are you doing?* The truth was agony after hiding so long in the shadows. He felt like a man kept too long in a dark and windowless cell and someone held a torch to his face. It stung. It was agonizing. But his body craved it, nonetheless.

"Like a Bow Street Runner?" she asked thoughtfully. "That is believable."

"Hardly." Oliver scoffed, the sudden exhalation irritating his injury so he had to clutch at his side with a grimace.

"Not a Runner, then…a spy?" Emily laughed airily at her foolishness, but it died on the air when she noted the severity in his expression. Oliver's heart began to race. "A spy." She mulled it over, the keenness of her mind evident in her flashing eyes.

Stop here. End. This. Right. Now. Turn and walk out that door never to see her again. Let her return to her life and forget all about you until you're naught more than a shadowed specter of an odd interaction.

That did not sit well with Oliver, however. Lying to this woman after all she'd done for him and then contemplating bringing her into his web felt more like a sin than any of the others he'd committed in his life.

"Truly?" Rather than fear or suspicion, her eyes glittered with fascination. She held him utterly entranced. "If that is the case, then why are you telling me this?" She propped a fist on a hip, revealing the delicious curve of her waist beneath her gown. "Isn't the ability to keep secrets rather integral to being a spy?"

Oliver nearly laughed aloud at that observation. It certainly was, and there he was, ready to lay it all at her feet. She had him addled. She made him trust her. And he was backed into enough of a corner that he was desperate to have anyone on his side.

He took a bracing breath, knowing he'd likely live to regret his next words. "Because, thanks to this injury, the Crown wants to pull me off the investigation I've been performing for months. I cannot give up on my mission. Lives are at stake—perhaps even the monarchy, itself." She didn't laugh or move; she hardly breathed. "I am injured and they will offer no aid if I pursue this on my own...and it is apparent that you are already too em-broiled in my situation." The last caused Emily to take a step back; the first fissure in her confidence. "I assure you, that was no threat. You have nothing to fear from me, Emily."

As he'd walked away from Scotland Yard, a purely irrational thought had begun to bloom in the darkest recesses of his mind. If he'd been a more honorable man, then he would quash it, but it had already taken root and he did not see any other option to resolve his current predicament. "I simply need your assistance," he said. "I require another set of eyes; capable hands to help pick up the slack until I am fully healed."

"W-what does this have to do with me?"

"Isn't it obvious? I am making you an honorary spy in service to His Majesty. And, in a few days, I need you to accompany me to a week-long house party in the country."

Her laugh was laden with incredulity. "Is this a jest? Are you trying to trick me into running off with you? Surely you must be feverish to believe such a ruse would work. I should have Dr. Bianchi return to ensure your head isn't damaged beyond repair."

"I am deadly serious," he said, cutting her off. The laughter died like a candle extinguished by a strong gust. "I was supposed to work beside another agent, but my superiors are no longer in support of the mission and they will not send her in if they feel I am an unfit partner. I require a woman brave in spirit and quick in mind to accompany me. This is no usual house party, but a pleasure party thrown by a man called John Hayes."

EMILY'S EYES WIDENED. The name was one that often came up in her ledgers; Lady Night's regularly supplied "entertainment" for him and his gatherings. Of course, she'd never met the man—or any of the brothel's other patrons, for that matter—but his range of appetites and the whispers from the ladies were enough to cause a chill of foreboding to slide down her spine. It took a woman willing to perform certain unsavory tasks to cater to his desires; and more than one employee had refused to see Hayes again after their first encounter.

"You know him?" Mr. Holden asked, having noted a change in her expression or posture.

"Of him. I have never met him and he would not know me." The lines beside his eyes relaxed somewhat, telling her that he truly believed his hopes were pinned upon her. She had never seen Mr. Hayes and she was never allowed out of the flat during business hours, so going unrecognized was not something with which she'd have to concern herself. Still...

"If I do believe this incredible story, what makes you think I'll agree to this?"

"Because you could have let me die." Holden's words rang like the tolling of a bell. "You could have run screaming from the room if you truly believed me to be a delusional madman. You did neither. Not to mention, you reside above a brothel and are probably no stranger to the things that transpire at pleasure parties."

Emily's cheeks warmed...though, against her better judgment, she did consider his words.

She *should* run screaming; she *should* believe him a madman. By all accounts, she shouldn't trust the stranger who'd fallen from the sky and landed injured and unconscious on her balcony. Something about everything he'd said made an insane sort of sense to her.

It explained how he'd come to be on her balcony, how he'd been injured, why he'd spoken in foreign tongues while he'd slept beneath laudanum's leaden blanket, why he'd been armed—from the looks of the sack on the bed that hadn't been there before Dr. Bianchi's arrival, much more than she'd been aware.

"What would you require of me?" she asked, her voice sounding very far away to her ears.

"Take the place of my companion. Assist me in locating the information and evidence I require. Help disguise the fact that I am not at my fullest physical capabilities."

"So I pretend to be your hired companion?"

"That is correct."

"Only pretend?"

"Yes," he replied with a deep frown, as if suddenly questioning his decision to include her in this scenario if she couldn't comprehend that most basic of facts.

"May I have some time to consider this?"

"I must leave in two days if I am to adhere to the schedule. If not…"

"Then you lose all the work you've done and lives could be in jeopardy," Emily finished for him.

His mouth formed a grim line when he nodded once in agreement. "I will not lie and tell you there is no danger involved, but I would not request it of you if I were not desperate—if I did not believe you could be an asset to this investigation. With your help, we could prevent tragedy."

She exhaled long and slow through parted lips.

Hadn't she just been contemplating how useless she felt? Wouldn't attempting to help her country—no matter in how small a way—bring more meaning to her existence than she'd ever thought possible?

"And I will protect you with my life," Holden added in a

growl that told her he most certainly would. The glint in his eyes would have been terrifying if she were his enemy.

For the life of her, Emily wasn't sure why she heard her voice agreeing to the insane plan laid out before her: "I can be packed and ready by the time you need to leave."

"Very well," Holden nodded. "I will return on Saturday at half past seven in the morning to retrieve you from the back garden. Is that acceptable?"

Emily nodded. "I should be the only one awake at that hour."

"Be sure to pack appropriate clothing. Tell no one." The warning in his eyes made it difficult to swallow past the lump in her throat.

"I do have one request." Her words stopped him as he turned to leave. She took his silence as a prompt for her to continue. "Tell me your real name."

He began shaking his head even after she finished speaking. "It's best you don't know."

"Oh…"

"It is for your safety."

"I understand." She knew it was probably true, but that didn't stop her from feeling crestfallen.

"You may address me as 'Holden' or 'Marcus' and I shall answer you."

She nodded.

"Very good. Until then, Miss Tailor."

"Emily," she corrected him. "And don't think I will stop asking after your true name because you have given me an alternative."

Unless she was mistaken, a hint of a smile tugged at one side of his lips before he turned to leave.

Chapter Seven

Emily awoke at sunrise the day of her departure with Marcus. As she dressed, she refused to dwell upon the fact that she didn't know his real name and, instead, that he'd given her leave to address him in such an informal manner. It felt intimate despite the oddness of their circumstances.

In the time since Marcus had left Lady Night's, Emily had begun gathering necessary items and pondering how she would explain her absence to the mother who'd kept her shut away in their flat like a Medieval fairytale princess. There was no way Emily would be allowed to simply walk out the door, trunk and valise in tow, as her mother wished her well. This meant Emily was left with only one other option.

She packed in secret.

Knowing she would have no help carrying the full trunk down to the back garden, she opted to move the empty luggage to a storage room on the bottom floor and gradually fill it during her trips up and down the back stairs while the rest of the building slept. The most difficult part was deciding which clothing to bring. She deemed one of her morning dresses adequate for what she suspected the climate of the party to be, but she couldn't very well wear the same thing over and over again. She was forced to dig through her mother's wardrobe at night when she was busy overseeing the brothel and Mary was occupied with other tasks. Emily was careful to select garments she knew her mother wouldn't notice were missing, and opted for pieces somewhere between casual and immodest. The two of them were close enough in size that alterations above a few pins in the hem wouldn't be required.

Before slipping from the flat that morning, Emily paused to scratch out a quick note. She hadn't intended to do so, but her conscience chose that moment to pipe up. In it, she let her mother know that she was unharmed and had left of her own volition to assist a friend; that she planned on returning in no more than ten days.

Standing at the door to her flat, wrapped in a borrowed traveling cloak, Emily looked around the familiar, comfortable parlor, cozy and intimate as it was. These floral-papered walls had been her world, her safe cage. The emerald velvet of the upholstered furnishings had been a part of the pretty prison her mother had created to keep Emily away from the dangers of Covent Garden and the harsh way life it fostered.

Now, thanks to Marcus, she would spread her wings and take a chance. She had the opportunity for adventure. She had no illusions that this would be a fun holiday, but that didn't bother her. She was ready to do something with her life, and an adventure—albeit a dangerous and quite possibly foolish one—was as good a way as any.

This was why, at the appointed time and against her better judgment, Emily dragged her trunk from its hiding place and alternated between pushing and pulling it out into the back garden. There, cloaked in wool and morning shadows, she waited.

To be honest, she half expected Marcus not to show—perhaps he had been just a deluded man with a head injury who'd taken one too many blows to his skull (despite some evidence to the contrary). She liked to think she'd be relieved if the hours ticked by without his return to Lady Night's, but that was not the truth. Now that she'd decided to accept the risk and go on this journey, to discover the entire thing would never come to fruition would be nothing short of devastating. She'd committed.

The rhythmic clop of horses' hooves on the cobbles echoed from the street back through the alley and into the gardens where Emily stood. Her body buzzing with excitement and nerves, she rushed to open the heavy barred gate. Waiting for her just on the other side was a devastatingly handsome man dressed in well-fitted traveling clothes of navy blue, his dark hair brushed back from his face and accentuating his strong features and piercing eyes.

In Marcus's absence, Emily had all but convinced herself that she'd been delusional; no man could live up to the figure her mind had created, could he? But, unfortunately for her, that was far from the truth. His face and body had been arresting when he lay prone in her bed. Now, freshly bathed and smelling of fresh air and warm male skin, impeccably dressed as he was, he was downright dangerous. Two additional days of recovery had done him well.

"Miss Tailor," he greeted her with a tilt of his head. The rumble of his voice was pleasing to her on a primal level.

"Emily," she corrected him, watching as his keen eyes scanned the garden, taking in the carved benches, small fountain, and cleverly designed archways to provide privacy to those wishing to be entertained out of doors.

"You said nothing to anyone?"

"Not at all." She omitted the fact that she'd left a note for her mother. She had been careful to leave out any details of where she was going or whom she was with, so she didn't think it mattered. He couldn't very well expect her to leave without doing that much; the disappearance of Lady Night's daughter would raise an alarm in Covent Garden as quickly as the cry to summon a fire brigade.

"Very good," he murmured, his praise strumming something deep within her belly. "Where is your luggage?"

Emily showed him to the nook where she'd managed to store her trunk and valise. She picked up the smaller item to carry it herself, but, rather than summon a footman, he shocked her by hefting the trunk onto his shoulder. His side must have pained him terribly, but the only sign of discomfort was a small grimace. She hurried in his wake, her slippers padding silently on the paving stone path. She was careful to ensure the gate was locked behind her and she could feel her fate being sealed with the metallic click of the latch.

She hurried after Marcus, but the length of his stride was so great that he'd already had her trunk loaded and strapped to the back of the hired carriage by the time she reached him. He offered to pack her valise as well, but she declined, preferring to keep it and its contents with her person. His manners were cool and impeccable as he handed her up into the conveyance and allowed her to settle herself upon the forward-facing seat. Climbing the step, he spoke a few words to their driver before ducking in and filling the remaining space inside the cab with his impressive size. Two knocks upon the ceiling and they were off.

It was still fairly early in the day, but all manner of merchants had already clogged the streets selling their wares and making deliveries while servants from great houses traveled to markets to haggle and obtain goods for their masters and mistresses.

Their conversation was pathetically nonexistent as they ambled through the busy streets until Marcus finally deigned to speak when they reached the outskirts of London.

"From here, we will have a journey of approximately four or five hours to the country estate," he said, not turning his eyes away from the slowly passing scenery. For her part, Emily was torn between admiring his profile and gazing in wonder at the scenery transitioning into the countryside. She'd never before had occasion to leave London, so this was her first glimpse of anything outside of their little corner of Covent Garden. There was so much color!

"Did you hear me?"

Emily's eyes snapped back to his. "No, I'm sorry. I was—"

"If you cannot pay attention to this, then perhaps we'd best turn around right now. Both of our lives depend upon you remaining aware and in tune with the situation."

"Well we are not yet arrived and you will have to forgive me for enjoying my first look at the world outside of London," she snapped. She wanted to tell him that she was the one doing him a favor and the least he could do was give her some grace in this singular situation, but she didn't.

Rather than biting back, one of Marcus's eyebrows rose and a muscle of his jaw twitched. He gave her a few minutes of silence before continuing as if their last interaction hadn't taken place.

"John Hayes is not who you believe him to be."

"I have never met him, so I do not believe him to be anything other than a man with certain appetites."

Marcus's sharp eyes met hers. "What of them?"

"Lady Night employs few women who are willing to tolerate his…" Emily paused, trying to find more delicate words, "his voraciousness and tendencies toward exhibitionism. For all his polish, he is a rough man behind the veneer." Several women had discovered this the hard way and Emily was grateful they worked for her mother because few brothels would have put a stop to any man's activities if he were a paying customer. The employees were viewed as assets rather than human beings at most of London's brothels; the comfort of her employees made Lady Night's establishment so unique.

Marcus nodded in understanding as if she'd confirmed a suspicion. "I've been following him since early Spring, learning his habits and his acquaintances. I believe that he has ties to a faction that would seek to weaken England from the inside out. He has aligned himself with some powerful monarchical dissenters and others who, while not as vocal about their leanings, hold sway and power elsewhere, which might be viewed as beneficial."

"How so?" she asked, growing more alarmed as he continued. It felt as if something shifted beneath the earth, taking hold with poisoned roots while she and everyone else trod upon it unawares until it was too late. This situation was quickly becoming very, very real, indeed.

"You should know that Marcus Holden is heir to a small yet financially sound shipping company," he said pointedly, referring to himself and the name he'd offered her. "Hayes enjoys rogues and wastrels in all their most reprobate forms. He is a man of vices and seeks the same in his companions; he prefers men who share in his hobbies. Playing the part of one such man is precisely what allowed me to ingratiate myself with him and earn this invitation. If Hayes does not outright invite me to join his cause, then I anticipate having the chance to ferret out any information I can."

"What do you expect to find?"

"You have already been given more than sufficient information to serve your purpose as my assistant," he replied coolly. "I shall apprise you of more should the need arise." Emily narrowed her eyes at him but stopped just short of a glare. "Now, you should know that my invitation to this party included the stipulation that I bring along a woman 'of a certain disposition to enjoy such entertainments.' As such, you shall be playing the part of my lover."

"Your lover?" Emily squeaked out as her stomach flipped uneasily.

"What did you think when I said you would be coming as my companion?"

"I don't know! Do *not* laugh at me." She leveled an accusatory finger at Marcus and willed her cheeks not to blush with embarrassment over her naivete.

"Only an act," he reassured her dismissively. "And it will help keep me close enough to protect you from the other guests."

"What?" she exclaimed in an even higher pitch. Now, regret was beginning to settle like an anchor in her gut.

Marcus looked at her as if he were trying to decide if her reaction was in jest. "There is a great deal of sharing one's partners at these parties," he explained matter-of-factly. "You, yourself, indicated you were aware of Hayes's proclivities; it stands to reason that the parties he hosts would be in the same vein. Do not be surprised if you are propositioned by any of the guests—male or female. And do not feel obligated to give in…that is unless you wish to." He shot her an assessing look from the corner of his eye.

Emily could only splutter in response.

Who did he believe her to be?

"If you decline these requests, however," he continued, "do try to let them down as gently as possible so as not to alienate anyone who may eventually be of use to my investigation. If there is any trouble, find me and I will make an excuse for you to remove you from the situation."

Lord, but what have I gotten myself into?

Emily began to feel a bit queasy.

"And…what will you be doing while I am fending off these hypothetical advances?"

"Naturally, playing the part of a debauched shipping heir."

"That seems far easier," she muttered, then wondered what it might entail.

Unbidden, her mind began to imagine another woman's hands exploring the gloriously masculine planes of his body…and she experienced an unanticipated pang of jealousy. It was absurd, really. She had no claim to him, no connection other than the fact that he'd happened to fall to her balcony and she'd taken pity on him.

And nursed him back to health.

It was nearly impossible for Emily to swallow past the lump in her throat.

"And how are we supposed to convince everyone that we are lovers?"

"The usual," he said with a negligent lift of a shoulder. "A few kisses, some touching—even heated glances across the room can go a long way toward creating the appearance of intimacy.

Her cheeks grew instantly, painfully hot at the thought of Marcus's mouth on hers.

Of his hands touching her as a lover's would.

Her imagination—fueled only by the naughty stories and accounts of Lady Night's female employees—began to run rampant, causing an unfamiliar ache to bloom and spread outward from her core.

"I—I do not think I can do this."

"Why not?" Marcus demanded suddenly, his brow furrowing deeply as if his mind was already racing to come up with an alternate plan even though he'd already stated that she was his only option. "It is nothing too extreme. Listen to the other ladies, act the part, and let me know if you hear anything of interest when you report back to me each evening."

"It's just…"

"Just what?" he snapped and then grabbed at his side when the outburst aggravated his wound. Unscrewing his eyes, he sighed and then turned them heavenward. "Apologies," he said more gently than before. "I never should have pressured you into this and it was unfair of me to expect someone untrained to assume a false identity and perform the duties of a spy. None of this is the occupation you have known and I should not have drafted you into this situation."

"It's not that," Emily eked out, rendered almost dumb when his eyes met hers across the carriage. She looked down at her gloved hands, though it did little to staunch her mortification when she said, "I have never before been kissed."

Chapter Eight

OLIVER'S JAW PRACTICALLY fell through the carriage floor. He couldn't recall a time when he'd last been so caught off guard—let alone something said by a woman not of his world of lies and shadows.

"What do you mean you have *never been kissed*? You live above a bloody brothel!"

Emily turned the brightest pink he'd ever seen, but her voice was remarkably steady. "Just because the women who share my roof choose to sell their talents and their bodies does not automatically mean I have done the same."

"Are you indicating that you are a virgin as well?" His voice had risen further, causing a fiery poker to prod at his wounded ribs, but he ignored it.

The aversion of her embarrassed eyes was enough of a reply for him.

Oliver spat a curse—not at her, but at his ill-considered choices and his horrible luck. Of all the women in that building, he'd had to choose the one *least* qualified to pretend to be his mistress and lover.

This was it. He was going to have to accept this as the final sign that his mission was not meant to be. The gods had conspired against him and all his meager options had been exhausted. No matter how it caused rage to heat his blood and annoyance to roil his gut, he had to concede.

He lifted his arm to knock upon the carriage's roof and have the driver turn around at the next opportunity, but he was stopped when Emily launched herself across the space between them and grabbed his arm.

"No!"

Oliver froze, his hand poised in the air as she hung from him. She was a flurry of deep raspberry skirts and ribbons, as delectable as a dessert. He found he enjoyed her looking up at him, her clear eyes wide, her cheeks flushed, and her pink lips parted. She presented an absurdly enticing image, especially now that Oliver knew just how innocent she truly was.

She seemed to return to her senses and wrenched her arms from him to slide back to her side of the carriage. She cleared her throat before she spoke. "That is, I want to help; really, I do."

"And how do you intend to do so, hm?" Oliver asked, his voice only slightly above a growl. "I am expected to bring a skilled, worldly woman to this play party and, instead, I shall be arriving with an ignorant virgin in tow."

"Simply because my virginity is intact does not mean I am wholly ignorant." She sat a little straighter, a little prouder. "I *did* grow up in a brothel...and women talk—especially when living in close quarters. I assure you, I am far from missish." Her eyes took on a challenging glitter. "And I would also wager that I know more tricks of the trade than you could fathom."

Oliver quirked a brow, deeply intrigued despite his frustrations. "As enticing as that sounds, I am not so sure." He raised his hand once more to alert the driver, but her next words stopped him as cold as the cocking of a pistol.

"Kiss me."

He could only stare at Emily.

It was far from his first kiss—far from the first time a beautiful woman had asked him or told him or begged him to kiss her— but something about Emily made a part of him stir in an unexpected way.

"Kiss me," she repeated bravely, and Oliver found it impossible to remove his gaze from her perfect lips, rosy pink and plump as they were. "You should kiss me so I can prove that not only am I no shrinking miss, but I am a quick study. My hesitation was not for fear of being kissed, but my unease with being perceived as inexperienced as I am. Will the evidence of an untutored lover not give us away and put us in danger?"

The war raging inside of Oliver was furious and desperate. He was drawn to this contrary woman—at once blinding innocence and the licking flames of passion personified—but he knew he should push her away for her own safety. He'd been rash and foolish to ever have dragged her into this, but now…he'd be hard-pressed to send her on her way.

Several moments passed before Oliver inclined his head in agreement with Emily's proposal. Moving slowly, he shifted to her side of the carriage, noting her slight intake of breath, the widening of the dark pools of her pupils.

He caught a whiff of the fresh rosewater scent that had haunted his dreams since those feverish laudanum-induced dreams he'd experienced in her bed. It could have been cloying, but, on Emily, it was heady and fresh, clean and intoxicating.

"Relax," he murmured, sensing the tension in her body even though he had yet to touch her. Ignoring the way his pulse began to race, he leaned forward to trace the line of her fey chin and jaw, to graze her lower lip with the pad of his thumb. She was so damned soft. He'd never been this close to something so good, so pure. It felt wrong and, yet, it also felt so bloody right.

The next moment, his fingers slid back into her hair to pull her head forward and his mouth was on hers. The kisses began slowly at first with tentative meetings of their lips. Small sips and tantalizing tastes gradually evolved into something more daring. Everything in Oliver's body screamed to press her back and explore every bit of her with his tongue and teeth, but he was able to rein it in before he acted upon it.

His patience was rewarded when Emily's posture melted away and she began mimicking his movements. He nibbled, and she nibbled back. He cupped the back of her head, and she did the same, raking her nails against his scalp in a way that made his entire body shudder. A jolt of lightning shot through him when she unexpectedly began using her tongue. It was all he could do not to groan when he learned she tasted of sugar and cinnamon—spice and sweetness in perfect proportions. He showed her how to tilt her head to provide them both with better access; how to stroke and taste until they were both nearly breathless.

She hadn't been lying when she'd said she was a quick study.

Every touch of her soft hands, every caress of her tongue made Oliver's hold upon his sanity slip further. He was so unnerved by how much he enjoyed kissing the innocent chit that he tore his mouth from hers and sat back, trying not to acknowledge how much his world had shifted as he watched Emily blink back to awareness. Her lips were deeper pink, slightly swollen and parted to reveal straight white teeth. The sight made it nearly impossible for him to breathe.

Oh, yes...he was much more moved than he should have been, to be sure.

When he finally spoke, his voice was slightly unsteady and their faces were only a breath's width apart. "Where did you learn to do that if you've never before been kissed?"

It was difficult not to be impressed with the nonchalant lift of her shoulder. "Women talk," she reiterated. "And how can women be expected to know how to please a client if they do not know what to do?"

An instant flood of heat filled his groin; the image of Emily and other women discussing the most delicious and scandalous things was exciting beyond measure. He had to force himself to lean back while draping a strategically placed arm across his lap, clearing his throat as a reminder to regain his composure. He'd only just given the girl her first kiss; he needn't expose her to the evidence of his rampant arousal.

Though her color was becomingly rosy and her eyes glittered joyfully, he could tell she hadn't been quite as physically moved by their kiss as he had been.

How interesting.

"Is that what I can expect from you, then? Kisses such as that?" Oliver bristled at her inquiry, nearly demanding she explain exactly what she meant by it when she added, "That was not so bad."

The comment tipped him over the edge, ruffling his usual cool and practiced composure. He could no longer resist teaching her a lesson.

"There will be touching as well," he said, lowering his tone. His groin throbbed with the possibility of unnerving Emily as she'd done to him.

"Touching?" Ah, there was the tremor in her tone he'd been expecting.

"Oh, yes," he murmured and nodded gravely before running a knuckle along her arm, tracing the curve of her neck and the line of her decolletage, showing her a taste of what she might encounter.

Emily's breath hitched and he savored the sound. He wanted more of it; wanted to hear it over and over again. He traced her kiss-plumped lower lip with the pad of his thumb while his other palm found her knee and trailed up her thigh. Her shape was more than pleasing beneath her gown, and she felt warm and firm with curves and softness in just the right places to make a man see stars.

"Maybe," he breathed into her ear, enjoying the blossoming gooseflesh it elicited, "some touching and kissing, together."

Turning her head just so, Oliver proceeded to kiss her deeply, hungrily, though he knew it was perhaps the least prudent thing for him to do at that moment, aroused as he was. He couldn't help himself. His body lit up in unexpected ways when she responded to him and the forbiddenness of it only made him want her more.

Their tongues dueled and tangled until he trailed his lips down her jaw to where her pulse pounded within her pale throat. He felt it leap against his lips and it was everything he could do not to latch there and suck, to sink his teeth into the virgin flesh and mark her as his. She was so delicate. So fragile.

"Sh-should I be touching you as well?" Her throat tightened against his mouth as she attempted to swallow. "Will that be expected?"

"Yes, do." Oliver's response was immediate and without forethought. Had he had one thread of rationality left in his brain, he might have considered that having her tiny hands on him could prove to be his undoing.

Immediately, she held him to her with surprising strength as he continued tasting the soft skin where her neck melted into her collarbone. The sensation caused by her short, manicured nails scoring his flesh through the fabric of his shirt and coat made his skin ripple with pleasure and his abdominal muscles clench. Those dainty fingers of hers trailed down his chest and ran along his flexing thighs as he kept them steady in the rocking carriage.

Emily was unpracticed, but there was not a doubt in Oliver's mind that she wasn't at least dimly aware of how these attentions from a woman such as she could affect a man.

Could drive him wild with need.

And that was precisely what he could not allow to happen.

Realizing their situation had, once again, been reversed, Oliver broke their contact with a sharp gasp.

What was it about her that threw him? How did she set him on his heels before he even recognized that he was under attack?

"Exactly like that," he said hoarsely, ripping himself away and adjusting his position as he once more sat back across the carriage from her. There wasn't nearly enough distance between them, but it would have to suffice for—he glanced at his timepiece—the next several hours…

Desperate for relief, Oliver turned his attention out the carriage's window. Emily may not have been in his direct line of sight, but she continued to own his other senses with her scent and her shallow breaths. He exhaled a very slow, deliberate breath through his nose before speaking again. "We shall be sharing a bedchamber at the house party."

He turned from the passing scenery to look at her when she made no comment. Her chest still rose and fell in a rapid rhythm, her eyes were aimed dreamy and unfocused at a point somewhere in the vicinity of his left shoulder, and she'd caught her lower lip between her teeth as if to capture any lingering hint of his taste. The sight made him throb and he was unaccountably pleased with himself that he'd finally managed to rattle her a little. It was only fair. What gave this chit the right to be so composed, so self-assured while he, who was supposed to be the more experienced of them, could think only of tossing her skirts up and showing her real uninhibited pleasure?

"And we should probably agree upon an alias and backstory for you." Still, she did not respond. He might have been worried that he'd terrified her or shocked her had there not been a healthy color to her cheeks and chest. "Miss Tailor? Emily?" Reaching across the space between them, he crooked a gentle finger beneath her chin so her wide blue-green eyes met his. He did his best to look past the pure beauty and innocence they contained to the soul beneath. The next bit was particularly important and she needed to understand him fully. "If you sense danger, then you must run. Leave me and run. I can take care of myself."

"If I leave, then you will be entirely without assistance."

He chose to ignore her observation and, instead, continued as if she hadn't spoken at all. He pulled his purse from his pocket and handed her a fistful of coins. "Take some time to sew several into the hems of each of your gowns in case you need to flee at a moment's notice. There should be more than enough there to return you safely to Lady Night's. Her eyes widened, but she did not protest and held out her reticule for him to deposit the coins into. "And you must defer to my expertise in all things."

They spent the rest of the journey inventing a persona and an assumed last name for Emily (she was now Miss Emily Tully). Despite her best attempts to craft a creative name and scenario, she was prohibited from adopting an exotic honorific or the backstory of a foreign princess of a faraway country. Oliver hadn't thought she'd been serious, but he couldn't help but be amused by her efforts. She even coaxed an unwilling chuckle out of him at her exasperation when he "refused" to even give her suggestions some thought. The banter brought some much-needed levity back into the space between them as they trundled down the country roads. Eventually, Emily did give in to Oliver's insistence that they keep things as simple as possible—the smaller the lie, the easier it was to keep to.

"You will be one of Lady Night's new girls, fresh-faced and relatively inexperienced," Oliver decided. "It affords logical explanations as to why you won't be recognized by any of the brothel's frequent customers who may be in attendance at this gathering, as well as any knowledge you may have of the building and its industry."

Next, he quizzed her on information about himself that may come up in conversation. Where "Marcus Holden" had been born and raised (Dover and then London, though Oliver had spent most of the first two decades of his life in only a small corner of London), where he'd been educated (private tutors and then a term at Cambridge before leaving to learn the family shipping business—even that was far more formal education than Oliver had ever received), and hobbies (shooting and sailing; while Oliver abhorred the water, was a brilliant shot only because he had to be, and quite enjoyed a novel now and again). He was careful to discuss only information related to his assumed persona and steered clear whenever Emily attempted to ferret out any nugget of truth in his words. She was wily, he had to give her that.

"Favorite color?" she asked.

"Whyever would you need to know Marcus's favorite color?"

"Wouldn't his paramour know it and make an effort to wear it to please him?"

"Blue," Oliver blurted out, feigning interest in an invisible string dangling from his cuff. He didn't know what possessed him to answer the frivolous question; Marcus's favorite color was about as important as if his cock hung to the left or right, but he hadn't been able to help himself. He'd given Emily *his* favorite color. And now he couldn't stop picturing her wearing it.

She nodded appreciatively. "Any siblings?"

"None.

"Pets?"

"No."

"And your real name?" she asked lightly, cleverly inserting it into her peppered barrage of questions.

Oliver's lips snapped shut and he cocked a brow at her. The mischievous look she shot him beneath her long, gilded lashes did funny things to his innards.

"You will have to try harder than that, Miss Tailor."

"Miss *Tully*, if you please," she replied cheekily.

And did he ever wish to please.

Chapter Nine

T HE STEADY ROCKING and bouncing of the hired coach did nothing to assuage Emily's growing nerves with each passing hour. The memories of that rather unorthodox first hour of travel kept intruding upon her every thought, causing the most unfortunate heating of her cheeks and flushing of every inch of her skin.

The first kiss had been enough to kindle a flame low in her belly.

The second with the touching...now *that* had just about made her combust.

She repeated to herself over and over again that she shouldn't read too much into it or Marcus's reactions to the intimacies. She, of all women, should know better than that. Still, it was tempting to believe that her very first kiss hadn't been as clinical as it should have been, were it truly only a lesson.

She did her best to focus on Marcus's description of the rented country estate where the party was to take place. The property was a popular one for these gatherings due to its secluded setting and well-trained, tight-lipped staff who remained in residence despite the frequent comings and goings of different renters. The building's existence and true purpose were a poorly guarded secret amongst the *ton* and even those who turned their noses up at it were often the very ones who resented never having received an invitation.

"You might be surprised at how many titled individuals, or

those with wealth and status, participated in such parties," Marcus had said, clearly noticing how high Emily's brows had risen throughout his descriptions of the goings-on at such events. She supposed it shouldn't have surprised her as much as it did; she knew quite well how human carnal appetites worked. Neither sex was exempt from the urges and she could see how such parties might cater to a specific demographic in a time when chastity, purity, and decorum were expected—and even demanded—in Society drawing rooms and ballrooms.

"I can understand the appeal," she had commented with a lift of one shoulder. "There is a certain freedom to them not widely appreciated or allowed. If all parties are…enthusiastic about attending, then I don't see why such events should not take place."

Marcus had said nothing, only nodding before turning his attention out the window once more.

To his credit, he spent a great deal of their journey displaying infinite patience, doing his best to make her feel as prepared as possible for this strange and unfamiliar situation. Not only did he give her details on the party and the other attendees, but he reassured her many times over that he would protect her should there be a problem. His calm confidence was comforting, but it did not entirely douse her trepidations. More than once, Emily had questioned her sanity.

Whatever had possessed her to trust this man she did not know?

What had made her so willing to put her life at such risk?

Perhaps because something in her soul believed him and longed to help him.

He did his best to remain professional and informational in his tone, but she would occasionally catch a gleam of something in his eye when she spoke that showed there was much more to him than he revealed. Far from being unnerving, it was stimulating and made him seem more human than the facade he usually presented.

Despite his efforts, Emily became so anxious that her fingers were wrinkling her skirts beyond all help. She needed something to busy herself lest she lose her mind before this entire scenario even began in earnest. Unlatching her valise, she attempted to read the latest novel from her collection back home. It had been published about three months prior, but it was one of the few she had yet to reread to death. That lasted only a quarter of an hour before the jostling of the letters upon the page made her nauseated. She set it aside, but the clatter of heavy coins in her reticule made her pause.

Now was as good a time as any, she supposed.

She'd been taught to keep a small set of basic sewing implements handy at all times—not that she'd ever had the chance to travel much of anywhere. But her mother's instructions had stuck and she'd packed the necessary pieces away in a small roll in her valise. She withdrew it now and, after only a moment's hesitation, she lifted her hem, pulled her feet up, and curled her legs beside her on the seat. She had enough layers of underskirts and petticoats to hide her legs, not that she would have been all that scandalized to have a bit of ankle show anyway. It was just skin.

"What are you doing?" Marcus's voice had an odd edge to it and, when she looked up, she found him staring at her most peculiarly.

"You told me to sew coins into my garments. We have a few hours to go yet and I couldn't focus on my reading." She busied herself by finding a discreet fold in the hem and turning it up to create a pocket for the first coin.

"Shouldn't you wait until we arrive? So you can do that in private?"

"Nonsense. It needn't be pretty because no one will see it. What else is there to do?" She finished the first coin and lifted another layer of her skirts to begin on the second.

The knot of his cravat bobbed slightly.

"Using a needle in a rocking carriage does not seem like a prudent activity."

"Pish." She brushed him off as she finished the pocket for the second coin, careful that each layer she wore held enough money for her to obtain a seat on a carriage back to London. This way, she wouldn't have to worry about what she wore, lest she be left penniless. It wasn't the most pleasant of things to contemplate, but she knew it was a necessary precaution; Marcus had told her as much several times over. She'd have to finish sewing the coins into the rest of her garments once they arrived at their destination as they were all stored in the trunk strapped to the back of the conveyance.

The carriage lurched through a rut in the road and Emily yelped as her needle pierced her thumb.

"I told you," Marcus said with a sigh of resignation before crossing the gap between them. He removed her thumb from between her lips, examined the puncture as it oozed a thick drop of crimson blood, and then pressed a handkerchief produced from his pocket to her finger.

"It's nothing," she assured him, but he refused to relinquish her hand.

"You cannot arrive with blood on your gown," he chided her and continued to hold pressure on her thumb.

Unable to do much else, she allowed him to see to her minor injury. His concentration allowed her to examine his fine profile. She was once more nearly overwhelmed by the heat of his nearness and it was unreasonably tempting to lean into him. She settled for sitting stiffly beside him until he was satisfied that she would not expire. He pocketed the soiled handkerchief and returned to the rear-facing seat.

The chill left by his absence was as unexpected as it was unnerving. Where did she get off feeling such things? She knew she had to place whatever this attraction was into a small box and bury it down deep; it had no place in this situation.

UPON ARRIVAL AT the manor house, Emily and Marcus were greeted by a bevy of servants dressed in sedate blacks and grays.

The eyes of maids and footmen alike were dutifully riveted straight ahead with almost eerie determination. No sooner had Marcus helped her step down to the crushed gravel drive than their luggage was immediately unstrapped and unloaded by two footmen with brisk efficiency. The butler, a man who was the very personification of the color gray, greeted them with cool politeness and ushered them inside.

Rather than be shown to their rooms to freshen up and rest after their travels, however, Emily's cloak was taken and she and Marcus were shown into a cavernous parlor already occupied by the rest of the guests.

Emily didn't know what she'd expected from a gathering of individuals willing to participate in the debauched activities Marcus had described, but it hadn't been this room of relatively normal-appearing individuals.

"Ah, Mr. Holden!" A tall man, lean of build and broad of shoulder with features as sharp and keen as a falcon, approached them with open arms in a gesture of welcome. He had hair the color of chocolate with several distinguished strands of silver at his temples, and his eyes were so pale a blue as to be nearly colorless. Marcus's forearm tightened beneath her hand.

"Mr. Hayes," Marcus returned the greeting and clasped his proffered hand. "May I introduce Miss Emily Tully?"

Emily had to school herself not to take a step back as their host's eyes turned to her. His disconcerting gaze raked her from head to toe and back again in blatant appraisal. He took her numb hand in his and pressed his lips to her knuckles, then, shockingly, he turned it over and kissed the skin of her wrist where her cognac-colored kid glove ended.

"I am pleased beyond measure to make your acquaintance, Miss Tully." His tone was dripping with sensual promise. She could well believe this was the same man whose sexual appetites intimidated many of Lady Night's employees.

Willing the nerves from her voice, she replied, "The pleasure is all mine, Mr. Hayes." She inclined her head and looked up at him from beneath her lashes as she'd seen other girls practice. His answering smile was just shy of wolfish.

"Come, let me introduce you to the rest of our guests." He smoothly extricated Emily from Marcus's care before she knew what was happening, and guided her to the rest of the couples on the far side of the room. Three men and four women sipped from crystal cups of lemonade and enjoyed a selection of small cakes and sandwiches, beautifully prepared refreshments to replenish them after their journey.

"This is a beautiful building," Emily said, trying her best to sound conversational. She could feel Marcus following closely behind her and she took comfort in his nearness. He would not leave her at the mercy of this man.

"Thank you." He grinned down at her. "I make a point to visit at least once or twice each summer. I find the atmosphere agrees with me."

A rectangular structure only three stories in height with no towers or outwardly jutting wings, the house was rather simple in its design and construction, but—though her experience with architecture was painfully limited—she recognized quality in every corner. It lay in the details, the high ceilings, the silk paper upon the walls, the thick rugs beneath her feet, the polish of the furniture. Everything smelled pleasantly of costly beeswax and herbal sachets tucked away in nooks and drawers. Her eyes spotted not a single speck of dust as she scanned the large room, before being drawn up before the rest of the party.

"Ladies and gentlemen," their host drawled dramatically. "I present to you, Miss Emily Tully." She was at a loss with how to greet these unnamed individuals, so she settled for a demure tilt to her head and a bobbed curtsey. "Most of you already know Mr. Holden." He gestured to where Marcus had stepped up on Emily's other side. She wished he would take her back from this man who held her too close to his body, but she knew it couldn't be done without raising some eyebrows. As it was, they already appeared to be of some interest to the other guests—rather,

Marcus was. The females each cast knowing glances at one another, their lips curving in delight as they looked back and forth between their companions and Marcus. Emily felt a trickle of unease graze her spine. So distracted was she that she nearly missed the rest of the introductions.

In attendance were Mr. Reginald Frye (a man with powerful ties to the board of a weapons manufacturing firm) and his current paramour, the widowed Mrs. Claire Wright; Viscount Satterly (who stood to inherit a powerful earldom once his chronically ill father finally succumbed) and his wife, Francesca (who was a handful of years his senior, but came from another prominent family); Baron Allyson (a man who was extremely vocal in Parliament) and his longtime mistress, Lady Mary Aaron (an earl's widow and mother to a powerful son who'd stepped into his father's place); and a stunning young lady called Maeve Murphy. The last was Mr. Hayes's companion for the party and Emily said a silent prayer of thanks that he hadn't hired one of the ladies from Lady Night's. That would have been far more complicated than Emily felt herself capable of handling. As it was, she recognized Frye and the Satterlys as patrons of her mother's brothel. Pairing faces with those names was an odd experience for her.

Pleasantries were exchanged for several minutes after that. She nearly sagged in relief when Hayes finally released her, but Marcus was right there to prop her up, smoothly sliding in beside her and slipping a proprietary arm around her waist. She fit so well beneath his arm and stood there, content to allow him to take the lead in the banal conversation.

"If you don't mind, I believe I should like to show Miss Tully to our room. We have not yet had a chance to freshen up." Marcus was already backing them toward the door.

"Ah, yes, of course," chuckled Hayes. "Forgive my manners; I took one look at your lovely partner and lost all sense."

"Understandable." Marcus grinned and squeezed her waist.

It's an act, Emily had to remind herself lest she allow the butterflies in her stomach to flutter out of control.

Shortly thereafter, they were shown to a room on the home's second floor with a view of the front drive. Though not the premiere vista that might have been offered by some of the other bedchambers, to Emily, it was still glorious. Fields of green and copses of trees were scattered as far as the eye could see. Never before had she witnessed so much of the sky, so clear and so blue. The room itself was large with the grandest four-posted bed she'd ever seen, a desk, a wardrobe, and an attached private dressing room. A looking glass larger than she was tall was propped in the corner and four man-sized windows took up the far wall. A marble-framed fireplace was clean and waiting to be laid. Everything from the walls to the upholstery and coverlet was done up in decadent shades of crimson and chocolate; heavy velvet draperies hung from the horizontal posts of the bed frame as well as the windows. Surely they would block out any light if drawn properly. She noticed her trunk and Marcus's stood open and empty near the wardrobe and turned to find him watching her stroll around and investigate.

"So that was John Hayes, then?"

Marcus grunted in assent. "Don't take his amiability for weakness."

"I shan't. Everything about him gives me a chill." She shivered dramatically, earning her a slight softening of the skin around Marcus's mouth. "What now?" It was hours yet until supper.

"Freshen up. Rest. Whatever you wish. I will come to change and retrieve you before the meal."

"What will you be doing in the meantime?"

He lifted a shoulder. "Having a look around. Mingling. Memorizing the layout of the house as best I can."

Right.

They were there for a mission; this was no simple party.

"Of course."

His eyes searched hers for a moment before he said, "You did well with Hayes." A swell of pride at the compliment blossomed in her chest. "Now, I want you to lock this door behind me and open it to no one other than me." The pride withered and died, replaced by unease.

"Why?"

"Because not everyone looks at you as a human being—that much should have been obvious the first five seconds we were in the parlor." He proceeded to show her the door's two locks and then how to prop a chair beneath the knob so it could not easily be opened even if one possessed the key.

"How will I know it is you?"

He cocked a brow at her. "I will tell you it is me."

"Oh."

"Were you hoping for a secret knock? A code?"

She averted her eyes and hated how her cheeks warmed.

Marcus gave her a soft chuck under her chin. "I will return. Use this time to gather yourself and prepare. It will be a long evening."

Chapter Ten

THREE HOURS LATER, Emily had washed her face and hands, finished sewing all the coins into her various hems, then sat upon the mattress to test it out for a spell—and it was unreasonably comfortable. The bedding was plush and soft. It called to her to curl up within its cloud-like folds and sleep away the rest of the day. Emily just barely resisted its siren's call and busied herself with selecting her clothing for that evening. Once that was done, she managed to read a few more pages of her novel before dozing off on the chaise lounge situated in the warm sunlight filtering through the window.

She woke with a start at a knock at the door and noticed the sky had shifted from its brilliant blue to shades of navy, purple, and orange.

Her heart pounded to a near deafening degree until she heard a muffled, "Miss Tully? It is Marcus; I have returned."

Her book tumbled to the floor with a thud as she sprang up and rushed to unblock and unbar the door to admit him. Momentarily absorbed with being greeted by his handsome visage, it took her a heartbeat too long to realize he was not alone. A mousy girl in a maid's gray uniform with a white cap and apron stood beside him.

"I hope you had a pleasant rest." Oliver's smile was so warm it nearly melted Emily from the inside out until she realized that it was naught more than a performance for this girl. "I've brought Ann here to assist you in dressing for dinner. I've been assured she's quite adept with a pair of hot tongs."

"Oh. Oh! Yes, do come in." Emily opened the door wider to allow the girl to enter. Rather than follow, Marcus remained in the hall, catching Emily's arm before she could turn away.

"I shall return in an hour to dress. Will that be sufficient time to prepare yourself?" he asked in a low tone so as not to be overheard by the maid currently sorting through Emily's wardrobe.

She nodded. He turned to leave, but not before reminding her to lock the door behind him. Of course, Emily did just that.

She was still staring at the door and basking in the remaining hint of Oliver's scent when the little maid spoke up. "Which dress would you like to wear this evening?"

She spent the next hour being brushed and combed and curled and pinned, then laced into a cerulean-blue gown she'd borrowed from her mother's collection. Sapphire-colored glass beads dangled from the low-cut neckline while the skirt was a cascade of ruffles and silk. Luckily, she'd had enough time and forethought to alter the hem before Marcus had returned with the maid.

Emily was slipping on the elbow-length ivory gloves when she thanked and dismissed the maid. As the girl left, Marcus ducked in with impeccable timing. He was so focused on locking and barring the door that he did not immediately notice Emily.

"I'll change in the dressing room." He spoke to his cuff as he fiddled with its plain silver fastening. "I shouldn't be more than—"

His words died as he looked up to find Emily standing before the mirror. His eyes ran from her cream satin slippers up the shape of her body accentuated by the well-made gown, the voluptuous curves of her bosom, to the plaited and curled coiffeur so carefully crafted by Ann. Hayes's eyes upon her body had felt dirty, but Marcus's made her feel…bubbly. Instead of calculating all he could take from her, he stared at her as if in awe. She barely suppressed a chill of excitement; he so obviously liked what he saw and it was empowering.

He cleared his throat and, with a stiff nod of acknowledgment, he strode across the bedchamber and ducked into the dressing room, shutting the door firmly behind him.

AT SUPPER, EMILY and Marcus were seated across from one another. Given the unorthodox nature of the guest list, the seating arrangements were informal; no one sat in order of precedence as they would at a normal meal. Instead, it was simply coordinated so each woman had a man on either side of her. To Emily's left was Mr. Frye and Baron Allyson sat to her right. Both men proved amiable conversationalists with amusing anecdotes and it was clear they knew one another previously from the way they chatted.

Mr. Frye was of middling height and build, and couldn't have been thirty years of age if he were a day. His blue eyes twinkled with mirth and his cheeks grew flushed from laughter and drink. The baron was barrel-chested and on the shorter side, but he had a kind face and infectious laugh. It was easy to see how he commanded such a presence in Parliament—his every word and burst of laughter boomed through the room like thunder.

Midway through the meal, Hayes stood and held his goblet aloft. Conversation died as all attention turned to him. "Thank you for joining me this week at my little party. I hope you will all enjoy yourselves as much as I plan to." The last was met with a knowing chuckle so filled with promise that it made Emily's skin crawl with the sensation of a thousand tiny bugs. She couldn't help but look to Marcus for reassurance, and she didn't know whether to be excited or unnerved when he winked at her.

The shift in his personality—even the way he carried himself—had been nothing short of a miraculous transformation since their arrival. This Marcus was far different from the serious, cool-headed one in the carriage. He was funny, boisterous, and seemingly well-liked by all. Now, surrounded by all these people, the transformation was complete. He was a charmer. A flirt. A man whose personality endeared him to one and all. And she had to remind herself that his casual touches on her person before they'd gone in to dine, every handsome smile he shot her way, was an act.

"To your health, longevity, and endurance!" Hayes concluded his toast and everyone held their drinks in kind with a chorus of, "Hear, hear!" Most of the attendees polished off what remained in their goblets, but Emily merely sampled a sip of the dry white wine. She noticed Marcus did the same.

Following the two-hour meal, the entire party congregated in the same parlor where she and Marcus had been introduced earlier that day. She was speaking with Maeve, complimenting how the Irish girl's choice of emerald green complemented the copper hue of her hair, when, out of the corner of her eye, she caught sight of the oddest thing.

It took her two glances to realize she hadn't imagined it.

Mr. Frye and Mrs. Wright were locked in a passionate embrace in the corner of the room as if there weren't ten other individuals sharing the space. Their lips met with desperate fervor as their hands began to wander. She did her best to focus on her conversation with Maeve and then the discussion Marcus and Baron Allyson were having a few feet away, but it was impossible. Her attention kept drifting to the couple in the corner. She felt like she shouldn't watch the display, but her eyes kept darting over there, her body becoming more flushed with each sigh and moan that caressed her ears, then the glimpse of a stocking and untied garter.

The buzz in her mind screeched to a halt, however, when Hayes came up behind her, wrapped an overly familiar arm around her waist, and tugged her to his side. Instinctually, she shot a look at Marcus for assistance and saw his keen eyes watch Hayes's possessive arm wrap around her. But instead of flying to rescue and protesting the liberties their host took with her person, Marcus actually *grinned*.

Emily held herself painfully still, trying to ignore the large hand on her body, the heat of the palm as it slid up the curve of her hip so his thumb caressed the underside of her breast. It was all she could do not to squirm away.

"You have found us quite a delicious little morsel at Lady Night's," Hayes commented to Marcus, his voice dripping with innuendo.

"I agree most wholeheartedly," Oliver practically purred, his eyes raking her up and down, but doing entirely different things to her insides than the man who held her against his side. "I predict we are going to have a great deal of fun this week."

"I am a regular patron of Lady Night's, yet I do not believe I have ever seen this beauty there before. I certainly would have requested her company if I had."

"She is new," Marcus replied flippantly. "I found her a virgin and paid a pretty penny to deflower her."

"You don't say?" Hayes looked down at her expectantly, one brow arched high.

Emily tried to mask her flaring cheeks with another demure tilt of her head. "It was quite memorable, indeed."

"I am certain it was, with Holden managing things…" Hayes leaned in and pressed his lips to her exposed collarbone, inhaling deeply. "She smells of roses. How delightful."

Emily bit her tongue to keep from telling him he reeked of wine.

Marcus finally took pity upon her and snatched her hand, tugging her so she followed him to the cushion of the nearby couch and smoothly draped her across his lap. She knew him well enough at that point to recognize the slight tightening of his face signaled how the motion had pained his ribs, but he disguised it well. Likely no one else noticed it. She almost shivered when he plucked a fallen curl from her shoulder and she felt his warm parted lips on the back of her neck.

"I am not quite ready to share her just yet," he said in a voice so low that it vibrated through her body. "This one is still enough of a novelty to keep it exciting." He proceeded to nuzzle the nape of her neck, sending delighted chills traipsing up and down her spine.

Just then, a deep, masculine moan came from across the room. During the minutes of their distraction, it appeared the drawing room had transformed into a festival of Bacchanalian debauchery.

Mrs. Wright had dropped to her knees and was busy using her mouth and hands to service Mr. Frye with a fervor that would make Lady Night proud. The top of her gown had been pulled down, her full breasts and red nipples exposed to the golden light of the room. Viscount Satterly was fondling one of her breasts as his wife busied herself kissing Mr. Frye.

Baron Allyson and his mistress had migrated to another of the sofas and recruited Maeve for their activities. He had an arm around each of them and they took turns kissing him deeply.

When it became clear that Marcus was not going to relinquish his possessive hold on Emily, Hayes cast them one more assessing look before draping himself beside Maeve and fisting a hand in her hair to firmly draw her backward to meet his claiming kiss.

Emily was held rapt by the sensual and scandalous scene surrounding them.

Using a gentle finger on her jaw, Oliver turned her to face him and covered her parted, shocked lips with his own. So taken aback was she that she remained motionless.

"You must kiss me back," he murmured against her mouth. "This is no longer practice—especially now that Hayes has his eye on you."

Knowing Marcus was right, she immediately did as she was told and sank into the kiss. His lips were at once soft and firm, pleasantly demanding and encouraging. Emily's senses dissolved until she amounted to nothing more than the points where his body touched hers and what he made her feel.

She parted her lips as he'd shown her in the carriage and allowed his tongue to stroke deeply. He tasted of sweet cream and ripe strawberries with a hint of mint—the sugared dessert they'd enjoyed at the conclusion of their meal. She suckled his tongue and, with a groan, Marcus repositioned her so she straddled his hips, her skirts hiked up to expose her stocking-clad calves to the warm air of the room.

Familiar sounds of pleasure filled the parlor around her, but she ignored them. Instead, Emily was focused on every point of contact between her body and Marcus's. Tangling her fingers in his hair, she pressed herself closer so her nipples brushed his chest. His large hands slid from her back to cup her bottom, splaying wide to knead and caress the curves. Having him touch her there while his tongue and teeth devoured her made her ache for more. She wanted to hear him emit the same sounds the other men were, and she knew in her soul he would make her feel the most wondrous things in return.

She pressed her pelvis down and gave a testing rock of her hips, her eyes snapping open when she felt the unmistakable ridge of arousal that was most certainly not being faked for their audience. Oliver gasped against her lips when she did it again. Her core went instantly molten.

He dug his fingers into her rear in a bruising grip, but Emily found it only served to further spur on her need for exploration. She was fast discovering that she liked experiencing the power and control Marcus held in check so much of the time.

She wanted more of it.

Before Emily could rock her hips again, Marcus braced his legs and stood. It must have pained his side, but he did it anyway, smoothly hoisting her up with him as if she were an insignificant weight. Her arms twined around his neck and her legs naturally hooked around his lean hips to lock around his firm rear. Their lips and tongues locked in a sensual duel, Marcus carried her from the room and into the darkened hallway.

Finally alone, Marcus pinned her against the cool wall, pressing his head against the papering behind her shoulder and breathing heavily for several minutes before he slowly released her. Emily had barely regained her footing before he silently took her hand and led her up the stairs to the bedchamber they were expected to share. Her pounding heart was deafening in her ears as she stumbled along half-senseless behind him, trying not to marvel at the strength and security of his powerful hand around hers.

ONCE HE HAD Emily safely inside their bedchamber, Oliver locked the door behind them and barred it by propping the chair beneath the brass knob before resting his head against the barrier. Despite his efforts, his breath and pulse refused to quiet. The things Emily had done to him—the things he wanted to do to her—sprinted through his mind on an eternal loop. How she tasted, how she felt, how she moved…she would drive him mad if he weren't careful.

When he'd finally recovered, he turned to find Emily looking nothing short of dazed.

"It's to prevent any of the other guests from sneaking in during the middle of the night," he explained, gesturing to the chair as if he hadn't already explained the necessity of the precaution.

"Oh," she replied a little shakily. Her eyes caught on the tenseness of his shoulders. "Did I do something wrong this evening?"

"No. Not at all." An awkward silence followed. Oliver glanced at the gilded clock positioned on the mantle. It was well after midnight and they'd spent much of the day traveling. "You must be fatigued."

Emily shook her head. "I am used to keeping odd hours…though I would like to change into something more comfortable." She gestured to the lush blue beaded gown that had set his blood on fire the entire evening. Blue. She'd worn his favorite color. From the moment he'd first seen her, he wondered if she'd done it for him. "I will just ring for Ann."

"You cannot do that."

"Whyever not?" she asked, freezing in place.

"Because everyone downstairs currently believes *I* have undressed you by now—especially given how we took our leave."

He watched as Emily's cheeks flamed painfully pink. It was a stark contrast to the ease and confidence with which she'd ridden his lap only minutes earlier. Oliver cleared his throat.

"I can help you undo your laces and stays," he offered evenly, trying not to allow his imaginings of her bare skin to arouse him beyond sanity. "Then, you may use the dressing room or I will turn around to afford you the privacy you require to undress and change your clothing."

There was a moment's hesitation before Emily nodded and turned to offer him her back. As Oliver lifted his unsteady fingers to the ties of her gown, he cursed his decision in as many languages as he could. The gesture of unlacing a woman's clothing without the sole aim of having her beneath him as quickly as possible was extremely intimate…and erotic beyond comparison.

The moment he was done, Oliver retreated to the far side of the room and faced the wall. His vision bore holes into the red-striped papering as the rustle of fabric rang nearly deafening in his ears. Of course she'd torture him and change right there in the middle of the room…

His mind too easily imagined Emily bare behind him, her rosy-pink flesh exposed to the air, her deliciously dusky nipples puckered and begging for his mouth. He clenched his fists until his knuckles were white and bloodless.

Not until Emily assured him that she was decent did he turn.

Though he tried to ignore it, the sight of her tucked beneath the deep-red coverlet, her knees pulled up to her chest—so sweet and so tempting—made his mouth run drier than the African desert.

Clenching his jaw against the vicious pang of desire, he strode over to her and snatched up one of the pillows and an extra blanket that had been laid out at the foot of the mattress. He tossed them with more force than necessary to the floor by the hearth.

"What are you doing?" Her voice was soft and curious.

"Preparing my bed," he grunted without looking up.

"The floor will be terribly uncomfortable for your injuries." There was a hesitation as she seemed to consider her next words before speaking. "Why don't you take the other half of this bed?"

"No," Oliver snapped as the last word left her lips. He refused to consider how her offer made his pulse skip.

"But this mattress is far too large for one person."

"No!" he said, more forcefully that time. Oliver righted himself from his task and, facing the hearth to glare into the flames, he began to struggle out of his fitted coat. The fashionable cut of the fabric left little room for movement, let alone with the hindrance of his wounds. His ribs continued to plague him with persistent throbs if he inhaled too deeply or turned too quickly. It had probably been too early, but he'd removed the stitches himself before retrieving Emily from Lady Night's. The site was painful, but not infected. He could tolerate all of it as long as he was cognizant of his physical limitations.

Suddenly, small hands began working from behind him to slide the clothing from his shoulders. Stiffly, he allowed it to happen, knowing all the while he had only to turn around to see the pink of Emily's skin beneath the virginal white of her nightshift. His cock pulsed with every heartbeat, throbbing to life and demanding relief. The sensation of her fingers on his arms reassured him that he most certainly could not share a bed with her without taking things much, much further than he should…

As soon as he was free, Oliver stepped away from Emily and began untucking his shirt from his breeches and then prepared to remove his boots. He watched from the corner of his eye as she neatly draped his coat and waistcoat over a chair. The action was so achingly sweet and domestic that it made him pause.

"Do you always wear your weapons?" she asked, tilting her

chin to gesture to the sets of knives strapped to his waist and back. The harness had been cleverly designed to be worn seamlessly beneath a fitted coat and the sheaths had been strategically placed where they would not create bulk to his form, yet they remained within easy reach.

"Danger can be unpredictable." He slid one boot free and removed the blade that had been concealed by the thick leather. Her eyes widened.

"Armed to the teeth, are you?"

Oliver's lips twitched, but he did not respond and set about removing his other boot. As comfortable as he could make himself, Oliver lay back upon his makeshift pallet and draped his forearm over his eyes.

"Go to sleep, Emily."

He listened to her sigh of resignation as before she padded back across the plush rug and slid back into bed.

What he wouldn't give to be alone so he could wrap his hand around his cock as he replayed over and over again the way it felt to have Emily in his arms, of her kissing him and riding his lap. He couldn't very well beat off with her less than ten feet away, so he rolled to his side and, grumpily, reconciled himself to little sleep and a raging cockstand while Emily danced teasingly through his mind.

Chapter Eleven

THE NEXT MORNING, Emily woke to a quiet room.

She was so used to the incessant din of her building and life in London that the silence was, at first, deafening. There was always something happening—some delivery being made, some cart rumbling over the uneven road, men deep in their cups shouting at one another, the cackle of women in the streets. Here, there was none of that.

It was almost disconcerting. Disorienting.

Because of this, it took Emily a few moments to gain her bearings and recall just where she was. She reached her arms above her head and blinked up at the ceiling. It instantly made her wonder if she weren't still in a dream because she saw her sleep-tousled reflection staring back at her from another opulent bed mounted high above her head.

Panes of mirrored glass affixed to the ceiling?

What an odd house.

She elongated her limbs in a luxurious stretch, enjoying the plush softness of the overstuffed mattress and thick coverlet. The flat she shared with her mother was comfortable and she had everything she needed, but it was nothing compared to the delectable bed in which she'd slept that night.

Alone.

A glance toward the hearth told her Marcus had already risen. His pillow and blankets had been collected and neatly folded on the foot of the bed, erasing every indication that he hadn't actually slept beside her. He was so silent that she didn't notice at first that she wasn't alone in the room.

Marcus was standing before the full-length looking glass in the opposite corner of the room, trying in vain to reapply the wrap around his wounded side.

"I did not expect you to be such an early riser." Emily nearly fell out of bed when Marcus unexpectedly addressed her reflection. The realization that he'd caught her staring made her abdomen flutter. "The rest of the guests will no doubt be abed for some time yet; it is only half-six in the morning."

"Just because I live above a brothel does not mean I keep their usual hours," she retorted, sitting up straight and doing her best to smooth back her hair. She'd always moved a great deal in her sleep and created a hopeless mess of her hair, and that night had been no exception. It didn't matter if she plaited it, donned a bonnet, or tied it up; she always awoke to the most disastrous of appearances. It hadn't bothered her before, other than for its inconvenience, but this was also her first time facing a man immediately upon waking. Despite her embarrassment, she mustered up as much dignity as she could.

"Fair enough," Marcus said. He was still occupied with his task, the tone of his voice indicating he either didn't believe her claim or didn't care overmuch.

She was tempted to explain further that she'd always been an early riser; it was often the only time she had peace and autonomy. She was the one who ensured the timely arrival of deliveries to Lady Night's, personally inspected the main rooms for any damage from the previous evening, and balanced the account books with the money locked securely away in a secret cellar safe. She didn't know why it mattered to her that Marcus knew she was more than a slugabed, but it did.

She watched as he fumbled with the wrapping for the third time and she could take it no longer. She flung back the coverlet and padded barefoot across the thick rug to assist him. She could feel his eyes watch her every movement in the looking glass while she washed her hands with water from the pitcher and, from the stiff way he handed the linen wrap over to her, she could tell he loathed relying upon anyone. Despite this, he did not protest and silently allowed her to finish the job.

Emily did her best not to notice the solid heat of his sculpted, naked torso beneath her hands, the smooth expanse of flesh with its mysterious silvery scars and marks, but it was nigh on impossible when he looked the way he did, smelled the way he did, watched her the way he did with palpable intensity.

She finished and neatly tied and tucked the ends of the wrapping away. "How fares your head?" she asked as she gently brushed a thick dark lock of his hair aside to examine the healing wound. The silk stitches had been removed and there was only the pinkness of kitting flesh. Luckily, there was no redness and swelling; it looked healthy to even her untrained eyes.

At once, she realized how very close her examination of his head had brought her to Marcus. All he had to do was turn his face and they'd once more be kissing. If the mere thought made her toes curl and her skin tingle, what would the real thing do?

Likewise, Marcus did not seem entirely unaffected by their proximity. She could feel even without touching him properly how taut his every muscle was, how each sinew was clenched to the point of vibration.

His sharp eyes darted to her lips and Emily practically jumped backward with an awkward laugh. "So…what did you need to do to earn an invitation to this house party?" she asked, effectively changing the subject as she helped him to shrug into his starched white shirt. "After last night, it is abundantly clear that such a gathering is comprised of a very select demographic."

Marcus's mesmerizing eyes met hers. "You should not be asking questions to which you do not wish to know the answers." His voice was flat, but not unkind.

Emily swallowed hard and did not press him for more information, knowing he was probably right. Having witnessed what she did last night, the answer likely wasn't something pleasant.

She could only guess at the debauched ways Marcus had gained the confidence of their host—of the things he'd witnessed and, perhaps, even done, himself, to make it known that he could be trusted and that he would fit in well with the rest of the guests.

The memory of Hayes's lascivious eyes and wandering hands made her skin feel greasy and uncomfortable.

No, she likely didn't want to know the answer.

She walked back to the bed and sat down upon the center of the mattress, crossing her legs beneath her nightshift. She leaned back on her palms and tilted her head to the ceiling with a sigh.

"From what I've seen of this house, it is like a brothel on a grander scale." She gestured above her head to the cleverly suspended looking glasses she'd noticed upon waking. "I have never seen anything like this. What would one wish to see from this angle?"

She found Marcus watching her intently. He fastened his cuffs before approaching the edge of the bed; rather than stop, however, he prowled over to her on hands and knees with his innate grace. He laid her back with his nearness, his body hovering so closely over hers that she could feel the heat of his skin beneath his half-fastened shirt front. Her breathing stalled and she was fairly certain he could hear the frantic thud of her heart.

"Look up," Marcus murmured huskily.

With some difficulty, she tore her eyes away from his handsome face—the rims of deep blue encircling his pupils—Emily looked over his broad shoulder to witness the reflection of his impressively long, lean body between her legs, the bunching of his muscular back and buttocks as he held himself as still as a marble statue. Her wide eyes shone back at her from the mirrors hung above them. Unbidden, she imagined how it would be if they were naked.

Oh my...

"Surely Lady Night's has rooms such as this one; everything has been designed with pleasure in mind." Without affording her time to respond, Marcus smoothly rolled off of her and gestured to the holes bored into each of the thick posts of the enormous bed—a bed she was certain had been designed to sleep many more than just two. She hadn't noticed the holes until he'd pointed them out; her eyes had passed over them, believing them to be a part of the intricate carvings. Whatever did they have to do with pleasure? Her mind tried and failed to create a likely scenario.

"I have never been permitted to be in any of the pleasure rooms at Lady Night's." It had been her mother's valiant attempt at retaining some of Emily's innocence. "I was only to see the employees in my rooms or their sleeping quarters."

"They sleep in different rooms from the ones in which they…work?" Marcus asked distractedly as he did up the remaining fastenings of his shirt. He'd returned to the task of dressing himself.

"You do not sleep where you work, so why should they?"

He shot her a droll look and Emily realized he'd done just that.

"Are you hungry?" he inquired, changing the subject. Emily nodded in reply. "I'll ring for a maid. A formal meal won't be served since no one else is likely to rise until well after noon. They all likely stayed up into the wee hours of the morning 'making merry.'" He tugged at a bellpull near the bed to sound a chime in the bowels of the kitchens before flipping a small lever near the door.

Nothing happened.

"What was that for?" Emily asked with a frown.

"In houses such as this one, the guests value their privacy above all else," he explained as he finished dressing. "While the staff is paid well for their discretion, there are other measures taken to ensure it. Rather than having servants enter rooms to inquire as to the guests' needs, this lever flips a flag outside the door to tell them food is required. The other switches indicate the request to have a bath drawn and things of that nature."

"I thought you'd never been here before; you seem incredibly knowledgeable for that to be the case."

"I haven't," he remarked wryly. "But I have been to other homes and establishments just like this one over the years."

"All in the name of King and country, of course," she commented, unsure where the snark in her tone came from and then appalled that she'd acted in that fashion.

Marcus stood after donning his boots. Nothing in his manner or speech gave her an indication that he'd taken offense. "Do you need assistance to dress? We likely cannot call a maid to help you do so for several hours and maintain the ruse."

"Why not?"

"Because I'm supposed to have tupped you past the point of exhaustion," he replied bluntly. "And the request for food is only to fortify ourselves for more. You need not dress simply to eat and remove it all over again."

Emily cleared her throat. "Well, then..." She slid from the bed and began rifling through her wardrobe to select the garments she required. Yesterday had been a raspberry-pink woolen traveling ensemble and the cerulean gown for supper. Today, she selected another of the creations she'd pilfered from her mother's collection: a seafoam-green morning dress trimmed in lace with a daringly low-cut bodice accentuated with artful pleating. Her ivory slippers completed the look.

Marcus had finished dressing himself by the time she was done and he ducked into the private dressing room to allow her to strip down, and don her undergarments. She took a precious few moments to freshen up, brush tooth powder on her teeth, and attempt to tie back her hopeless hair with a ribbon in a fashion that was only partially successful. She turned her back to the dressing room door and called out for Marcus to return. Once he did, he immediately set about assisting her with all the tugging and tying and fastening that went into being a fashionable woman of the day.

By the time he'd helped her into a dress—with surprisingly

deft ease, mind you—there was a knock on the door. Marcus strode over, but, instead of opening the door, he swung aside a painting hung beside the levers he'd previously shown her. Behind it, there was a hidden cabinet! He produced a silver tray piled high with berries and eggs, glistening sausages, and even two fragile china cups of chocolate.

"How clever!" Emily exclaimed, unable to contain her appreciation. She dashed over to the secret cubby hole to examine it. The other side was closed behind paneling in the hallway. "No one needs to see the room's occupants at all."

When she looked back at Marcus, a smile more genuine than the one he'd used since their arrival graced his face.

And it was glorious.

The man wasn't simply handsome; he was beautiful.

And he was amused by her excitement over something so trivial as a secret door in a wall.

Emily smiled self-consciously and retreated to the room's small round table by the window. He followed her, set the tray down, and gestured for her to begin breaking her fast.

She nibbled on a strawberry while watching as he wound a length of fine fabric around his neck for his cravat. Instead of standing before the mirror, however, she was amazed to see he closed his eyes and tied an impressively intricate and perfectly formed knot against his throat without any visual assistance whatsoever. He held her rapt with unmasked appreciation while she sipped the warm, velvety chocolate.

Marcus continued to amaze with each new thing she learned about him.

OLIVER OPENED HIS eyes to find Emily's gaze trained upon him. She was angelic sitting there in the golden light of early morning, even with her hair so messy it appeared to have a life of its own. God, if she looked like that after a night alone in bed, what would she look like waking up after an evening spent being thoroughly worshipped?

"You are quite good at that," she stated.

"Yes, well, I've had a fair amount of practice." He took the seat across from her.

"Tying cravats or taking care of yourself?" she asked innocently.

"Both," he replied without thinking, plucking a blueberry from the plate between them.

"Whose cravat have you been tying like that? You seem to have had a great deal of practice doing that somewhere."

Masquerading as a duke's valet for eight years, Oliver had been thoroughly versed and skilled in such things, careful to maintain nothing short of the height of fashion. Now that he was parading about as Marcus Holden, well-off heir to a shipping company, he was expected to dress the part. He did so without thinking—styling his hair just so, donning well-fitted fashions and fabrics, all of it came with his role and he managed it single-handedly. He'd never relied upon anyone else before and he never intended on doing so. He'd learned decades prior that it could only lead to pain and disappointment.

Of course, Oliver told her none of that.

He shrugged and replied cryptically, "I've picked it up here and there."

She arched a perfectly shaped brow at him. "You *can't* or you *won't* tell me?"

Oliver remained silent, chewing on a bite of sausage.

"Both, then." Emily sighed and took another sip from her cup of chocolate before returning it and its saucer to the table. "You know, you should offer me a little something true about yourself. We are going to be working together in these close quarters, after all." She eyed him thoughtfully. "I know Marcus Holden is not your real name and you have refused to confide even that much in me."

Oliver nodded once, unable to tear his eyes from her lips. A daub of the creamy chocolate was left on the corner of her mouth. As sweet as she'd tasted the night before, he couldn't help but ponder how much sweeter she'd be with chocolate on her tongue.

He imagined licking it from her lips...and elsewhere.

"From where do you hail, then?" she asked, snapping Oliver's eyes to hers once more. "Are you even listening to me?" She giggled lightly.

He touched his lip to demonstrate and said, "You've a bit of chocolate. Just here."

"Oh!" She touched her face and then reached for her napkin, but it slid from her lap as she scrambled to swipe at the offending smudge.

Oliver handed her his, but, instead of releasing it, he used it to tug Emily to him and kissed the chocolate away with a deep sweep of his tongue.

Yes.

She was *delicious*.

He melted into the kiss, tasting her, licking into her, wishing he could sink inside of her warmth and never resurface.

When he finally pulled back, her eyes were dreamy and glazed. As collected as she usually was, he liked knowing he had this effect on her when he caught her unaware.

The only issue was that she was beginning to do the same thing to him...

Oliver sat back in his chair and did an admittedly poor job of masking his intentions when he said, "You must expect things like that here. Even the most benign interactions can turn intimate."

She pulled her lips between her teeth and nodded, turning her attention back to the food between them and selecting a strawberry. He was utterly entranced as she took a bite and licked the juices from her ripe lips...and Oliver knew he was in serious trouble.

He could not watch her eat, not when everything Emily did—every glance and every motion—was so unconsciously sensual. The way she tilted her head and leaned toward him when he spoke, the erotic curve of her lips, the sway of her hips when she walked, all served to set him on edge and prime his body fit to bursting with desire. He should have known the daughter of London's most renowned madam would have inherited her mother's innate sexuality. Even if Emily was still a virgin, that made her all the more dangerous. She said she had learned some of the tricks of the trade from the women at Lady Night's, but she couldn't know how they affected men—and to what lengths some men would go to capture her for those natural wiles and instincts.

She was an untrained hunter with a loaded weapon, and he was as good as her prey.

He wanted her.

Badly.

And that could mean nothing but trouble for him and his mission. The last twenty-four hours had proven to him even more than before that he had to protect her from Hayes.

And he had to protect her from himself.

"I was born in South London," Oliver blurted out before he could stop himself.

Emily's answering smile was devastating in its sweetness. "That wasn't so difficult, was it?"

Little did she know, the admission had cut him more deeply than the knife he'd taken in the side. To disclose even this little bit of information went against all of his training. It rubbed him raw like sandpaper on bare flesh. It felt like spiders crept beneath his muscles. He needed space. Clearly, fresh air was in order. Oliver stood and pushed back from the table, tossing his napkin beside the food as he did so.

"I should begin my search. Under no circumstances should you leave this room unattended and you must lock and wedge the door behind me. I will return for you when it is safe to come down."

"Is that necessary? It is morning."

"Not all of the other guests will treat you with as much re-spect as I have," he replied soberly.

Her mouth snapped shut and she nodded in agreement. "I shall spend my morning reading. Alone. Hopefully, I do not expire after too many hours of boredom."

Oliver fought a smile and tilted his chin to the novel she'd left on the bedside table. "I doubt that is possible; that story is particularly good. I never took you as someone who enjoyed tales of derring-do." Her lips parted in surprise. "I shall bring Ann when I return to help you tame that mane of yours as well."

Emily huffed in indignation, aimed, and flicked a blueberry so it smacked him square in the chest. He narrowed his eyes at her, but the effect was lost when her bubble of laughter escaped from behind her palm.

OLIVER CREPT DOWNSTAIRS as silently as possible until he reached the parlor in which they'd spent the most time. The gaudy, gilded clock atop the mantle told him he should have a few hours yet before any of the guests began to move about. This was likely his best opportunity to finish learning the house's layout and begin mapping potential hiding places for damning correspondence and other tangible evidence.

He was already familiar with the dining room and had performed a cursory review of the drawing room before supper the prior evening. The house, however, was large and there were plenty of rooms in which to hide things. He needed to start soon if he was going to find what he needed. Oliver began by touring the library, which would have proved more daunting had the room's disuse not been so evident in the film of dust on the higher shelves. For all their efficiency elsewhere, the staff had found ways around performing certain tasks that the usual clientele were unlikely to notice.

There were a couple of sitting rooms, a music room with a piano and harp—both untuned—a small glass-walled conservatory devoid of plants, but filled with furniture for naughty romps beneath the sun or moon. In the hall, there was a cleverly disguised entrance to the servants' stairwell, which allowed them to travel unseen from their attic rooms to the kitchens below, and every floor in between.

And then there was the study.

Oliver crept closer to the last room in the line of polished doors, listening all the while for signs of life. When there were none, Oliver turned the knob and entered the study.

He wasn't alone.

He quickly masked his annoyance at finding the room occupied with an apology for the intrusion. "It seems I've gotten a bit turned around."

Hayes looked up from the papers on his desk, smoothly sliding them beneath another stack, and stood to approach Oliver. He clasped a companionable hand on his back. "It is easy to do here. The halls are like a maze." The casual, yet deliberate, way in which his host locked the study door and stored the key in an inner pocket of his coat was not lost on Oliver. "I was trying to finish up a bit of work before the day began in earnest."

"Do not feel as though you must abandon what you are doing to entertain me. I am perfectly capable of occupying myself."

"Nonsense. Have you broken your fast yet this morning?"

"I have." It was difficult not to imagine Emily back in their bedchamber, bent over a novel as she nibbled on berries.

Hayes guided them back the way Oliver had come, effectively leading him as far away from the study as he could. "I thought you might have been abed quite a while longer this morning, Holden. You and Miss Tully appeared quite enraptured. If I had been you, both of us would have been so spent, we wouldn't have shown our faces before luncheon." Hayes chuckled thickly, oblivious to how the comment caused Oliver's blood to boil. Luckily, he'd had a great deal of practice masking his emotions behind a carefully crafted veneer. "I plan on having her before the week is out, mark my words." Hayes spoke casually enough, but his words rang with innuendo and dark promise. "It is a crime that Miss Tully's only experience thus far has been you; she deserves something to compare it to."

"It is up to the lady," Oliver replied as lightly as possible, trying to inject nonchalance into his tone. "Though she seems rather content just now, if you ask me."

"That is because she does not know what she is missing," Hayes laughed heartily and slapped Oliver on the back slightly more firmly than necessary.

Oliver's fists clenched at his sides.

Chapter Twelve

THE REST OF the day was rather tame in comparison to the previous night's entertainment. After Oliver retrieved Emily from their bedchamber, they joined the rest of the party for a light luncheon. To their credit, the guests seemed to have recovered quite well and were more than ready for another evening of debauchery. The juxtaposition of these normal conversations and relatively well-behaved exteriors compared to what she had witnessed the night before initially threw Emily off kilter. How was she supposed to look Mrs. Wright in the eye after what she'd seen her do to Mr. Frye? For that matter, how could she look at Mr. Frye when she'd seen every inch of…him? She wasn't prudish, but it was one thing to discuss such things with her mother's employees, and another entirely to face people whom she'd seen in flagrante delicto the night before.

Fortunately for her, Marcus's easy attitude and joviality helped her to relax and, soon enough, she was enjoying casual conversation with the other guests as if everything had been nothing more than a very vivid dream.

Following a late supper of chilled watercress soup, whitefish in a creamy lemon sauce, roast fowl with vegetables, and dessert of decadent iced cakes topped with sugared fruits, the spirits flowed heavily. Wine, brandy, whiskey, and port were served, slurring voices, increasing their volume, and lowering already questionable inhibitions. Throughout it all, Emily took Marcus's silent lead and only sipped the drink that had been poured for her.

She watched in amazed appreciation as Marcus played up his inebriation. It was utterly fascinating to witness his remarkable acting ability. The way he drew attention like a moth to a flame, how he captivated everyone with amusing anecdotes and witty banter, more than made up for and helped to mask Emily's lack of experience in such a situation. Everything he did took the focus off of her and drew the guests' eyes to him.

Several rounds of drinks later, everyone was coaxed into a game by the Satterlys. Lady Satterly—cheeks and bosom quivering in excitement—explained how one of their party would stand blindfolded in the center of a circle of bodies and then be spun. That person would then stumble, laughing, until they encountered someone. They would then kiss that person, whomever it might be, male or female. This often resulted in uproarious laughter and cheers, in which Emily couldn't help but participate.

Mrs. Wright wound up in their host's lap when they both tumbled onto the sofa to share a kiss. Mr. Frye tipped straight over as soon as he was done being spun. Sputtering and laughing, Lady Satterly had bent to assist the man and was pulled down beside him in a heap of sloppy kisses and titillated laughter.

Emily's eyes caught Marcus's across the circle and her laughter abruptly died. He was suddenly remarkably sober—his stillness underscored by the cacophony around them. His eyes were riveted upon her, unblinking and unwavering. Her body went cold, then unbearably hot; her thighs clenched around the blossoming ache at their crux. It was everything she could do to not cross the circle, step over the couple in their lurid embrace, wrap her arms around Marcus's neck, and kiss him.

IN ALL, OLIVER thought Emily was being a remarkably good sport given their unique situation. She'd overcome some initial awkwardness to fall in well with the rest of the party. He might attribute it to her rather unconventional living arrangement above Lady Night's business, but to do so would do her spirit a disservice.

Where most women would have run screaming from a similar situation, Emily had straightened her spine and gone into it with full trust in him and his ability to keep her safe. Her confidence shone like a beacon on a stormy night. She was amiable, witty, charming, and downright lovely. Any man would have to be daft and blind not to notice and be inexorably drawn to her charms. To be sure, Oliver hadn't been her sole victim.

Oliver watched as the red-haired Irish girl, Maeve, staggered blindly toward Emily. She caught Maeve, who then removed her blindfold, giggling in delight when she saw it was her. She leaned in and pressed her lips to Emily's. The room went silent.

Much to Oliver's surprise, Emily's eyes closed and she kissed Maeve back. He hoped his unbidden groan of instantaneous lust wasn't audible above the rising cheers of the other spectators. He, like the others, watched raptly until the contact broke.

Maeve turned to him. "Now I know why you are so keen to keep this one to yourself," she said in her lilting accent, raising a suggestive brow, a saucy tilt to her lips.

"She is quite the natural," he murmured in response, trying to disguise how flustered he was beneath a false haze of inebriation. His eyes flicked to Emily and he noted the flush of her cheeks and throat, but he couldn't tell if it was from embarrassment or pleasure.

Oliver had to force himself to turn his attention back to the game rather than the enchanting woman across from him.

When it came time for Emily to be blindfolded and spun, Oliver found himself praying to a God he did not believe in that Emily would come to him and no other. As erotic as watching her be kissed by another woman had been (and, judging by the ravenous look in Hayes's eyes, Oliver was certainly far from the only man to appreciate the sight), he didn't think he'd handle it well at all if another man kissed her. It likely would go quite poorly if he had to knock a man out cold for touching Emily.

After being spun 'round and 'round by Lady Satterly, Emily

stumbled dizzily, her dazzling smile visible beneath the edge of the blindfold. Some deity must have heard Oliver's pleas because she fell toward him. She might have been caught by Mr. Frye, who stood to Oliver's left, but Oliver's reflexes were much faster than his. He easily caught Emily's waist when she would have tumbled, and hauled her to him. His entire body shivered when she reached up and found his lips with her thumbs, tracing them with light back-and-forth strokes. Smiling, she stood on her toes and kissed him sweetly, tenderly.

It rocked Oliver to his core.

He'd just begun to give himself over to the kiss, passing his tongue over the seam of her pillow-soft lips, when Emily leaned back and lifted her blindfold. The glint in her eyes told him she knew it had been him all along.

The two of them ignored the complaints the crowd had as to the tameness of the kiss—this was meant to be a game of twisted passions, not affection. He gritted his teeth and, as good-naturedly as possible, told everyone in the room to sod off. This comment was met with shrieks of laughter. His limbs felt heavy and rusted as he forced himself to accept the blindfold from Emily, release her from his arms, and stand in the center of the circle.

Rough hands and groping fingers spun him several times over and he made sure to stumble dramatically when he was released. The skirts he encountered reeked of perfume and the sourness of spilled spirits, not the light scent of rosewater. It was for the best, though. It wouldn't do to seem more attached to Emily than he already was.

The woman (Mrs. Wright, judging by the scent and heavily beaded gown) raked her nails through Oliver's hair, roughly tugging his mouth down to hers. She devoured him with wet, open-mouthed kisses that tasted of wine instead of the earthy sweetness of chocolate. Her hands began to roam, measuring the breadth of his shoulders, creeping beneath his silk waistcoat to hook her fingers in the waistband of his breeches. Throughout it all, Oliver kept his blindfold on, making it easier to throw himself into the act.

Mrs. Wright rubbed her voluptuous curves against his body, grazing his chest with her erect nipples. She moaned against him like a cat in heat, pulling him forward until he collapsed on top of her on an oversized wingback chair.

From the cheers and lewd remarks surrounding them, they were the center of the party's attention. His stomach soured knowing Emily was watching as well, and what she must think of him as he reached down to push Mrs. Wright's skirts up past her knees and give a testing rock of his hips. The resounding encouragement confirmed his suspicions that the game had been abandoned for this new show.

Oliver ripped the blindfold from his face and found Mrs. Wright panting beneath him. Her dark hair fell from its pins and one of her full breasts had slipped from the bodice of her gown in their tumble, revealing to all her large, puckered nipple.

Oliver knew what he *should* do.

He *should* accept her blatant invitation to take her right then and there, thereby further endearing himself to the debauched Hayes and earning a spot in his inner circle.

But he couldn't do it.

"Touch yourself for me," Oliver commanded her instead. Her eyes darkened and her lips parted in delight. Hiking her skirts up higher, she did as she was told as Oliver disentangled himself from her limbs under the guise of spectating with the rest of the guests. As Mrs. Wright moaned breathily and spread herself for the crowd, Oliver stealthily moved aside to find Emily in the back of the group looking vastly discomfited. As much as he would have liked to remove her from the situation entirely, he knew they couldn't exit as early as they had the previous night without drawing unnecessary notice.

Instead, he retrieved a bowl of strawberries and raspberries which had been laid out for their pleasure and, taking Emily's small hand in his, he guided her to a chair close enough where they were a part of the group, but far enough that their whispers wouldn't easily be overheard.

Oliver settled her in his lap, feeling slightly more relaxed now that she was in his arms once again, but she remained tense. He ran a calming hand down her spine and it elicited a delightful little shiver from her body. He had to turn his mind to other things lest the movements and weight of her in his lap create a new crisis. It was more important at that moment to ensure she was well.

He set the bowl of berries on the chair's arm and selected a plump strawberry, holding it to her lips. Stupidly, he'd thought of little else besides feeding her strawberries just like this since they'd broken their fast together that morning and he was well past beating down that temptation.

Reluctantly, Emily took a bite.

Oliver leaned in, absorbing her scent of berries and roses, the clean musk of a woman who had no idea she was beginning to drive him mad. "Are you alright?" he asked the soft skin behind her ear.

"That display was rather enthusiastic of you," she whispered after a short delay.

"It was all an act," he replied softly, trying his best to keep his reluctant smile out of his voice. "Trust me when I say that, if I had truly wanted to take her, I'd be inside of her right now." Emily leaned back, her wide eyes meeting his and causing a burst of satisfaction to bloom in his chest. He ran his lips along her throat. The beginning of a mewl escaped her before she was able to tamp it down. "Your performance was well-done as well. The kiss was rather…moving." Even thinking about it now made his groin pulse with heat.

Emily inhaled a shaky breath and melted against him, making his breeches grow uncomfortably tight despite his best efforts to remain even keeled. "I admit it wasn't the first time I've shared a kiss with a woman." She curled her fingers into the lapels of his coat, holding him where he was when he found a particularly sensitive bit of skin. "It was how I learned to use my tongue."

Oliver had to reach between them to surreptitiously adjust himself after he was assaulted by that mental image. It took him far too long to remember how to breathe. "Is that something you enjoy?" His voice was barely above a raspy whisper.

"I pretended she was you," Emily admitted with a sigh.

The words hit Oliver like a hammer to the gut and he had to school himself to remain as impassive as possible. His pulse pounded and something deep within him roared with pride. This woman wanted him. Or, at the very least, she enjoyed their interactions enough to use them to her advantage. Either way, it was more than he deserved.

He was there on a mission and he could not risk the distraction Emily presented. He had a part to play and his life depended upon it—Emily's, too. He must keep his wits about him, no matter how tempting he found her.

Out of the corner of his eye, Oliver watched as two more bodies lowered to the floor to join Mrs. Wright's writhing form. Flashes of pale skin and flexing muscles could be seen in glimpses between doffed pieces of clothing. A keening cry signaled a woman's climax and was immediately followed by a flurry of vulgar and appreciative comments.

He also did not miss how a sharp pair of pale blue eyes watched him and Emily.

Enough talking.

Catching a strawberry between his teeth, he gently urged Emily to take it with her lips...which she did, delicately. When she was done with her bite, he kissed her deeply, sinking his tongue past her lips and teeth. He claimed her in no uncertain terms. She hooked an arm about his neck and hauled them closer together, tilting her head just as he'd shown her so he had complete access. He tasted and stroked every part of her, sucked her tongue between his teeth, nipped her lower lip before soothing the sting with another kiss. All the while, his hand ran along her shapely leg and up her flat stomach, stopping just below her breast.

"May I touch you?" he growled against her lips.

Emily did not hesitate a moment before nodding in assent.

Her pert, firm breast filled his palm as if it had been made for him. He tested the soft weight and did everything in his power not to moan with pleasure at how perfect she was—how right she felt. Her nipple pebbled into the caress of his thumb; he swirled around it again and again, hardening the bud further until she wriggled and arched into his touch. Her little gasp at the newly unleashed sensations stoked his ardor as no woman ever had.

Behind them, there was the rustle of voluminous fabric dropping to the floor as gowns and petticoats were shed and tossed in a heap. Oliver was aware enough to witness a naked woman clad only in sagging stockings before she was eclipsed by two men. Soon, the room was filled with the sounds of wet flesh colliding violently, the thick musk of sex, feminine squeals, and the guttural grunts of male participants. For his part, Oliver was fully content to focus on the woman in his arms, the rest of the world be damned.

Emily, noting the change in the room's tone, turned to look, but Oliver stopped her with a gentle finger on her jaw. "You needn't look unless you truly wish to. Otherwise, focus on me."

She nodded and he leaned in to press more kisses and licks to her delicate throat while her fingers wove through his hair.

The rest of the room fell away until their chair began to teeter precariously. Oliver just managed to plant his boot and save them from toppling only to discover Maeve had been forced across the arm, practically landing in Emily's lap. Hayes stood behind her, face flushed and jaw clenched. He pushed the woman's skirts up over her hips and jerked at the falls of his breeches. Maeve moaned as he entered her roughly, her hands grasping their chair for purchase.

Oliver's blood ran cold when he noticed that Hayes's dilated eyes were locked onto Emily's face as he pounded into the other woman with a punishing pace and force. The intensity of his stare made the hair on the back of Oliver's neck stand on end. His gaze was nothing short of predatory and Oliver vowed at that moment to put him down like a rabid dog if he ever laid an untoward hand upon so much as a hair on Emily's head.

Emily, on the other hand, did not show any outward disquiet from the attention. Unflinchingly, she stared Hayes down as if he were an inconvenient annoyance before turning her attention back to Oliver. No, she was no shrinking flower. And he was proud of her.

IT WASN'T LONG before the partygoers were too embroiled in their sexual escapades—some having ducked off to rooms and others sampling one another out in the open—to notice Emily and Marcus's retreat.

Emily allowed him to sweep her back to their bedchamber, where she flopped back on the mattress in exhausted relief. Tilting her head, she watched as he bolted and blocked the door as usual. His dark evening kit made him appear at once more elegant and more dangerous.

She sat up abruptly, not caring for the direction of her thoughts. "Their appetites certainly are voracious, are they not?"

Marcus rewarded her with a rare laugh, so quick she might have missed it. "They haven't even brought out the potent herb yet. It's purportedly able to make those sessions last for hours."

"Impossible!" Emily gaped.

"I assure you, it exists." He gestured for her to stand so he could begin unlacing her dress. She pondered how curious it was that they'd already become so comfortable with one another to have developed such a routine—how much trust had taken root between them in this very odd, very unique situation.

"And you have first-hand knowledge of this mystical herb?

"I have attended events where it was used."

"But you have never partaken?" The inquiry was inappropriate, but she couldn't help herself.

"My dear," he chuckled once low in his throat, "I do not need it."

Oh my…

The things that image did to her body, the sensations it released between her thighs, the poorly formed images it unleashed in her mind, were unholy. And delicious.

Emily's cheeks warmed, but she said nothing more as Marcus continued to help her undress down to her shift so she might change for bed. He turned his back to allow her to finish as he began unwinding his cravat and undoing the fastenings at his wrists and down the front of his shirt. After donning her nightshift, Emily proceeded to help Marcus out of his coat as she had the night before.

"Have you had any luck with your mission?" she asked softly so anyone out in the hallway might not overhear. She heard only silence, but the last thing she wished to do was place either of them in danger when there were still others milling about. Even then, trills of laughter passed through the walls and the thud of a closing door echoed down the hall.

"I had time this morning to examine the layout of the main floor, but I was thwarted in my search of the study. Hayes was already there." He rolled his shoulder and twisted his torso, wincing slightly as he pushed himself a little too far. He was improving, but still had a way to go. "Judging by the way he hid his work from me, I believe the room shows promise."

"Keeping important papers in the study seems rather obvious," Emily commented as she gathered the items necessary to change the wrap around Marcus's ribs.

"It stands to reason that Hayes will have brought with him some damning paperwork. He told me earlier today that he has plans to stay for at least another fortnight following the party's conclusion, and I doubt a man such as he would be able to remove himself from his business for that long. I'll not be disappointed if I can discover everything I need in that study; I just require a bit more time alone to complete my search."

Together, they worked in silence with synchronized movements to reapply the linen and binding to Marcus's injury. Emily had seen his naked chest, back, and arms, many times over at this point, but they never ceased to amaze her in their rugged glory. Biting the corner of her lower lip, she imagined she could still taste him there.

He was a master of the art of seduction and she was dangerously close to falling into the trap of believing he felt more for her than he did. When she could taste his desire and feel the long, hard, mysterious length of him beneath her bottom, the line between acting and reality blurred. When he palmed her breast and touched her in such a way that every pass of his finger shot a zing of awareness straight from her nipple to the liquid heat between her thighs…now, that was wicked.

Emily felt her skin begin to flush and had to busy herself with tidying up to distract her wayward thoughts. Meanwhile, Marcus moved to once more prepare his bed of blankets and pillows on the floor near the hearth.

"Will you sleep on the floor again?"

"It does look that way, does it not?"

"Do you think you might perhaps be a little less surly if you slept in an actual bed?" She watched with satisfaction as Marcus froze and then his spine went ramrod straight when she added, "The mattress is far too large for one person. I wager I'd be able to stretch out completely and not be able to touch one side and the other at the same time." He'd begun shaking his head even before she finished speaking. "Oh, don't be so pigheaded. You were clearly sore this morning from spending the night on the floor. It is foolishly unnecessary when there is a perfectly good bed right here. We need not touch at all."

Marcus's face was taut when he met her eyes, a surprisingly haunted look floating behind the silver orbs. "You…trust me enough to invite me to share a bed with you?" he asked softly.

"You have had numerous opportunities to take advantage of me. You may have tested my limits, but you have never forced me." She paused. He seemed determined to decline despite her logic. "I trust you if you trust me." The last had been said in jest, but Marcus didn't seem to take it as such. In fact, to Emily, his hesitation hinted that he might not trust himself.

Weary of the back and forth, Emily began to gather up several of the pillows and blankets he'd already laid out, carried them back to the mattress, and tossed them down. She turned, hands on her hips, to see what he would do with that.

He held himself impossibly still for long moments before exhaling a deep sigh of resignation. Comfort had won over virtue.

Separately, they finished preparing for sleep, with Emily crawling beneath the coverlet first and watching as Marcus finished moving about the room. He laid out his clothing for the next day with brisk efficiency. His actions were economical and unconsciously elegant; even more beautiful was the play of orange firelight on the hills and valleys of his exposed skin. In that lighting, he appeared crafted of molten bronze, shaped and polished by the hands of an artist. She wanted to run her hands over his skin—and not just in an inadvertent fashion when she helped him to dress or to change his bandage. She wanted to count the ridges of his abdomen with her fingertips, to rake her nails through the short, crisp hair trailing down toward his navel. She wanted to taste the salt on his skin and hear the sound he would make if she nibbled on his throat as he liked to do to her.

"Are you certain you don't mind this?" Marcus asked, shocking her out of her reverie so quickly that Emily gave a little jump. She was mortified to realize how damp she'd grown between her legs thanks to her inappropriate musings and she prayed he wouldn't somehow know just where her mind had been headed.

"Of course," she stammered.

His mouth drawn into a thin line and his angular jaw set tightly, Marcus pulled back the coverlet and laid himself down as far away from her as he possibly could. She might have been offended if she hadn't known he was doing it out of respect.

"Don't be ridiculous," she laughed. "You are half off the mattress already. There is still plenty of room." He did not budge. "I shall come over there and drag you onto the mattress if you do not do it yourself."

"Don't," he commanded, holding up a hand that brooked no argument. "Don't," he repeated a little gentler and then, more than a little begrudgingly, proceeded to scoot himself toward the center of the mattress. The bed was so large, she hardly felt the shift of his body. In actuality, there was probably enough space to fit another entire person between them, but she swore she could still feel the draw of his body's warmth.

"Better?"

He only huffed a sigh in response.

Emily accepted it as a reply and doused the candle on the table beside the bed. They were immediately plunged into the flickering darkness with waving shadows cast across the walls by the low fire. As they settled, it was Emily who questioned the strength of her wisdom as she listened to Marcus's nearby breathing. She didn't believe he'd fallen asleep and he was likely as awake and attuned to her as she was to him.

Rolling onto her side, Emily lay awake a long while, picturing Marcus's strong hands on her body. Of course, these thoughts did nothing to assuage the molten ache of her core. She tried to press her thighs together to dull it, but it did no good. Were she alone, she might have reached beneath her nightshift to touch her feverish flesh, caress the slick, swollen center of her desire, stroked and rubbed herself until she reached a shuddering climax, Marcus's name on her lips and his voice in her ears.

Now, with the very same man mere feet away, she had to settle for the incessant pulse of longing dragging out her desire for an interminable amount of time.

It was a very long while until the sound of Marcus's even breathing lulled her into sleep.

Chapter Thirteen

T HE NEXT MORNING, Emily awoke alone yet again. It took her a few minutes to unbundle herself from the coverlet and swipe her hair from her face, but one glance around the room told her she was its only occupant. The rumpled pillows on the far side of the bed told her Marcus had slept there, but it was clear he'd already vacated.

His clothes were no longer draped across the chair where she'd watched him lay them the prior evening. She wondered, as she rubbed the sleep from her eyes, how he'd struggled to dress himself without her help, and how it hadn't woken her.

Then, she saw the chair remained propped beneath the door-knob and froze.

How had he left the room with that in place?

Frowning, Emily slipped from the bed. He wasn't in the adjoining dressing room and, though she felt ridiculous, she confirmed he wasn't beneath the bed. The only other way out would have been the window.

Just as the thought crossed her mind, the glass panes swung inwardly, pushing aside the heavy crimson velvet draperies and revealing the glorious pink and yellow morning sunlight.

She took a frantic step backward and collided with the bed-post when a large black mass crept through the window and dropped to the floor with a small grunt.

Marcus stood straight, tugged down his shirt, and ran a hand through his dark hair where it had fallen into his face. He was healthy and handsome; his smile when he saw her up and out of bed made her knees weak. A stirring and a flutter tickled her somewhere below her navel, reawakening the liquid need that had plagued her throughout the restless night.

"How long have you been awake?" she asked, suddenly self-conscious of the fact that he was impeccably dressed while she was rumpled and wore nothing but her thin nightshift.

"Since before dawn," replied Marcus. He moved on to slapping the wrinkles from his charcoal breeches. "I thought it might be a good time to look around."

"There are easier ways to leave the room than the window."

He shot her a droll glance, but she recognized the amusement in his eyes. "I couldn't risk detection in the halls and didn't wish to leave you entirely unguarded while you slept." He met her gaze, his eyes darkening, and added in a grave tone, "I also do not trust Hayes anywhere near you. You should keep your distance as much as you can, and do not goad him, Emily."

"Goad him?" She reared back. "Whatever do you mean?"

"You have this…" Marcus paused, gesturing to her from head to toe and looking oddly pained. "Unconscious sensuality about you." He averted his eyes as if regretting the words that excited her beyond measure. He noticed her. "Just take care."

It took Emily some effort to swallow past the lump in her throat before she could reply. "We have been here several days now; what has prompted this warning? Did you stay awake all night pondering the way Hayes watches me?" Her good-natured chuckle dissipated when Marcus's only response was a noncommittal grunt.

He couldn't have.

Could he?

Gnawing on her lip, Emily turned her attention to the window. It remained ajar to allow in the crisp morning air. The lush branches of the single oak in the center of the circular drive swayed slowly in the gentle breeze smelling of grass and earth…abruptly reminding Emily just how high they were from the ground.

"Marcus!" she squealed and dashed over to the window. "We are not on the first floor!" She peered out to the gravel drive far below, noting only the slim decorative ledge wrapping around the building and realizing that Marcus must have traversed it.

"Indeed. And I appreciate your concern, but I have been in far more precarious situations than this."

Emily's stomach plummeted. "However did you descend?"

"There is a sturdier tree around the corner of the building. And not easily." He pressed a palm to his sore side. "It would have been a damned sight easier without this bloody injury."

She tore her eyes away from the window to watch Marcus wince as he rotated his shoulder. "Can I get you anything?" He shook his dark head, a lock of his hair falling across his forehead. It was all she could do not to brush it away. "Did you at least find anything of use?"

Marcus proceeded to describe how he'd crept from the window to shimmy along the ledge toward the tree he'd spotted during his first exploration. After silently thanking the gardeners for trimming the tree too few times, he'd descended to locate the exterior door to the study.

"I gained access and managed to locate some ledgers written in complex code. Some banal correspondence. Nothing much above the fact that our host is a careful man who wants no one in his business."

"That is rather disappointing," Emily said, trailing off. She retrieved her wrapper, trying to keep her disappointment from her voice. It wasn't that she minded continuing to spend time with Marcus, she just didn't enjoy the thought of him putting himself at risk any longer than necessary. "I am certain you will eventually discover what you are looking for." Marcus was watching her as if in awe of her faith in him. It was an unnervingly intense stare, so she turned her attention back to the glorious day. That, however, only served to bolster her disappointment that she would likely be cooped up in their bedchamber for the better part of the morning, if not the better part of the day.

"Dress," Marcus commanded brusquely as he picked up his coat.

"Now?"

"You wish to see the gardens, do you not?"

Not half an hour later, Emily had donned a morning dress of pale-blue and ivory lace and allowed Marcus to escort her through the small, well-kept gardens behind the house. While the grounds were expansive enough that not another home could be seen in any direction, little development had been done. The building exuded rich excess, but the simplicity of the clean garden beds with their common flowers and neatly trimmed bushes spoke of the minimum effort expected for a house such as this. Still, Emily found them charming. She stopped to examine the white-and-yellow daffodils and the fragrant miniature pink roses. What the gardens lacked in variety, they made up for in neat efficiency.

Emily turned her attention to the fields in the distance. The hills were dotted with colorful wildflowers in watercolor sprays of pink and blue and white amongst the green and gold of the grasses. Large trees stretched their branches toward the sky, so high they seemed to be propping it up like great marble columns. Birds swooped here and there, gracing her ears with their unfamiliar songs.

"I have never seen half these plants or wildlife before," Emily commented, enjoying the heavy scent of a lilac bush with its delicate purple bursts of blooms. "I have spent my entire life in London; the open sky and cleared fields are so foreign to me."

"My youth was very much the same," Marcus surprised her by admitting. "I did not see much of the world until…"

"Until?" she coaxed.

"Until I joined the military," he responded flatly.

Emily knew he was being purposefully obtuse, only hinting that his world had been quite small until he'd become a *spy*. It felt unnecessary because they were alone on the garden path, but she deferred to his expertise.

"How does one 'join the military'?" she asked, feeling silly for the face value of her words, but knowing Marcus would catch her meaning.

"Drafted," he grunted in reply. The honesty of his answer wasn't what she'd been expecting. Beyond telling her the general area where he'd been born, this was the most he'd revealed to her about his past. "I possessed a particular set of skills and knowledge, and it was either consent to the draft or live the rest of my short days out in prison before being hanged. Neither option presented the possibility of a full and lengthy life, so I opted for the one with a more imaginative ending."

Emily was taken aback by his candor, the cool way he spoke of his past, and what quite possibly lay ahead of him. An icy chill wrapped around her spine. "You truly had nothing to lose, then?"

Marcus shook his head. "Nothing to fight for, other than my own skin. As it would turn out, I'm pretty good at what I do and pretty difficult to kill."

Emily swallowed hard, not in the least enjoying the thought of Marcus in peril. "How many men have you killed?"

"Haven't I already warned you not to ask questions to which you do not want the answers?"

That many...

Emily pondered this as they strolled. Of course, he'd had to kill to survive in his career as a spy for the Crown. Was that any different from if he had been an actual soldier in the Wars? She didn't think she could kill someone, but she wasn't foolish enough to believe the circumstances might be different were her life in real danger.

Like Marcus's had been.

Whatever his past had been, he'd fallen into circumstances where he'd been forced to choose between certain death and spending the rest of his life in what amounted to dangerous servitude.

She slipped her arm through Marcus's as they walked and she

could feel the heat of his eyes watching the connection.

WORD TRAVELED THROUGHOUT the party that Hayes had coordinated an outdoor activity to take advantage of the weather, and the housekeeper and staff had prepared a picnic to accompany it. Emily, escorted by Marcus, followed the rest of the guests to the east lawn to find the pleasant array of white iron tables, chairs, and a spread of blankets with mounds of pillows. Small, frivolous bouquets of wildflowers had been gathered to decorate the tables. Emily picked one up to examine the blooms. A miniature daisy came loose, but Marcus caught it and tucked it behind her ear, making her heart skip.

Wicker baskets had been carried out from the kitchens. Pristine white porcelain plates, polished silverware, and even crystal goblets were laid out beside the trays of cucumber and cold-cut sandwiches, bowls of fruit, and other foods easily consumed outdoors. One basket overflowed with bottles of wine in a variety of colors and vintages. She knew from experience that those would be finished in a shockingly short amount of time.

"Gentlemen!" Hayes bellowed, dragging everyone's attention from the spread. He stood in his tailored brown coat, buckskin breeches, and green silk waistcoat with one arm cocked at a ninety-degree angle, a gleaming pistol held casually in that hand and pointed at the sky. His gaze scanned the group, making Emily's heart thud painfully in her breast. Hayes had always seemed dangerous to her, but him holding a weapon was downright frightening—especially when witnessing the ease with which he handled it. "A bit of shooting?"

Emily and the rest of the ladies reclined upon thrones of pillows, chattering and drinking and eating as the men took turns selecting their weapons from the array before them and then shooting clay discs tossed up by steel-nerved footmen. Emily knew next to nothing about firearms, but she recognized that pistols and rifles were among the choices.

Soon, bets broke out between the men. Money was laid

down and two men would square off, each aiming for the same disc or competing to see how many they could strike in a row.

Emily watched Marcus as surreptitiously as possible and, though he did a very good job of disguising it, she could tell he intentionally missed some of his shots. Of course, the action brought his abilities more on par with the rest of the guests, but she did not enjoy the ribbing he took as he handed over his losses.

Hayes, on the other hand, was far more prideful. He placed his abilities as a marksman on full display, demonstrating how trained he was at shooting and lapping up the praise. At one point, Emily caught Marcus's eye, and saw he'd also noticed that Hayes was no ordinary marksman.

The latest round finished and Marcus made a great show of examining the pistol he'd used just before Hayes took his final turn. Their host tossed his empty rifle to a footman and performed a flourishing bow.

"Might I interest any of you beautiful ladies in a shooting lesson?" Hayes asked in a tone dripping with an overabundance of solicitousness. His cold eyes swept over the women who, one after another, demurred.

Her mind sharp despite the glass of wine in her hand, Emily realized that this presented a unique opportunity for their mission.

"I will," Emily chirped with a wobbly smile. As she stood, she could feel Marcus's eyes upon her and hear his warning from earlier that morning. Did attempting to endear herself to Hayes and gain his confidence under the guise of a shooting lesson count as goading him?

She liked to think it didn't.

However, as she shook the wrinkles from her skirts, she could feel Marcus's subtle glare upon her and hear his warning as loudly as if he'd just called out to her. It was obvious he didn't agree with what she planned.

Emily approached Hayes, nonetheless. She did her best to ignore the feline smile curling his lips as he took her hand. Thank goodness she had the protection of gloves between them because she didn't think she'd have been able to bear having his skin on hers—not after witnessing the way Hayes had stared at her the night before. It made her blood run cold to think about it.

"Pistol? Rifle?" Hayes asked.

Emily pasted a saccharine smile on her face. "A rifle seems so much more exciting." She gave a dramatic little shiver.

There was a small twitch over Hayes's shoulder and she saw Marcus watching them with interest. Evidently, he did not care one bit for Emily's choice…but there was no going back now.

For his part, Hayes cocked a brow, though he didn't argue. Picking up the weapon, he proceeded to explain to her the parts of the weapon, how it functioned, and the power of its recoil.

"You are such a brilliant shot, Mr. Hayes," she purred. "Wherever did you learn?"

He arched a brow at her. "You do not believe a man can be born with such talent?"

"I believe there are *some* talents with which a man can be born."

"Indeed," he murmured.

"But the use of a firearm is not one of them. Were you in the Wars?"

Hayes's grin never faltered, but the tightening around his eyes gave him away. He was displeased by her inquiry. "I did my part," he replied cryptically. "Now, shall we resume our lesson?"

He moved to stand behind Emily to press the entire length of his body against hers and wrapped his arms around her so they stood chest-to-back, thigh-to-thigh, indecently close in any sense of the phrase. He smelled of cigar smoke and pomade. He proceeded to press his pelvis against Emily's rear and she recalled the savage way he'd pounded into Maeve. Bile rose to the back of her throat, but she remained steady.

Hayes's lips brushed her ear as he instructed her on stance and aim, and inhaled the scent of her hair. This man was nothing short of a predator and Emily felt suddenly very out of her depth.

He interpreted the slight tremble of her muscles to be excitement and said, "Isn't it thrilling to hold something so powerful in your hands?" There was a vulgar lilt to his tone. "Do not be afraid. You might find that you like it more than you thought possible." He positioned her fingers and stepped away.

Emily locked her joints and squeezed the trigger, missing the clay target by a large margin. The rifle's recoil jolted her body, but she remained uninjured and on her feet even if her shoulder would be sore the next day. The shot's loud bang was still ringing in her ears when Hayes said, "We can try again." He gestured for another clay target to be readied. It was tossed after a count of five, but it caught the wind. "Hold!" Hayes commanded. "No need to waste the shot when it is out of range."

The crack of another weapon beside them made the entire party jump in shock. The disc, which should have sailed well out of range for any accuracy of the weapon Marcus held, exploded into dust.

Everyone gaped at Marcus, who only shrugged in response. "Lucky shot," he said nonchalantly before thrusting the pistol grip-first at a footman and storming back to the blankets and the lounging ladies. He reclined on a pillow between Lady Satterly and Lady Aaron. The viscountess began feeding him grapes. She squealed in delight when his teeth nipped at her fingertips.

FOR THE MOST part, Emily and Marcus kept their distance from one another for the remainder of the afternoon, spurred by an unspoken agreement fueled by their mutual displeasure with one another's actions. It was evident to her that he cared not one bit for how she'd drawn Hayes's attention; for her part, she was irrationally irked with how he'd smiled at the female guests…whispered in their ears…pressed his lips to their wrists…in all, everything he did was bothersome. He seemed quite content to enjoy the attentions of the female guests while she kept herself busy with the less threatening males in attendance. Baron Allyson again proved himself the adept conversationalist; Mr. Frye was a jovial and gregarious drunk. To their credit, both men took Emily's coyness in stride. Neither blinked when she leaned just out of arm's reach or dodged a kiss. She instinctively knew there was a fine line when dealing with people who attended a house party such as this and she was careful when she tapped into her as-yet-untried bank of knowledge regarding the art of enticement. While they lapped it up and were politely and earnestly attentive, they still seemed much more harmless than their host.

Emily would deny it if asked, but she'd caught Marcus watching her on numerous occasions. The fact that she'd noticed so many times would speak of just how often she'd glanced in his direction. Despite being occupied with a busy rotation of other guests—particularly those of the female persuasion—he somehow found time to keep a watchful eye on her every movement.

Brushing that aside, she decided that she could be of far more use than an accessory for Marcus to parade about and use as a cover. She may not have been trained in the finer points of espionage, but she'd been prepared in the ways of conversation and entertainment. She knew how to charm. She could put that knowledge to good use and, now that she'd resolved to try that tack, refused to be deterred from her course by Marcus's glares.

She poured Mr. Frye another glass of wine. After spending the better part of an hour chatting with the man, she'd managed to learn his lineage as the grandson of a marquess, and even how he'd met their host during a "chance" encounter at a Covent Garden brothel. She listened intently as he described how both his father—third brother to the current Marquess Byrnham—and twin brother were on the board of a prominent weapons manufacturing company that had gained momentum supplying firearms for the British militia during the Wars. He was remarkably forthcoming with all the information. It became clear to her that Frye had been sought out for his familial connections (even Emily knew the marquess's family was known for being critical of the monarchy these last few decades), industrial wealth (someone with access to plenty of weapons would certainly be a boon for anyone angling for support of a coup), and his penchant for more elicit sexual exploits. The last would be a way to wheedle into his life, gain his confidence, and perhaps even be used as blackmail or leverage if Frye ever balked at what was being asked of him. It didn't take a great imagination for Emily to guess what Hayes wanted from Frye, and she suspected it was a similar situation for each of the men present. Marcus had told her that Hayes believed him to be a shipping heir; such an alliance, for example, could prove invaluable in smuggling goods, money, weapons, people... Their host was aligning himself with men he believed would benefit his cause. She couldn't wait to report to Marcus the knowledge she'd amassed.

Emily chanced another glance around the room and noticed Lady Aaron, Baron Allyson, and the Satterlys had quietly slipped off to locate more privacy. Only about half of their party remained in the warm, glass-walled conservatory. The angle of the fiery sun indicated it would soon be time to dress for supper. Frye was sloshed, but he accepted yet another glass from her. She gauged his flushed skin and his nodding head and wondered if she might make one more charge before excusing herself to prepare for the evening meal.

"What do you know of Mr. Hayes?" she asked as she leaned in conspiratorially.

Frye gestured with his glass, the burgundy liquid splashing over the edge and splattering the floor and cushions. "He's a frightening man, but he throws one hell of a party!" Frye slurred. Much of what followed was along the same vein. Hayes was wealthy, mysterious, and knew how to get what he wanted. He had rougher, more daring sexual appetites and this created a siren's call to men and women of the same ilk. He was the piper of debauchery, earning loyal followers by supplying them with everything their hearts desired.

Frye's finger began tracing a line up and down her arm, tickling the skin from her wrist to the bottom of her sleeve. "When will I"—he hiccoughed loudly—"have a chance to sample your nectar, Miss Tully?"

She shot him a shy smile and decided her work there was done. "We shall just have to see, won't we?" She pressed him back with a finger in the center of his chest. He fell without resistance, beaming at her with a ridiculous smile before his eyes rolled back. With any luck, the man would return to his rooms and sleep the rest of the evening. She quickly made her excuses and escaped the room to bathe and dress for supper.

She also needed space to breathe some air that didn't reek of wine, cigars, and spilled spirits.

OLIVER COULDN'T HELP but watch Emily leave. Maeve, who had draped herself across his lap, followed suit only a short time later. Soon, only the men were left—though Frye had fallen asleep on the chaise he'd once shared with Emily.

Hayes dropped on the cushion beside Oliver with an exaggerated sigh, swirling his cut crystal glass of whiskey. Oliver had been nursing the same portion of brandy the entire evening— notably *French* brandy.

"Are you enjoying yourself, Holden?" Hayes asked as he stared into his glass of rich amber liquid.

"Immeasurably," Oliver slurred, leaning back against the cushions and spreading his legs wide, affecting the posture and mannerisms of one deep into his cups.

"Have you had occasion to speak with Satterly? His views on the current political climate are fascinating."

"I can't say that I have."

"He has some…rather interesting things to say."

Oliver paused for long seconds before speaking. Hayes's line of conversation was phrased cleverly, pointing to Satterly as an instigator rather than himself. "If it has anything to do with the wasted excesses and the atrocious state of the monarchy, then I most certainly will need to speak to him." Frye emitted a nasal snore from his nest on the other sofa. "Perhaps when all of us are less foxed."

Hayes gave a calculating smile; something unnerving flickered behind his eyes. "Fascinating. And the regency?"

Oliver scoffed. "Madness in the bloodline. Prinny is unbalanced. He hasn't been the same since he lost the princess." That last was true. The man had been prone to outbursts, unreasonable demands, and outrageous spending before the death of his only legitimate heir in childbirth, but he'd been inconsolable and even unstable after. It was a common argument amongst dissenters of the monarchy that a new rule was in order. After George III's loss of the Colonies and subsequent madness, followed by the regency rule of his son, disillusionment with the monarchy was at an all-time high. Oliver didn't necessarily disagree, but he was far from supporting a violent uprising. Violence would only beget more violence; a civil war was never going to be the answer. Plus, regardless of his personal opinions, it was his duty to protect his country from such threats. He was honor- and duty-bound to carry out his mission.

"Precisely," Hayes murmured appreciatively before clapping Oliver on the shoulder. "I would love to hear more of *your* thoughts on the subject." He leaned in conspiratorially. "Especially on how, say, a shipping company might benefit those who would see a more worthy leader on the throne of England."

Treason.

Now, all he required was the tangible evidence that would hold up at a trial and expose this dangerous cell for what it was.

Hayes excused himself to call for a footman to assist Frye to his chambers and Oliver slipped from the room. He all but ran back to his bedchamber, heart pounding in his ears. This was the indication he needed to reassure him that he was on the right path. Hayes was growing more comfortable around him and Oliver knew it wouldn't be long before everything was laid out between them. He *knew* he'd done the right thing in continuing his mission despite the perils.

Much to Oliver's chagrin, he discovered the door to the bedchamber was unlocked. Rage and frustration boiled up inside of him. Hadn't he made himself clear that she needed to be careful?

That no one was to be trusted? What if something had happened to her in the hour since she'd come upstairs?

Bursting into the room, he immediately launched into an admonishment for Emily's foolish behavior.

"What did I tell you about locking this door and barring it?" he demanded, proceeding to turn and do just that after he entered. "You have left yourself exposed. Do you have any idea how idiotic—" Oliver's words died in his throat when his eye processed the sight before him.

Emily was submerged in an enormous brass tub with just her head visible above its lip.

Chapter Fourteen

"D O YOU MIND?" Emily squealed.

The sight of her flushed face and damp hair set Oliver off all over again. All thoughts of his conversation with Hayes fled as Emily was shoved to the forefront of his mind. "What if I'd been Hayes seeking you out? What would you have done then? Thrown a cake of soap at him?"

"I can handle myself," Emily barked back. That was very difficult for him to believe when her skin was an alluring rosy pink and her hair was slicked back from her face; she looked about as intimidating as a wet kitten...but as enticing as a mythical mermaid to a man who'd been lost at sea for months on end.

"Oh? Like you willingly allowed yourself to be groped earlier?" He tossed a bathing sheet at her, which she deflected to the ground, but not before offering him an accidental glimpse of the upper curve of her full breast. "You must be more careful—I cannot watch out for your well-being every second," he snarled, more angry at himself for his visceral reaction to finding her naked. He had to take a slow, deliberate inhalation in an attempt to slow his rushing blood and the subsequent throbbing in his groin.

Emily's fingers clenched the rolled lip of the brass tub. "Why? Because I am a nuisance?"

"Yes!" Oliver snapped. "And a distraction." He heaved a sigh and speared a hand through his hair. "And I'll never forgive myself for dragging you into this if you wind up hurt." His stomach plummeted when the raw admission slipped unbidden past his lips. He spun away from the tub. "I will send you home in the morning."

A minute of pregnant silence was broken by the sound of dripping water as Emily rose and stepped from the tub. His eyes slid closed, his chest constricting, his cock throbbing and heavy and twitching in his breeches, as he listened to her drying her naked body with the toweling. He imagined rivulets of water racing one another down each curve and hollow, dripping from her puckered nipples and sluicing through the curls at the juncture of her thighs. She would taste as sweet and clean as she smelled. The entire room was filled with her rosewater scent—if one could ascribe a color to a scent, he would say she smelled pink. Not the pink of a sunrise, or the rosiness of a flower. No. Emily was pink like her lips after he kissed her, pink like the flush of her skin when she was aroused, pink like the petals of her sex as he imagined her dripping with need for him. How he would lap it up like a man too long denied sustenance…

Oliver practically melted when she placed a warm, damp hand on his shoulder. Reluctantly, he turned to find her standing in a white bath sheet, whisps of her white-gold hair curling around her face from the steam.

He felt weak.

It terrified him.

"I want to stay," she said softly, erasing all signs of her earlier frustration with him. "I want to help you. I apologize for being so careless. You were right. I shouldn't have been so lax. But…" she paused and leaned in conspiratorially, "I *was* able to obtain some interesting information." She proceeded to summarize her interactions with Frye, all she'd learned about Hayes, and her suspicions as to why Hayes had targeted this particular group of individuals. "He seeks to gain something from each of them for his ultimate aim," she finished proudly.

"You've quite the knack for espionage," Oliver replied as a

reluctant smile tugged at the corner of his mouth. "You knew precisely which person to target and how to obtain the information you desired. Still..." Unable to help himself, Oliver reached up and swiped a water droplet from her cheek with the pad of his thumb. The skin there was impossibly soft. "You have no idea how difficult it is for me to watch you shower attention upon another man," he rasped.

She blushed prettily. "You say that as if you were jealous."

To his surprise as much as Emily's, he admitted, "I was."

The little hitch in her breathing was nearly Oliver's undoing.

Her eyes flew to his face, but, before she could speak, there was a scratch at the door. Gesturing for her to stand off to the side, Oliver answered it to find Ann, the maid, standing there.

"I've come to help Miss Tully dress for dinner," she stated, seemingly not surprised in the least to find Oliver there when Emily had just stepped from her bath.

Emily peeked her head around his broad frame and smiled at the girl. "Yes, thank you. Do come in." She gave a little tug on the back of Oliver's coat and he was as helpless against it, as if it had been a ship's anchor strapped to his back and pulling him overboard.

Ann stepped into the room and looked Oliver up and down. "Will you be staying?" she asked flatly. There was no hint of censure in her tone, merely a question.

Emily, at a loss, spluttered incoherently, but Oliver bit his tongue. He was eager to see how this would play out. The maid jumped in as he hoped she would.

"It's common here for men to stay and watch the women dress," she explained.

Meanwhile, Emily looked about ready to swallow her tongue, and Oliver couldn't resist raising a questioning brow at her. The panic in her eyes would have been hilarious if he respected her less.

After allowing her another moment to stew in her anxiety, he saved Emily with a charming smile, bowed his head, and made a smooth retreat from the room.

The hallway felt impossibly chilly for the warm day outside, though he suspected it had little to do with the weather and more to do with the woman he'd left behind in the steamy room.

MARCUS'S ADMISSION PLAYED over and over again in Emily's head. Jealous. He'd said he was *jealous*. She might have thought it was an act, but there had been no one else around to witness it; therefore, it stood to reason that it was the truth. Considering that possibility made her pulse flutter so frantically that she grew concerned she was about to experience a health crisis.

Was it possible that he'd begun to experience some of the attraction from which she'd been suffering?

She'd felt the hard evidence of his arousal when she straddled him, she knew the long, thick ridge in the front of his breeches couldn't be feigned—not when it had reappeared so suddenly after encountering her in her bath. She'd tried not to stare at it, but *good Lord*, everything about the man was proportionately larger than life.

This, she believed, coupled with his actions and his words was evidence that he was affected by her nearness, just as she was by his. Beyond wanting her in the physical sense and feeling a moral obligation to look after her, Marcus desired her and experienced a possessiveness above and beyond what might be expected.

When he returned after she'd dressed, however, he'd behaved as if he hadn't said anything of the sort. In fact, he seemed to go out of his way to be cordial and proper. It left Emily feeling an unfamiliar mixture of annoyance and confusion.

She especially didn't know what to make of it when Marcus showered his attention upon Mrs. Wright. *He must be a brilliant actor, indeed, if he can so easily switch his outward affections*, she thought sullenly. More than once, she had to tear her eyes away from him and shake herself as a reminder that he was only doing his job. He was doing whatever was necessary to perpetuate his assumed identity and keep Hayes's suspicions at bay. Still, it stung to have him tell her sweet, moving things one minute, and then welcome another woman draping herself across him in another. She was inexperienced in the delicate art of separating one's emotions from one's duties. She'd heard it took a great deal of practice for some and came naturally to others.

She was someone who would need to practice it…if she even could fully accomplish it where Marcus was concerned.

This internal struggle contributed to Emily's indulgence of wine at supper that evening. Rather than feign drinking, she'd downed two glasses of it at the meal and accepted two more after, spurred on when Mrs. Wright suggestively caressed the solid length of Oliver's thigh and he nibbled the woman's throat in return. Emily leaned in more closely to Viscount Satterly, immersing herself in the thick cloud of his oddly floral cologne and inclining her head close as he spoke.

She'd just thrown her head back in an exaggerated laugh at something the viscount said when she saw Hayes making his way toward her. Prowling would have been a more apt description for the way he moved with his eerie eyes focused so intently upon her. Emily fought to swallow past the lump in her throat. A glance in Marcus's direction told her that he seemed very comfortable in the arms of both Mrs. Wright and Viscountess Satterly and wasn't about to offer her any immediate rescue.

Instead, Emily was saved by the arrival of the very stiff, very formal butler. A few whispered words were exchanged between Hayes and the butler; their host's features wrinkled in a frown of annoyance and frustration at being thwarted when he thought he might finally have his first opportunity to get her alone without Marcus's interference. He made a quick, grudging excuse to the room at large and departed with the promise to return.

It must have been something important to tear him away from the evening.

Emily caught Marcus's eye and immediately knew he thought the same.

She also knew he needed a distraction if he was going to be able to slip from the room unnoticed. She turned to the viscount beside her.

"I should like to play a game!" she announced brightly.

Drunkenly, Satterly assisted her in rallying the rest of the guests to play a scandalous game (the rules of which Emily had yet to sort out).

Marcus's tall, dark frame ducked from the room out the exterior door and she prayed to God she hadn't just gotten in way over her head.

OLIVER SLID OUT the veranda door and into the velvety shadows of the night. He crept stealthily along the building's perimeter until he reached the study—the only other room with windows showing life, glowing gold from lit candles within. Like many of the windows, the ones leading into the study were left open an inch to admit the fresh evening air that followed the pleasant day. Crouching low, he listened to the cryptic—yet still incriminating—conversation.

He could not see the other man's face from where he hid, but he could hear both of the rooms clear enough.

"Some of our men in London have gone missing," hissed the newcomer.

"And this is something you needed to convey in person?" Hayes growled in response. "I have *guests.*"

"Others are nervous…"

"You mean, *you* are nervous," spat Hayes. "You always were a coward." Despite this, there was a thoughtful pause before he added, "Names?"

The other man proceeded to list off several in response, some of which Oliver did not know, others he recognized as men he'd investigated in the past. To him, it sounded as if Ramsay and other agents had moved in after anticipating Oliver's withdrawal from the mission.

"No trace of them."

There wouldn't be—because they were likely being so thoroughly interrogated that it made the Spanish Inquisition look like a holiday.

Oliver wondered how long it had been before Ramsay realized that Oliver disobeyed the order to step back from the mission. Seeing as how he and Emily had left London only a few days ago, it hadn't been long. He cursed silently.

"We need to move more quickly," Hayes growled. "I am reasonably sure weapons will be guaranteed, but all movements must take place simultaneously to lessen the chance of sounding an alarm and preventing further preparations."

"This arrived before I left the city." Oliver imagined the man handing something—a piece of parchment from the sound of it—to Hayes. Heartbeats passed as, he assumed, Hayes read it and then there was the wooden click and slide as a drawer was open and shut.

"Vigilance is of the utmost importance—especially now. We are so near to the end and every step is vital. Keep your eyes open and your ears perked."

"Sir, I—"

"Enough."

"But I believe—"

"That is enough," Hayes snapped. "No more of this now. We will speak later."

Unfortunately for Oliver and Emily, Ramsay's movements against Hayes's faction meant the man would be even more on guard than he already had been, making their job a great deal more difficult and dangerous.

It was more important than ever that Oliver locate the tangible evidence he required so he could get Emily out of there and back to safety…and they could move on with their lives.

Separately.

He listened as Hayes instructed the unseen man to remain hidden from the party, rest, eat, and drink before he returned to his post—he would see him once more before he left. Oliver stayed as long as he dared before making his way back through the shadows, his boots sliding silently along the edge of the house and across the veranda. He waited until he was certain that he would be unnoticed before he ducked back into the parlor…only to discover that Emily had somehow become the center of attention.

The sight wasn't confusing in the respect that eyes were not naturally drawn to her, (they most certainly were), but because she usually did her best to remain unobtrusive. Now, however, she was in the middle of the room, garbed in her shimmering rose-red gown, singing a horrendously bawdy song at the top of her lungs.

She spun in graceful circles, her skirts billowing out around her as if she were a child's top or a doll in a music box, as she sang rhyme after rhyme about a farmer named Todd, his homely wife called Maude who made up for her looks with her ways with his rod.

On and on the song went, verse after gay verse, inviting hysterical laughter with little waves of her hands as the rest of the guests chimed in on the choruses. It was such an infectious scene that Oliver lost himself and, soon, was chuckling, grinning, and clapping along despite the dire undertone the evening had adopted.

Oliver was quickly learning life was like that with Emily. It didn't matter how serious the situation was, there was something about her that made him feel lighter despite himself. He wanted to smile. He wanted to laugh with her. She made him long for things he never had before.

He made a point of not turning when he heard Hayes reenter the room, choosing instead to focus his entire attention on the performance before him. The drinks continued to flow, filling the air with the sharp tang of spilled spirits and raucous laughter, and Oliver grew more concerned for Emily as the evening wore on. He'd noticed early on that she hadn't been pretending to drink as she normally did. Though she seemed to be enjoying herself, so everyone else was as well; that could very well spell disaster.

The crack and tinkle of a dropped glass briefly snagged Oliver's attention. Mrs. Wright simply abandoned her mess, stepping over it with her wine-stained white satin skirts, and hooked her fingers in Oliver's waistcoat.

"How clumsy of me," she tittered like a schoolgirl half her age before leaning in so her moist, wine-scented breath poured into the shell of his ear. "I do believe I should be punished for it. Why don't you use your large hands and larger cock and teach me—" Oliver was saved when Baron Allyson swooped in and grabbed her around the waist to abscond with her like a ruddy-faced Viking. She laughed and squealed and flailed dramatically as Viscount Satterly and Mr. Frye—both stripped down to their shirtsleeves, trailed in their wake, bellowing about knights coming to her rescue. Oliver could only shake his head.

When he looked back at Emily, he found her standing perfectly still and gorgeous as a Grecian statue, her large eyes watching him intently. The unflinching appreciative gaze made his pulse quicken and his cock thicken. He barely suppressed the urge to press a firm palm to it to stifle the aching throb.

He cursed beneath his breath when she began to saunter over to stand very, very close to him. As unconsciously sensual as every one of her movements and mannerisms usually were, they were magnified exponentially by her lowered inhibitions. The wine had made her bold as brass. He shuddered when she traced a finger up his chest to tug at his cravat and bring his head lower to hers. He let her. God help him, he didn't want to resist her anymore.

Every one of his senses screamed for him to reach out to Emily. He wanted to sink into her body, mind, heart, and soul. She made him feel seen in ways he'd never experienced.

His eyes slid closed of their own volition as the tip of her nose grazed his and her lips passed so closely to his mouth that he felt their warmth.

Did he...actually *groan* when she pressed a kiss to the hard line of his clenched jaw? He hadn't intended to do that, but there it was and there was no reeling it back in.

"Take care," Oliver cautioned her in a low growl, though his fingers itched to do anything but push her away for her own safety.

"What if I don't wish to?" The sensual effect was immediately wrecked when Emily listed to the side and plopped onto an ottoman in a giggling heap of skirts.

Huffing a sigh and shaking his head, Oliver decided enough was enough. He needed to get Emily back to their rooms before she was either sick, became injured, or got herself into more trouble than she could handle. He stooped and smoothly lifted Emily into his arms.

"We are to bed!" he called as he strode from the room without waiting for a reply.

Every step was a new sort of hell as Emily flung her arms around his neck and snuggled close to his chest. The tickle of her satin hair on his cheek made him imagine wrapping it around his fist; how it would feel against his bare flesh. The press of her silken lips against the point where his jaw met his cheek and the rasp of her kiss across his evening whiskers teased a new kind of intimate friction. He imagined how much softer the skin of her inner thighs would be against his cheek, how the fragrance of her most secret of places would be even headier and more intoxicating than the mouthwatering rosewater scent of her skin.

Oliver said a silent prayer of thanks when Emily tired herself out with her teasing and simply relaxed in his arms, allowing herself to be carried up the stairs to their bedchamber. She tucked her head beneath his chin and curled up like a sleeping cat. He could almost imagine her purring.

After what felt like the longest walk in history, they finally arrived at their rooms. He pressed open the door and, after checking to ensure Emily was still awake, he set her on her feet to close the door and barricade it. Turning back, he noticed the unnaturally pale hue of her skin and the glassiness of her eyes; she did not appear well at all. She'd propped herself up against one of the sturdy bed posts and looked for all the world like a woman lost on the tilting deck of a ship in a storm. She screwed her eyes shut, but it only seemed to worsen her dizziness.

Seeing her sway, Oliver rushed to her side and scooped her up into his arms once more before lowering her to the mattress, all the while whispering soft words of reassurance into her hair. He didn't recall what he said, he only knew that it felt right to do so. He needed her to know that he was there for her.

He brushed loose gossamer strands of her white-blonde hair from her forehead. Hearing her whimper in his arms was like another knife slammed between his ribs. It struck him with unnerving force how badly he wished to wave his hand and take away her discomfort.

Oliver recognized the moment nausea overtook her and he retrieved a basin from the washstand just in time. Fisting his hand in Emily's loose curls to keep them clean, he steadied her and returned to murmuring nonsensical words of comfort. He could well remember the last time he'd overindulged in spirits, though that had been nigh on a decade ago at that point—just before he and his talents had been enlisted in espionage. Back then, he, like many of the other slum dwellers, drank cheap gin to oblivion. He felt a great deal of empathy for Emily as her stomach cast out its poison, but more so for the hellish morning he knew awaited her the next day.

Even when there was nothing left inside her, he continued to care for her. He settled in with her amongst the layers of blankets and pillows; he wiped her brow with a cool, damp cloth as she reclined in his lap. There was nothing sexual about having her lying against him, and there was no hidden motive or undertone to his actions or words. Instead of arousal, a comfortable warmth diffused through Oliver's limbs.

Just when he thought she'd dozed off, he began to feel Emily's hands grasping his thighs on either side of her hips. Gradually, the caresses turned into languorous massages deep into the muscles. It felt delicious as well as dangerous when her hands crept higher and higher, her inhibitions dropping entirely in the haze of alcohol.

"You should rest," Oliver insisted gently as he tried to brush her hands away. He'd already removed what remained of her hairpins and her soft, fragrant curls tickled his lips when he spoke.

Emily made weak, almost incoherent protests, but didn't fight him overmuch when he slid out from behind her and helped her strip down to her shift and stockings. He had to create a conscious separation between his mind and his body as he did so. He wanted to help her, not seduce her.

When he went to tuck her beneath the coverlet, however, she begged him to stay. "Please," Emily whispered, her eyes already closed, though her fingers gripped his tightly.

"Angel…you need to sleep," he reiterated, though his resolve screamed in pain. He firmly believed he deserved sainthood for turning this goddess down.

How many men would have done so—let alone when she practically begged for him to take her? Surely the blow to his head had addled his brains. Since when did he possess such scruples and employ a conscience? He'd thought those parts of him long dead and buried.

When he would have left the room for his sanity's sake, Emily continued to plead for him to stay. "Please, Marcus. I don't want to be alone." Her words were a mix of slurred and drowsy, elicited by the drink. Her sleepy eyes glittered up at him and the pout of her lip was his undoing.

With a pained groan, Oliver divested himself of his coat, cravat, and boots and laid beside her atop the coverlet. Emily immediately curled up against his chest, her chin resting against his chest in the vee of his shoulder, her soft body a forbidden delight. She fit. He silently marveled at the realization and held as still as humanly possible. Despite the coziness of the situation, however, Emily continued to fight sleep…much to Oliver's chagrin.

What was worse, she began asking questions.

"What is your favorite food?"

"Food?" Oliver frowned in confusion. What logic was this that she'd just been sick and was already contemplating eating again?

She nodded heavily against his chest. "Yes, food. I would give absolutely anything for some of the caramel cake the cook back home makes for me on my birthday." The appreciative groan that followed went straight to Oliver's cock and tightened his balls.

He cleared his throat and roughly forced his mind back to the task at hand. Food? What was that again? "A good steak and ale pie—the kind with the flaky crust, not soggy." Oliver was transported back to the first time he'd gotten his hands on one from a tavern. He'd been earning a few extra pennies running errands for the owner and then, one day, he'd been paid with a thick slice of the gravy-filled pie made by the proprietor's wife. He didn't remember ever having tasted something so warm and rich and comforting since his mother died.

"That sounds delightful," Emily cooed. There was an extended pause, and then, "I like Spring."

Oliver's lips curled in an unbidden smile. "Are you asking me which season is my favorite?" His thumb had begun tracing lazy circles across the soft expanse of her naked upper arm.

"I wager you like winter, all dark and bleak and moody," she said with exaggerated vowels and a yawn.

"Autumn." He enjoyed the colors. It made London come more alive than the rest of the year. It was a bit of beauty for someone who had seen so little of it in his life.

"Autumn is nice." Emily nodded in grave agreement against his chest. "I love it when the trees are so colorful they look like they are aflame."

Oliver's chest constricted when her words so closely echoed his thoughts.

They continued like that for an indeterminate amount of time with Emily peppering him with silly inquiries and Oliver responding to her with nothing but honesty. He found it was easier when he addressed the dark ceiling; it felt less dangerous than speaking to her directly.

Gradually, Emily melted against him, her entire body fitting to his as she hooked a leg across his thigh. He listened as she spoke in endearingly rambling sentences about how she'd grown up in Covent Garden, how her mother had seen to her education, how she helped her run the business and worked to make it the most unique establishment in London with both women and men vying for opportunities to work in the clean environment for fair wages and respectful treatment, free to leave at will and never beholden to Lady Night. He could easily see how this garnered a great deal of respect for the madam.

In return, Oliver described how he'd spent most of his childhood with his father—his mother having died from the drink when he was quite young and he retained precious few memories of her. He told her how he and his father had never gotten on well, to say the least. They hadn't been a well-off family to begin with, but his mother losing her position as a maid when she became pregnant with him and then Oliver being another mouth to feed only increased the resentment.

He never knew why his father hadn't just dropped him at a workhouse and wondered if it had been out of some dying promise he'd made to Oliver's mother. More than likely, however, his father had just wanted to keep around a whipping boy upon whom to take out his frustrations. Either way, Oliver had suffered through his early years at the hands of a man with a violent temper. That childhood was part of the reason he'd become so good at sneaking around: pure self-preservation.

"Is that where all your scars came from?" Emily asked in a voice barely above a whisper.

Oliver paused. "Some of them." Others had come from his years on the streets after he'd finally gotten sick of being pushed around by his father. "You know, I looked forward to the day that I was finally big and strong enough to give the old man a taste of his own medicine; instead, I learned years later that my father died on the docks following a brawl over some perceived slight in a pub." Even thinking about it rubbed an old wound raw. Upon hearing the news, he'd experienced a mixture of relief, regret, and anger at learning the news: relief over never again having to worry about running into his childhood demon; regret because he could never get the answers he so futilely sought—Why had he hated an innocent child with such vitriol?—and anger over having been made to suffer such a miserable childhood and never being able to repay the man who'd caused it all.

Emily slung her arm around his waist and tugged herself closer. She could have been snuggling up to him so she could finally drift off to sleep, or she might have been hugging him to offer silent comfort. Either way, Oliver appreciated the gentleness. She asked nothing of him other than to let her remain near to him.

"There is something..." Emily began softly, sounding far soberer than she'd been when they first laid together. How much time had they passed talking? "There is something my mother tells the women and men who come from terrible situations." She sighed gently, as if she had some difficulty locating the words but was still determined to do so for him. "Our pasts can define us, but they can also be the tools with which we shape our futures. We can either choose to define ourselves this way or create an entirely new path—as you did. You bettered yourself." Her hand tightened around his side. "Instead of allowing the abuse of a cruel man to crush your soul, you recognized your strengths and forged ahead."

Oliver immediately began shaking his head in denial even before she'd finished speaking. He would not allow her to make him out to be noble or some sort of saint; he would always be a gutter rat at heart. No amount of education, primping, or training could ever change what was the most essential part of himself.

"Stop that," Emily chided him gently, swatting softly at his chest. "You can try to deny it all you want, but only a man with a kind heart and a good soul would have taken care of me like you did."

The warmth of her against his side forestalled any further protest he might have attempted to utter. She nuzzled against him in total and complete innocent trust. And, when her breathing deepened and evened out, it made his throat tighten as he stroked the curve of her back and pressed his lips to the crown of her head. Never in his life had Oliver experienced such a thing—this level of trust. It made him feel as though he might just possibly be enough for someone.

For a man who had been made to feel less than worthless throughout his youth, who had been forced to scrape and scrounge while viewed as nothing more than filth, who had never done anything except fight for his life and be seen as the sum of his talents rather than appreciated as a man, this was a gut-wrenching feeling.

Rather than analyze the way it—the way Emily—made him feel overmuch, he lay there stiff and still, willing his mind to ponder anything but that.

"Will you finally tell me your real name?" Emily asked, her voice meek and just above a whisper. How wasn't she asleep yet? Oliver didn't doubt that, if she'd seen his face, the pain of his indecision would have been evident there. "I'll understand if you can't...I just cannot help but wonder."

"Oliver," he said softly, as if the world was foreign to his tongue.

"What did you say?" Emily's entire body went still; he even felt her hold her breath.

"Oliver. Oliver Black," he repeated more confidently. Emily tilted her face to his and gifted him with the most beautiful smile he'd ever seen; it nearly broke his heart to look at her.

It was worth it.

"I quite like that. Pleased to meet you, Mr. Oliver Black."

Relief washed over him, as if her approval of his name was somehow tantamount to his survival.

As if her acceptance of this most basic facet of his identity was vital.

Emily rested her head upon his chest once again, sighing in contentment as she settled in once more. Oliver knew with every fiber of his being that this was perilous territory upon which they'd begun to tread.

Chapter Fifteen

WHEN OLIVER WAS finally certain Emily was in a deep enough sleep that she wouldn't be easily woken, he smoothly replaced himself with a down pillow beneath her cheek, into which she promptly buried her face. He moved about the room, cleaning the basin and placing it nearby for her along with a fresh glass of water on the side table should she need it. Then, he slipped from the room, pocketing the key so no one would be able to enter or exit. The last thing he needed was a tipsy Emily wandering the halls in search of him.

It was too tempting to lie there with her in his arms and pretend the rest of the world had faded away. A part of him screamed in protest, begged to stay and listen to more of her kind words—wanted desperately to believe them—but he beat it back. He couldn't be foolish. Foolishness led to sloppiness. Sloppiness led to death. And there was more than just Oliver's life on the line in this situation. He needed room to breathe and clear his head a bit.

Rolling his shoulders, Oliver donned his "Marcus Holden" persona as he skulked back through the halls, down the stairs, and up the corridor. The sounds of high-pitched laughter and masculine voices grew louder as he neared the parlor that had been informally relegated as the den of debauchery. Just as he approached the door, however, it was flung open and the hallway was flooded in golden light. A half-naked woman landed in his arms with a drunken roar of laughter. Her dark hair marked her as Viscountess Satterly. Oliver steadied her as Baron Allyson—missing his coat and waistcoat, his linen shirt untucked from his breeches and his cravat eschew—followed in her wake. Oliver handed the giggling woman over to her partner as they disappeared into the shadows of the hallway.

Injecting an inebriated swagger into his step, he rejoined what remained of the party. He wasn't surprised when Hayes's eyes immediately tracked his entrance and noticed he'd returned alone.

"Where has our lovely Miss Tully gotten off to, hm?" Hayes's posture was that of an indolent sultan reclining upon a throne of cushions. Legs spread wide, shirt open at the collar, hair mussed, falls of his breeches half-undone, he personified hedonism.

"Unfortunately, she is not very practiced at holding her liquor."

"Perhaps she should have someone to care for her…" Hayes suggested, his tone full of disgusting promise that had nothing to do with altruism. Oliver's fists clenched at his side, willing himself not to punch the man's teeth in and shove them down his throat.

"Already done," Oliver replied with what he hoped was a disarming smile. "Poor kitten is rather ill."

"Ah." Hayes wrinkled his nose. That should keep him away from Emily for the time being, and Oliver would be able to concentrate on his work.

Oliver took up the vacant cushion beside Hayes and he was quickly straddled by Maeve. The girl wore nothing more than her sheer drawers, garters, and stockings. Naked from the waist-up, her bright-red hair hung loose to graze the swells of her small, high-set breasts topped in bright cherry-pink nipples. Gripping her hips in his palms, Oliver grinned up at her appreciatively, though his body stirred not one bit.

Maeve leaned in and began skillfully licking and kissing her way up his neck to his mouth as she rocked suggestively against his lap. This was a woman who knew how to please a man—to wring every last shudder from him.

What he wouldn't give to lose himself in a mind-numbing release and reset his mind.

Oliver shut down, existing in a surreal haze as Maeve ground against him, pressed her naked breasts to his chest, took his hand, and pulled him to stand before leading him out of the room, up the stairs, and into a darkened bedchamber. She immediately divested herself of the last scraps of her clothing and leaned back on the bed.

Oliver wanted nothing to do with any of it.

"A drink," he barked and strode over to the dressing table where a half-empty crystal brandy decanter sat unstoppered.

Behind him, Maeve emitted an unattractive whimper of protest. "But I've already been waiting so long for a moment alone with you."

"Oh?" he tossed distractedly over his shoulder as he prepared them each a drink, slipping a small portion of powder in Maeve's from a wax paper packet he pulled from his pocket.

"There have been whispers about your skills…among other things." She cast a pointed glance at his groin and accepted the proffered glass, her lips curling seductively.

"All good things, I hope." Oliver offered her a half-hearted wink, relying upon the shadows in the room to mask his distaste.

"Of course," Maeve purred before tossing back the brandy in one go. "How could they be anything but?"

His mouth twisting into a wry smile, he took her empty glass and set it aside with his untouched drink and leaned against the bedpost. "How did you meet our generous host?"

"Is that really what you wish to discuss?" Mave asked, leaning back and running her hands along her body. Oliver's eyes stayed firmly upon her face. He watched for the telltale fluttering of her lids, the yawning of her pupils in her blue eyes. "I was so hoping to do other things with our mouths." The last word was more slurred than the rest.

"Come now, Maeve. I think you'd rather enjoy a good night's rest more than anything."

She frowned and shook her head, clasping her skull when the room began to spin. "N-no," she stammered. "I want to see if you're...you're as good as they say..." She began crawling toward him. "So many men care nothing for the woman's pleasure." Her arm slid out from under her and Oliver had to catch her with a hand on her shoulder so she didn't tumble face-first off the mattress.

"Then you must try to find some better bed partners," he suggested flatly as he helped her maneuver back onto the bed and slide beneath the coverlet. Though she fought it, it wasn't long before she was snoring softly.

Oliver turned to the window and cursed his treacherous body, wanting only the angel sleeping in a room down the hall. His injured side ached as he climbed from the window, gauged the direction he needed to take to find his way back to his rooms, and proceeded to creep along the edge with catlike grace and precision. The last thing he needed was to be caught out in the hallway when he was supposed to be in Maeve's bed.

He took his time, checking each window for movement before he crossed over it. Even though many of the windows were left ajar to admit inside a hint of the sweet, warm evening air, most of the rooms he passed were dark and unoccupied or had their drapes drawn. The last window before he turned the corner to round to the front of the building emitted the sound of hushed voices.

Voices speaking in rapid French.

Propping his back against the wall, Oliver settled in to listen. He willed his breathing to even out and his muscles to remain steady even though they burned from exertion. It seemed the messenger from earlier still had not moved on.

"What are you saying?" Hayes demanded.

"I tried to tell you earlier, sir. The man at the meeting place beside Lady Night's...it is believed he was working for The Phantom."

Hayes spat a curse. *"Why do you say that?"*

"He was too well-trained. The last thing everyone wants is The

Phantom on their trail."

"He isn't."

"How can you be certain? Men are disappearing!"

"Do not worry so," Hayes demanded. There was almost a note of desperation in his tone. The last thing any enemy of the Crown would want was Ramsay nipping at his heels, but that was precisely what was happening…and precisely the situation Oliver helped facilitate. *"You said he was stabbed and fell from the rooftop. There is no possibility that he survived all that."*

"How can we know for certain? The Phantom must have received the information from somewhere. Nicolas remains missing after his arrest. Pierre and Armand have gone missing. It is as if they are being snatched by the shadows." This man was growing more anxious by the second.

"Do not be ridiculous," hissed Hayes.

The voices grew more hushed as their footsteps retreated across the room. Oliver took his opportunity to cross and continue toward his destination. This conversation only solidified Oliver's belief that their time was running out. And now, more than ever, he needed to keep his wound hidden lest the injury give away his identity.

The window to his bedchamber remained unlatched, just as he'd left it. He stepped down into the room and found Emily's delicate form sleeping soundly in the moonlit bed, right where he'd left her. She still clutched the pillow to her body, her wild blonde hair tumbling like spilled whiskey across the mounds of pillows and blankets.

Oliver watched for several minutes as she slept, the mere sight of her content and peaceful like a balm to his weary soul. Oliver shucked his clothing into a pile on the floor, unable to stand the stench of expensive, cloying perfume any longer. He replaced them with a comfortable set of trousers, took the time to check his healing wound and remove the bandages, pleased with the progress of its healing, and then—before he could overthink it—he crawled into bed beside Emily. There was plenty of space that he could have lain far enough away so they needn't touch, but she drew him like a fire on a frigid night.

Sensing his movement, Emily stirred and smiled in sleepy recognition before curling up against him once more. Oliver planned to sleep for a few hours and wake well before dawn. It was in that early hour he hoped to finally find what he was looking for.

For now, however, he savored Emily's warmth and softness.

OLIVER'S INTERNAL CLOCK woke him before dawn without fail. After dressing as silently as possible, he slipped from the window, crept along the ledge, and swung down to the grass with the aid of the fortuitously positioned tree. He stifled a hiss as his side burned with the exertion. He couldn't wait to be back to full form.

The fields around the manor house were blanketed in a thick mist. The world was bathed in the deep lavender of the earliest hint of morning. Even the birds remained silent and sleepy at this hour.

Keeping to the foggy morning shadows, he slid along the building's perimeter until he came to the exterior door of the study. He extracted the small leather kit he'd stashed in his waistband, selected the correct tools, and unhinged the simple locking mechanism with a few deft flicks of his wrist. He was careful to keep it intact so no one would easily notice the door had been forcibly opened.

The grate of the hearth was cold and the room was silent and dark. It was early enough that the charmaids had yet to make their rounds to lay the wood in the grates. Even though the weather outside was pleasant, these large manor houses could remain chilly.

He slipped into the study, ducking through the curtains and pulling the door nearly shut behind him. He was enfolded in a shroud of darkness. Luckily for Oliver, he'd been raised in a hole far darker than this. His job was made easier because he'd already committed the room's layout to memory during his brief visit earlier.

He found the desk and popped each locked drawer one by one, discovering some interesting notes with dates and times, but nothing damning enough when taken as a piece of the puzzle. He needed something that would form a whole enough picture to condemn the cell…he needed to find something he hadn't already seen. His gut told him if he could locate whatever the messenger had brought Hayes the night before, then he'd be on the right path.

Rifling through a small drawer to the left of the chair, he nearly abandoned it for another when his hand touched a tightly folded piece of parchment stuck to the underside of the desktop. Oliver gently plucked it free. Turning it over in his hands, he began to unfold it and quickly skimmed the minute writing.

His blood ran cold.

Normally, when he located a piece of written evidence he would make a careful copy and replace the original, but there wasn't the time. The house was already coming alive; the charmaids would be wandering from hearth to hearth ensuring the old soot was swept away and fresh tinder was laid; the lower kitchen servants would be lighting fires and preparing food for early risers.

As it was, the faint creak of floorboards signaled the impending entrance of one such sleepy little charmaid to the study. Oliver silently closed the drawer and slipped unnoticed behind the heavy curtain framing the window. He slowed his breathing, every last one of his muscles tense with anticipation as he listened in perfect stillness. There was the scrape and brush of grit, then the soft knock of wood and the strike of flint as the grate was cleared, set, and the new logs caught in a fragrant wisp of smoke. He listened as the girl gathered her tin bucket and crept from the room, but waited several more minutes of frozen silence until he stepped from his hiding place.

The sunlight through the window was quickly warming to

the pinks and oranges of dawn when he reached into his pocket, unfolded the note he'd stashed there, and read the list of names once more.

There were more than a dozen…and Sterling St. John, Duke of Morton—his friend, and former partner—was near the top.

His heart began to pound with worrying ferocity.

What did it mean?

Were these potential allies for Hayes's cause?

Targets?

Suspected threats?

All Oliver knew was he had to sort it out before anyone else was caught in the flames.

Chapter Sixteen

EMILY AWOKE SLOWLY and cursed every moment that full consciousness grew nearer. She groaned painfully and yanked the coverlet over her head. The throbbing ache and the needles piercing the backs of her eyes were things she'd never before experienced, and vowed never to do again so long as she lived.

A gentle hand reached inside her coverlet cocoon and brushed her wild tangle of curls from her face. Carefully, she unscrewed an eye to find Oliver smiling down at her. Actually smiling. She had to blink several times to confirm she wasn't, in fact, dreaming. Or dead. His name. He'd finally revealed his name to her. The words "Oliver Black" had pirouetted through her hazy, nonsensical dreams, and now she was faced with the real thing.

"Good morning," he murmured in greeting and left a quick, light kiss on her temple before disappearing from her narrow line of sight. She didn't have time to process the gesture before he returned with a cup. "I requested a headache powder for you. Drink this."

Emily tried to decline his offer with a shake of her head—the mere thought of swallowing anything made her stomach turn—but the motion sent a new wave of pain screaming through her skull. A pathetic moan eked through her throat.

"Please drink it; I promise it'll help." His voice was gentler than she'd ever heard from him before. "For me?"

Her mind too foggy to analyze what he'd said overmuch, she allowed Oliver to incrementally help her to a sitting position and then accepted the drink. She loathed every sip, but she did as he asked. When she was done, he took the cup from her and then did the oddest thing: He set about the task of taking care of her for the better part of the morning.

Ignoring every one of her protests, Oliver saw to her comfort and needs. He rearranged her pillows and brought her a clean nightshift when she realized she'd slept in some of her garments from the prior evening. He took his time, moving her carefully so as not to aggravate her aching head or roiling stomach. Emily couldn't recall a time when anyone had cared for her with such tenderness, such selflessness. He didn't give her an opportunity for embarrassment because she was too busy being overwhelmed by his actions. She was nothing short of taken utterly aback by his tenderness.

Tears stung the backs of her throbbing eyes and she finally had to brush him away lest she make a bigger fool of herself than she already had.

"Fine, fine." Oliver held his hands up in mock defense. "I need to change anyway." For the first time, she truly took stock of his garments. He was garbed in black from head to toe. His boots, breeches, and fine lawn shirt were all dyed the color of the deepest shadows. And, now that she examined him closely, a bright green leaf clung to the hair on the back of his head, standing in stark contrast to the dark locks. Turning away from her, he untucked his shirt and pulled it over his head. Emily could only watch in mute rapture as he moved around the room, her eyes catching on the scars covering his body.

Then, snippets of the previous night began to emerge from the hazy cloud of her memory one by one. Had he truly opened up to her as much as she remembered? Had he held her against him as she savored the way his deep voice resonated up through his chest and tickled her cheek?

Good Lord, had he held her hair back for her as she tossed up her stomach's contents?

And he still wanted to be around her?

She barely suppressed the urge to pull the coverlet back over her head and never reemerge.

"Is there something you'd like to try eating?" Oliver asked, motioning to a domed tray she hadn't previously noticed on the table near the window. She pressed the back of her hand to her mouth to stave off a wave of nausea. Oliver, however, persisted. "It is nearly luncheon time and you've yet to put anything in your stomach since supper last night—and that was short-lived." She cursed the charming hint of a smile on his lips. "You must at least try to eat. I had them bring some porridge, scones, tea." He persisted even when she shook her head, sitting beside her on the bed, so close that the mattress dipped beneath his weight and rolled her toward him. To be fair, she didn't fight gravity all that much—not when he smelled so divinely masculine. "May I fetch some bread from the kitchens for you?" he asked gently.

Realizing her continued refusal was futile, she groaned, "If you must," when she really only wished she could burrow back beneath the covers and sleep away the miserable day.

Emily snuggled back down into the nest Oliver had created for her and listened as he slipped from the room. She curled back up into a protective ball, taking deep breaths and finding comfort in Oliver's lingering scent upon the sheets. Its existence left no doubts that he'd slept beside her the night before, yet, was it odd that she didn't worry one bit that he'd taken advantage of the situation? When had she come to trust him so?

She turned that thought over and over in her mind as she gradually drifted back to sleep.

MEANWHILE, OLIVER SLIPPED downstairs to the kitchens. He could have rung for service, but he couldn't pass up the opportunity to both personally see to Emily's needs and do a bit more poking around.

The heavenly smell of fresh bread wafted up the back stairwell he used to descend to the basement kitchens, calling to him like a siren's song. The scent could still make his stomach growl in fierce anticipation.

How many nights had he lain awake starving, fed only by the memory of just such a smell? How many times had he sat outside bakeries and cafes in wait to catch a whiff, only to be chased off for deterring customers with his filthy presence?

Now, he had all the food and luxuries he could ever possibly hope for, yet it seemed some memories from the streets would never leave him.

He entered the kitchens, a wide and charming grin plastered upon his face. At once, the gray-haired cook and her red-faced maids turned to him wide-eyed, their hands frozen mid stir, chop, and scrub. The little maid who'd been scouring the long worktable was so distracted by his sudden appearance that she slipped and landed on her rear.

"Good morning, ladies," Oliver greeted them. They responded in kind, but it was clear from their shifting glances and uneven tones that they were unsure what to expect from his presence. It likely wasn't often that one of the guests in this house of sin and excess made his way to the servants' areas, and his motives were being met with an intense level of suspicion. Even unease. He loathed the thought that these women might be afraid of what he could do to them, so he immediately set about putting them at ease. "I hope you don't mind the intrusion, but the scent of bread was far too tempting. I realize it's unusual that I've come to fetch it myself, but might I trouble you for some?"

"Why, of course, sir. It won't be done baking for another ten minutes or so. I can have a girl bring it up to you when it's ready?" offered the cook as she wiped her hands on her apron. She was obviously eager to have him out of her domain.

"That won't be necessary. I can wait here if it's all the same to you, of course."

This took them all aback. Several attempts were made at trying to redirect him to a more comfortable waiting area—the breakfast room or perhaps the solar—but he refused to yield. Instead, he fell easily back into his knowledge and the habits he'd maintained during his time as a valet. It was easier to build a rapport with servants when you were one yourself, but this would have to suffice given his current circumstances. Servants were often his best source of information, and he'd have been remiss had he skipped over this veritable untapped fount of knowledge.

Oliver adopted an unassuming posture, spoke politely and kindly, was careful about where his eyes went as they traveled the room, and made no sudden moves. The last thing these women needed was to fear having him in their midst lest he try to charm his way beneath their skirts. Regardless of whether or not it was agreed that the household staff were off-limits, he didn't doubt that some guests believed themselves above the rules.

"May I?" Oliver asked, seeing an opportunity to ingratiate himself as a girl sat across from him to peel apples for that evening's dessert. She stammered, looking to the cook for assistance. "I used to help my mother peel apples," Oliver said honestly. "I promise I am quite adept with a knife." The last bit was truer than they could know.

"It'll look bad to have the guests put to work," fussed the cook, looking for all the world like a harried robin.

"I'm merely finding a way to pass a bit of time until that delicious bread is ready," he said with a disarming smile. "In fact"—he paused and fished a coin from his pocket—"one pound to the girl if she can prepare better apples than I." The girl's blue eyes glittered hungrily, but the cook's eyes narrowed in his direction. "And a pound to you as well, ma'am, if she wins—for who else could have trained her so well?"

"Have at it," the cook harrumphed and turned back to another maid and told her to fetch some onions from the root cellar.

Oliver accepted the knife the girl offered and he shot her a kind smile in return. "Ready?"

She picked up her blade and selected an apple from the pile and nodded.

As they worked, the little maid began to come out of her cell. It was slow going at first since he was playing the role of a guest rather than a servant, but the rapport eventually evolved. She answered his questions about her position at the house, then her family who lived in the closest village and raised pigs. She became so comfortable with Oliver's presence and the purposefully soothing tone of his voice that she didn't realize when he began peppering in inquiries about Hayes. It wasn't long before he learned some of their host's notable habits.

For one, he refused to allow maids into his room to tidy unless he was present. He also kept a locked armoire in there and no one was certain what was in it, not even his valet. While the furniture belonged in the house, the armoire presented a puzzling secret to the staff when his clothing was kept in an attached dressing room, along with the rest of his luggage. The girl's cheeks burned a stunning shade of red when she regaled some of the rumors—that the cabinet held a chest of treasure and gold, that he stored a body in it, among other things. Oliver smiled, but not unkindly. Rumors such as this—even outlandish ones—could spread like wildfire amongst staff. For one, they needed escape from their lives of endless tasks for others; for another, it was easy for gossip to expand and explode as it passed from person to person. He'd witnessed it firsthand during his time as Sterling's valet and they'd used it to their advantage—it was how the ruse of the duke's supposed licentious ways was perpetuated so thoroughly that it had traveled from the Continent all the way back to London.

Regardless of what the servants believed might be stored away, Oliver knew that Hayes's bedchamber was now first on his list of places he must investigate.

The pile of apples was soon peeled and cleaned, ready for judging.

"Admirable work," muttered the cook as she eyed the pale flesh of the fruit.

"Thank you, but I do believe Miss Mary has done a better job than I…and I am a man of my word." Grinning, he slid the coin across the table to the maid, her mouth gaping in disbelief. "And you," he handed another to the cook as he stood. "My compliments on your staff."

The cook's eyes widened, but she didn't argue even though a few bits of the girl's apples were mangled. The coin quickly disappeared between the ample swells of her bosom. "Thank you, sir." She bobbed a curtsey more gracefully than she should have been able to accomplish and handed him a loaf wrapped in a towel. It was still warm as he held it against his side.

"Many thanks for tolerating my company." He turned to the room at large. "A pleasant day to all."

Oliver returned to the darkened bedchamber and found Emily sleeping once more. Despite her hair which spread out every which way as if it had a life of its own, she really did look like an angel. Her lips with their perfect cupid's bow parted in a gentle breath, her face was as smooth and soft as a rose petal, long pale-gold lashes fanned out upon her cheeks like butterfly wings.

She stirred and so did the organ in Oliver's chest. It wasn't difficult to picture her waking like this each morning, slowly and languidly like warmed honey.

Needing to separate himself from this dangerous train of thought, he busied his mind and body by helping her to situate herself once more and did his damnedest not to watch the rise and fall of her breasts as she inhaled the yeasty scent of the fresh bread. He portioned his spoils from the kitchen and, together, they made a picnic in the middle of the bed.

"You're certainly an accomplished thief, having stolen freshly baked bread right out from under the cook's nose."

"You remember that, do you?" He experienced an unexpected wave of embarrassment, but it dissipated quickly when he noticed Emily's smile was impossibly kind rather than chiding.

"I do, indeed. I remember it all…I only wish I didn't remember how foolishly I behaved." Her face scrunched in a dramatic cringe.

Oliver couldn't help but chuckle. "I quite enjoyed the song and dance—especially the naughty bits."

Emily's blush was immediate and she dropped her head into her hands. "You shall never allow me to forget that, will you?"

"Never." Oliver's grin was wolfish. "Wherever did you learn such a song?"

"One hears things," Emily replied after nibbling a bite of bread.

"And commits them to memory, apparently." A laugh burst free from his chest when she swatted his arm. "Would you like some more?" he asked when he noticed she'd finished the portion he'd given her.

She declined with a small shake of her head and then sat back against the nest of pillows he'd created for her. "Tell me, have there been any further developments? Any progress? I apologize for having been such a distraction for you last night. I hope it wasn't harmful to your investigation."

"You were just the right distraction," Oliver reassured her, trying not to see if he could make out the dusky shadows of her nipples beneath her shift. He went on to tell her what he'd learned from the kitchen maid and how it was likely Hayes was hiding vital evidence in his bedchamber.

"I am no expert, but I think you may be right." Her eyes roamed his face and, unfortunately for him, she'd come to know him too well...or he was losing his touch when it came to hiding things from Emily. "There is...something else?"

He hesitated before pulling the folded bit of paper from a hidden pocket in the waistband of his breeches and turning it over in his fingers. "I am uncertain what, precisely this is, but I have some suspicions—none of which are very good."

"May I see it?" Emily held out her hand.

Oliver waited several more seconds before handing it over. He watched as she unfolded it slowly, carefully, and skimmed it twice.

Chapter Seventeen

EMILY READ THE scrap of parchment again and again. Oliver had handed her a collection of names, a full half of which Emily recognized as patrons of Lady Night's.

While the brothel's tabs were kept under code names, Emily and her mother knew the true identities of the high-class and powerful patrons—all the better to help cater to their specific tastes, make sure a particular girl was available for a scheduled visit, or have his favorite vintage of spirits on hand. One name on the list gave her pause: "Sterling St. John?" She met Oliver's eye. "Is this the same Sterling you mentioned in your sleep?"

Could it be? A duke? What did a duke have to do with all of this?

Oliver's mouth thinned into a tight, pained line until he eventually said, "Consider him an acquaintance."

Emily's eyes lit up and she leaned in close, a powerful suspicion prodding at her. "The Duke of Morton is a spy?" she hissed. Oliver remained steadfastly silent, but she took his determinedly stoic expression as an answer. Why else would Oliver be an acquaintance with a duke? And one who'd notoriously been on the Continent for many years. Was it so far out of the realm of possibility that he'd been on a mission, too? Emily did not think so. "He *is!*" She bounced a little on the bed in excitement and instantly regretted it when her stomach flipped dangerously and her head throbbed. Despite this, she began launching into her characteristic flurry of questions. "When did you meet? Did you work together? Were you with him while he was away on the

Continent?" She gasped. "Were the rumors true about all the things he did? Did you—" Oliver cut her off with a finger pressed to her lips. He smelled of warm bread and...apples?

"Please stop, so I do not have to lie outright to you."

Emily emitted what she hoped was a light laugh when he removed his finger. "You are a terrible liar for a spy; I saw right through you."

He chuffed. "I never would have survived this long if I *weren't* a talented liar." He frowned thoughtfully before his handsome features softened again. "Have you ever considered that I do not *want* to lie to *you*?"

Oh...

Emily's heartbeat kicked up its pace and her mouth went dry. This man—this brilliant complex man—never ceased to amaze her. She looked back at the organized list in her hand to try to steady her stomach once more. She slowly considered it in its entirety when she had an idea.

"Could the rest of these men also be spies?"

Oliver shook his head. "It could be possible, but I don't believe so. Of course, I don't know everyone in the society, but the odds of this many members of the *ton* and government is unlikely. Some could be aliases, though my name is not on the list, nor are any of the other identities I've used in the past."

Emily found the last bit particularly intriguing. How many names had Oliver assumed? How many lives had he lived? It was on the tip of her tongue to ask, but she stopped herself. As fascinating as it was, this was no game. Lives were at stake. And as much as she longed to know everything about Oliver and his life and his past, now was not the time.

"My best guess," Oliver continued, "is that these men are ones Hayes has had his eye on. Potential allies. Marks. Targets. You said so yourself that he aligns himself with men who can offer him a gateway into a beneficial industry or venture."

"It is possible—especially given some of these men's reputations," said Emily thoughtfully.

"Reputations?"

She probably should not have been as thrilled as she was to know something Oliver didn't. "Yes. Many of these names are patrons at Lady Night's. They all have rather sordid backgrounds."

"So Lady Night's ties many of them together?"

Emily grinned and nodded, feeling truly helpful for the first time. She began to tell him what she knew of some of the men listed and felt only the tiniest bit of guilt knowing her mother would fly into a fit if she knew Emily was revealing such private secrets.

She pointed to a name on the list. "This man has a proclivity toward being tied up and...whipped." She ran her finger down the row and indicated another. "This one enjoys the attentions of other men, though he and his wife have been married for nearly a decade." Several of the others were fairly run-of-the-mill patrons of the brothel, while others had more damning habits.

Some involved begging on their hands and knees for women to do unspeakable things to them...even as their wives and mistresses watched. Some with the inclusion of particular items of food...

"I am not at all implying that I judge these men," Emily added quickly. How could she, when her mother was the one enabling them, their money put food on her table and clothing on her back, and she could now better comprehend the way passion could drive someone to the point of irrationality. "But not everyone in London is as understanding. Since Hayes has patronized Lady Night's in the past, it is possible he may have observed some of these men there, and it is likely, too, that they were the sort to be lured into friendship by a man like Hayes. I can see how they might be drawn to someone who can provide the activities they crave, and fear the man who might expose them. This house is an example of that." She gestured to the room around them.

Oliver nodded thoughtfully. "He picks men who might further his cause, lures them in with sex, and then has the ammunition to blackmail them if they don't agree to go along with whatever he wants." He accepted the list back from her. "It would explain why Morton's name is on there. Hayes believes he's a good target and the sway of a duke would be a boon, indeed." She was surprised when he released a single chuckle. "Won't he be in for a disappointing surprise."

"What does that mean?" She knew of the Duke of Morton's lurid past from the gossip rags passed around by the brothel's employees, though it was suspected that he'd turned over a new leaf since his return from the Continent. Lord knew her mother had been sorely disappointed when the duke didn't so much as visit their establishment once. She'd mourned the loss of the duke's coin ever since.

She suspected that, if anyone knew the truth of it, it was Oliver.

"You would be surprised how much most men's exploits are exaggerated," he said cryptically. "Not everything is as it appears." She didn't interrupt his ensuing thoughtful silence with more questions. "It is possible," he finally resumed, "some of these men are supporters of opposing the Regency; others are Tories and would be instrumental in this opposition; some are just downright powerful and their voices raised against the Crown would cause quite the stir."

"Is that truly what this all is?" Emily asked as reality truly began to dawn on her. "The goal is to tear England apart from the inside. They're slowly working toward creating a revolution and a civil war."

The grim set of Oliver's mouth told her she was correct.

It made her nauseous all over again.

This was far more serious and dangerous than she'd ever imagined. This wasn't romantic or exciting; this was life and death on a grand scale. Memories of the Wars were still strong in the hearts of English men and women. The possibility of more loss and bloodshed—especially on their own soil—was horrifying.

She looked into Oliver's face, searching his intense, surprisingly soulful eyes. This was *his* life. And he'd given her a chance to be a part of this thing so much bigger and more important than herself. She really *had* sprung from her shelter and into the flames the moment she'd decided not to let him die on her balcony.

Oliver must have read the myriad emotions on her face because he was very serious when next he spoke. "Emily, I must apologize for my stupidity. I never should have dragged you into this. I was so consumed with my mission and single-minded—"

"Stop."

"—in my desire to see this through. It was—"

"Oliver."

"—unconscionable for me to drag you into this, no matter my motiva—"

Emily fisted her hands in the front of his shirt and wrenched him to her, crashing their mouths together in a silencing kiss. Oliver was, at first, rigid with shock, until her tongue tentatively swept out to trace the seam of his lips. His arms enfolded her in his warmth, crushing her chest to his in a way that was not at all unpleasant. In fact, the chafe of his hard body and the fabric of her nightshift against her rapidly hardening nipples was torture of the most delicious variety. Both of them were panting by the time she broke away.

"What do you need me to do?" she asked, her breath whispering across Oliver's lips, though her tone was more confident than she'd have believed herself capable. She might have laughed at his wide eyes and stunned expression were the topic not so serious. He was trying to brush her off, to absolve her of her agreement to provide assistance, to lay all the blame for their situation at his feet, but she refused to allow any of it. He hadn't forced her into this, he'd merely presented her with the opportunity—the chance to make a difference. Now, she was determined to give him no other option than to continue involving her in this, no matter the cost. "What is your plan and how can I help? I am already here and you already explained that you have no assistance from the

Crown in this task. To abandon you now might mean your death...and I didn't save you once just to allow that to happen now."

His lips parted, but no sound came out; his eyes danced across her face as if trying to gauge her sincerity. Or her sanity. Maybe both.

It was then that Emily realized he'd probably never felt like his life was important enough for anyone to willingly risk themselves.

Finally, Oliver cleared his throat and released her, able to find his words once more. "We must find a way into Hayes's bedchamber. And we will require another distraction."

IT WAS AGREED that Emily would spend much of the rest of the day recovering in their bedchamber as best she could to prepare for what was planned later. Oliver, meanwhile, joined the party and made her excuses, which the other guests readily accepted (and some looked as if they regretted not having done the same).

There was no sign of the mysterious houseguest who had arrived the prior evening and provided Hayes with the worrying list of names. Of course, it wasn't as if Oliver had expected the man to join them for meals, but he'd surreptitiously paused outside the room the man had been given and heard not a single breath or creak of floorboards. He'd likely taken his leave in the wee hours of the morning and returned to whatever nefarious assignments Hayes had given him. While not ideal, this didn't much hinder the plans Oliver and Emily had crafted.

Together, it had been decided that it was time to change tactics—they needed to move things along more quickly. There were only a few days left in the house party and their mission was growing more dangerous by the day. Allowing Hayes to take the lead and suss Oliver out at his leisure was taking time they did not have.

He made one last go of it, though, with little else that could be done before the house party was distracted by supper and the evening's usual festivities. He produced a quality bottle of brandy from his trunk and sought out Hayes, eventually locating him in the conservatory, lounging on a sofa with a cheroot dangling negligently from his lips.

"Holden," he greeted Oliver and sat up, capturing his lit cheroot between his fingers after one more long drag.

Oliver held up his offering. "Apologies that I did not bring this out sooner. Slipped my mind."

"Ah, what is this?" Hayes examined the bottle. "French?"

"Only the best."

Hayes made an appreciative sound. "Shall we?"

Soon, the two of them were ensconced in Hayes's study, a snifter of brandy before each of them. Just as he'd anticipated, Hayes was particularly receptive to the gift and enjoyed the contraband French spirits with gusto. Oliver waited until the time was right—until Hayes's eyes held just the right gleam and they'd shared enough small talk and amiable banter—before he began to employ his finely honed interrogation skills. He deftly steered their conversation in the direction he needed it to go.

"You said the other day that Satterly had some interesting views on the current political climate."

"Did I?" Hayes drawled and took another nip from his snifter. He, however, wasn't fooling Oliver.

"You did. And I must say, I quite liked what he had to say. I found it perfectly reasonable and markedly more appealing than anything currently in place." He paused for effect. "And I assume you must feel the same."

"What makes you say that?" Hayes balked and sat back in his chair.

Of course, Oliver hadn't actually spoken to Satterly, but he had a solid suspicion of exactly why Hayes had brought them all together, and the views he desired to confirm they all shared— without saying as much, of course.

Oliver leaned forward and braced his elbows on his knees. "Come now, Hayes. We are two intelligent men. Ambitious men.

Men with powerful friends and strong opinions." He watched his host's eyes narrow ever so slightly.

"I am sure I don't know what—"

"No more smoke and mirrors, Hayes. No more."

The pregnant silence that immediately fell between them was a turning point. Oliver had either misjudged his host and would need the weapons he concealed on his person, or Hayes would finally speak freely.

"Tell me why we are here," Oliver said flatly. "I am not a man who wastes his time, and I do not believe you are either."

Hayes finally offered him a single nod and then steepled his fingers. "Tell me, Mr. Holden…how do you view the path upon which England is headed?"

Even though his features remained perfectly placid, Oliver's heart began to race.

LATER THAT EVENING, Emily smoothed the skirts of her deep-rose-pink gown and straightened the tiers of beaded organza. The effect of the fabric was lovely in motion, making her appear as if she floated when she walked, but she felt the immodest neckline left much to be desired. The pleats created an almost heart-shape to the bodice, but dipped lower than she would have preferred, given the size of her bosom. It would have to do, though, because she'd just about run out of borrowed gowns at that point. She was grateful that this adventure was finally coming to an end for many reasons, the least of them being that she was almost out of clothing.

She looked forward to the predictability of her old life and couldn't wait to be herself once more.

Then again, it also meant she might never see Oliver again.

"Are you ready?"

Said man materialized at her side as if conjured from her imagination and wrapped an arm around her waist. It was nearly impossible for her to keep herself from melting into his side. The image they presented together in the mirror was a striking one, to be sure. They contrasted nicely, and yet, they were somehow complementary. Her heart-shaped face, doe-like eyes, and fair coloring paired well with Oliver's dark, angular features, strong jaw, solid frame, and midnight-black hair. It was painful for her to think of never hearing his voice again, of never having his hand hold hers, of missing the way he took care of her in ways both subtle and blatant. It was utterly ridiculous, but true. They'd hadn't known one another for more than a couple of weeks and yet...Emily couldn't rid herself of the feeling that having him removed from her life would be akin to losing a limb. She didn't rely upon him—she'd survived just fine without him for more than two decades before him and she'd go on surviving after— but to imagine the comfort of having him as a partner, someone who appreciated her and saw her as an equal, who respected her as a woman and also desired her, was so tempting.

"I am," she finally said.

"How are you feeling?"

"Much better." She met his smoky eyes in the mirror. "But please keep all spirits as far away as possible from me."

Oliver emitted a sympathetic chuff and squeezed her into his side.

They walked arm in arm down to the dining room. The plan was to attend dinner as a pair as usual and then part ways to spend time with other members of the party. Oliver had insisted that they could no longer remain exclusive and go unnoticed.

Something that also hadn't gone unnoticed by Emily was the way his fists had clenched in stark contrast to the cool detachedness of his words.

It was decided that Oliver would slip away with whichever woman was deepest into her cups and most amenable to ducking out as early as possible. In his absence, he would rely upon Emily to once again create a distraction where Hayes wouldn't retire to his rooms while Oliver was completing his search.

Emily did her best to be as engaged as possible during the meal—she chatted with Mr. Frye and Baron Allyson, exchanged quips and hoped she laughed at all the appropriate times—but her anxiety only continued on its upward slope as the meal wrapped up. Her pulse followed suit as they all meandered into the parlor for their usual after-dinner drinks and activities. She felt as if her heart might burst straight through her ribs as Oliver accepted and encouraged the attentions of Lady Satterly. It was unexpectedly painful for Emily to watch—which was absurd because it wasn't the first time she'd witnessed it—but she bit her tongue. Literally. She wasn't surprised when the metallic tang of blood stained her mouth.

It was difficult for her to put her finger on what was different between them. The only conclusion she came to was that things had changed since he'd admitted to feeling something for her, and he'd trusted her with his real name. She took solace in that and held the pearl of knowledge close to her breast, reminding herself that this was not about her and any inappropriate feelings she may or may not have been fostering toward this dark and mysterious man.

Sooner than she'd thought possible, Oliver and Lady Satterly prepared to slip from the room.

His dark eyes caught Emily's just before they disappeared.

Chapter Eighteen

T HE MINUTES TICKED by and still Oliver did not return to the parlor. Emily watched impatiently for his return in between serving more drinks to the men and coercing the party to split into groups for rounds of cards where the stakes were garments rather than coins. The activity proved to be such a success that no one seemed to notice how conservatively she wagered during play. She'd only lost her gloves, slippers and a single stocking while Mr. Frye was naked from the waist-up, his pale, hairless chest nothing compared to Oliver's. Hayes had done away with his coat, waistcoat, and cravat; Viscount Satterly—entirely unconcerned with his wife's absence—was barefoot and down to only his breeches; Maeve had lost everything but her stays and shift; Lady Aaron's gown was long gone and she wore only her nearly-transparent shift; Mrs. Wright's ample bosom was on full display as she sat only in her stockings.

Emily was quite sure the woman had lost several hands on purpose.

Fifteen, twenty, thirty minutes passed without a sign from Oliver. After an hour, Emily began to grow nervous—more so when she realized Hayes had made a silent exit while she'd turned her back to refill Allyson's whiskey.

Heartbeat deafening in her ears, Emily muttered a quick excuse—something about experiencing a relapse of that morning's poor constitution—and left the parlor as quickly as she dared. Her only thoughts were of warning Oliver or preventing

Hayes from discovering him; she had no idea how she would accomplish the latter, but she knew she had to try.

Especially because there was not a doubt in her mind that he would do the same for her.

Her pace increased as soon as she was out of view of the parlor. She gathered up her skirts and flew up the stairs, dashing down the hallway toward the room on the second floor Oliver had indicated was being used by their host, slowing only when she found the corridor empty and lit by intermittent candlelight. Though she tried, it was nearly impossible for her to quell her heavy, panting breaths—as much from nerves as they were from exertion. She counted the doors until she reached the proper one.

She heard nothing from within.

She glanced up and down the hallway once more and wrung her hands in indecision before holding her breath and placing her hand on the brass knob.

It was unlocked.

She peered into the darkened room, frowning when it appeared as deserted as the hall.

Where has he gone?

Stepping lightly forward, though, Emily was immediately wrenched against a hard wall of masculine chest and a large hand was slapped over her mouth. She was about to open her mouth and sink her teeth into her attacker when he spoke.

"What the hell do you think you are doing?" Oliver growled in her ear, sending a thrill through every one of her nerves.

She pried his hand away and whispered harshly, "You were taking too long." Her heart resumed its pounding all over again. The heat of his body bled through her back and engulfed her, making her knees more than a little unsteady.

Without freeing her from the strong bands of his arms, he pressed the door closed with silent movements before pulling her more deeply into the large, shadowed chamber. She could barely make out the shapes of an oversized bed, a hulking armoire on the far side of the room beside a table with a washbasin set with silver grooming implements, and a pair of spindle-legged chairs set before the banked hearth.

"Lady Satterly refused to be set aside," he whispered, his breath warm on her cheek. "I was forced to give her something to sedate her."

"You drugged her?" Emily squeaked.

"I assure you, she is sleeping quite happily. It is not the first time I've done so to someone; I know what I am about. Besides, you are far from someone who should turn her nose up at drugging someone," he added the last with a sardonic lilt to his tone, referencing how she'd dosed him with laudanum to force him to rest after his injury. Her cheeks flushed and she was grateful for the darkness.

He finally released her and she found herself strangely bereft of his warmth and touch. The danger hadn't passed, but she seeing him, hearing him, feeling him, smelling his now-familiar scent went a long way toward helping her believe all would be well.

Emily's eyes were beginning to adjust to the lack of light in the room and she spied a gap in the doors of the oversized armoire. It appeared that its trio of iron locks had proven no match for Oliver.

"I gave you an hour and then Hayes left the room while my attentions were elsewhere. I've no idea where he went. I thought only to warn you...I was worried."

She could feel his eyes on her in the still and shadowed room, but he said nothing in response to her words.

Oliver strode back over to the cabinet with silent steps and swung the door open to reveal two hat boxes brimming with sheaves of letters and correspondence, notebooks filled with tightly cramped writing.

"It's encrypted. All of it." He swore. "It would explain why Hayes was willing to carry it with him; anyone who saw it in passing would be unable to read it. Obviously, there is no key conveniently placed and this one is not a code with which I am familiar."

"Is there someone who might be able to decode it?" Emily joined him at the armoire and squinted at the writing.

"Without a key? It could take years—if ever. Patterns would need to be established and even then that is no guarantee. What if the code changes from one month to the next?"

"Is all of this not enough?" Panic edged its way into her tone. Had they come this far only to be thwarted?

"Not if the code cannot be broken," Oliver said with a shake of his head. "I could bring both these boxes to my superiors, but, without a key, these could easily be argued to be nothing more sinister than the ravings of a madman."

Emily paused with her hands pressed to the papers, feeling a hopeless helplessness rising within her so agonizing that she closed her eyes against the burn of tears. They were *so close*. If Oliver was stymied, then what hope did she have to provide him with any sort of help? Where would that leave him? For that matter, what she knew about codes amounted to less than a thimbleful. But—

Her eyes flew open.

Codes.

In one of the books she'd recently finished, Emily had read a small passage about an imprisoned queen.

One who had ties to France.

Beside Hayes's bed, there was a delicate, spindle-legged table. She strode over to it and, with trembling fingers, she slid open the single slim drawer and plucked from it a brown leather-bound Catholic Bible. The discovery was interesting enough in their Protestant country where the Church of England ruled, but more so because Catholicism was also the chief religion of France. Her limbs began to tingle with excitement.

"Emily?" Oliver's voice was close, but she did not look up from the book in her hands.

She couldn't.

She turned it over again and again, examining the seams of the covers until the edge of her nail caught on the paper pasted to the inside board of the back cover. Her heart instantly filled her throat and nearly choked her when she gently lifted the flap to uncover a hidden pocket. She was just able to work a thin scrap of opaque paper from its hiding place.

She handed it over to Oliver, careful not to allow it to slip from her trembling fingers.

He unfolded it with gentle fingers, his eyes skimming it again and again until his jaw dropped and he looked up at her in astonishment. "How did you…?"

"Mary, Queen of Scots, kept her code in her Bible," Emily explained, blushing in pleasure from Oliver's unabashed admiration of her cleverness. "She was also a French princess. It was a lucky guess that these spies might employ the same tactic."

The air rushed from Emily's lungs as Oliver suddenly hauled her to him, kissing her soundly. He cupped her face in his hands and pressed his forehead to hers as she clung to his forearms. "You are bloody brilliant!" he praised her. Though his voice was barely above a whisper, she felt his words to the very core of her being.

"Not brilliant," Emily laughed quietly, though she was thrilled by Oliver's reaction, "only a voracious reader. There isn't a great deal I'm allowed to do other than the books for Lady Night's."

Oliver's eyes glittered with pride; his lips parted as if he wanted to say more, but the sound of approaching voices and footsteps forestalled him.

"Oh no," Emily gasped.

Releasing her, Oliver rushed over to the armoire, snatched up a handful of letters from the stacks, shoved them into an inner pocket of his coat, and deftly relocked the doors with his tools.

Emily spoke before he had a chance to turn around and bark orders at her. "Hide behind the curtains."

"You cannot be serious," he hissed, his brow furrowing in consternation. "What about you?"

"Don't worry about me," she commanded, shoving him

toward the wall though her efforts had little effect on his large frame. "Go!"

Rather than listen, Oliver pulled a small but deadly-looking stiletto from his boot and pressed the hilt into her palm. It wasn't lost on her that it was the same one she'd found on her balcony.

"Use it if you must," he instructed evenly. "Aim for the stomach—it is a larger target. Do not worry about killing him if you believe your life is in danger. Incapacitate him and run."

"But, if I kill him…" she began, stammering, "then you will lose all chances of a confession or of having him lead you to anyone else."

His piercing eyes met hers and they almost glowed in the darkness. "You are more important."

Those words were still ringing in Emily's skull as Oliver disappeared behind the curtain and the door to the bedchamber swung open, casting a golden ray of flickering candlelight upon her as if she were an opera singer on a stage.

Rather appropriate.

She slid the knife behind her back as the man in the doorway froze and paused for several tense moments before he spoke. "How did you get in here?" Hayes asked. His tone was so flat it was entirely unreadable.

"A maid let me in." Emily hoped the crack in her voice would be construed as excitement rather than terror.

"Which maid?" he demanded, advancing one menacing step into the room.

"Does it matter?" she replied, doing her best to placate him with a slow, sultry tone in her voice. "I had to beg and bribe the poor thing to let me into your rooms to surprise you."

"Surprise me?" One of his full brows arched high and his ice-chip eyes softened slightly.

Though her body screamed in protest, Emily nodded and began to approach Hayes, keenly aware of Oliver listening from the space behind the curtain. "I wanted a chance to be alone with you," she said employing her best seductive voice and movements. This had its intended effect as his skepticism lowered further, beginning to win out over his wariness.

He closed the shadowed gap between them with predatory grace, but she stood her ground. Once she was within his reach, Hayes began to touch her. He ran his fingers down the soft skin of her arms and twisted a lock of her hair around his finger again and again until he gave it a sharp little tug.

"You couldn't stand to be held captive by Holden any longer, hm?" He pressed his wet, parted lips to her neck, making her skin crawl.

"He is terribly possessive." She tried not to grit her teeth when she spoke. The hold on her restraint was tenuous, but she told herself again and again that Oliver needed her to keep her head. They hadn't made it this far for her to jump and destroy the best chance there was at a successful mission.

"I wonder, Miss Tailor…what are you hoping to gain by coming here?"

"Excitement," she purred and watched Hayes's pupils dilate.

"That, I can supply in good measure."

His tone lowered and his proximity became nearly over-whelming until Emily worried she might be forced to use the stiletto lest this game go too far.

Suddenly, Hayes froze. His eyes were no longer on her.

She turned to see what had riveted his gaze and noted a bare-ly perceptible twitch of the curtains. Emily's heart skipped and then thudded so hard, she feared it might give out when Hayes stepped around her and crept toward the window. Her hand tightened around the hilt of the knife behind her back as she followed, ready, she realized, to attack Hayes for Oliver's sake.

She held her breath and tensed her muscles when Hayes reached out and abruptly wrenched the curtain back. He found only the window cracked open with too small a gap to emit a cat, let alone a man. Emily nearly sighed in relief, but Hayes wasn't convinced. He proceeded to fling the window open wide and peer out into the night nonetheless, his head tilting this way and that as he scanned the shadows.

When he was finally satisfied, he closed the window and latched it carefully. Emily's breath left her lungs in a slow, quavering release. She didn't know how Oliver had accomplished his escape, but she was relieved he had.

Unfortunately for Emily, Hayes interpreted her trembling nerves as excitement rather than fear for Oliver's safety. He approached her once more and ran the back of his hand across her cheek, trailed it down her neck, and traced the scalloped and beaded neckline of her gown.

"You are…quite one of the most delectable morsels I've seen in a long while," Hayes rasped, inhaling the scent of her hair. "I wonder how you'll sound when I pound into you and make you scream." His tongue darted out to lick the shell of her ear. She shivered in revulsion, bile rising to the back of her throat, but Hayes either ignored it or chose to read it as acquiescence.

Just when she thought she might be forced to act, the door to the bedchamber banged open and Oliver strode in, looking for all the world like a vengeful dark angel. It was nigh impossible for Emily to disguise her relief when she realized he must have scaled the ledge to reenter through their bedchamber window, doubling back through the hallway to rescue her.

"There you are," Oliver said, smooth as silk and deep as the ocean. "I've been looking everywhere for you."

Hayes was most displeased by the interruption and made it known. "What do you think you are doing, Holden? How dare you barge into my rooms?" Hayes's hand clamped around Emily's upper arm so tight, it would surely leave finger-shaped bruises. Oliver's eyes flicked to the point of contact and his jaw hardened for a moment before his features morphed into an amiable mask.

"Like I said, I've been searching high and low for Miss Tailor. Imagine my surprise when I found her in the very last place I looked." Despite Hayes's murderous expression, Oliver approached Emily and, under the guise of wrapping his arm around her, tugged her free from Hayes's grasp and removed the knife she still held hidden behind her back. She felt him slip it up the sleeve of his coat to conceal it. "Naughty girl sneaking away from me," he said in a growl and gently chucked her beneath her chin.

"I thought you and Lady Satterly were occupied," Hayes gritted out.

"Unfortunately, the viscountess wasn't up to my appetites." Oliver shrugged nonchalantly and turned back to Emily. She knew it was an act, but the smolder in his gaze made her clench her thighs together. "This one knows exactly what I crave."

Without giving Hayes a chance to reply, Oliver bent and tossed Emily over his shoulder. She yelped in surprise but didn't fight it. Hayes on the other hand, was none too pleased with the development.

"Where do you think you are taking her?" Hayes snarled.

Emily squeaked when Oliver firmly swatted her behind with great theatricality and swept her from the room. Hayes followed in their wake, bellowing protests as she watched the patterned carpet of the hallway come into view.

"She chose me!" Hayes spat. "You were to bring a woman to share in everyone's pleasures and you have gone back on your word. You have kept her to yourself when she would rather lie in my arms this night."

Oliver paused in his exit and turned halfway to face their pursuer. "I do not hear the lady protesting." Tilting his head back to address Emily, he asked, "Should I put you down so you might enjoy a taste of variety?" Her teeth gritted so tightly they squeaked in objection—if he didn't get her out of there soon then she might just kick free and bolt. She didn't know how much longer she could stand in Hayes's vile presence. When she didn't vocalize a protest, Oliver patted her rump once more and murmured, "Good girl." Her body was instantly set aflame by the praise and she throbbed most unexpectedly.

He continued down the hallway at a steady pace, past two other couples gawking at the scene created by their trio. He didn't slow and when confronted with their confusion and questions, swept her into the room, kicking it shut with the heel of his boot and then bolting it. He set her gently upon her feet before wedging the chair against the door.

Harsh pounding immediately rattled it on its hinges.

"I demand you release her, Holden!" Hayes snarled through the barrier. "You cannot hold her hostage!" The jangle of keys was quickly followed by the snicking of the lock, and Emily thanked God that Oliver had had the foresight to further bar the door from entry. She silently promised to apologize for ever thinking he was being dramatic; Hayes could have entered the room at any time, just as Oliver had suspected.

There was a muffled string of vile curses from the other side of the door and Emily dropped to the edge of the bed, her legs suddenly weak and jelly-like after the close and disturbing encounter with their host.

She watched as Oliver leaned toward the door and called through it in a light tone. "Don't worry; I assure you she shall be quite satisfied with her time in 'captivity.'"

If anything, the pounding on the door increased.

"That won't satisfy him," Emily hissed, her wide eyes darting between Oliver and the shaking door.

"What do you suggest?"

She pressed a palm to her forehead in indecision, her imagination reaching and failing. How could they make him go away? How could they convince him to leave them alone? Hayes had to believe the opportunity was past. But how—

Emily's eyes sprang open and, for the second time that night, a dip into her past brought her the answer.

She pressed her fingers to her lips and signaled for Oliver to be silent.

Chapter Nineteen

OLIVER FROWNED BUT nodded in agreement as Emily cleared her throat and closed her eyes. The silence dragged out, broken only by Hayes's furious shouts from the other side of the door. Fists clenched, he fought the urge to shake her—how could sitting on the bed with her eyes closed be the solution? Were he alone, he would have ducked out the window and fled back to London with the damning paperwork tucked into his coat. But Emily…he'd never leave her defenseless. He'd just about reached his breaking point when she began breathing heavily.

The hair on the back of his neck stood on end as the pants shifted into moans as palpable to Oliver as if fingers were being raked down his abdomen to his groin. His mouth fell open in astonishment. Her sounds were rhythmic. Seductive. Incredibly, unnervingly realistic—enough that Oliver was sure if he were in Hayes's place and couldn't see her placid exterior, he'd have bet money that Emily was experiencing passion of the highest level.

Emily's voice rose in convincing gasps and cries, sighs and filthy words of praise that made Oliver's cock painfully hard. The hammering at the door halted and it seemed as if their host was as captivated as he was with the performance. So powerful was his erection as he watched Emily and listened to her that he had to press a firm palm to it. It was everything he could do not to stroke himself to relief.

He knew damn well it was all an act, but, *God*, now that he had heard the sounds of false pleasure torn from her lips, he would never be able to forget them. Even her false climax left his head spinning. Her "orgasm" crested gloriously and Emily was left pink-cheeked, bosom heaving from her performance. Like the blackguard he was, he hoped the seams wouldn't contain her luscious breasts much longer. She came down slowly while Oliver remained painfully aroused and shaking with need.

Furious footsteps retreated down the hallway.

Emily hesitantly opened one eye and her face immediately ignited when she met his gaze.

"D-Did it work?" she whispered.

Oliver's nod dissolved into a shake of disbelief as he flung his arms open wide, not caring one whit that the thick, hard ridge of his arousal was on blatant display. Let her see what she did to him. "Where did you learn such a thing?" he croaked.

"Exactly where I've learned everything else," she replied somewhat bashfully.

"So they teach women at Lady Night's to do…*that?*"

Emily's breathy sighs still rang in the space between his ears, and he knew he'd give his right arm to hear the real thing.

"Some men prefer it when…" Her voice trailed off and she lifted a shoulder in a shrug.

With a curse, Oliver approached her, dropping the stiletto to the rug with a muted clatter. He hauled her to her feet and kissed her with unmasked need and pleasure and desire, murmuring endearments and admonishments against her lips. She was soft and sweet, intoxicating in her earnestness and refreshing lack of artifice, so at odds with the performance she'd just given.

"You brilliant woman. You stupid, brave, intelligent woman," he said harshly as he sipped deeply of her mouth, his tongue dueling with hers. These were no pretend kisses, but the unleashing of a fount of longing. This had been building between them like steam beneath a lid.

It pained her to do it, but Emily, unable to resist, reared back and asked more than a little breathlessly, "How can I possibly be all those things at once?"

The curve of Oliver's lips caused a rush of dampness to pool between her thighs. "You are brilliant because you can think more quickly on your toes than some professional agents. You are intelligent because your mind contains such an amazingly untapped plethora of knowledge and skills. And you are stupid," he explained as desire deepened his voice, "because you put yourself at risk for my worthless skin." His fingers dove into her hair and cupped the back of her skull with enough force that she couldn't have looked away had she wished to. "Don't ever do that again." Oliver's fathomless eyes searched her face for a moment before he continued. "I also find you beautiful, beguiling, intoxicating, and so bloody desirable that I've been hard-pressed to focus on anything else since I woke to your face after my injury. Not even the pain of my injuries and my pounding head could make me think I faced anything other than an angel."

Emily stared wide-eyed at him, lips parted in shock.

The ensuing silence was heavy.

Oliver instantly realized how foolish his words were, and he was as close to mortified as he'd felt in his years as a grown man. He averted his eyes and cleared his throat as he attempted to step back. His retreat was halted, however, when Emily's small hands held fast to the lapels of his coat. She refused to allow him to back away from the words he'd dropped between them.

"Was that the truth or another lie?"

Oliver swallowed his pride as if it were crushed glass in his throat. "Only the truth for you." Her breath hitched and it sent a new shock of arousal to his cock. His balls ached. His hands flexed against the urge to throw her to the bed and act upon his baser needs. Instead, he apologized. "I never should have said that, Emily. It wasn't—" The woman actually clapped a hand over his mouth.

"Why are you doing that?" The question was posed far more softly than the pointed look in her eyes. Oliver knew there was no disguising the way he felt any longer. "I've been shuttered away, protected for so much of my life. No one has ever spoken to me like that before—no one has ever been given the opportunity." Her hand lifted from his mouth but was quickly replaced by her lips and tongue. She licked her way into his mouth to stroke his tongue with hers, nibbled his lower lip, pressed her pelvis to his, and reveled in the hardness of his member pressing insistently against her belly. Everything about him called to her like a beacon in a storm.

He'd just begun sinking into the kiss when he suddenly stiffened and groaned, tearing his mouth from hers.

"I can't...this must stop." He covered her hand with his when she would have tilted his face back to hers.

"Whyever not?" she asked earnestly. "This is far from the first time we've kissed." She'd said it lightheartedly, but the tautness of his face melted her smile.

"Because...because I..." Oliver was unable to finish. He pulled free of her grasp and stepped back to turn away from Emily and scrub at his face with his palms.

"Because you're a street urchin?" The words slammed into his back as if a board had been broken between his shoulders. He whirled on Emily. "Oliver...when will you see there is so much more to you than that?"

"Don't pretend to understand," he ground out, stalking over to her. "I am not a good man. The only difference between the man who lived on the streets and the one you see before you is a bloody good disguise. At least now, I get paid for the men I kill." He towered over her, but she refused to be cowed. He needed her to understand. "My hands are dirty. My conscience has long since deserted me. And I do not deserve to touch you. Surely, my desire has damned what shriveled remnants of my soul remain."

Emily shocked him, reaching for his hands and tracing the scars on his knuckles, the pale mark of a healed wound that bisected the heel of his palm where he'd once cut himself on the glass of a broken window in a brawl.

"Do you know what I see?" she asked gently. "I see a survivor; a man who fought the odds, tooth and nail. Life treated you unfairly and unkindly. You could have so easily turned into a monster, considering your circumstances, but you didn't. You've shown me respect and a remarkable sense of duty. What pains me is you believe you have so little to lose that you risk your life with nary a second thought. I understand how you might believe it after hearing those vile words so often—I've seen it often in those seeking employment at Lady Night's—but I hope, one day, you see yourself as something so much more…as someone brave and admirable." She kissed his palm and Oliver was lost.

Emily's words had simultaneously built him up and shattered him.

He couldn't, wouldn't believe her…but there was something in her eyes—an innocent sincerity that he'd witnessed in no one but she. He ached to protect it and nurture it, to guard her from the world. He was convinced she really must have been an angel; there was no other reason for her to be so willing to absolve him of his sins.

She was a balm to his tattered soul.

She breathed life into something he'd thought long dead—his sense of hope.

Oliver groaned her name and caressed his cheek with his knuckles.

She was so soft.

"Will you make love to me, Oliver?"

He froze.

And he was fairly certain his heart stopped and would never restart.

"All my life, I've wondered about the passion between a woman and a man—especially growing up in the environment I did. I hold no illusions that I'll one day marry a respectable man who will take me away and give me a family, for what man of quality would wed Lady Night's daughter? Having spent the entirety of my life in brothels, it isn't expected that I will be chaste and virtuous, no matter the claims I or my mother make. So this may be my only opportunity to be with a man whom I trust."

"This is merely a product of your recent experiences," Oliver rasped, trying to reason with her. "It is natural to crave physical closeness after a harrowing event."

Emily calmly shook her head. "Do not diminish my mind because of your sense of duty. I know what I am about."

Despite what his head told him and his heart argued, this was no jest. The raw truth of Emily's decision was evident in the burning blush on her petal-soft cheeks.

"Once done, this cannot be taken back," he cautioned her, though he knew deep in his soul that it was pointless. Emily was no fool. She would have thought this over inside and out; she'd likely thought about it for days, and the idea that she had considered it so carefully sparked lust in his blood. He held her body flush with his, barely fighting the filthy urge to grind against her.

"I know that." She nodded, her eyes soft and the corners of her mouth tilting in the slightest of smiles.

"And you will be mine," Oliver added. Her brows lifted at the words, but she nodded once more. She couldn't know what she was agreeing to. She would be his forever, and only his. Once he claimed her body, he knew all hope of relinquishing Emily would be lost, and he'd kill any man who dared touch her.

Unable to restrain himself any longer, Oliver swept her into his arms and carried her to the oversized bed, hoping to live up to whatever expectations she had.

No.

He vowed to do so; she deserved nothing less.

Emily deserved a gown made from the heavens, and jewelry crafted from the stars themselves, she deserved the world in a pretty little box. He couldn't give her all those things, but he could give her his loyalty and his protection, his trust and every ounce of his desire. Dare he think it, he'd give her his heart if he discovered he still had one.

As he laid her down, he asked her for a favor. "As much as I enjoyed listening to your earlier display, I don't ever want you to pretend with me." He met her eyes to ensure she comprehended his seriousness. "I've had enough deceit in my time, and you are too good to be a part of that aspect of my life."

"I swear it," she murmured as she wrapped her arms around his neck and tilted her head to accept his kiss.

EMILY OPENED HER thighs to cradle Oliver between them, and he fit more perfectly than she could have imagined. Having his weight there, where she ached and throbbed was delicious. Having Oliver be the man she shared this with was nothing shy of exquisite. There was something so raw and unpracticed about the way he kissed her. His touches remained as skilled as ever, but it was as if a veil between them had been lifted. There was nothing to dampen the desire or mask it behind false identities and crafted stories.

There was a languid eroticism to the way he stroked her tongue with his, explored her mouth as if discovering a new and wondrous land. He groaned unabashedly when she kissed him back and grazed his mouth with her teeth. She took her opportunity to run her hands along his broad shoulders, to feel the flexing bulge of his biceps as he hovered above her. Careful of his injured ribs, she instead moved her hands up to the strong tendons of his neck and traced the hard angle of his jaw with its rasp of early stubble, the angled lines of his cheekbones. She reveled in the softness of his hair, the dips and swells of his back.

Oliver was performing an exploration of his own. Using his mouth and teeth and tongue and lips, he memorized the slope of her neck, learned the taste of the skin covering her collarbone, savored the softness of the swells of her bosoms. She shuddered when his tongue dipped into the valley between her breasts, as his palm stroked her in large and steady circles, pebbling her nipple into an achy, needy peak. She arched into his touch, seeking out more pressure as she rocked her hips up into his pelvis. Emily cursed the layers of clothing separating them and, though her heart pounded furiously with nerves, her excitement far outweighed any trepidation.

It was odd for her to realize that she didn't feel the anxiety she thought she would have, but it was simple for her to chalk it up to her unconventional lifestyle and, perhaps, even some inherited sensual confidence. Despite the newness of the situation—of the sensations Oliver was firing through her body one by one—she wasn't the least bit frightened. She wanted more, more, more.

He began undressing her with infinite care, helping her to sit up and unlacing the gown to free her, then removing her stays and chemise. His hands were remarkably, frustratingly delicate. He was far too gentle for the roar of desire welling up from her soul.

"Do not treat me with kid gloves," Emily demanded. "I will not break, no matter what you do to me."

"Very well," he said with a wolfish smile and sidled around to face her as he knelt on the mattress. "If you are so brave and bold, then you should show me how you like to be touched."

"I—I am untried. I do not know—"

"How do you touch yourself, Emily? How do you bring yourself to orgasm in the heavy shadows of the night? What makes your body shudder as it comes apart?"

It was scandalous, what he asked of her, but oh so exciting.

She couldn't resist following his order.

Leaning back against the pillows, she inched up the hem of her thin shift with tantalizing slowness. The glide of the soft linen upon her sensitized flesh was almost too much to bear. She watched Oliver, held rapt by the gleam in his smoke-dark eyes as they hungered for her. This, coupled with the sight of the thick outline of his member as it strained against the confinement of his breeches, spurred her on with a level of confidence she didn't know she possessed.

Emily watched as his lips parted when he caught the first glimpse of her dewy sex and the golden curls. He was unblinking as she bent her knees and gradually inched them apart for his view. His groan made her core clench tightly as she spread her slick folds with her fingers, showing him what he did to her.

"Emily," he rasped, his fists balling so tightly that they blanched.

She slid her fingers lower and began to tease herself, dipping and stroking, rolling and plucking just the way she liked…only now, instead of closing her eyes and losing herself to a fantasy, she held her eyes wide open and watched the man who she knew in her soul would fulfill her deepest desires and dreams.

She concentrated on spreading her slickness with her two longest fingers, staring at Oliver as he stared at her, unflinching and with a blatant appreciation that made Emily's mouth water. Her body bloomed beneath his appraisal, swelling and throbbing as the yearning within her ebbed higher. Her clitoris sparked with awareness as each passing flick of her fingers and press of her thumb strummed her as if she were a tuned instrument of pleasure. Her moans and sighs filled the air between them as she climbed, her eyes falling to where his palm pressed firmly against the evidence of his arousal.

"Now you do the same," she said, the flush of her cheeks deepening until she was certain she was the brightest red. "It is only fair that you show me what you like."

Oliver nearly swallowed his tongue at Emily's demand, but he couldn't have denied her had he wanted to—not when she looked and sounded like she did at that moment, a pagan goddess of carnal pleasures. He undressed with reckless haste, flinging aside his clothes and dropping his brace of knives to the ground, nearly growling with pride when her eyes widened at the sight of his rampant arousal springing thick and ruddy, reaching for her from the nest of dark hair between his thighs.

He began his ministrations slowly, running his palm along the thickly veined underside in a whisper of a touch. Up and down. Up and down. He wrapped a fist around his cock, working it in pumps that deliberately matched the rhythm of Emily's fingers as they stroked and slid through the pink folds of her sex. She increased her speed; he did, too. She moaned, and his balls tightened, threatening to spill before he even experienced the sweet tightness of her sheath.

Emily found the sight of Oliver working his body into a frenzy to be one of the most beautiful things she'd ever seen. He gripped himself tightly and used prolonged, hard jerks on his member. He was thick and long, flushed with arousal, and ridged with pulsing veins. She wanted to touch the velvet flesh that slid over the hardness beneath with every pump of his hand, test the pendulous weight that swung below, and experience how it felt slapping against her as he thrust in and out. The flexing of Oliver's muscles, the ripple of his abdomen with his every groaning breath only spurred her on. Even though she slid two, then three fingers inside of her body, it was nowhere near enough. She craved Oliver's impossibly large body over her, under her, behind her, inside of her, filling her to bursting, his hands gripping her so tightly she would wear the marks of his fingers for days. The thought of his feral strength matching her need was heady. Her muscles clenched as the first flares of her climax tore whimpers from her throat and she screwed her eyes closed. Just as it was upon her, Oliver's hands covered hers and removed them from her straining body.

She writhed and whimpered, but he held her fast and lowered his face to hers. His breathing was as erratic as she felt when he said, "I want your first orgasm with me to come from my body."

"First?" she asked, her floating mind latching onto that word.

"Oh, yes, Angel. There will be many."

Chapter Twenty

OLIVER SLID DOWN Emily's body, his large hands branding a fiery trail between her full, heaving breasts, his fingers only grazing their sensitive peaks despite her desperately arching into his touch. He coasted down her abdomen, skimmed her navel, before reaching the rucked-up hem of her shift. He paused, savoring the heat and scent of her sex for several interminable moments before finally lifting the garment to reveal her to his eyes.

Her thighs and the petals of her sex were slick with her juices and it was all he could do not to dive in and taste her—to become drunk on her nectar. Instead, he took his time. He nuzzled her, licking and nipping the sensitive skin of her inner thighs as he gradually spread her wider and wider until not a bit of her was hidden from his view. He inhaled and filled his lungs with her as if it was his last breath in this life. His fingers flexed against her legs, loving the sleek lengths of them as he imagined them wrapped around his head as well as his waist. He nudged against her with his nose, pressing deep until his face was all but buried between her thighs.

Oliver savored Emily's gasp at the contact, but he growled with pride when she cried out in response to the long, bold strokes of his tongue. It wasn't long until his face was covered in her slickness and the bedding beneath them was damp with their shared enjoyment. Her little moans and gasps of surprise as he explored each new hollow and fold were nothing short of delightful. The erotic movements of her body made his blood burn for her and it became nearly impossible for him to rein in his need. Still, however, he focused on her pleasure, dipping his tongue deep inside her tight channel before replacing it with his longest finger. He'd watched with devilish elation when she'd used her fingers on her body, but his were far, far thicker and longer…

Emily shuddered and moaned at the new sensation he unleashed within her with every flick of his tongue on her clitoris and every slow stroke of him within her body. She was so bloody tight, surely she'd kill him once she took his cock.

"D'you like that, Angel?" he demanded through clenched teeth. "Can you take more?"

She panted, breasts heaving, and nodded her head. "Yes!"

His chest rumbled in approval as he added a second finger to his machinations. Her inner muscles gripped him so well, so sweetly. He moved slowly at first, allowing her to grow accustomed to the new girth, but, when he curled his fingers upward to hit that special place inside of her and returned his tongue to its job, she went feral.

Emily rode his fingers and mouth, rocking against him, bearing down on him where she needed more pressure. And Oliver was only too happy to oblige.

He worked her higher, maintaining a steady pace when he found one that made her cry out and knot her fingers in his hair. Meanwhile, desperate for relief, he resorted to grinding his throbbing cock against the bed. He'd never yearned for a woman like this before, never had his body scream and rage for her, demand to stop the play and fuck. He was painfully aroused, the hardest he'd ever been in his life, and dangerously close to coming right then and there. With her heels digging into his back as she pulled him closer, her intoxicating scent and taste overwhelming his senses, Oliver was lost.

"More," she sobbed.

Without hesitation, he added a third finger, groaning at the tight stretch of her slick channel. God, how good she'd feel wrapped around him. Emily was Heaven—at least as close as a man such as he could hope to get.

He continued using his tongue on her and plunging his fingers deep until the telltale flutters of her inner muscles began to signal an impending crisis.

His sudden withdrawal was immediately followed by a flurry of incoherent complaints and exclamations from Emily. He ignored them all. He'd meant what he said earlier, and he would not let her come unless it was with him deep inside her.

Her limbs trembling, his name on her lips, drove Oliver past the point of sanity. Prowling up her body, he kissed her deeply, his tongue plunging into her mouth to let her taste how delicious she was. Reaching down between them, he ran the broad, blunt head of his member through her dripping folds, notched into place, and then pressed forward.

It took every ounce of his considerable restraint not to slam to the hilt and drive deep again and again and again. The little minx gasped and moaned, sinking her teeth into his shoulder and undulating against him in a manner born of pure instinct. Every muscle trembled with his strength and need held in check, but he was keenly aware that his hold upon it was wearing thin, like a rope above a flame. Sooner or later, it would snap and he would be unleashed.

He carefully yet firmly rocked forward a little more each time he felt her body adjust to his length and girth, greedily accepting every inch she afforded him and reveling in its glory. She took him well and without complaint. She must have experienced some discomfort, but her near frantic need for release far outweighed it.

"You shall split me in two," Emily moaned into his neck, licking at his skin and tasting his sweat as it collected there.

"I thought you wanted more," he chuckled gruffly. "If you want me to stop—"

Her nails raked his scalp as she pulled his face down to meet hers. Emily's blue-green eyes were wild. "Don't. You. Dare."

Sweet angel.

Grinning like the fool he was, stinging sweat dripping into his eyes, Oliver seated himself fully with one final thrust of his hips.

"Christ above," he moaned, his eyes screwed shut against the blinding white light overtaking his vision.

"Yes!" Emily cried as she clawed at his back, trying to gain as much purchase as possible. Her movements were jerky and uncalculated as she desperately and blindly fought for more. She rotated her hips and earned a guttural moan from deep within Oliver's chest.

"If you don't stop that, then I'll not be held responsible for what comes next," he gritted out. That rope holding him back was beginning to singe and fray.

"I can't help it," Emily panted. "I need to feel more of you. I want *more*."

He snapped.

His head whipped up and he sat back on his heels, careful to keep their bodies joined as firmly as possible. Snatching up one of the pillows, he lifted her hips and shoved it beneath her to lift her pelvis to a new angle. Curiosity flashed across Emily's beautifully flushed features, but she allowed him to position her as he wished. She gasped when the position caused him to be seated differently inside her. She was so full and tight; it was exactly what she'd requested, but her untried body tensed around him.

Oliver immediately set about urging her to relax. Holding perfectly still within her even though he was certain it would eventually kill him, he slowly dragged his palms from the hammering pulse in her throat to her bright pink erect nipples, hard and begging for his touch through the thin fabric of her shift. When she moaned at the contact, he continued his circular ministrations, plucking and pinching until she clenched around his cock hard enough to make his hips jerk in response. He tested the tender weights of her breasts, traced her heaving ribcage, and traveled lower to the delicious lips of her sex split open and weeping for him. He proceeded to stroke her there just as she'd shown him she liked and she immediately arched off the pillow, grinding against him in a way that made him hiss a breath through his teeth.

He plucked and rubbed, rolled the sensitive bud between his fingers, coated it in the slickness he collected as it seeped from the place they were joined. Emily's sheath convulsed around him and he knew she was close again...and he hadn't even begun to thrust. He was hugged so tightly that it caused him to see stars behind his eyelids.

When her breathing grew more ragged and the ripples of her muscles became more frantic, he stopped touching her, grinning wickedly at her cry of frustration as he denied her yet another orgasm. Every bit of her skin was coated in a fine sheen of sweat from the torture and the fabric of her shift had grown sheer with it.

"Oliver!" she ground out and he immediately clapped his palm over her mouth. Her hands flew up to meet his, her eyes opening wide in shock and then squinting in apology when she realized what she'd done.

He lowered his lips to her ear. "Be a good girl and don't use that name again tonight—no matter how badly both of us wish for you to scream it."

And then, Oliver began to move.

His thrusts began slow and deep, increasing in pace as Emily spread her legs wider to accept more of him and met his movements with wild bucks of her own. His large hands mercilessly gripped the soft flesh where her hips met her thighs as he pounded into her, fueled by her cries of relief and joy at being filled again and again, taught what it was to be truly claimed by a man.

By him.

Their flesh slapped together with each of Oliver's powerful thrusts. He filled her to the brim, stretching her, as she demanded more, more, more. Emily wanted all of him. She wanted him fast and furiously. He was afraid of what his weight and strength might do to her, but she took it all—and gladly, given her cries and gasps of pleasure. He was in awe of her, there was no other way to state it. The room filled with the suck and glide of colliding flesh, the musk of desire, Emily's moans as she tossed her head and palmed her bouncing breasts to tweak her nipples, Oliver's thick, pained words of praise.

"God, you're beautiful, Emily. So—"

Thrust.

"—damned—"

Thrust.

"—beautiful."

Thrust.

"Perfect in every way."

And mine.

Regardless of what the future held in store for them, Oliver knew he would never be able to see her as anything else. Emily was his and he was hers, body, heart, and soul. He didn't know when or how it happened, but he'd somehow fallen for this angel in his arms. Both his past and his present didn't make him fit to touch her—let alone claim her—but a primal beast inside roared with triumph that he had ignored his better judgment and grasped the one ray of light that had ever dared to shine upon his life. His claiming of her was nothing short of obscene, but he didn't care, not so long as she didn't.

His ribs ached and throbbed with his every movement, hot little stabs of pain prodded him relentlessly, but he paid them little mind. He focused on Emily. Only Emily. And he'd deal with the soreness later.

Oliver experienced the tingling in the base of his spine as his orgasm approached. Thankfully, he could tell Emily's climax neared as her inner muscles convulsed around his rock-hard length. Pressing the heel of his palm firmly against her mound, he rubbed with the same punishing rhythm of his pistoning hips.

"So good," she cried amidst incoherent sobs, clawing at the

blankets around them.

"Yes love," Oliver grunted. "So bloody good." He tossed his head back and sank into the sensations crashing over him in wave after wave and caught the most glorious sight. "Look up," he commanded hoarsely.

It was a struggle, but she did as he said, her pretty mouth gaping at what she saw. The mirror suspended above the bed placed them on display. At first, she didn't recognize herself. Who was that wanton girl with locks of her white-gold hair plastered to her sweat-slicked flesh? Her parted lips were rosy and plump from forceful kisses. She was able to watch Oliver's well-formed flexing buttocks as he thrust into her, the thick stalk of his sex as it slid in and out of her body. The latter held her entirely rapt. She could feel everything he did to her with his skilled hands and body, but to watch it with the removal of a third party was…exciting.

So exciting that she could not stave off her powerful climax any longer.

Emily finally shattered in an explosion of sobs and keening cries, her back arching to present her breasts to him as if she were the most sinful of buffets. His balls tightening, Oliver froze and released his control. Burying himself fully within Emily's body, he allowed her orgasm to milk his climax from his body, nearly doubling him over in relief and ecstasy as he filled her with his hot seed.

As soon as he could form a coherent thought, Oliver cursed himself for his carelessness. He bloody well knew better than to finish inside a woman and risk planting his babe within her belly, but he couldn't truly bring himself to care—not when Emily sighed contentedly as the last tremors of her orgasm rippled through her body and she gazed up at him with sleepy eyes and open arms. Oliver lowered himself and buried his face in Emily's neck, closing his eyes and savoring the way she enfolded him with her entire body even as his erection gradually flagged within her.

This was acceptance.

As far as Oliver was concerned, this was love.

His heart felt fucking broken.

Chapter Twenty-One

I T TOOK EMILY a long while to float down from the clouds into which her glorious climax had launched her. She'd brought herself pleasure many times before, but it had never, ever been anything like what she'd experienced at Oliver's hands.

And teeth.

And lips.

And tongue.

And cock.

Even the thought of what they'd just done made her flesh flush anew, even though her body still pulsed with awareness. He'd shown her a new world and she didn't think she would ever be able to go back to the way things had been. Oliver had forever changed her, just as he'd said he would.

She whimpered when Oliver finally slid from her body, but he soothed her with a kiss on her forehead and tucked her against his side. Even sweaty from exertion, she thought he smelled utterly delicious—especially when the heady musk of their coupling hung heavy in the air. She closed her eyes and listened to the drum of his heart.

"Are you well?" Oliver finally asked, his deep voice vibrating through his chest and tickling her cheek.

"Perfectly," she replied on a languorous exhalation, gently dragging her nails through the dusting of dark hair on his sculpted chest and the ridges of his abdomen. "I told you I would not break."

"You are not broken, but I don't doubt you will be sore and bruised in the morning."

"And I shall cherish every last ache."

He laughed at that and placed another kiss atop her head. She loved it when he did that. And she adored that she was privy to a part of himself he kept locked away. Knowing the secrets of his past made her appreciate his moments of tenderness all the more. He was a born carer, whether he realized it or not. One had only to see the way he looked out for others, how observant he was to her needs, how he took care of her even in her worst states without a question or hesitation. This was a man she would never grow tired of.

That she'd come to care for him so deeply was a sobering realization, indeed. She'd found him intensely attractive ever since the first night when he'd lain rain-drenched and unconscious on her balcony. Now, having gotten to know so many different facets of this mysterious man, she knew she could spend a lifetime sussing out everything there was to him. And she would do it gladly.

Emily sank into the feeling of being held close to Oliver's side. She allowed each of her senses to wander through the moment. She could still taste his kiss on her tongue—the mixture of his unique flavor and the musk of her arousal coating his lips. She filled her lungs with his scent of evergreen, clean air, and masculine sweat from exertion. She savored the contrast of his skin against hers, the feel of the coarse hair on his thigh as it tickled her leg, the places where he was solid muscle in comparison to her curves and pliant flesh. She was lulled into sleep by the perfectly even beat of his heart.

Oh, yes, she could spend a lifetime doing this.

Even if it was just a dream.

"YOU KNOW…YOU NEVER did explain to me what these were for," Emily said, gesturing to the holes bored in varying heights up the height of the four thick bedposts. She'd dozed for a little while until her arm had fallen asleep. The pins and tingles were remarkably unpleasant until she realized that she was, indeed, still naked and pressed flush to a man she was convinced was the most beautiful of the male species. More than just physical beauty, she adored how he placed her needs above his own, how she never doubted for a second that he would fight to the death for anyone in his care. Trust was too simple a word for the way she'd grown to feel toward Oliver since they'd met.

She would have been entirely content to snuggle back into his warm body and inhale his scent until it lulled her back to sleep, but the sight of the silver fire in his eyes told her rest was not something she'd experience anytime soon. She didn't mind that in the slightest.

She welcomed it.

Her stomach performed a rapid set of somersaults at Oliver's wicked smile.

Then, he proceeded to educate her.

Reaching off the bed, he retrieved his discarded cravat and then made quick work of threading each end through a pair of holes on the posts flanking the ornate headboard. Chills danced across Emily's skin as he helped her shuck her shift, placing tender kisses along every inch of exposed flesh, then gently, loosely bound one end around her wrist and then the other until she was trussed.

Until she was at his mercy.

She watched Oliver's beautiful face as he assessed his work and then appraised her body with the eyes of a starving man.

"Now, sweet Angel, you are mine to do with as I please."

The place between her thighs was wet in an instant; the secret hollow already throbbing and begging to be filled by him once again. She longed to touch herself to relieve the ache, but this, she realized, was the purpose of the bindings. An experimental tug of her arms showed the knots were loose. She didn't doubt Oliver possessed the skills to well and truly tie her up if he so desired; the fact that he'd taken such care to ensure her comfort was endearing beyond measure.

Rather than free herself, Emily twisted her wrists to wrap the fabric more tightly, shortening the length so her arms were stretched high above her head, and she gripped the cravat and held on. She bent her knees and spread her legs wide to expose the dripping folds, loving the way the banked coals in his gaze burst into an inferno.

"I am yours," she murmured.

Oliver required no further encouragement and immediately set upon her like a ravenous beast. He began by devouring her mouth, his tongue tangling with hers in a vicious war, his teeth nipping at her, stroking her, tasting her. It wasn't long until his mouth made its way lower to her neglected breasts.

Emily hissed a plea as he eyed the puckered rosy buds that had so long begged for his attention. He, being the caring man he was, obliged. Fastening his mouth on one nipple, sucking as much of her into his mouth as he could, he covered the other with one large, calloused palm. His tongue soon joined the battle, swirling and flicking until she was writhing beneath him. The hot length of his turgid member pressed against her leg and she spread herself even wider, trying to angle her hips and entice him. If only he would enter her and take her, she knew she could come again with just that contact. Everything about him made her burn.

He worked her mercilessly, trading one breast for the other, then returning to the first until Emily was digging her heels into the mattress and imploring him to give her release.

"Please! Please, please, please…"

"Oh, Angel…" Oliver purred and then licked the valley between her breasts and up her throat to place a peck upon her lips. "You're so lovely when you beg."

He proceeded to lay the underside of his cock between her thighs and rocked back and forth through the slickness gathered there. The pressure was nowhere near what she craved, though it still felt impossibly wonderful. Up and down he stroked her, grinding against her slit and the sensitive pearl at the crux. Her body screamed for her to break free of her bindings and enfold him in her limbs—to wrap his cock in her hands and feed him into her body until he was as mad as she—but she refrained, taking her stress out on the taut cravat holding her immobile.

She growled in warning.

"What, love?" he asked teasingly. His expression remained unchanging as if he were wholly unaware of the way the word struck her.

"I—I cannot take much more," she stammered.

"I think you can. You proved as much earlier."

She sobbed and attempted to rock against him, but he remained maddeningly gentle with his strokes.

"I swear upon all that is holy, I will exact my revenge upon you if you do not immediately take me properly. *Immediately.*"

"D'you promise?"

Oh, heaven above, but he was wicked.

Despite his teasing, Oliver finally positioned himself at her entrance and slid home in one drawn-out thrust that stole her breath. The sting and stretch of the intrusion were agonizingly good. She loved the feel of him inside her, how his large size forced her body to accommodate him and accept him. This was the feeling she'd longed for, and it was better than she'd dreamed. *He* was better.

Oliver was so in tune with her every pant and sigh, her every plea for more pressure, more force. His body claimed hers again and again, thrusting and retreating with just the right rhythm, grinding his pelvis into her sensitized flesh at the perfect angle to pluck at the taut strings of her arousal. Everything he did dragged her higher and higher out of her body, pulled her muscles rigid and made her melt at the same time. She was molten, liquefying from the inside out.

It wasn't long until her orgasm began to ignite within her, spiraling outward from her core and expanding with every stroke of his body on and inside hers. She wanted to sink her nails into the flexing muscles of his back, clutch him to her so they were flush, her curves to his hardness, but she had to settle for tugging at the bindings until the bed began to creak with the force.

"You feel so good—so tight," Oliver growled into her neck before pressing a kiss to her lips. She could taste his desire on his tongue and, when she kissed him back, she met him with equal fervor. "And you taste like heaven."

"Oliver!" She sobbed his name again and again as quietly as possible while he drove into her, stroking her higher until, finally, her every muscle went rigid and her climax struck her with brutal force. She came with a keening cry of relief. He continued his steady, relentless onslaught of her senses as wave after wave of blinding pleasure flowed through her veins.

As the last dregs of her orgasm shuddered through her muscles, Oliver released a gruff string of curses. His hips bucked wildly until, with a guttural groan, he throbbed and swelled as his orgasm filled her. He collapsed on top of her, covering her body with his heavy bulk, but she did not mind in the least. In fact, she was quite pleased to discover that she found a thrill in being at the mercy of his skilled body. Even restrained as she was, not once did she ever experience so much as an inkling of trepidation.

With a quavering sigh, Oliver raised his head and set about unbinding her wrists. He rubbed them with infinite tenderness—even placing kisses upon the light red marks left behind.

"I hope you weren't hurt," he said, staring at her skin with concern.

As soon as she was able, she wrapped an arm around his neck and pulled him down to meet her lips. "Not at all." She cupped his cheek and met his eyes. "I did tell you I trusted you, didn't I? That hasn't changed. I trust you. I always will."

THE NEXT MORNING, Emily and Oliver awoke late in each other's arms. Limbs tangled, sheets warm from the shared heat of flesh on flesh, they savored the peace.

Oliver was keenly aware that it could not last.

Oh, but how he wanted it to when he woke up with Emily in his arms, the sweet curve of her bottom nestled against his pelvis, his cock hard and straining for her even though he'd had her several times the night before.

He was insatiable.

She was insatiable.

And he wanted nothing more than for this safe and comfortable sphere they were in to last forever—where they could take their time learning, exploring, and nurturing whatever this was between them.

Well.

Oliver was fairly positive he knew what he felt.

It was illogical. It was dangerous. It was foolish. It was unbelievable.

But he knew with everything in him that he'd fallen in love with Emily Tailor.

When she looked at him with her drowsy eyes, red smudges on her cheek from a deep sleep, her hair wild and chaotic as it was every morning, he knew only that he wanted this forever. He had no right to, but he did.

He'd spent his life going without many things and he'd survived. Going without Emily, however, felt unfathomable now that she'd wheedled her way beneath his armor. There would be no removing her at this point.

"G'morning," Emily slurred adorably. Never had Oliver smiled as much as he had since he met this woman.

He plucked a heavy lock of hair from her face and held it aloft. "You are quite the sight in the mornings."

She giggled and batted his hand away. "Don't be unkind."

"It is not unkind if it is a fact. Your hair has a life of its own—oy!" Oliver jumped away when she nipped his earlobe.

"Forgive me for being exhausted. I seem to recall that wasn't entirely of my own doing."

"It most certainly wasn't." His mouth tilted once again as he rubbed at his ear.

"Now I know why all the guests at this party make a habit of remaining abed until so late in the day."

Oliver chuckled and kissed her. He couldn't help it.

"And if we don't get out of this bed soon, we never will." He thoroughly enjoyed the way her skin pinkened from her hair to the pert tips of her breasts.

He almost enjoyed, even more, the way her eyes followed him appreciatively as he rolled from the bed and strode fully nude across the room. He could feel her gaze caress every curve of muscle before finally lingering on the heavy evidence of his arousal.

And, if she didn't stop staring at him like that—as if she wanted nothing more than to run her tongue along every inch of him—then the entire day would fall apart.

Begrudgingly, he tugged on his smallclothes and then his breeches before refreshing himself at the washstand and applying tooth powder. It took a tremendous feat of willpower not to turn when he heard Emily rise from the bed and search out her dressing gown.

"What do we do now?" she asked.

It was on the tip of his tongue to tell her that he could very easily spend the next several weeks teaching her all the things they could do, but he stopped just shy.

"We leave."

"Today?"

"We have the key and some correspondence; I have to hope there will be something incriminating in there once it's decoded so this viper's den can be exposed once and for all. We have the list of names. I've extracted what information I can from Hayes. I need to take you back to London before our luck runs out. We've made it this long without a grand incident."

"What was last night, then?" Emily crossed her arms beneath her bosom, pressing them together in (what he hoped) was an unintentionally mouthwatering display.

He cocked his brow at her before pulling his shirt over his head.

She groaned and gestured vaguely in the direction of the bed. "*That* aside. I mean what happened with Hayes."

"That is precisely why you will stay here to oversee the packing. Stay out of sight while I duck downstairs and have a hired carriage summoned to return us to London, pleading business as an excuse. We should be prepared to leave as soon as it arrives and we can be on the road by early afternoon." He tugged on the bellpull, removed the chair propped against the door, and flipped the switch to signal a request for a maid's services before retrieving his navy coat and brace of knives. He winced harshly when he attempted to shrug into them as pain gouged his side. The prior evening's activities had aggravated his injury more than he'd thought.

"Here," Emily said, rushing over and assisting him. "Do you require anything for the pain?"

Oliver shook his head and covered her hand with his. "Only this." He bowed his head to kiss her until she began to melt into him. His heart did its dangerous flip before diving into his stomach.

You love her.

You love her.

You love her.

The words fired in his head like cannon blasts, rattling him to his core. He broke their kiss and, after raking her hair out of the way, he pressed his forehead to hers.

"Emily," he sighed. "Angel."

She reached up and held his forearms, her thumbs stroking his wrists and the pounding pulse beneath. "Hm?"

Oliver closed his eyes, unable to believe what he was about to say, but knowing his life was one of few sureties and fewer comforts. One had to take joy where and when one could. "You'll think me mad for saying this."

"Go on."

He blinked and found her steady gaze. Looking into her eyes, he saw for the first time in his life the possibility of a future. "I have fallen in love with you, Angel."

Emily's lips parted and her breathing quickened, but no words could be exchanged before Annie scratched at the door and let herself into the room.

"Would you like a bath this morning, miss?" the maid asked, not sparing Emily and Oliver's embrace so much as a glance. "Or shall I organize an ensemble for you?"

Oliver pressed his lips once more to Emily's forehead and stepped away from her. "I will leave you two to it, then."

He slipped from the room before Emily could say a word.

Chapter Twenty-Two

OLIVER STILL HADN'T returned to their chamber by the time Ann was done helping her dress and pack their things. The maid had assisted her in donning her raspberry-dyed traveling dress—nicely brushed and stored since their arrival days ago—and, together, they'd organized their belongings in their trunks. Oliver had tucked away the precious papers before he left.

Before he *declared his love for her* and left.

What man did *that?*

Certainly not the men her mother had led her to believe existed in this world.

Of course, Emily would be the first to admit that the information had not necessarily come from the most unbiased of sources. Her mother had first only been a victim of men, and then she'd found her strength and learned to control their vices. However, from what Emily had seen, Oliver was a different breed altogether—someone driven and powerful, tender when needed, and only in private.

And she didn't believe he was a man who used the word "love" with the reckless abandon others did.

Something told her that—with a background and a past like he had—it was quite possible he'd never used it before.

This entire situation was confusing and exciting, maddening and thrilling all at once. Their proximity and forced reliance on one another meant they'd gotten much closer than any other pair might have in this short amount of time. She could admit to herself that she was well and truly infatuated with Oliver, she adored the way he cared for her, she was giddy with his shows of strength and impressive abilities, his physical skills made her entire body hum, and there was something about his personality that spoke to her on the deepest levels. She was jealous when other women touched him…and he'd expressed the same. Now that she considered it, a great many of her inner feelings echoed things Oliver had told her he felt about her.

Did that mean she loved him as well?

She closed her eyes and tried to imagine returning to her old life at Lady Night's, resuming her solitary existence without Oliver's laughter and teasing, his smile and his touch. It wasn't about the excitement and danger of his profession, she was drawn to the things that were inherently *him*.

And that, coupled with how unbearable she feared her life might now be without him, provided Emily with her answer.

She paced at a furious speed while waiting for Oliver's return so she could divulge her realization to him, but the minutes ticked by and still he did not show.

Deciding a distraction was in order, Emily moved toward her valise lying atop their trunks to pull out her book for some reading. Her hand paused, however, when she neared Oliver's case. She hadn't yet seen a carriage arrive, so it seemed there was still some time before footmen retrieved their luggage to load it. She knew she shouldn't, but she couldn't help her hands as they set aside her book, unlocked Oliver's trunk, and dug the coded papers and their key from their hiding spot within the lining. She located a scrap of paper, ink, and a quill in the room's writing desk tucked away in a far corner. She settled in.

The code was a complex collection of runes, dots, lines, and intricate symbols. A direct pattern would have been too simple— there was no easy one-to-one translation from the code to the key. What she thought was the letter *A* in one space was slightly different in another…until she realized that symbols were combined when consecutive vowels were used. After much scribbling and grumbling, she was able to decipher a few scattered words that appeared several times on the first document. And they made no sense. It was not in English, of that she could be certain.

Her spine snapped straight when she remembered these men were from France. French hadn't been a large part of her education, but she could still recognize some words because the modiste her mother hired was French and the woman often sang and muttered to herself in her native language while she worked. She picked one word that came up often. It still was not a word she recognized. She deflated once more until she read it backward. Her fingers began to tremble as she wrote out, *"Roi."* King.

Angleterre.

England.

Prudence.

Caution.

Espionnage.

Espionage—spy…

Not only did the documents employ a complex code, but they were written in backward French.

She needed to find Oliver and tell him of her discovery; she needed him to know his suspicions about Hayes had been correct and they must leave as soon as possible.

Quickly, she bundled up her work and stored it away. Her heart was already pounding in her ears when there was a knock at the door. Two large footmen garbed entirely in black entered and collected their luggage. She'd been so absorbed in her task that she hadn't heard the approach of the hired coach.

Not a moment too soon.

OLIVER WAS STILL berating his foolish honesty with Emily when he discovered Hayes brooding over a newspaper in the conservatory. He'd just requested someone from the staff be sent into the village to hire a coach. Knowing they had at least an hour or two to kill, he figured he'd give Emily some time to pack her things—

and unpack her thoughts and reactions to his declaration—and he'd be remiss if he didn't keep an eye on their host. They needed to make as clean and quick a getaway as possible.

"You have a lot of nerve showing your face here after the stunt you pulled last night." Hayes spoke while glowering at him over the edge of his paper.

Oliver, adopting his nonchalant persona, brushed off Hayes's ire and sauntered further into the room. "You should have locked the door. Leaving a beautiful little bit like that open to be absconded with is a crime." His gut roiled in reaction to speaking of Emily in such a way, but it was necessary. The last thing he needed was for Hayes to catch wind of just how much Emily meant to him.

Hayes carelessly flicked his paper onto the cushion beside him and crossed his arms over his chest. His mien paralleled the gray weather brewing outside. The glass walls and ceilings of the conservatory provided views of only gray skies and tall grasses rippling in the wind. There was a charged undercurrent both in and outside of that room.

They were saved from further conversation by Baron Allyson's arrival. "I thought I heard voices. Good morning, gentlemen. Join me in breaking my fast?"

"Thank you, no," Oliver replied. There was no sense in pointing out the fact that it was mere minutes until noon at that point.

"Are you certain, Holden?" He clapped Oliver on the back. "That was quite the scene last night—right Medieval!" Allyson chortled. "You appear quite content, though I suppose I would too if I managed to coax those sounds from a woman like Miss Tully. I've suspected all week that she's a proper minx in bed."

Oliver forced a wooden smile but said nothing.

Allyson turned to Hayes. "You're not too sore about it, are you, chap?" he asked with a laugh. "All's fair in tupping, eh?" He butchered the quote and jabbed a conspiratory elbow right into Oliver's healing wound and damaged ribs.

Oliver did his best to mask the grunt of pain with a chuckle, but the flicker in Hayes's cold eyes told him he'd failed.

"An injury, Holden?" Hayes asked with a raised brow.

"Still recovering from a fall I took from my horse just before leaving London," Oliver explained smoothly.

"Oh? You never mentioned it."

Oliver met his eyes with an unflinching stare. "I didn't feel it was pertinent information—not when it didn't hamper my attendance...or performance."

"No, indeed!" chortled Allyson, entirely oblivious to the silent exchange playing out in front of him. "I'm certain Miss Tully would attest to that!"

"It appears you have spoken her into existence," drawled Hayes, causing Oliver's heart to choke him.

Sure enough, he turned to the open doorway and there she stood, garbed in her raspberry traveling gown. Oliver barely resisted the urge to curse. Why didn't she ever stay where he told her to?

"Greetings, gentlemen. I hope I am not intruding."

"Not at all," Allyson answered for them all and grinned. "I was about to excuse myself for a meal; would you care to join me, my dear?"

"Thank you, no." Her warm smile appeased Allyson and the baron went on his merry way.

"Did you need something, Miss Tully?" Oliver asked.

"The carriage has arrived and it is being loaded as we speak."

"Very good."

"Carriage?" Hayes asked, one of his brows rising in interest.

"I'm afraid business is calling. I'll be certain to take our conversations under advisement."

Much to Oliver's surprise, a malicious smile curved across Hayes's lips as he looked at Emily. "Did Holden ever tell you how he came to be a part of our little club?"

Oliver tensed.

"No," she replied with a shake of her head before looking up at Oliver. "He didn't." She was so open and trusting; he couldn't meet her gaze. He knew Hayes would read any apology he attempted to silently convey to her—that the softness he would find would instantly betray just how much Oliver cared for Emily.

Hayes's smile turned wicked. "Holden is quite the performer. He serviced two women simultaneously in front of our group. The man has no qualms or inhibitions."

"It would seem not," Emily responded evenly.

Oliver felt disgusted and ashamed, but, still, he could find no words. He wanted to tell Emily that he'd had no choice, that earning Hayes's trust demanded full submission to his depraved ways and a public performance was not only a demonstration of this, but also a way for him to obtain damning information about his targets. Now, knowing what he did, Oliver was certain the intent was to hold it above their heads as a way to keep them in line if their commitment to Hayes's cause began to falter.

The task was different for everyone—specifically designed to offer the greatest level of discomfort as a way to weed out the weak from his ranks. As debauched Marcus Holden, Oliver had very little leverage for Hayes to take advantage of, so his womanizing, skilled lover persona was created and then taken full advantage of. He believed Hayes anticipated taking Holden's actions public anonymously and submitting the lurid details to the board of his family's shipping company to have him ousted.

Of course, in reality, there was no shipping company and Oliver had no family to embarrass. What he'd done, he'd done out of duty; shoving down his distaste and raging resentment, he'd completed the task with the efficiency of any other mission to which he'd been assigned. And it had worked. He'd gained Hayes's trust and earned an invitation to this house party as a result.

He wanted to say all of this to Emily—to reassure her that there had been no emotions or true desire involved. He needed to tell her that everything they had shared together was entirely different from anything else he'd experienced in his life.

He ached to remind her that he loved her, and only her.

"That was until he brought you," Hayes drawled. "He has been uncommonly protective of you, Miss Tully; he forgot how to share."

"You say that as if I am some object to be passed around." Oliver could practically see the frost falling from her words. Hayes didn't refute her comment. If he was taken aback by the difference in her personality that morning, it did not show. The coy, acquiescent miss had been replaced by this regal lady, and Oliver loved her all the more for her strength and bravery.

Hayes's eyes shifted between Oliver and Emily, then back again. "Care to share a brandy before you leave, Holden? Miss Tully?"

"Thank you, no," Emily replied for the both of them. "The carriage is waiting."

"I really must insist," Hayes said gravely, standing and straightening his coat. "The bottle you brought is quite fine. Come."

He gestured for them to walk ahead and Emily glanced at Oliver for guidance. There was nothing to be done at that moment, but he silently vowed to find a way out of this for her. He tilted his head to urge her forward and slipped her arm through his.

Oliver's mind raced as their trio headed up the hallway. He was uncertain whether Hayes was armed, so bolting was not a viable option—especially not when the nearest exit was down a long, straight corridor. He covered her cold hand with his and she squeezed his arm in silent understanding of his reassurance. It was all he could do to will his heart to slow so his thoughts came at a more manageable pace. Preserving his own well-being was one thing, concerning himself with the life of the woman he loved was entirely different. It escalated the stakes to a height he'd never before experienced.

He needed a distraction. Even if both of them were unable to slip away, he could take solace in giving Emily enough time to escape in the prepared carriage. She'd already said their luggage had been loaded and awaited only their boarding to be off. He was confident in his ability to stay alive if he could only have Emily safely away from this den of debauchery and danger.

The answer came in the form of egg-and-sausage-scented air wafting from the breakfast room.

As expected, Allyson's voice was present; it was also accompanied in conversation by that of Frye and Satterly as the men shared the meal. Oliver halted their progress in front of the open doorway, ignoring the barely veiled hostility in Hayes's eyes as he did so.

"Gentlemen," he said by way of greeting. The men stood when they noticed Emily on his arm. "I am sorry to say that Miss Tully and I will be off shortly."

"So soon?" Satterly almost sounded aghast—as if he couldn't fathom why anyone would wish to leave such an event any earlier than necessary.

"Unfortunately, yes." Oliver chanced a glance at Emily, growing proud at the pleasant smile she'd pasted on her face. "Duty calls and I should return Miss Tully to her establishment before she's missed overmuch. I'd hate to have to pay additional fees for keeping her past our arrangement." Allyson chortled at Oliver's salacious wink.

"Sorry to see you go, chap," said Frye, who stepped around the table and held his hand out to Oliver for a hearty shake. "And you, Miss Tully. It was a pleasure." He kissed the back of her hand.

Oliver took his opportunity. "I told Hayes of our earlier conversation, Frye. The one regarding the unfair allocation of royal contracts to weapons manufacturers. Our gracious host had quite the interesting opinions." He'd been cornered by the man following the prior day's luncheon and filed the information away for later use. Now was the perfect time.

"Did he?" Frye's thin brows rose and he turned his attention to Hayes. Oliver didn't miss the way his lips thinned; Frye, however, was entirely oblivious and immediately launched into a lengthy oration on the topic.

Knowing they had but a minute or two before Hayes was able to extricate himself, he guided Emily back two steps so they were just outside of the doorway. Without removing his eyes from Hayes, he inclined his head and whispered out of the corner of his mouth.

"Do you remember what I said when you agreed to accompany me on this mission?" He saw her barely perceptible nod out of the corner of his eye. "You run when I say run. Now is that time. Go to London. When it is safe, bring everything to Scotland Yard. Find the furthest clerk in the main office and request the file on Windsor, 1791."

"What does that—"

"Windsor. 1791. Understand?" She caught her full lips between her teeth and nodded once. "A man named Ramsay will meet you. Give what you have to him and no one else—not even if they demand to see them." Oliver finally turned to look at her and hoped he was capable of conveying in his eyes everything he felt for her, but knew it was impossible. There weren't words and looks enough to describe the way she'd seeped into his soul and filled the cracks. He wasted precious seconds memorizing her features, the curve of her cheek, the bow of her lips, the color of her eyes. "I know it goes against who you are to leave me, but you must. I cannot do my job unless I know you are safe." He paused and took a breath. "Run," he whispered. "Do not turn around. Do not stop. Do not come back for me."

Her lips parted, but Oliver knew time was running out. To argue about it now would ruin the only chance he had of getting her out of there safely. He released her arm and jerked his chin.

He thanked a God who'd long ago forsaken him when she did as she was told and moved down the hall toward the foyer as quickly as she could without raising an alarm. He didn't breathe until he saw the flash of sunlight down the corridor as she disappeared.

"I'm sure we will discuss this more later, Frye," Hayes said loudly, finally fed up with the man's diatribe. "Holden will be leaving and I'd like to chat with him one last time before he and Miss Tully take their leave." Hayes turned on his heel and immediately registered the void beside Oliver. "Where has Miss Tully gone?"

"You know ladies," Oliver said as nonchalantly as possible, praying Hayes wouldn't hear the carriage pulling away. "She stepped away for a private matter, but I expect she will join us in your study presently."

OLIVER SAT ACROSS the desk from Hayes. Though he affected a relaxed posture, every one of his nerves hummed with awareness and anticipation. Both men eyed the glasses of brandy set between them, though neither partook.

There was a light knock at the door. Oliver refused to turn away from Hayes even as he looked to see who required his attention.

"Well?"

"No sign, sir."

"The carriage?"

"Gone, sir."

Hayes waved an irritated hand to dismiss the servant and narrowed his gaze on Oliver. They eyed one another in steely silence until Hayes finally deigned to speak first—in the fluent, perfect French of a native speaker.

"I must commend you—not only for infiltrating my party but for surviving that fall in Covent Garden. My men were positive you had dropped to your death."

Oliver smiled coldly and replied in French as well. *"Perhaps they should learn to make sure their victims are dead. We English are remarkably hardy."*

Hayes emitted a bark of laughter before lifting his drink in a salute and tossing it back. *"You did well hiding your injury for this long...however, it was not the only thing that gave you away."* Hayes paused and fished something small from an inner pocket of his coat, dropping it beside Oliver's drink with a small click. The bead was in the shape of a water droplet, shining clear in one direction and throwing a rainbow of light if one's head was tilted the other way. And Oliver recognized it.

"Miss Tully was quite beautiful in that gown, was she not? Good enough to eat." Hayes licked the corner of his lips in a blatantly lecherous gesture; Oliver's fist clenched at his thigh despite his best efforts to prevent it. *"I found it in my armoire, if you can believe it. I thought at first that it may have stuck to my clothing and fallen there when I opened it after you so rudely absconded with her from my chamber. But then...you revealed that you suffered a recent injury to your side—the same side where my men indicated they'd stabbed a spy not three weeks prior. And now, Miss Tully is gone. A coincidence? I think not."*

Oliver experienced a thrill of relief to learn that Emily hadn't been located—that she'd successfully fled the estate and was on her way back to London.

"Did you think yourself so cunning that you could infiltrate my party unnoticed?" Hayes asked him with bone-chilling coldness.

Oliver weighed his options and decided the truth would serve him best in that situation. *"I believe it worked fairly well until today."*

Hayes shot him a murderous glare. *"A pity you couldn't heal more quickly."*

"I am but a man at the mercy of nature."

"Nature seems to have betrayed you, my friend."

Oliver settled for a disarming smile, mentally calculating where his weapons were on his person. Several had been tucked away in his trunk, but he still wore his brace and sheaths beneath his coat and one knife strapped to his calf. This gave him five weapons at his disposal.

"I must say, I am impressed you were able to track me down. The General is not a man who is easily located."

Oliver's blood ran cold. The General. *Le Général.* This man, John Hayes— Louis —was the very one Ramsay had been attempting to locate for the better part of a year. Ruthless. Cold. Cunning. He had a following of loyal men and women who would sacrifice their lives for whatever cause he deemed worthy. And Oliver had unwittingly located him.

"Surely you know now what must be done," Hayes said with mock remorse.

"But of course."

He leaned toward Oliver until he could smell the brandy on his breath. *"And after I finish with you, I will hunt down that pretty blond bitch and fuck her until she begs me for a lead ball between her eyes."*

"There is just one problem with your plan," Oliver said with impressive calm though his pulse roared in his ears. He picked up his glass and sipped the brandy, allowing it to sear his tongue and throat, letting the burn of it spur on his rage.

"And what is that?" Hayes's eyes were so dark they were nearly black.

Oliver caught the glimpse of gunmetal reflecting in the window behind Hayes. *"I am not dead yet."*

Oliver whipped his crystal glass at Hayes just as the man raised his pistol above the desktop. He shrieked as it shattered against his face in a spray of crimson shards and brandy droplets.

He dodged to the side and reached beneath his coat for one of his knives just as the crack of a pistol echoed throughout the study.

EMILY'S SENSE OF dread overwhelmed her as the carriage jerked into motion.

What am I doing?

She couldn't leave Oliver.

Her heart was torn between her need to protect him and her desire to keep her promise to him that she'd run and keep herself safe. She'd sworn to deliver the information they'd collected.

She could only watch out the window as the grand house receded from view.

Hot tears coursed down her face and heartbreaking sobs were

ripped from her chest, none of which the driver could hear above the jangle of tack and the crunching of the gravel drive.

Everything about this felt wrong. She couldn't abandon him. She couldn't leave him like this.

Her mind made up, she launched herself at the door, only to find it locked securely.

"No." She cursed. "No, no, no, no, no!" she cried, pounding on the barrier.

She stumbled across the space as the carriage took a turn, but she managed to reach the hatch that led to the driver. She pounded on it again and again with her palm until it finally slid open.

"We must turn back!" she cried, rivulets of tears coursing down her face at that point.

"I thought ye said ta drive 'n' drive fast wi'ou' stoppin'," the driver replied, clearly confused with her about-face.

"I did, but we have to go back for someone. Please!"

"Are ye certain?"

Emily would have nodded, but she paused. Oliver's words played out in her head again and again. He needed her to go. He needed to know she would be safe so he could focus on keeping himself whole and not worry about her. Besides, what could she hope to accomplish?

She had no training. She had no special skills which might be of use to him. If anything, she'd be more of a hindrance than an aid. And she could never live with herself if Oliver was killed protecting her.

"Miss?" the driver asked again above the clatter of tack and crunch of gravel.

She shook her head. "No. Forgive me. Continue to London."

The hatch was closed and Emily instantly deflated into a puddle of skirts. She held her face in her hands and sobbed.

She cried for the man she'd left behind. She cried for the unfairness of their circumstances. She cried out of fear and rage.

Most of all, she cried because Oliver could very well die without knowing that she loved him, too.

Chapter Twenty-Three

HOURS LATER, THE hired carriage rolled to a stop in the street before Lady Night's in Covent Garden. The grueling journey had been made without pause from the country house to this corner of London. The conveyance's sole occupant was numb, kneeling on the floor with her head resting on the cushion of the seat. Her tears had long since stopped, but not for lack of trying; her body had simply run dry.

It took her several moments to realize the motion of the carriage had stopped; another few to realize the door had opened and the driver was speaking to her.

"Miss?"

It took a tremendous feat of strength for Emily to lift her head. Blinking was a struggle. Her eyes ached like sand had been stuffed beneath her lids, but she was eventually able to focus enough to see the wiry, weathered driver's hand extended into the carriage to help her to her feet.

"Did ye fall?"

She shook her head and rather ungracefully hauled herself to her feet. Stepping down to the cobblestones on knees barely strong enough to support her, she was immediately greeted by the familiar stench of the gutters and refuse mixed with wafts of perfume and candle smoke, the grime and grit grating beneath her boot. She could only tilt her head back and look up at the building she'd at once called home and silently considered a tower of isolation. Night had fallen and the business was bursting with life at that point. Every last one of the windows glowed golden, casting halos of light into the misty, dreary darkness of the street.

The driver asked her where she wanted her luggage to be set, but it took him several tries for her to hear him. Even then, Emily could only gesture vaguely to the scrubbed granite steps of her mother's building. The man looked around and, for the first time, seemed to truly register just where he had delivered her.

"Are ye sure, miss? I can take ye somewhere else. The fare is more'n paid fer." She'd tossed the man several gold coins ripped from the inside of her bodice as she'd careened out of the country house and into the carriage.

While she appreciated the sentiment, she had nowhere else to go and not a single notion of where else someone might accept her…nor did she feel she had the capacity to complete such a task then.

"Yes, I am certain. Thank you."

She stood stock still as the trunks were unstrapped and, one by one, deposited on the steps. She was forced to face the fact that, rather than feeling as if she'd come home, Emily dreaded her return. The little kernel of hope she'd harbored that she would not have to do so alone had been well and truly smothered.

One of Lady Night's burly guards exited the building and the music from inside swelled and danced out the door and down the steps to greet her. Dressed all in black and nearly a head taller than most men and broad as a blacksmith, Felix Dawson possessed the perfect burly frame and imposing demeanor to frighten off even the most seasoned of troublemakers from their establishment. Only Emily and Lady Night's employees knew of Dawson's unerringly kind disposition masked beneath his imposing glower.

"Miss Tailor," he greeted her with brows arched in relieved surprise. "I had to see for myself when one of the girls said they saw you standing out here on the walk."

She was too exhausted, too deflated to offer him more than a nod of her head. Seeing a friendly, familiar face helped, but Emily's spirits were too low to be resurrected at that point.

"Wha' 'bout this trunk, miss?" the driver asked, interrupting Emily's morose musings once more. He gestured to Oliver's slightly battered plain black trunk, so different from her brown leather ones that it was clear it did not belong to the set. She could only stare dumbly for several moments until she finally waved a hand, hoping he'd accept it as some sort of answer. Vaguely, she heard Dawson saying he'd take over as Emily dashed up the stairs and in through Lady Night's front door.

She sped through the foyer, past open doors to receiving rooms and parlors swathed in rich jewel tones and dim candlelight, ignoring the few girls milling about who noticed her and exclaimed her name. Emily hurried by and slipped through a concealed doorway to the back staircase, climbing them with such haste that her chest began to burn beneath her stays.

Bursting through the door, she ignored Mary's startled greeting as she crossed the main room and slammed her bedchamber door closed behind her. She leaned her back against the barrier and slid to the floor in a heap of wrinkled raspberry skirts, covering her face and sobbing into her palms.

How could she have abandoned Oliver?

What if he was—

No.

She refused to consider his demise, even though it was a very real possibility.

Somehow, her body found the strength to produce more tears. They stung her chapped cheeks as they fell to her skirts, staining them with small, dark circles of her pain. Emily railed against Oliver's blasted sense of duty. He shouldn't have stayed behind. He shouldn't have insisted that she save herself and leave him to his fate. Emily ignored Mary's repeated knocking on the door and inquiries as to her well-being; she could only choke on her tears.

It was only much later that Emily calmed herself enough for

the numbness to set in once again and she could stand to allow Mary to help her undress and bathe. The older woman wisely remained quiet and patient as she did her duties as if sensing that the slightest bit of pressing might cause Emily to shatter all over again. She didn't know what story Lady Night had come up with to explain her absence, but Mary hadn't seemed all that surprised at her return.

Dawson had seen that Emily's trunks were safely delivered to her room, but Emily couldn't bring herself to open them. She opted instead to don an old worn nightshift from her dresser and curl up on her bed, hugging her knees to her chest.

After plaiting Emily's damp hair, Mary moved to begin unpacking her trunks.

"Don't." Her single word was like a door slamming in the silent room. Mary's brow furrowed, but, for once, she didn't argue. The maid nodded, gathered up Emily's traveling clothes, and left.

Emily didn't know if or when she'd be able to face the contents of the trunks, but that night was certainly not the time.

She was still sitting there immobile and barely blinking when her mother arrived.

Lady Night burst into the room with all the subtlety of a warship and swept her daughter into a crushing embrace. The warmth was short-lived, though, as her mother released her and gripped her upper arms in a way that was just shy of painful.

"Now. Tell me. Where 'ave you been? An' no lies."

Emily's lips parted, but she found herself unable to answer— for more reasons than one. What was she supposed to say? That she'd gone to the countryside to assist in an espionage operation? That she was so upset because the man she was now certain she loved had been left behind when she fled for her life?

Seeing the tears twinkling in Emily's eyes, her mother's harsh expression softened slightly. "Wha's 'appened?" she asked gentler than before.

Tears threatened, but Emily managed to rein them in. She

shook her head, at a loss.

"A man?"

She remained silent.

"Ah… The man from the balcony?"

She sat still and quiet, her eyes downcast as she fiddled with the hem of her nightshift like she was a girl all over again. Lady Night nodded.

"I knew it'd 'appen sooner 'r later—a man would come along 'n' appeal to your sexual nature. 'S in your blood."

"He did not seduce me," Emily protested as strongly as her hoarse voice would allow. If anything, it had been the other way around…but her mother didn't need to know that bit.

"Did 'e promise ya pretty fings? A ring for ya finger?" Harshness ebbed into her mother's tone. "I thought I'd raised ya to be smarter 'an that. Men lie. They tell ya what ya want to 'ear for the night 'n' then they disappear the next mornin'." The words pinched Emily like bee stings, but she did not interrupt. "It's precisely why, 'ere, we teach all the women 'n' men that they's in charge. They 'old the cards. They's the ones who's bein' sought out 'n' chased after. They 'old the power. 'Ow does it look that me own daughter runs after a man?"

"It wasn't like that," Emily snapped. "He never made any promises." Her own words startled her into a pause. He hadn't made any promises other than to keep her safe. Was a declaration of love in and of itself a promise? Or wasn't it?

Either way, he'd very likely paid for it all with his life.

Emily fisted her hands in her coverlet before continuing. "Not all men are like the ones you've known. And, yes, you raised me never to need a man or be at the mercy of one…" Her voice broke. "I don't need Oliver, but, God, I want him. I never thought to feel that way about anyone, but I do. And he is a *good* man."

"Oh?" her mother said with a sniff. "And where is this 'good man'—this paragon of masculinity and chivalry?"

To this inquiry, Emily was at a loss. It took her time to craft a response that both did him justice and did not betray his confidence.

"Something has happened. I cannot explain it, but something bad has taken place. I know he would be with me otherwise." And she did. Emily felt in her soul that Oliver was not a man who would abandon her were it not for extenuating circumstances. The explanation she offered her mother was admittedly pathetic, but, short of spilling the entire story, Emily didn't know how she would even begin to go about explaining why she knew this was no ordinary parting of lovers.

"Well," sniffed Lady Night. "If I raised ya so well, then ya should know better 'an to allow anything to stop ya from gettin' what ya desire."

With that, her mother stood, shook out her scarlet-red skirts with their glittering jet beads, and turned on her heel to return to her business. Lady Night was not known for her comforting words or gentle disposition, but there was a reason she was widely touted as the most caring of employers and vicious protectors of those beneath her roof. As such, Emily's childhood had been filled with bolstering words instead of kisses, demands for strength when tears threatened, and instructed to use her brain when her whims fought for supremacy. It had not been the perfect childhood—Lady Night hadn't been the perfect mother— but it had been right for Emily because it made her the woman she'd become.

Feminine laughter tinkled up from the floor below hers, mingling with the words echoing in her skull. Frustration blossomed in her breast, spreading like a drop of blood on fabric. She was helpless. She couldn't very well go back to the manor and see for herself what had happened to Oliver. Would she just show up on the doorstep, knock, and ask Hayes if he'd killed the man he'd once known as Marcus Holden?

She couldn't drop by Scotland Yard at that time of night—it wasn't safe to traverse the streets and she thought it would be more likely that she'd run into someone helpful during the daytime hours. She'd go at first light.

Unfortunately for her, morning was still many hours away and she didn't feel capable of any restful sleep.

Her eyes snagged on Oliver's black trunk in the corner of the room. Taking a deep breath and strengthening her resolve, Emily unfastened the latch. Opening the lid, she was instantly assailed by Oliver's familiar scent. Her body threatened to be overcome by her emotions, but she rallied and fished out the stack of papers from where she'd hidden them. Carrying them to her desk, she lit a few more candles and spread her work out before her.

THE NEXT DAY, Emily waited in the bustle of Scotland Yard's main entryway. The number of men darting back and forth made her head spin; the sheer chaos of it all was overwhelming. She did her best to stand off to the side, yet she was still nearly run over on several occasions.

She'd donned her most respectable powder-blue gown and matching spencer embroidered with forget-me-nots. Still, the curious looks every other man shot her made her supremely self-conscious.

She had arrived early that morning and followed Oliver's instructions to the letter, seeking out the proper man at the proper desk, providing him with the requisite phrase, and then she'd been left alone for what felt like an hour. Emily, however, refused to be denied or give in to her nerves and discomfort. She'd promised Oliver she would not leave without completing her task and she would do just that.

She'd just been considering going back up to the man when he was approached by another attractive young man garbed in the darkest black and brightest white, from the tips of his polished boots to the crisp lines of his cravat. He was unnervingly still, like the most realistic statue she'd ever seen. He was the only point of stillness in the otherwise loud and chaotic building.

"Miss Tailor." His tone was flat and even, unnervingly clear—as if it sliced through the din like a rapier.

She tightened her hold on the bound packet of papers she'd carefully prepared and carried through London. It felt wrong to hand over what she and Oliver had worked so hard to obtain, but she knew it was what Oliver needed her to do.

"Mr. Ramsay?" His reply was only a raised brow in acknowledgment. "I was told to bring you this." She held out the packet and prayed she wasn't making a grave mistake.

"Thank you," he said, inclining his head and accepting the package…and then he simply turned to leave.

"What about…?" Her eyes darted back and forth, unsure how to inquire after Oliver's well-being without stating his name.

The man's mouth twitched. "Black?" She couldn't deny the leap of her heart in hearing his name. "He chose to act on his own. Anything he did and any resulting consequences are none of my concern." Then, he pivoted on his heel and slipped through the crowd like a specter, ignoring every one of her calls after him.

Just as she was about to follow him, a hand clasped her upper arm.

"You have a pleasant day, miss." The man's voice was light enough, but his hold on her brooked no argument. Before she could get a word out, Emily found herself on the street outside of Scotland Yard, alone, feeling almost more lost than when she'd arrived there.

THE NEXT COUPLE of weeks were just as maddening. Emily doggedly returned to Scotland Yard several times, but each man she spoke to denied Ramsay's existence. She'd harassed the clerk countless times, but he stated again and again that he had no idea what she was talking about when she provided him with the same passcode that had worked so well the first time. She'd been escorted from the premises several times, tears of frustration burning her eyes as day after day she was made to feel mad. The sleepless nights and ensuing nightmares nearly made her believe she'd dreamed up the encounter.

She would have made inquiries elsewhere, but the last thing

she wanted to do was bandy Oliver's name about town, not knowing who was friend or foe. Besides, he'd also mentioned to her that he used several aliases—there was no telling who he might be known as. And, if he'd somehow escaped Hayes (and Emily refused to believe otherwise, despite the prolonged silence), then he could be using any of them. It could prove as dangerous as it might be fruitless.

Still…she had to find out what had happened to Oliver. She'd never forgive herself if she went the rest of her life knowing she hadn't done everything within her limited power to discover the truth of his fate.

There had to be someone who knew something…

Emily arrived back at her flat following a particularly frustrating day where she'd been flat-out denied entry into Scotland Yard by an oversized brute who'd threatened to toss her into the Thames if she kicked at his shins one more time. She chucked her reticule onto her bed with a snarl of helpless rage.

Then, her eyes snagged on the small pastoral painting hung above her desk. Concealed behind it, she'd affixed the copies she'd made of the key and documents from Hayes's estate. She'd spent many nights poring over them when sleep evaded her. She tuned out the sounds of revelry and ecstasy bubbling up from the floors beneath her and stared at those papers until she nearly had them memorized.

Discarding her spencer, she took down the painting and carefully peeled away the backing she resealed with a daub of paste each time she returned it to the wall. As she had so many times before, Emily laid the documents out before her and stared at them for what felt like the hundredth time. There was nothing she did not know about them after painstakingly deciphering them and translating them through carefully peppered questions to those few acquaintances of hers who knew French and her own abilities to interpret context. They contained some allusions to meetings, shipments, and a few names—none she knew.

Then, with all of the documents laid out before her, a moment of recognition struck. Her eyes caught on the word, "duke." This duke was never named directly, but it was clear to even her that he was being viewed as a possible asset—much like Allyson, Frye, and Satterly.

Though she'd finally allowed Mary to unpack her trunks and return the borrowed clothing to her mother's wardrobe, Oliver's black trunk remained untouched in the corner. She hesitated but knew what she needed to do.

She sat on her heels, took a deep breath, and lifted the lid. His scent struck her like a punch to her stomach all over again, and that was precisely why she'd avoided delving into it. Now, however, she was on a mission. Setting aside a few sheathed knives she uncovered, along with a small leather pouch filled with organized silver picks and hooks, she rifled through pockets and seams, eventually locating the particular scrap of parchment she'd been looking for.

Emily had been so concerned with the coded messages that she'd forgotten about this list entirely. One option was to return to Scotland Yard and try to bribe Ramsay out of hiding with additional information, but she didn't think it was wise to taunt an elite spymaster (no matter how satisfying it might be). The other was to strike out on her own and contact the only duke listed.

The only duke Oliver had mentioned.

She had to see the Duke of Morton.

Chapter Twenty-Four

S TERLING ST. JOHN, Duke of Morton, was reading a report from his steward in his study when his butler rapped upon the door.

"Enter." Maxwell's impeccably professional mien was a little less perfect than usual, immediately setting Sterling on alert. "What is it?"

"A visitor, Your Grace."

"What is the matter?"

"I beg your pardon, Your Grace. I told the woman that you were indisposed, but she insisted you would wish to hear what she has to say. That it is a matter of great importance. She has no calling card." The last was added with such gravity that it clearly offended Maxwell's sensibilities.

"And you found yourself incapable of turning this woman away?"

"I assure you, I did tell her to quit the premises."

"And?"

The poor man looked supremely uncomfortable. "When I indicated that she would be forcibly removed, she said she'd stand across the street until you saw fit to admit her."

This was intriguing.

"Show her in, Maxwell. I shall deal with whatever it is she feels is so vitally important."

Sterling stood as the objectively pretty young woman with white-gold hair was shown into his study.

EMILY WAS TAKEN aback by the obvious wealth and opulence of the Mayfair Townhouse; the regal bearing and handsomeness of its lord and master. It had taken the better part of half an hour, but she'd finally managed to gain admittance to the residence of the Duke of Morton. Now, one of the most powerful peers in England was staring at her with hawk-like hazel eyes set in a classically handsome face. Tall, well-dressed, and imposing on several levels, he watched her with such keen intelligence that she felt stripped down past her skin to the soul beneath. So unnerved was she that she momentarily forgot herself before dipping into a low and deferential curtsy.

"Thank you for seeing me, my lord."

He cocked an imperious brow at her. "One should typically address a duke as, 'Your Grace.'" The words were not unkind, but they cut her nonetheless—she felt as if her ignorance and inexperience had been exposed in less than five seconds of meeting the man.

Her face burned and she stammered an apology while dipping into an even lower curtsy.

"And you are?" he asked.

"I am Miss Emily Tailor…a friend of one Mr. Oliver Black."

"Am I supposed to recognize that name?" The flat expression on the duke's handsome face and his bored inflection made Emily feel foolish…until she remembered that the Duke of Morton had likely also been a spy and, as such, was a liar of more than passable skill. She should have expected him to deny knowing Oliver—the duke had no idea who she was or what she wanted.

Emily realized she had to make him trust her enough to help her before he kicked her out on her impertinent rear. Or worse.

She hastily produced from her reticule a copy of the list of names Oliver had found in Hayes's desk, along with one of the deciphered and translated letters mentioning a duke, whom she strongly suspected of being the man before her.

"These came into Mr. Black's possession and I was entrusted with their care. I have worked these last several weeks to decode and translate them, and I believe they refer to you, Your Grace." She watched in tense silence as his eyes skimmed the documents.

"You are responsible for the translation?" he asked with just a touch of curiosity.

"I am."

"Where, precisely, did these documents come from?"

Taking a deep breath, Emily briefly explained the strange sequence of events, praying she'd been correct in believing the Duke of Morton was a friend of Oliver's. She detailed his injury and how she'd cared for him; she described how he'd convinced her to accompany him on his mission and their experiences with Hayes, the discoveries they'd made, and how, finally, she'd been forced to flee as Oliver was left in a dire situation.

Throughout it all, the duke remained pensive and silent. As he reread the documents yet again, she mentioned to him that Oliver had indicated to her that not all rumors about the duke's past were true.

"I have reason to believe that you are not the same man who filled the tabloids for all those years."

Those words captured his attention and his head whipped up.

"Please," Emily begged, clasping her hands in front of her to still their trembling. "I must know what happened to Oliver. I have to find him. I cannot rest until I know…" Her voice cracked on the last word and it trailed off between them.

Morton provided no more answer than inclining his head, tucking the papers into a drawer of his desk, and gently guiding her to the door.

As she stood out on the street once more, Emily closed her eyes and tilted her head back, silently praying that her judgment hadn't been poor.

If this didn't work, she didn't know where else to go.

OLIVER STARED UNSEEINGLY out of the foggy leaded window of his rented flat on the top floor of a small building near the Thames. It was a neighborhood he could disappear into. A man with his head bent against the rain, his rough clothing soiled from work, and the scruff of a beard cloaking his jaw would no more create a stir than a robbery or assault.

He'd spent several weeks moving from place to place to prevent being tracked, living quietly and beneath Ramsay's notice. He was lying low until he was certain he would not be hanged for going against orders, but he was beginning to itch from the constraints.

He'd personally deposited Hayes—Louis—on Scotland Yard's doorstep, along with the boxes of evidence he'd carted from the countryside. *Le Général* was a bit worse for the wear, but he'd survive.

Whether he'd survive Ramsay's interrogation was another story entirely.

Oliver couldn't find it within him to care whether the man suffered. As far as he was concerned, the world would be a better place without that cruel, violent, instigator around to harm others. He deserved whatever pain he endured.

After Emily's flight from the estate, Oliver had been free to focus on his opponent. The man was quick with a pistol, but Oliver was quicker with a knife.

He closed his eyes, remembering the confrontation, hearing the crack of glass, smelling the acrid scent of gunpowder, the enraged screams.

A knock at his door snapped Oliver from his reverie; another knock followed in quick succession. He unsheathed the knife he'd set aside on the rough-hewn table behind him and crept with feline silence to the door. A third knock sounded.

Standing to the side, he opened the door. He wasn't a man easily surprised, but finding Sterling standing in the hallway was not something he'd expected in the least.

"Put it away, Black," said the duke, brushing past him in a whirl of black woolen greatcoat before surveying the sparse living quarters. "So this is where you've been hiding out?"

"Obviously, not well enough." Oliver sheathed his blade. He

and Sterling had always had a unique friendship; an odd mixture of trust born of necessity and camaraderie influenced by circumstances. They could vacillate between formal deference and brotherly ribbing. After nearly a decade spent with only each other for support while working in the field, they'd formed quite the bond. To have Sterling on his doorstep now must mean something dire, indeed.

"You are too trusting."

Oliver scoffed. "You're the first one to describe me as such."

"I know all your safe locations."

"You know *some* of them," Oliver conceded. He owned or rented several properties of varying locations and descriptions; he'd also taken great pains to make sure his superiors were unaware he kept them. He could afford to do so because he'd always been accustomed to living frugally, and all fineries during his missions were funded and supplied by the government when he was assigned a cover story and identity.

"This is only the second one I checked."

Lucky guess, Oliver groused to himself.

"Then to what do I owe this visit?" He gestured to the other chair and Sterling seated himself.

"You have a very persistent pursuer."

Oliver's heart tripped…and then stopped altogether as Sterling began to detail Emily's visit to Morton House following her frustrating trip to Scotland Yard. His chest swelled with pride over the fact that she'd not only followed his instructions, but she'd brilliantly translated the documents and even tracked Sterling down.

He'd longed for any word of her, a single glimpse to tide him over, but he didn't dare lead any danger to her doorstep. Even if he received word that Ramsay was not out for him and had accepted completion of the mission as recompense for disobeying direct orders, he was unsure if he would seek her out. There would always be an element of danger for anyone involved with him. Despite the way he felt about her, his rational side argued that it would be better for her if she never saw him again.

"She's remarkably brave and intelligent to have located me and linked my name to both you and this anti-monarchical plot." Sterling's eyes met his with boring intensity. "What happened?"

Oliver briefly explained how he'd successfully fought Hayes and completed his mission.

"I'd have given anything to see Ramsay's face when he saw the present you left him," Sterling chuffed. "I did some poking and it does seem like your intelligence was able to accomplish the intended outcome." He leaned back in his chair, stretching his long legs out before him. "Twenty-three arrests in all—French spies; English dissenters actively funneling weapons, goods, and money in and out of the country; even a few peers were charged, though you and I both know they likely won't see the inside of a courtroom."

"Such are the privileges of your class," Oliver quipped and received a raised brow in response.

"Ramsay was furious, of course, but it's difficult to argue with tangible results. Give him another few days and I suspect he'll be ready to welcome you back into the fold. You know how his ego is."

Oliver scratched his beard thoughtfully. He trusted every word of what Sterling told him, but he didn't care for the little hopeful voice in the back of his head screaming that he could very soon see Emily again.

If he wanted to.

Of course, he bloody well wanted to.

"Now…the real question is why are you hiding out when you have a woman like Miss Tailor so concerned for you?" The question dropped like a leaden weight between them. "She thinks you may be dead."

"She is a distraction," Oliver replied flatly.

Sterling, on the other hand, smiled knowingly. "It is terrifying, isn't it?"

"What is?" Oliver asked though he had a sinking feeling he

knew what his old friend would say.

"When someone comes to mean so much that you can think only of them."

Oliver remained pensively silent before stating, "I'm not a good man. And I do not deserve her."

"Do we ever deserve them?" Sterling asked with a self-deprecating laugh. "If Alaina can forgive me for abandoning her for eight years, your determined woman can overlook your imperfections. She already seems to have done so."

"Well, don't you wax poetic?" Sterling scoffed in response and Oliver added, "You've gone soft."

"Perhaps a little softness is preferable to a lifetime of loneliness. Give it a try; you might discover you quite like it."

AFTER STERLING LEFT his flat, Oliver quit his rooms to prowl the streets. A part of him ached for Sterling's words to be true, and he'd give anything to believe the things Emily had told him…but he'd spent so long believing he wasn't enough.

He hadn't been enough for his mother to live.

He hadn't been enough for his father to love.

But, God, did he want to feel the way he felt when Emily smiled at him. For once in his life, he felt full.

He felt whole.

He felt at home.

Oliver found himself in Covent Garden as if his feet had carried him there of their own volition. He was drawn to Emily's side as if an invisible string reeled him into her orbit, whether he wanted it or not.

He sized up the street and its buildings and alleyways, cringing a little when he saw the building from which he'd fallen that rainy night several weeks prior.

The building was beside Emily's flat on the top floor of Lady Night's.

He wagered it would be safe for two reasons: Anyone with half a brain wouldn't reuse a site where they'd already been discovered and had an altercation, and the cell had been dismantled per Sterling's information.

He slipped inside without incident and climbed the stairs.

Chapter Twenty-Five

OLIVER WAS PERCHED on the rooftop of the Covent Garden building, perfectly disguised with his dark clothes as he leaned up against a crumbling brick chimney. It was not the first time he'd come to this location to watch.

It had been a week since his visit from Sterling and his friend's words still rattled through his mind like a street gambler's dice. Every night since then, he'd watched Emily's balcony and her window, staring intently until he caught a glimpse of her. Safe.

It was remarkable what even a flash of her hair or snippet of movement did to him. He experienced a fluttering of peace. Even at this distance, she quieted his soul. Each beat of his heart sang persistently, *I love you...I love you...I love you...*, confirming to Oliver that she would be a part of him whether he liked it or not. She'd wound her way past his defenses and seated herself inside, as much a part of him as his blood and his breath. He ached to be nearer to her, longed to touch her and hold her, and desperately needed to hear her voice again, but he resisted. He made do with these little bits of Emily he could collect, and he filed them away for safekeeping.

That particular night, a light rain had begun to fall. It was so reminiscent of the night that he'd met Emily that a chill traipsed down his spine as he stood in his usual place. Oliver pulled his black woolen cap over his ears and propped his collar against the wetness. He scanned the glowing windows, but Emily's bedchamber, with its well-placed balcony, was dark. The similar dimness of the parlor window he could glimpse just beyond the balcony told him she was not there either.

It was far too early an hour for her to sleep, that much he knew. Not for the first time, he judged the distance from the flat roof upon which he stood to Emily's balcony and considered that it was only by the grace of some deity that he hadn't missed or broken both his legs. Heaven had smiled upon him, indeed.

Not only had he survived, but he'd all but landed in Emily's arms…his angel.

A flicker of color in the street below caught his eye and he crossed the roof to obtain an unobstructed view. Through the glistening rain, he watched as a woman in sodden green skirts and matching spencer trudged up the street. She held no umbrella with which to shield her head, offering him an unimpeded view of her movements.

She walked with a purpose and had a rhythm to her steps that Oliver had committed to memory.

EMILY CURSED HER rushing. It had looked like rain all day, but she'd been so overcome with nervous excitement that she hadn't wanted to waste time running back up to her flat to bring her umbrella along. She'd been spared poor weather on her journey to Morton House in Mayfair in a hired hack.

The duke's note had arrived by courier shortly before Lady Night's opened for the evening and she'd been glad that a liveried servant hadn't been sent—that would have been much more difficult to explain to her mother. She had, however, been silently impressed by the duke's ability to locate her without any difficulty, which only solidified her belief that he was of the same ilk as Oliver. The brief missive indicated that he had news for her and invited her to call at her earliest convenience. Unable to sit still until the next day, she'd immediately readied herself, asked Dawson to hail a hackney for her, and bounded up the duke's front steps just at the tail-end of acceptable calling hours.

If the duke had been annoyed by the immediacy of her arrival following his note, he made no indication. He took the time to introduce her to his wife—a well-dressed, elegant, beautiful blond woman with an irreverent sense of humor. The duchess greeted her without any hint of derision or condescension for Emily's social status. Though she'd been practically crawling out of her skin with anticipation for news of Oliver, she remembered to curtsy deeply and "Your Grace" whenever appropriate.

She was offered tea and other refreshments but found that she could take it no longer. She looked at the duke and said, "I sincerely appreciate your assistance and hospitality, Your Grace, but I have been waiting weeks for this moment and I fear I shall burst if I wait any longer."

"Of course, Miss Tailor," the duke said with unexpected kindness. "Our mutual friend is alive and well."

Emily nearly collapsed with relief, barely stifling a sob with the back of her hand. Lady Morton took her elbow and helped her to sit, offering her something to drink. Emily declined with a trembling voice and asked, "Where is he? May I see him?"

The duke's face shuttered instantly. "That is a bit more difficult." Emily's stomach dropped out. "He is a man whose life has long been dictated by his profession. He must take stock of where he stands…as well as where he sees his future."

"So…you will not tell me where I might find him." It was more of a statement than a question.

"I cannot betray him; it must be his decision." There was a drawn-out pause. "My apologies. I know this is not the answer you wished for."

"Are you saying he does not wish to see me?" The words were nearly unbearable to speak, but Emily commended her strength.

There was a hesitation before the duke spoke again: "Yes and no."

"What on earth does that mean?" Emily demanded with a frown, momentarily forgetting just to whom she spoke.

"His lifestyle does not permit him the luxury of attachments."

Emily did not miss his meaningful glance at his wife beside her. "Just know that what he does, he does with you in mind."

Fiery tears threatened and Emily knew she had to leave quickly or else she would become a blubbering heap in the duke's parlor. She thanked them both and excused herself as quickly as possible.

She'd been attempting to button her spencer for the third time when Lady Morton caught up to her and stopped her with a gentle touch on her arm. She smiled warmly and said, "These men"—she gestured over her shoulder to indicate her husband who remained in the parlor she'd vacated—"have spent so long thinking about duty and self-preservation that it's often at the expense of their happiness. They're stubborn and pig-headed, but they will do absolutely everything in their power to protect the ones they love." She gave Emily's arm a friendly squeeze. "Give him time. The good men usually come to their senses eventually—if they know what is good for them."

Emily couldn't help but crack a hint of a smile at that. She could see herself being friends with this woman. They came from worlds on opposite ends of the social spectrum, yet here was proof that a good heart and an open mind could transcend all barriers.

Lady Morton then offered her the use of their carriage, but Emily declined and opted to take a hired hack back to Covent Garden. Arriving in a splendid carriage would cause even more of an uproar than a liveried servant carrying a letter for her.

She'd had every intention of taking the time to compose herself and process the news she'd been given, but her nerves eventually ran out and she could no longer take the confinement. Emily leaped from the hack, tossing the jarvy her fare, and began the walk home. She was still a few blocks from Lady Night's, but she needed space. She needed air.

As her furious feet ate up the distance, she'd silently damned Oliver's sense of duty, his misplaced sense of worth. How dare he tell her he loved her and then disappear?

The blasted idiot.

The sky split open when she was only two blocks from her building.

"Really?" Emily snarled at the sky. She tucked her reticule against her side and wrapped her arms around herself as she trudged on.

The pattering of rain and water sloshing through the gutters drowned out the sound of footsteps behind her.

Her slipper—impractical and not made for walking far in the streets, let alone during a rain shower—skidded across a slick cobblestone. She was forced to clutch one of the infrequent lampposts to keep from landing in a filthy puddle.

"Bugger!"

Before she could fully right herself, a thick hand closed around her wrist in a bruising grip, wrenching her arm in the air to grant its owner better access to the reticule dangling there. Emily yelped in surprise, finally registering that two men were attempting to rob her.

"Give it 'ere!" growled the pockmarked man holding her arm.

"Jus' rip i' off!" cried the other, his nose snub and crooked, his frame equally as rough and imposing as the first one's.

Both reeked of stale gin and body odor. She barely managed to stifle a retch.

Instead, Emily gathered up her courage and her rage. She refused to give in without a fight, just managing to close her fingers around the strap of her reticule before it was wrenched away.

Perturbed by her spark, Pockmark raised a hand to deliver what would no doubt be a stinging backhanded blow. Emily closed her eyes in anticipation of the strike, but it never came. She cracked one eyelid to witness a black blur dispatching one and then the other attacker with well-placed blows and a preternatural grace. Each strike resulted in a smack of flesh and a crack of bone. He used the men's bulk against them, flipping them over his back and dropping them to the grimy street. They wheezed and struggled to catch their breath.

Snub Nose was able to add one more facial injury to his tally after a well-aimed kick. He flailed in pain, his leg knocking Emily to her knees. Jolts of pain zinged up her legs and through the heels of her palms, but it was nothing compared to what the criminals were experiencing.

She watched in horror as Pockmark struggled to his feet, his left arm dangling at a nauseating angle. The glint of a blade shone in the pitiful light as the man brandished a small knife he'd hidden in the pocket of his coat. He had eyes only for her savior.

Before he could move more than two steps, Emily pulled Oliver's small stiletto from her garter and pressed it to the unexpecting man's throat. Pockmark froze, his mouth agape like a fish's, his eyes wild and pain-addled. He was quickly dispatched by the blur of a flying fist to his jaw and he crumpled to the ground in a messy heap.

Panting, her blood singing with adrenalin, Emily turned to the black-garbed man. His collar was pulled up, a cap covered his head, and a dark beard covered the lower half of his face, but there was no mistaking Oliver's silver eyes. Despite the effort to save her from her would-be attackers, his chest rose and fell in even breaths. He was beautiful. He was glorious. And he was standing before her.

The stiletto fell from Emily's frozen fingers and clattered sharply to the slick cobblestones.

Chapter Twenty-Six

OLIVER DRANK IN the sight of Emily. She was shocked and disheveled—her mouth forming a perfect *o*, her gown damp and ruined from the scuffle, sodden locks of her hair tumbling from the pins—but she still looked perfect to him. Her doe eyes grew even wider than usual and she paled in recognition.

His heart was threatening to burst through his chest, but it had nothing to do with his abrupt descent from his viewpoint using drainpipes and rotted balcony railings, or the tussle with the muggers. It had everything to do with Emily's nearness…and he was suddenly reminded why he'd stayed away. Now, faced with her as he was, he didn't think he'd ever be able to walk away.

Then, his mind acting a little slowly through the haze created by her nearness, his joy was quickly overtaken by anger.

"How could you be so stupid?" he demanded with a roar. "What were you thinking walking alone at night—let alone in an area such as this? Did you want to be attacked? Or worse? Well?" He added the last when she didn't immediately respond. Did she know how much she worried him? How it would have killed him if something had happened to her?

Emily only gaped at him…and then she did the most curious thing.

She started hitting him.

She pounded her tiny fists against the hard wall of his chest, smacking his arms and railing against him with all her might.

Oliver didn't fight back; he made no attempts to stop her. Tears—of anger, confusion, maybe even relief?—spilled down her rain-dampened cheeks as she took her turn yelling at him.

"How could you abandon me? I thought you were dead! How could you? Stupid, stupid man!" Her voice was so broken, her pain so palpable that it lanced through him.

Oliver grabbed her upper arms to hold her still. "I did it for your own good. You need protection. You need stability I am unsure I'm able to provide. I did it all for you." All the while he spoke, she shook her head in denial.

"Never. Never do it again." Then, she pulled his head down to hers. Their mouths met in a desperate kiss as the rain fell around them, unheeded. She tasted of rain and salty tears, honey and shortbread. She tasted of everything he never knew he'd wanted and now knew he could never live without.

When Emily finally pulled away, Oliver moved a strand of her hair from her forehead. He gazed down at her, hardly daring to believe she was in his arms once more. His chest ached from the possibilities before him.

"Come. Let's get you out of this weather." He moved to retrieve her discarded reticule as well as what he now recognized as one of his stilettos. He raised a brow at her from his crouched position, to which she shrugged entirely unapologetically. He slid it into the side of his boot. She'd clearly been riffling through his trunk.

He liked the thought of her hands on all of his things.

RELIEVED TO FINALLY be out of the rain, Emily moved to continue toward the glowing beacon of Lady Night's, but he grabbed her hand. "I am tired of worrying about interruptions," he said.

Instead, Oliver steered her in the opposite direction, leaving behind the unconscious thieves and leading her down streets and up alleys, taking so many turns that Emily couldn't have guessed what part of London they'd wound up in.

She was pleasantly surprised when they reached the front

door of a pleasant-looking Townhouse in what seemed to her to be a comfortable and safe neighborhood. This particular building appeared to be a home converted into roomy living quarters.

"Bachelors' flats," Oliver explained, fishing out his set of keys. "Tenants can come and go as their lifestyle dictates, but they need not concern themselves with running an actual household and maintaining a staff of their own. The site is managed by an older couple who reside in the basement flat." He glanced at her. "Women are not allowed, but I'm sure the landlords will be willing to overlook it this one time if I offer them an advance on the next month's rent."

"This is where you live?" she asked in awe, trying to come to terms with the fact that this is where he might have been hiding out all these weeks.

"Sometimes."

"What does that mean?"

"It means that I have six residences of varying location and quality. This one happened to be the closest."

He proceeded to guide her to the topmost floor and, using another key, let them inside. It was an impersonal space with white walls and simple furnishings, but it was clean and warm and dry. It was, she realized, far better than anything a younger Oliver ever could have dreamed of.

He removed his hat and cloak, then helped Emily remove hers, chafing her chilled arms with his large hands. There, surrounded by him, she was suddenly inexplicably shy.

This was the first time there were no secrets between them. No danger. It was just the two of them.

Contrary to what she believed Oliver's fears to be, Emily was afraid that *she* would not be enough for *him*. How could she ever hope to live up to the life he was used to? The excitement? The danger? The intrigue? How could she hope to satisfy a man who had seen and experienced so much of the world?

Ever observant, Oliver interpreted her silent uncertainty and set about systematically dismantling it. "I've missed you, Angel."

He moved closer until the toes of his filthy boots disappeared beneath her skirts and the erect peaks of her breasts just barely brushed the lapels of his coat. His hands gently took hers and he examined her scraped palms. "Are you injured elsewhere?"

Emily took stock of her body. Her knees throbbed from her fall, but she'd managed to walk to this flat without incident, so they couldn't be in too bad of shape. "Not really." She barely resisted the urge to squirm beneath Oliver's skeptical stare. "Well, my knees are probably bruised, but—"

She was cut off as Oliver firmly guided her into one of the chairs. He set about lifting her skirts to her knees and, his mouth turning down when he saw how the silk of her stocking had been stained and torn through. She didn't doubt that he'd have gone back to finish off the men in the street if he hadn't been so absorbed in taking care of her.

Emily swore her heart nearly burst through her chest as he removed her slippers and rolled down her stockings to daub at the scrapes with clean linen and spirits he pulled from a cabinet. She hissed through her teeth at the sting, but he quickly bent his dark head and blew a gentle stream of air on the wounds. Gooseflesh rippled across her body.

"I was so worried about you," she whispered, her eyes drinking him in. His hands curled around her calves and squeezed her reassuringly. The adoring heat in his eyes made her heart ache.

"It wasn't safe to be near you. I didn't know how my superiors would react when they found out I'd disobeyed orders."

"I went to Ramsay—I went to Scotland Yard—"

"I know," he murmured and caught her hands in his, bringing her knuckles to his lips. "You did so well, Angel."

Hearing praise on his lips instantly warmed her soul. "What happened with Hayes?" Her fingers squeezed his.

While he cleaned her palms and then tidied up the items he'd used to see to her minor injuries, he described his confrontation with Hayes. The truth of how close he'd come to serious injury—even death—chilled her to her core, made the edges of her vision fade to red. He continued his story as he quickly, efficiently lit a fire and explained how the party was disbanded and Hayes, along with his co-conspirators scattered throughout London, were arrested for questioning in connection to the French plot to assist dissent and unrest to take root in English soil and threaten the monarchy. Once their usefulness came to an end, they would be dealt with in such a way that it would send a warning message to anyone else who thought to tread on Ramsay's territory—likely involving a great deal of pain and the shipping of dismembered body parts. She didn't find it a pleasant thought, but she did feel better knowing Hayes and his men would no longer be able to spread their poison…or come after Oliver.

"None of it would have happened without you," Oliver said in a low tone, watching her with his fathomless eyes. Somewhere along the way, he'd stripped down to his shirtsleeves and worn black trousers.

"You give me too much credit."

"You do not give yourself enough." He crossed the room back to her and tugged her to her feet. Before she realized what he was doing, he had unbuttoned her spencer and guided her to the warm glow of the fire. Once she was seated, the soft weight of a blanket was draped over her shoulders. She held her hand up to Oliver and, after a moment of hesitation, he accepted it and sat beside her, though not nearly close enough for her liking. Emily scooted herself closer and wrapped the other end of the blanket over his shoulders until they were both cocooned together, staring into the flickering orange flames.

"Did you mean what you said?" She somehow knew she didn't need to provide additional details for Oliver to understand what she was referencing.

"I told you I never wanted to lie to you," he finally replied and Emily's heart sang with the reassurance of it. That was until he continued speaking. "You are so precious and allowing you to get too close to me is dangerous—even now that I am no longer a target of Ramsay's. I told myself it would be easier and safer if I stepped away and allowed you to return to your life…regardless of how I felt. How I feel."

"But that is not what I want."

"I am not worth wanting," Oliver retorted adamantly.

"That is idiotic and you know it, Oliver Black," she snapped before her bravado deflated. "How can you say that when I am unsure if I am worthy of you."

"That's—"

"Perfectly valid." She cut him off and her cheeks began to burn. "You have lived a remarkable life. I believe you when you say you love me. But I fear love may not be enough when any life we might live could never hold up to the excitement to which you are accustomed."

"Are you honestly worried I will grow *bored* of you?" Aghast was the only way to describe the contortion of his handsome features. "Trust me when I say that that will never happen. Never." He pulled her roughly into his arms, running his hands up and down her back. "You are the only ray of light in my otherwise bleak life. How could you ever believe you wouldn't be enough?" His voice broke and he had to clear his throat before he could continue. "You are so much more than any man could ever deserve, let alone a lowlife like myself."

"Stop speaking so ill of the man I love," Emily mumbled against his hard chest as she clutched him to her. Almost instantly, Oliver released her and leaned back, slipping from her grasp and making her feel oddly bereft though he was still only inches away.

The feeling deepened when he abruptly stood and began to pace, scrubbing at his face with both hands.

"Oliver?" she asked, a wash of cold crashing over her as she stood and clutched the blanket around her chilled body. "Did I say something wrong?"

Oliver hadn't been this unsure and afraid since he'd been a boy spending his first night on the streets. Everything was new and strange. He was petrified of letting go—of Emily and his guard.

He whirled on his heel in another lap of his path across the main room.

"It's alright," Emily said, trying to calm him, but he spun on her.

"I've never needed anyone before," he ground out, "but I need *you*. I hate my weakness, but I need you, Angel."

Emily recognized the torture through which Oliver was suffering. This was not about his lack of feelings for her; she knew now that that should never be questioned. This was about a war within himself. He'd never believed himself worthy of love, so he struggled to accept it. His unfairly difficult life had conditioned him to be so; it had hardened him. Showing emotion was crippling and could very well kill him in his line of work. His soul was the battlefield of a war between the man he was in his heart and the man he'd been raised and trained to be.

She held out her hand to him, palm up, offering him the security and unconditional love fate had so long denied him, and he took it.

"You may not believe it now, but I will spend the rest of my life convincing you that you are worthy of everything I have to give." She brought his hand to her lips and pressed a tender, lingering kiss to his palm before pressing it to her cheek. "I trust you with my life. I trust you with my heart. A part of me always knew I would be safe with you." The softening of his eyes nearly broke her. "And I hope, one day, you might trust me with the same devotion. I know with everything you have been through that it might take time—"

Oliver covered her mouth with his, hungrily devouring her as he hiked her up into his arms and wrapped her legs around his waist. His tongue slid past her lips, invading deeply, tasting her in long, erotic strokes.

"Don't ever doubt my love," he growled against her lips. "I would give my life to see you safe and happy."

"You must promise never to do that."

Laughing, Oliver covered her grinning mouth with his.

The blanket fell from her shoulders and he laid her down atop it, her body clinging to his as he nestled his hips between hers. She could feel the insistent press of his arousal at her core and she instantly grew slick and ready for him. She'd been aching for him for weeks at that point, and she didn't want to wait any longer.

Emily tore at the collar of Oliver's shirt as her tongue tangled with his. She raked her nails down his flexing abdomen and untucked it from his trousers.

"Angel," he groaned and she knew his restraint was wearing dangerously thin.

"I know," she gasped and arched into his grinding pelvis, desperately seeking the pressure her body needed. The dampness between her thighs spread with each passing thrust of his clothed body against her. Her core pulsated for him, begging for him to fill her and claim her.

Suddenly, Oliver reared back and reached behind his head, tugging his shirt up and over before tossing it away from the hearth. He was beautiful; the stark lines of his sculpted chest and abdomen cast in harsh relief by the flickering light. The thick ridge of his member strained the front of his trousers until she thought the seams might give.

He immediately set upon her, undressing her as quickly as possible, but their position made it difficult. There was the sudden rending of fabric and popping seams and she felt the warm air caress her naked flesh. There was a glint of steel as Oliver slung aside his knife with uncharacteristic abandon.

"Did you just—"

"Rip off your dress because I couldn't wait another moment to have you bare beneath me?" He grinned wolfishly, making her nipples pebble and zing with awareness. "Why yes. Yes, I did." He covered her body with his once more and the heat of his skin against hers made her cry out in relief.

Oliver bent his head to suckle and nip the ripe tips of her breasts until she was so sensitive she could have screamed. Her hips bucked against his weight, her heels scrabbled against the floor, but she made no headway in convincing him to take her. Even as her nails scored his scalp and shoulders and she begged him for mercy, he continued his onslaught with his teeth and lips and tongue, the rough scratch of his beard abrading her raw in the most delicious of ways.

Oliver finally lifted his head when she swore she'd do anything if he'd stop his torture. "What, precisely, are you willing to do in exchange for my mercy?" he asked, his teeth flashing white in his dark beard as he grinned up at her.

Emily stared down at him, panting, her mind taking time to catch up, until she finally said, "I will take you into my mouth."

Judging from Oliver's reaction, this had been one of the last things he'd believed she would offer.

"Emily," he croaked, his silver eyes wide enough to place his shock on blatant display, "you needn't do that."

"I want to," she reassured him as she pressed a hand to his shoulder and urged him to roll over. "I have wanted to for some time."

Oliver relinquished control with a curse and flopped to his back in surrender. She wasted no time in reversing their positions so she knelt between his legs and eyed the object of her desire. Her inner muscles clenched as she lightly ran her fingers along the length, teasing it from root to tip as she located the garment's fastenings. He sprung free in all his thick and needy glory, bobbing before her like a man waving a flag in surrender—for that was what Oliver had done. He'd made himself entirely vulnerable to her, spread his arms wide like a man about to be crucified, and allowed her access to his most sensitive of places. She couldn't help it, she bent forward and placed a kiss upon the broad, blunt crown of his sex.

"Fucking hell…" he hissed viciously, but she didn't pull away. If anything, this chink in his armor spurred her on, emboldened her further. She licked the slit in the head, moaning as she tasted the salty pearl of moisture already beaded there. For her. All for her.

"Tell me if I do something you do not like," she said, entirely preoccupied with the feel of velvet over steel as she gripped him and worked her hand up and down in a painfully slow and deliberate rhythm.

"Angel. There is nothing you could do to me that I would not like." His chest heaved with carefully controlled breaths, but the contractions of his muscles as she sank her lips down on him revealed just how moved he was by her efforts. It was awkward at first, but trial and error helped her to find a formula they both enjoyed. Using her mouth in tandem with her fist, she worked his thick cock up and down, swirling her tongue around its head when she reached the tip before plunging back down. He was too large for her to take all of him, but it was obvious in his shuddering breaths, muttered curses, and groans that he appreciated everything she did, regardless of her inexperience. His hips began to buck and, several times, his hands flew to her hair, stopping just shy of touching her. She looked up the vast expanse of his glorious body to find his eyes fastened on her...begging her for permission.

She nodded, not once breathing her stride. Instantly, Oliver's fingers speared into her hair and fisted there. "Pinch my thigh hard if I do anything you do not like, alright?" he said in the most strangled voice she'd ever heard from him. She nodded once, and Oliver took the lead.

He pressed her head lower and held her still as his hips bucked up, sending his cock to the back of her throat. She nearly gagged, but swallowed instead, learning to time her breathing and relax into Oliver's control.

"Your mouth, Angel..." he growled. "It's almost as good as your tight cunny. So hot. So soft. So wet." Her whimper of excitement spurred him on. His eyes darkened and never left hers. "You amaze me. I could watch your lips around my cock for the rest of my days and die a happy man."

Emily reached down and slid her fingers through her dripping folds, working herself toward a shattering release as she matched

Oliver's rhythm. Heat flooded her limbs and she began to tremble. Just when she was about to lose control, Oliver lifted her head from his lap and hauled her up to straddle him.

She was dripping with need for him, so it took very little effort on his part to position her and slide inside to the hilt in one great thrust. Her body welcomed him, pulled him deeper, gripped him tighter than he'd ever dreamt possible. Coupled with the sinful pleasures her mouth had provided, the wet heat of her slick channel nearly sent him over the edge. Digging his fingers into the flesh of Emily's thighs, he held her immobile and tried to breathe through it, willing his orgasm to subside.

Emily, however, fought against his grip, doing her damnedest to rock against him and assuage the unstoppable pressure of her impending release.

"Please," Oliver hissed through clenched teeth. "Hold still, love. I don't want this to be over yet." The sight of her atop him, her legs spread wide to accommodate his hips, her hands gliding up her body to cup and caress the full pale globes of her breasts and tweak her bright pink nipples nearly did it. She pulsed around him, trembled from head to toe, inside and out.

"I want to feel you move," she whimpered. "It feels so good when you move."

"Damn it all." How could he deny her when she sounded like that? Oliver clutched the indentation of her waist, lifted her several inches, and began to pound into her from below.

"Like that!" she gasped in elation, continuing to knead her breasts.

Her body fluttered around him, coating them both in her wetness as his body slapped against hers relentlessly, colliding again and again with the swollen bud at the crux of her slit. His balls tightened and the base of his spine tingled. He was going to finish, but not until she did.

"Come for me, Angel," he growled and gripped the back of her neck, bringing her face down to his. "I want to feel your body milking mine."

As if a trigger had been pulled, every muscle in Emily's body clenched and she screamed through wave after wave of her orgasm. As she rocked and trembled above him, her teeth buried in the flesh of his shoulder, Oliver finally permitted himself to find his bliss.

His release was blinding in its intensity, rippling through his limbs and rocketing from him with incredible force. With jerky thrusts, he spilled into her and dragged her mouth down to his to kiss her deeply. They took turns swallowing each other's moans of pleasure.

"WHAT IS THIS?" Emily traced a fresh pink scar slicing horizontally across the outside of his left bicep. She was still draped across his chest before the fire, both too content to move to the bed or even allow him to withdraw from her body although he'd softened inside her.

"I was grazed by a lead ball."

"It looks fresh."

"Just a few weeks old."

She sat up. "Are you saying this was Hayes?" Her eyes flitted from the healing injury to his face. "You didn't say anything about being injured!"

"I survived," he said somewhat flippantly, but the depth of her emotion moved him. He'd never had anyone so concerned about him before and it caused his words to stick in his throat. He ran his hands along the curve of her spine to the globes of her rear. She was so beautiful it hurt to look at her, especially when he could read her heart in her eyes. "I am fine."

"Just fine?" She arched a brow at him.

"Much better now." He wrapped a lock of her hair around his finger and tugged it gently. "I am fairly certain I'm the best I've ever been...thanks to you."

Epilogue

THE DAY AFTER the incident with the footpads, Oliver had safely deposited Emily back at Lady Night's, traveled to Scotland Yard, and resigned from his post. He'd have been a liar if he claimed he hadn't been nervous about it.

Ramsay greeted him with icy silence and Oliver took his cue to follow him, wagering it was equally likely that it was to a private place to speak as it was to his death. If it were the latter, then he'd sure as hell take as many down as he could.

The two men sat in silence for several interminable minutes eyeing one another across Ramsay's desk until Oliver spoke first.

"Did you enjoy your delivery?" It likely wasn't wise to goad the man, but he'd put his life on the line—and Emily's—the least the man could do was thank him.

"You were lucky."

"Luck had nothing to do with that outcome. We both know that."

Ramsay narrowed his eyes. "If you're angling for your payment—"

"I don't give a damn about the money. I want to confirm what Morton said was true; I've been pardoned for following my gut and going against orders."

"It was decided that you won't be hanged if that's what you're asking."

"Or assassinated." Ramsay remained silent. "*Or assassinated.* That won't end well for whomever you send after me or mine."

Ramsay cleared his throat. "You and Miss Tailor are safe. I must say, I admire her tenacity and her codebreaking skills. For those reasons alone, I would have let her live despite her role in aiding your insubordinate and foolhardy actions. You never should have drafted an uninitiated woman into this situation."

"You also have her to thank for the discovery of the key." Oliver's chest still swelled with pride whenever he thought of how she'd so brilliantly located such an integral piece of information.

"Impressive."

"She is. And she is precisely the reason why I am resigning."

This time, both Ramsay's brows rose.

Resignation and retirement had never been topics of discussion between them. When he'd been drafted out of prison, it had been his only option if he wanted to avoid the hangman's noose. Since then, Oliver had served loyally and effectively, but he'd also never had a reason to consider another existence for himself. Now, he had to know if he'd be expected to remain indentured and indebted to the spy society for the rest of his days, or if his faithful service would be considered a debt paid.

Ramsay leaned back in his chair, eyeing Oliver thoughtfully. "You wish…to resign?"

"I have proven myself a thousand times over, and I feel I have earned my right to resign from the field."

The corner of Ramsay's lips twitched up ever so slightly.

"AND, JUST LIKE that, they allowed you to walk away from your work?"

"Well, yes and no."

Emily propped a fist on her hip. "What does that mean?"

"Ramsay isn't letting me go without a bit of payback."

"And that is?" Her skin flushed cold with dread.

"He is trying to have me knighted." Oliver cringed dramatically.

"Knighted?" she laughed incredulously, nearly overwhelmed

with the immediacy of her relief. "How is that payback?"

"Because he bloody well knows I would hate every moment of it. I told him I'd take a healthy pension instead." He tugged her close to his side as they strolled through the remote corner of Hyde Park. "I will sell off my various safehouses and, together, we can choose a place to live. A new home."

Grinning, Emily pressed him up against the trunk of a tree and pulled his head down to hers, showing him how grateful she was.

EMILY HAD SUSPECTED Oliver to be a man who would love with every fiber of his being when he finally opened his heart; the months following their reunion solidified this. Oliver had, indeed, been allowed to resign from his post, though Emily strongly suspected the spy society would miss his steady and accomplished presence. He'd avoided the knighthood, but just barely. One of the most impressive feats, however, had been his unerring determination to win over her mother. Lady Night wasn't known for her forgiving nature.

Oliver came to call daily, always bringing with him gifts for the infamous madam. Despite the unconventional nature of Emily's living conditions, he made a point to keep their "courtship" as traditional as possible. The first afternoon when he came to call, he appeared at the back entrance of the brothel. Emily happened to be assisting with inventory in the larder at the time and nearly swallowed her tongue when she answered the door to find him freshly shaven and impeccably dressed, bearing an enormous bouquet in every shape, size, and shade of red imaginable.

"Oliver!" She clapped her hand over her mouth. They hadn't discussed what he would be called.

"I believe 'Mr. Black' is more appropriate," he tsked, then snuck a peck on her cheek when he was certain no one else in the kitchens would see.

"You look so different," Emily giggled. "I'd become used to

your beard."

"I thought it chafed your thighs," he murmured low enough for her ears only, and she felt herself flush bright pink from her chest to her hairline.

Evening tea with Lady Night before the brothel opened for business that evening was a chilly affair. Even though her mother all but refused to acknowledge Oliver's existence, he continued to return day after day, enduring slight after slight until, finally, Lady Night turned to fix him with a stare.

"You love Emily." It was not a question—in fact, it was more accusatory than it was a statement of a fact.

"Completely," Oliver replied without missing a beat even though he and Emily had been discussing a novel he'd brought for her.

"You think ya can provide for 'er."

"I know I can. And I'm more than happy to hand over banking statements to attest to that fact."

"Don' make tha mistake of thinkin' yer better 'n me 'cause ya come from a better part 'a Town."

"Actually, I don't—on all counts." He met Lady Night's gaze squarely. "My mother was a maid. My father was a butcher who liked to inflict pain almost as much as he enjoyed a cheap drink. I was born only three blocks from here. I have no breeding to speak of, no title, and I certainly do not think myself above the woman who has single-handedly created a successful business and done a service to Covent Garden and its inhabitants. I know you are viewed as a heroine for the way you protect your employees, treat them fairly, and empower them. I wouldn't dare to think myself above a woman such as yourself, Lady Night."

Never before had Emily seen her mother so set back on her heels as she was in that moment. Emily might have laughed were she not so stunned by the perfection of Oliver's reply. Her throat tightened as she gazed at him, grateful and so in awe of this man who held her heart and proved to her time and time again that she'd made the right decision in trusting him all those weeks ago.

"You'll marry 'er." Lady Night narrowed her eyes at him. "I'll not be tolerating empty promises; Emily deserves better."

"I'd marry her today if she'd have me, but we're a little late for that. I suppose I can settle for tomorrow. Is that agreeable to you, Angel?" Oliver turned his attention to her and Emily swore she melted into a puddle right then and there.

THREE MONTHS INTO their life as husband and wife, Emily and Oliver were well settled into their Townhouse. The lovely brick building was comfortable, in a desirable part of London with shops and other necessary businesses nearby, and it overlooked a tidy park.

Moving into the home and learning to live with one another had been the simple part. Helping Oliver to adjust to a life of normalcy had been interesting, to say the least. At first, he'd been constantly on guard, peering out of windows, double- and triple-checking locks, even refusing to enjoy a meal at a restaurant on several occasions. His protective instincts were fierce—especially when it came to Emily. She dedicated herself to proving to him that she was all right, danger did not lurk behind every corner, and they could live a peaceful life together.

Emily took great pains to reassure Oliver that he was loved, that he made her happy, and that he could—for the first time in his life—truly plan a future. It had taken some doing, but one of his favorite activities was now lying naked in bed together and discussing all the things they'd like to do and see (which was second only to *how* they'd wound up naked in bed in the first place).

One consistent hurdle they encountered was what Oliver would do for work. It was the first time in his life that he wasn't scrambling for survival or at the beck and call of Ramsay's society. While he'd been educated as part of his training, his other skills weren't exactly in demand outside of a very niche area.

"An assassin?" Emily pillowed her cheek on her fist as she and Oliver lay in their bed.

"Now you're being ridiculous," Oliver chuffed, cracking one eye open to look at her.

"I don't think it's that far-fetched."

"The point was to remove myself from these dangerous situations so I might be around to share my life with you, Angel." He cocked a brow. "Unless you're sick of me already and trying to do away with me." He rolled her beneath him in one swift movement, pinning her as she squealed and pounded playfully at his chest.

"You know that's not true." She pressed a kiss to his chin and held his face between her hands. "I'm being creative. I hope you don't feel pressure from me to decide. We have funds enough for the time being, and I'm continuing to help at Lady Night's. We are comfortable and there is time enough."

Oliver hadn't been thrilled when Emily announced that she planned on continuing her role at the brothel, though he'd been assuaged when she agreed to allow him to escort her to and from the establishment each evening, and that she would continue to work unseen by the public. She'd been safe all these years, so it stood to reason that the same would hold up even better with Oliver keeping an eye on her. At first, she thought she might resent having him watching her every move, but it quickly proved quite pleasant having her husband nearby. He was stealthy and cunning enough to spirit her away for the most delicious of interludes whenever she needed them most. He was remarkably talented in that respect.

Additionally, he'd settled into a role helping wherever it was needed at the brothel. Some days, he helped make quick work of unloading the deliveries; others, he offered his imposing presence as a deterrent for would-be troublemakers. They both knew he wouldn't be working at her mother's brothel for good, but for a while, it was a good fit for him. She could tell he enjoyed feeling useful and the sense of community provided by Lady Night's. Emly quite liked it when he allowed his menace to show just a little…

"You know," she said, admiring his rugged features, "you once let slip a rather impressive Cockney accent." Oliver cringed and groaned. "Is that your 'real' voice?"

"I don't quite know what 'real' is anymore." He paused to nuzzle her throat. "But, yes, that is probably as near to 'real' as it would ever be."

"Can you do it again?"

"Honestly, I've been masking it for so long that it would probably take more effort to use the damned dialect than not."

"Please?"

"But, Mrs. Black…I think I've proven I can take you just as hard and rough as any dockworker, even without the accent. Haven't I?" The man had the power to make her core melt with just a word. "Perhaps I need to refresh your memory…"

"It seems we have found a good use for your talents after all." Emily was already breathless.

"I'm only getting started, love…"

And he proceeded to show her how imaginative he could be.

Again.

And again.

And again.

Author's Note

Hayes's debauched party might seem far-fetched, but these gatherings of sin and vice weren't unheard of in Regency England! Not every country party was as picturesque and tame as those so often portrayed in books and media. Events like this were a way for men and women to break free of Society's constraints and explore another, less inhibited side of themselves. Naughty games and even orgies took place, if you can believe it!

Establishments like Lady Night's were popular as well. Patrons donned masks, disguises, and costumes to explore their darkest desires behind closed doors. Wealthy men paid good coin to be whipped. Nude employees stood like statues in erotic poses.

While I took imaginative liberties with some of the details of Hayes's party and the behind-the-scenes peeks at Lady Night's high-end brothel, the essence remains the same. Even Regency-era people had their kinks—and indulged in them, too.

The moral? Not all history is as "vanilla" as you might think!

I did also want to mention my fudging of Scotland Yard's timeline. The original location for the first headquarters of the Metropolitan Police had a front entrance off Whitehall and a rear entrance off Great Scotland Yard. It was founded in 1829 by Robert Peel. Of course, this is several years *after* this book takes place. I claimed the creative right bestowed upon authors (even though it grated against my Historical Accuracy Nerve) and bumped up the timeline to suit my needs. I did, however, remain true to the building's original location.

Ready for more secrets and swoon-worthy passion?

In *Marrying the Marquess*, a case of mistaken identity shatters everything Oliver Black believed about himself...and a surprise pregnancy brings together a rake and a hellion whose relationship snubs Society most deliciously.

Coming soon from Dragonblade Publishing!

Acknowledgments

I first drafted Emily and Oliver's story years ago and I'll be honest when I say it was one I was both excited and terrified to write. The plot was so different from anything I've written before, but I think it was worth all the sleepless nights and stress. Finding the balance between mystery, intrigue, espionage, realism, and spicy romance was difficult. Revision after revision, though, this exciting and unique love story has turned into something I adore, and I sincerely hope you feel the same way!

This book wouldn't have been possible without so many people along the way because one thing I've learned in the past few years is there are more amazing, brilliant, talented people involved in this process than you'll ever know. Thank you, Kathryn, for recognizing my passion and giving me the chance to share my stories. Thank you to Holly for the amazing artwork for this series! To Brenda, Shawn, Juliana, Evelyn, and everyone else who worked with me at Dragonblade Publishing—your support is truly appreciated and so integral to this journey.

Thank you to my friends for their love, support, and understanding. My writing may not always be their cup of tea, but having them in my corner is amazing—especially when they're so forgiving as I face down a deadline (or space out because I'm trying to work on a plot hole even when I'm not sitting at my computer). As always, a special thank you to Amy for not blocking my incessant texts about my writing (and for taking me out for a boozy brunch to celebrate the completion of this draft)!

A special thank you to my readers! You are so vital in making my dreams a reality. I love hearing how my stories have impacted you, moved you, and touched your hearts. There are few things more personal than putting your heart and soul onto paper and sending it out into the world. You make it worth it.

As always, thank you to my family for their unwavering support. To the cheerleading aunts and grandparents, a mom who talks about my writing at every opportunity, my indulgent husband and our patient son, I know I would not be where I am today if it wasn't for all of you. Each of you has shaped me and helped me along this journey. To have a support system like you has made this dream possible. I love you all.

About the Author

Kelsey is an Illinois native, author, wife, mother, animal lover, and owner of an obscenely large To-Be-Read book stash. She fostered her love of reading and writing after a heart condition sidelined her childhood. Early one, she learned the joy of living a thousand lives, experiencing hundreds of new worlds, and, eventually, the true pleasure of providing that same escape to others with her writing. Her passions continued to develop long after surgery restored her health and, to this day, it's difficult to find her without a book in her hands. She dove headfirst into the romance genre (perhaps) a bit earlier than the recommended minimum age and became rather adept at disguising her reading material. Once exposed to the glittering world of historical romance, she was forever changed. Her love of writing and all things British translated into her future collegiate studies in both English (with an emphasis on British Literature) and History (mainly British and European). She would go on to earn Bachelor's Degrees in both English and History, as well as a Master's Degree in English. She finished penning her first story fresh out of high school and has never looked back. Her debut novel, *The Baron's Folly*, was published in 2023.

When she's not reading or writing, she's usually watching reruns of her favorite shows, streaming just about any true crime show or podcast; obsessively collecting architectural designs, crafts, and recipes on Pinterest; or sketching, crocheting, cooking, and spending time with her family making the amazing memories she's always dreamt of. She is a diehard supporter of the Oxford Comma and is glued to the TV whenever le Tour de France is on. She is on a never-ending mission to convince her husband that they need pygmy goats, highland coos, and silkie chickens to make their lives complete.

authorkelseyswanson.my.canva.site